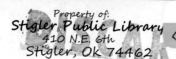
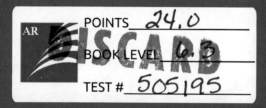

SUPERNOVA

Marissa Meyer

FEIWEL AND FRIENDS • NEW YORK

A Feiwel and Friends Book
An imprint of Macmillan Publishing Group, LLC
120 Broadway, New York, NY 10271

Our books may be purchased in bulk for promotional, educational, or business use. Please contact your
local bookseller or the Macmillan Corporate and Premium Sales Department at (800) 221-7945 ext. 5442
or by email at MacmillanSpecialMarkets@macmillan.com.

Library of Congress Control Number: 2019931347
ISBN 978-1-250-07838-4 (hardcover)
ISBN 978-1-250-22016-5 (ebook)
ISBN 978-1-250-25782-6 (international edition)

Book design by Patrick Collins
Feiwel and Friends logo designed by Filomena Tuosto
First edition, 2019
1 3 5 7 9 10 8 6 4 2
fiercereads.com

For Uncle Bob, who helped me be myself.

CAST of CHARACTERS

THE RENEGADES

SKETCH—ADRIAN EVERHART
Can bring his drawings and artwork to life

MONARCH—DANNA BELL
Transforms into a swarm of monarch butterflies

RED ASSASSIN—RUBY TUCKER
When wounded, her blood crystallizes into weaponry; signature weapon is a grappling hook formed from a bloodstone

SMOKESCREEN—OSCAR SILVA
Summons smoke and vapor at will

THE BANDIT—MAX EVERHART
Absorbs the power of any prodigy in his midst; has spent most of his young life in quarantine

WONDER—CALLUM TREADWELL
Eternally optimistic; can alter the perception of others by filling them with a sense of awe

FROSTBITE—GENISSA CLARK
Creates weapons of ice from water molecules in the air

THE ANARCHISTS

NIGHTMARE—NOVA ARTINO

Never sleeps, and can put others to sleep with her touch

ACE ANARCHY—ALEC ARTINO

Leader of the Anarchists and the world's most feared villain; was once the most powerful telekinetic in history; also Nova's uncle

PHOBIA—NAME UNKNOWN

Transforms his body and scythe into the embodiment of various fears

THE PUPPETEER—WINSTON PRATT

Turns children into mindless puppets who do his bidding

QUEEN BEE—HONEY HARPER

Exerts control over all bees, hornets, and wasps

CYANIDE—LEROY FLINN

Generates acidic poisons through his skin; also a talented chemist

THE RENEGADE COUNCIL

CAPTAIN CHROMIUM—HUGH EVERHART

Has superstrength and can generate chromium weaponry; he is allegedly invincible

THE DREAD WARDEN—SIMON WESTWOOD

Can turn invisible

TSUNAMI—KASUMI HASEGAWA

Generates and manipulates water

THUNDERBIRD—TAMAYA RAE

Generates thunder and lightning; can fly

BLACKLIGHT—EVANDER WADE

Creates and manipulates light and darkness

CHAPTER ONE

E veryone has a nightmare.

Nova was pretty sure her worst nightmare was walking back into Renegade Headquarters, wearing her Renegade-issued patrol uniform, less than twenty-four hours after her alter ego had infiltrated the building, stolen the most dangerous weapon of all time, stripped three Renegades of their powers using her stolen batch of the substance known as Agent N, started a fight that destroyed most of the building's lobby, and witnessed Max Everhart nearly bleed to death amid the shattered glass of his demolished quarantine.

It wasn't only surreal that she was returning to the wreckage in the first place, it was that she was doing so willingly. Nova had believed she would never come back here again. After months of working as a spy in the Renegades' midst, she had successfully stolen Ace Anarchy's helmet. She had what she needed to give Ace his power back, and together they would watch this organization crumble.

But things never went according to plan, and she hadn't known that while she was fighting for her life in this very lobby, a masked vigilante known as the Sentinel had discovered and arrested Ace Anarchy—the leader of the Anarchists and the uncle who had raised her.

Sweet rot, she hated the Sentinel. He was always around at the most inconvenient times, striking his ridiculous comic-book poses and spouting absurd catchphrases like "I'm not your enemy" and "You can trust me."

Except, no one fully trusted the Sentinel, as far as she could tell. Vigilantism didn't fit with the Renegade code, and despite his attempts to seize criminals and aid the Renegades, his stunts had often made the organization seem incompetent and ineffective. Perhaps the only thing Nova liked about the vigilante was his uncanny ability to get on the Council's nerves. Meanwhile, his determination to hunt down Nightmare and his capture of Ace Anarchy hadn't made him any friends among the villain set, either. The only people who appreciated the Sentinel's efforts were Adrian, who seemed to have a rebellious appreciation for the guy, and the public, who saw him as a true hero, one who believed in justice and answered to nobody but himself. That reputation was solidified with his capture of Ace Anarchy.

Though she knew nothing was ever easy, Ace's arrest had almost been enough to make Nova throw her hands in the air and succumb to the inevitable. Anarchists and prodigies like them would go on being hated, villainized, and oppressed for all eternity. She was almost ready to give up.

Almost.

That had been hours ago, and now Nova was back, because . . . where else could she go? As far as anyone here knew, she was still

Nova McLain, alias Insomnia, a Renegade through and through. Her secrets remained the best leverage she had, and now that her enemies had Ace, she knew she would need every bit of it.

Nova hadn't realized the full extent of the destruction wrought upon Renegade Headquarters until she found herself moving shakily through the rubble. She was surrounded by Renegades, but no one was paying her any attention. Even the Council members were combing through the remains of the glass quarantine that had fallen from the second story and shattered the tiled marble of the main lobby. From where she stood, she could see Captain Chromium holding the glass clock tower that had once topped the courthouse from Max's miniature Gatlon City.

Now it was destroyed. All of it was destroyed.

The signs of battle were everywhere. Steel beams bent at odd angles. Wires dangling from the ceiling where chandeliers had been pulled from their sockets. The information desk mangled on one side. Plaster and tables and chairs and tile and glass—so much glass from where the quarantine had fallen. The glittering shards were almost mesmerizing, the way they caught the light streaming in through the front doors.

And there was blood.

Most of it was dried in a puddle where Max had fallen. Where Frostbite had driven a spear right through him.

Nova tore her eyes from the spot and saw Adrian picking his way toward her. His shoulders were hunched and there was none of the usual grace to his demeanor. He had a shadow over his features, one that served as a reminder that Max, who was as close to a brother as Adrian would ever have, was in the hospital. The doctors had put him in a coma to stabilize his vital signs, but they weren't filling anyone's head with false optimism. He was hanging by a thread. There was only one saving grace—that Max had, in the last moments of the battle, managed to absorb all of Frostbite's ability. He had taken in her control of ice and used it to stanch his own bleeding, to freeze over his own wound.

It might have saved his life.

Then again, it might not.

Nova swallowed the lump in her throat as Adrian drew closer. His dark expression was about more than Max. He was full of a new burning hatred, like nothing Nova had ever witnessed before . . . at least not on calm, cheerful Adrian.

A burning hatred for Nightmare, who he was convinced had been the one who attacked Max. No one had seen it happen other than Frostbite and her comrades, and they weren't about to correct anyone's mistaken beliefs. Nightmare was too easy a target to put the blame on.

And Nova, whose secret identity remained, miraculously, unknown, couldn't exactly clear her alter ego's name, no matter how she yearned to defend herself whenever she saw Adrian's eyes smolder with restrained hostility.

"When you said Nightmare had infiltrated headquarters," Nova said, once Adrian was close enough, "this isn't what I pictured."

Lying through her teeth, as usual. She was always lying these days. She hardly even realized she was doing it anymore.

"Yeah, it's pretty bad." Adrian's focus was distant as he scanned the destruction. "They found the Silver Spear over there. We think Nightmare got it from the vault and used it to steal the helmet. And . . ." His voice caught and he coughed to clear it. "We're pretty sure it was the weapon she used on Max, too. There was blood on it. They're going to run tests."

Her teeth ground.

Adrian sighed and looked down. For the first time, Nova noticed something in his hands. A sphere with a small crown on one side and an open seam around its circumference. Nova recognized it immediately—one of Fatalia's mist-missiles, or so it had been, before she had stolen it from the artifacts department. She and Leroy had reconfigured the devices to release a gaseous form of Agent N, the noxious substance that had been developed using Max Everhart's blood. Though harmless to civilians, it was poison to prodigies. As soon as they inhaled, imbibed, or were injected with the substance, they would permanently lose their powers.

As Nightmare, Nova had detonated two of the devices in this lobby. Those, along with a stolen dart loaded with Agent N, had resulted in both Gargoyle and Aftershock being stripped of their abilities. She had orchestrated the neutralization of Frostbite, too, though she didn't need Agent N that time. She'd simply dragged the girl closer to Max and let the Bandit do what he needed to do.

Now she found herself staring at the shell of the device, already forming a series of lies she could tell when someone bothered to check them for fingerprints. She had touched the mist-missiles one day while working in the vault . . . that must have been before Nightmare stole them . . .

But the lies were flimsy.

The higher her lies piled up, the more precarious they became. Sometimes she felt that if she dared to exhale fully, the whole thing would topple.

"It looks like one of Fatalia's mist-missiles," she said, keeping her tone even.

"That's what Callum said, too," said Adrian.

"Callum? Is he here?" Nova's thoughts turned back to the night before, when she had left Callum unconscious in the vault.

Adrian nodded. "He went back upstairs to check if the mist-missiles are missing."

"Maybe Nightmare took them when she took the spear."

Adrian's brow furrowed over his dark-framed glasses. "I don't think so. Mack Baxter said Nightmare had some sort of bomb filled with Agent N. That's how she was able to neutralize Trevor. I think this is one of those bombs."

Nova silently cursed Aftershock and Gargoyle, even if she couldn't blame them for telling the truth. "Well, maybe she was inspired by the mist-missile design. She is supposed to be some genius inventor, right? She must have created these herself."

Adrian hesitated, and she could see him battling with his own thoughts. Finally, he conceded, "Maybe. We'll see what Callum finds."

Unconvinced.

Nova wouldn't have been convinced, either. No matter how hard she tried to deflect scrutiny away from herself, her arguments just weren't all that convincing these days.

"The thing is," said Adrian, tossing the empty device into the air and catching it again in his palm, "if Nightmare was setting off Agent N bombs . . . it would have affected her, too. Why wasn't she afraid of losing her powers?"

"She wears a mask, doesn't she?"

"Yeah, but I'm pretty sure it isn't a gas mask."

She shrugged. "We don't know that."

"Okay, but she was also right next to Max when"—Adrian cut short, his gaze darting toward the blood on the floor—"when he was draining Genissa of her powers. He should have been draining Nightmare, too, but she ran out of here like nothing was wrong. No one is immune to Max."

"Your dad is."

He scowled. "No one other than Captain Chromium."

"I'm just saying, there might be ways around Max's ability and Agent N. Maybe Nightmare found something . . . like you stumbling onto that Vitality Charm." The Vitality Charm was an artifact Adrian had discovered that could protect a person against disease, poison, and just about anything that would weaken them, including substances like Agent N. The artifact that was, even at that moment, tucked between the worn mattress and the wooden floorboards at Nova's house on Wallowridge. "There could be dozens of artifacts that would protect someone's ability and we just don't know about them."

"And you think that Nightmare and I happened to each find one around the same time?"

"Sure. Maybe."

"Or . . ." Adrian's voice dropped to a whisper, though all of the nearby Renegades were too busy sweeping up glass and pulling debris from the wreckage to care about their conversation. "Maybe Nightmare has the Vitality Charm."

Nova had expected this rebuttal. It made so much more sense than her argument, after all. But she kept her expression neutral. "Don't *you* have it?"

Adrian grimaced. "No. Pops had it last. I gave it to him so he could visit Max. You know, outside the quarantine for once. But now it's missing."

"So . . . you think she stole that from the vault, too?"

"It wasn't in the vault. Simon swears he brought it back to the house. That's the last we've seen of it."

She cocked her head to one side. "So you think Nightmare broke into your house?"

"Yes. No. I don't know. In theory, she could have done it while we were all at the gala, but there's nothing on any of our security cameras. And that doesn't explain how she would have known about the charm in the first place. I haven't told anyone other than you and Max, and I know my dads didn't, either." He rubbed the back of his neck, and she could tell he felt a little guilty to even ask—"You didn't mention it to anyone, did you?"

"Of course not," she said. "But Tina and Callum knew about the charm, too, and Callum can't keep his mouth shut around anyone. Maybe they let something slip, not realizing how valuable it is."

"Yeah. Maybe. I was actually hoping the team could get together later to discuss what we know about Nightmare. Maybe there's something we've overlooked. It's just . . . there seem to be some pretty strange coincidences."

"She's an Anarchist," Nova said, daring to settle a hand on Adrian's forearm. She felt his muscles tighten briefly beneath the fabric of his uniform. "She's devious and cunning and probably has a lot of connections in the world of . . . *villains* that we know nothing about. If she could do all this, if she could even steal Ace Anarchy's helmet, then who knows what else she's capable of? Finding that charm or figuring out some other way around Agent N—none of it seems like a stretch."

Adrian stared at her hand for a moment, before a wisp of a smile crossed his lips and he settled his own fingers on top of hers. His other hand, still clutching the mist-missile, dropped to his side. "I'm glad you're here," he said. But just as Nova's heart began to flutter, he added, "I'm glad you're on my side."

She allowed a wisp of a smile in return. "What other side would I be on?"

"Adrian! Nova!"

They turned to see Ruby and Oscar slipping through the crowd. Ruby latched on to Adrian's other elbow. "How's Max?"

His jaw flexed. "Still in critical."

She shook her head. "I am so, so sorry. She's a monster, Adrian. How anyone could do that to Max——!"

Nova winced.

"I hate to say it, but I'm not surprised," said Adrian, as if this had been an inevitable attack. "Of course Nightmare would try to kill Max. Any of the Anarchists would. It's because of him they were defeated in the first place. They've probably been plotting his murder for the last ten years."

Heat rose in Nova's cheeks. The more she heard about Nightmare's attempt to kill Max, the more she wanted to scream the truth. It was Genissa who stabbed the kid, not Nightmare. She would never hurt him. Hell, she'd tried to save him!

But she bit her tongue. There was no point in trying to argue Nightmare's innocence. They wouldn't believe her, and it would only raise suspicion.

"We'll find her," said Ruby. "We'll put an end to this. And Max——he's going to be fine. He's a strong kid."

"I know," said Adrian. He sounded grateful and like he wanted to believe her. Like he'd been telling himself this same thing all night. But there was still an echo of doubt beneath his words.

Nova exhaled slowly. Adrian had come to her house early that morning, after the dust had settled, to tell her about Max being in the hospital and about Nightmare stealing the helmet. He had seemed so defeated, and yet, at the same time, bolstered by a new desire for revenge. She shuddered to remember his words, spoken even as she held him against her, trying her best to comfort him.

I'm going to find Nightmare, and I'm going to destroy her.

CHAPTER TWO

"I HEAR NIGHTMARE really whupped Frostbite and her crew," said Oscar as he took in the massive amount of destruction to the lobby.

"More or less," said Adrian. "Frostbite, Gargoyle, and Aftershock were all neutralized."

"I hate to say it, but . . . I mean, that's sort of a point in Nightmare's favor, right?"

Ruby smacked Oscar in the shoulder. "She almost killed Max, you dunce!"

"No, I know. But if anyone was going to get neutralized, I can't say I'm sorry it was Genissa and her minions."

"It's okay," said Adrian. "I'm not too upset about that, either. And like you said, Max is going to be fine." He paused before adding, quietly, "He has to be."

"Holy smokes, what is *that*?" Oscar barked. He lifted his cane, as if prepared to stab something on the shattered tile floor.

A tiny creature was scuttling toward them out of the mess of broken concrete and plaster—a fierce little velociraptor, no larger than Nova's thumb.

"No way," muttered Adrian. "Turbo!" He crouched and scooped the creature into his palm.

It screeched and bit him.

"Ow!" Adrian yelped, dropping it. It landed on the floor and darted between Oscar's legs.

Nova leaped after it, grabbing the creature by the back of its neck. It made a pathetic mewing sound and flicked its clawed arms at her, leaving tiny nicks on her fingers. "How is this thing still alive?" she asked.

It seemed like ages ago that Adrian had drawn the small beast onto Nova's palm, in an effort to prove that his powers hadn't been drained by Max when he'd gone into the quarantine to rescue her.

Adrian bent down to inspect the tiny dinosaur as it squirmed in Nova's fingers. "Alive, but not doing so hot. Look, he's turning gray. And see how his movements are sort of awkward now, more like a machine's? That always happens when I draw animals. Still—he's lasted longer than I would have thought."

"Excuse me," said Oscar, eyeing the creature with trepidation. "But what *is* it?"

"A velociraptor," said Adrian. "I drew him a while back, and Max has been keeping him as a pet. His name is Turbo. Here." Stooping down, Adrian took out his marker and drew a palm-size cage on the white tile. With a swipe of his fingers, the cage emerged into reality, a three-dimensional carrier for a very small dinosaur. He held open the door while Nova dropped the creature inside. "I'll take him to Max at the hospital. He'll be happy to see him when he wakes up."

When, Nova couldn't help but note, and for the first time, Adrian sounded truly optimistic about the possibility of Max coming out of his coma. Perhaps he was seeing Turbo's survival as a good sign.

"He's probably hungry," said Ruby. "I mean, your drawings still need to eat, right?"

"I guess so." Adrian looked like he'd never given it much thought. "Max used to share snacks with him."

Ruby nodded. "I'll run up to the cafeteria and grab him . . . I don't know, chicken strips or something. I'll be right back."

She was gone before anyone could speak, darting between the Renegades who were milling around the destroyed lobby.

"Uh . . . ," started Adrian, too late, "I don't think they've reopened the cafeteria yet . . ."

"She'll find something," said Oscar. "They have turkey jerky in the lounge vending machines." The second the elevator doors closed and Ruby was no longer in sight, Oscar eagerly spun on Nova and Adrian. "Okay, now that she's gone, I need to talk to you guys. I mean, I know with Max and Nightmare and everything, this may not be the best time, but I was up all night thinking about what you said at the gala, and I have a plan." He fixed his attention on Nova, and she stiffened in response, wondering what on earth she had said. Though the gala had been just the night before, only a couple of hours before she'd broken into the HQ vault, it felt like weeks had passed since then.

"A plan for what?" she asked.

"You know," said Oscar, insistent. "Telling Ruby how . . . how I feel about her. Nova was right. I'm awesome, and I am ready to sweep her off her feet."

"Oh, that." Nova glanced at Adrian, who appeared equally relieved that Oscar's plan was for something so mundane. "That's great."

"Yeah, go for it, Oscar," said Adrian. "Way to take the plunge."

"Thanks, man. So, I'm calling it . . ." Oscar lifted his hand, as if highlighting invisible words in the air. "Operation Crown Jewels."

Nova and Adrian gawked at him, speechless for a moment, before Adrian cleared his throat. "Uh . . . what?"

"You know. Crown jewels . . . rubies . . . get it?"

Nova's eyes narrowed skeptically. "Isn't that a euphemism for . . ."

Oscar waited for her to finish, looking so adorably emphatic that she stopped herself. "Never mind. Just . . . why is there an operation name?"

"Because I have ideas," said Oscar. "Like, a gazillion ideas. This is going to be a calculated, multistep strategy."

"So you're not just going to ask her out?" said Adrian.

Oscar snorted. "Please. Ruby deserves better than that. There will be serenades, gifts, cloud writing . . . you know, some real grand gestures. The stuff girls go nuts for, right?" He looked at Nova, but she could only shrug. He sighed. "Okay, so I thought we'd start with a poem. I wrote it at, like, five o'clock this morning, so keep that in mind. But I was thinking of leaving a card on her doorstep some morning this week. Here's what I've got so far." He cleared his throat. "Rubies are red, your eyes are blue . . ."

"Stop," said Nova.

Oscar froze. "What?"

"Her eyes are hazel," she said. "And also, this is not really the time for poetry." She gestured around at the destruction.

Oscar huffed. "But you didn't even—"

A burst of red and blue sparks exploded over their heads. Nova ducked, panic rising.

Adrian squeezed her hand and sent her a look that bordered on teasing. "Just Blacklight."

At the front of the lobby, the five Council members were standing on the street-level balcony, silhouetted by a wall of glass and the hazy afternoon sun. Shadows of journalists and curious civilians could be seen on the sidewalk, held back by caution tape and a handful of Renegades tasked with keeping out anyone who wasn't a part of the organization.

As the remnants of his fireworks dissolved, Blacklight angled his palm to the doors and dragged his fingers through the air, as if shutting an imaginary set of blinds. A veil of darkness fell over the windows, obscuring both the sunlight and the citizenry.

"Thank you, Evander," said Captain Chromium, stepping to the front of the balcony, with the rest of the Council forming a semicircle around him. Nova scrutinized the Captain and the Dread Warden—the two adoptive fathers of both Adrian and Max. Though she could guess that neither of them had slept the night before, the exhaustion that was evident on the Dread Warden was lacking entirely from the Captain. His skin was as luminescent as ever, his baby-blue eyes as striking and bright. Only his slightly disheveled hair suggested he was less composed than usual.

But the Dread Warden wasn't the only one who looked exhausted. Thunderbird's black-feathered wings were drooping from her shoulder blades, and the ever-present serenity was, for once, gone from Tsunami's face, replaced with a taut brow and tense lips. Even Blacklight, usually the most laid-back among them, had his arms crossed tight over his chest.

"Fellow Renegades," said the Captain, his voice booming through the lobby. "A great blow was dealt to us last night. I won't bother to sugarcoat the details—you can see the truth of last night's events for yourselves. It is"—his mouth tightened as he searched for a word—"discouraging, to say the least. That we could be infiltrated on such a level by a single villain. That Nightmare was able to disarm our security system and defeat one of our best patrol units. That she could steal from us. That she could"—his voice snagged—"harm one of our own, in such a cruel, senseless way. And not just a Renegade, but a boy, a *child*, who is good and smart and kind. It's unthinkable. It is a reminder to us all that there is evil in this world, and it is our responsibility to stand strong against it."

Nova's fists clenched as she resisted the urge to scream—*I. Didn't. Hurt. Max!*

"But we are Renegades," Captain Chromium continued, "and we do not cower before evil. No—in the face of evil, we stand taller! We fight harder! Adversity only strengthens our resolve to be the protectors of this world, the defenders of justice!"

A few whoops echoed from the audience.

"We will not dwell on our losses, but look to the future and how we can move forward into a brighter tomorrow. Because—there were losses yesterday. But there was also a great victory. I want to confirm that the rumors you've heard are true." He paused, his attention sweeping over the room. "Ace Anarchy, who we believed to be dead these past ten years, is alive. And he is in our custody."

If he expected an approving cheer, he must have been disappointed. If anything, the knowledge that their greatest enemy had survived the Battle for Gatlon was met with a murmur of concern, regardless of his capture.

"What about his helmet?" cried Alchemist. "We were told it was destroyed, but now they're saying that's what Nightmare came here for."

The Captain curled his hands around the railing that divided them. "This, also, is true."

Nova swallowed.

"After the Day of Triumph, I did my best to destroy Ace Anarchy's helmet," continued the Captain, "but it was indestructible. The Council and I decided it would be best to tell the world that the helmet had been destroyed, to ease the concerns of our people while we worked on rebuilding society. I convinced myself the helmet would be safe here at headquarters." A flash of resentment curled his lip. "But it seems I was wrong. Nightmare did come for the helmet, and she did manage to escape with it last night." A rustle of chatter flooded the room, but the Captain lifted his hands. "Listen to me. We must remain calm. Let me remind you—the Anarchists may have gotten the helmet last night, but they lost their leader. Without Ace Anarchy, that helmet is nothing but a costume accessory."

Nova wondered if he believed that, and how many of the Renegades would believe *him*.

She didn't know much about Ace's helmet, but she had always assumed that it would amplify the powers of any prodigy, just as it had amplified Ace's. Otherwise, why would the Renegades have been so determined to destroy it, once they believed that Ace was dead?

Nevertheless, the Captain's words had an immediate effect. The crowd hushed. "I implore you," he went on, "for now, news of this theft cannot reach the general populace. Do not speak to the media. Do not tell anyone. The last thing we need is for mass panic to spread while we're on the verge of finally subduing the threat of villainous prodigies everywhere. From this point, we have two immediate matters of business to address. The first is undoing the damage that was wrought on our headquarters last night and initiating new security protocols. For that, my fellow Council members and I will be reaching out to our international syndicates, enlisting the help of any prodigies with powers that lend themselves to construction and repairs, and we will be assigning those in our home organization tasks based on their skills in the days to come. We are grateful for all your cooperation as we rebuild. If you have any thoughts on this project, I encourage you to speak with Kasumi, who will be heading up this undertaking." He gestured at Tsunami, who bowed her head in return.

"And, second," the Captain continued, "by the end of today, we will have a date scheduled for the public reveal of Agent N, after which all active patrol units will be equipped with the substance. This will allow us to defend ourselves against future such attacks, and convey to our citizens how very seriously we will be dealing with prodigies who choose not to follow our code of protection and honor."

Nova squeezed Adrian's forearm, though she didn't realize she'd done it until he took her hand, lacing their fingers together.

"Additionally, we have decided that part of the reveal will include a public neutralization of all prodigies who have been heretofore convicted of villainous behavior . . . including Ace Anarchy himself."

Though a chill ran down Nova's spine, his statement was predictably met with applause—albeit somewhat nervous applause. Agent N had seemed like an exciting development to most of the organization when it had first been unveiled, but that was before some of the substance had fallen into Nightmare's hands. That was before three of their own had been neutralized, right here in this very lobby.

Now it seemed that everyone was feeling a bit more apprehensive about the Renegades' newest weapon.

"And what about the patrols who refuse to cooperate?" rang out a voice, shrill and spiked with anger.

A flurry of interest passed through the crowd as Genissa Clark, formerly known as Frostbite, picked her way through the rubble.

Rather than the usual Renegade uniform, she was wearing drawstring pants and a loose T-shirt from the medical wing. Her bare arms were littered with bruises and scratches from her fight against Nightmare.

Nova tensed upon seeing one of the prodigies she had fought the night before. Though she had been hooded and masked, her heart still pounded to think that Genissa might have recognized her.

Genissa wasn't alone. The rest of her team followed in her wake: Trevor Dunn, who had been Gargoyle before his powers had drained away. He was still taller than an average man, but not as gigantic as he had been before, and his skin showed no hint of stone. Then there was Mack Baxter, no longer Aftershock, who moved with a peculiar gait, like he was so used to making the ground shake from his steps that he would have to relearn how to walk now without the ground swelling up to meet him.

Of their team, only Stingray—Raymond Stern—remained a prodigy. Nova had put him to sleep in the surveillance room before she disabled the security cameras, and he had missed the rest of the battle. His barbed tail slid behind him, scattering bits of glass as it flicked back and forth.

"What did I miss?" whispered Ruby, appearing behind them. She had an open bag of turkey jerky.

"Uh . . . we'll explain later," said Adrian, taking an offered piece of jerky and stuffing it through the bars of Turbo's cage.

"Genissa," said Thunderbird, stepping to the front of the balcony. "You have not been given clearance from the healers to—"

"Screw the healers," yelled Genissa. "What are they going to do? Bring my powers back?" She snapped her fingers—as if ice crystals might burst from their tips—but of course, nothing happened. Her scowl deepened. "You said yourself. The effects of Agent N are irreversible. So I don't see much point in lounging around in a stuffy waiting room just so someone can pat me on the head and tell me it could have been worse. I could be *dead*." She paused in the middle of the room, where the red-tiled *R* had been decimated by one of Aftershock's quakes, and let her gaze travel around the gathered Renegades. "But let's all stop and ask ourselves . . . really, would that be worse?" She returned her attention to the Council. "I'm not convinced."

"Genissa——" started the Captain.

"*Frostbite*," Genissa snapped in return, her nostrils flaring. She drew herself to her full height, her bob of white-blonde hair swinging against her shoulders. "We were here, on duty, protecting your organization. Your headquarters. I believed in the Renegades. I would have done anything to protect what we stand for. And look where it got me. Where it got us!" She gestured behind her at Mack and Trevor. "We stood up against Nightmare. We risked our lives, because that's what superheroes do. But it wasn't exactly a fair fight, was it? Because somehow, she had Agent N. She had *your* weapon."

Nova's jaw tensed, irritation flooding through her. How convenient for Genissa to skip over the fact that she, too, had Agent N at her disposal—and illegally, as the Renegades weren't yet supposed to have access to it. Nova guessed Frostbite had swiped some during their training sessions, and she hadn't hesitated to shoot Nightmare with a dart full of the stuff last night. If Nova hadn't been wearing the Vitality Charm, she would be just as powerless now as they were.

"I want to know how," Genissa continued. "How is it that you manage to develop a substance that can sap our enemies of their powers, only for it to fall into an enemy's hands before we've even made a public announcement about it?"

Captain Chromium cleared his throat loudly. "Gen—Frostbite poses a fair question, and we will be investigating this at length."

"Oh, you'll be *investigating* it?" Genissa flung her arms to the sides and faced the crowd. Though the Renegades closest to her backed away, it was clear that they were hanging on her every word. Expressions were full of pity for the three former prodigies. To lose their gifts—it was what they had all feared from the start. "Just like you investigated Nightmare's death after the Detonator supposedly blew her up?" Genissa said. "Or how about your investigation into the death of Ace Anarchy? Forgive me if I question your ability to figure out how Nightmare had access to Agent N, much less how you plan on keeping anyone else from getting it and turning it against us, just like she did." Her voice rose as broken glass crunched beneath her feet. "It's time we face the truth. Our leaders are incompetent. The Council is playing with things they don't understand, things they have no real control over, and worst of all, they are risking our lives and our abilities in order to do it!"

Nova traded stunned looks with Adrian. But while she imagined that Adrian was shocked that anyone would dare speak to the beloved Council that way, *she* was shocked to think that she actually agreed with Genissa on something.

"That's enough!" barked Blacklight, but he was silenced by the Captain lifting an arm across his chest, blocking him from moving to the front of the balcony.

"No, let her speak," said the Captain. Though his jaw was tense, there was compassion in his gaze as it shifted between Genissa, Mack, and Trevor. "We do carry some responsibility for what happened here last night. Tell me, what can we do to make amends?"

"Amends?" Genissa laughed dryly. "That's hysterical." Shaking her head, she reached for the band wrapped around her forearm.

"Honestly, I don't care what the Renegades do after this. I'm not one of you anymore. My time as a superhero is over." Peeling the band from her skin, she threw it at her feet. Mack and Trevor did the same, tossing their wristbands into the rubble. "I hope everyone here realizes that they're nothing but pawns to you. Just a bunch of pretty foot soldiers to do your bidding, so you don't have to worry about a bunch of pathetic villains ever showing up to take your power away. Or worse . . . those pesky vigilantes. But let's face it, we didn't become superheroes to play by the rules. We became superheroes because we believed in our ability to change this world for the better, at any cost. Well . . ." She wriggled her fingers. "Almost any cost."

Genissa marched through the lobby toward the main staircase. The crowd parted for her and her cohorts. "All I know," she called over her shoulder, "is that any prodigy who willingly runs around with Agent N strapped to their belt is a damned idiot."

No one moved to stop her or Mack or Trevor as they reached the balcony. Genissa paused once, seemingly surprised to have only two minions in her wake. She found Raymond Stern—Stingray—in the lobby, unmoved from where he had been standing at her side. A sneer twitched across her face, then she and her companions shoved through the waiting glass doors, letting in a blinding burst of daylight. An excited roar from the crowd outside greeted them, but was hushed the moment the doors shut behind them.

CHAPTER THREE

Nova had been to Adrian's home once before, and she hadn't fully recovered from the experience. Not only because this was where he had kissed her for the first time, a memory that still made her knees weak, but because there was something painfully unnerving about standing outside a palatial mansion and knowing to the core of her being how much she did not belong there. He lived in the old Gatlon City mayor's mansion, with more square footage than all the row houses on Wallowridge combined, and a lawn spanning almost an entire city block.

She tried not to think too much about it as she approached the gate and buzzed for entry. A device on a brick pillar scanned her wristband, confirming her identity, before the wrought-iron gate swung open.

By the time she reached the end of the walkway, Adrian was waiting for her on his front porch, framed by Grecian pillars and large urns with topiaries sprouting from them. The last time she'd been here, he'd been wearing sweats. Now he was donning his Renegade uniform, and the difference in his demeanor was startling.

This was a business meeting.

Still, Adrian was smiling as she approached. "The others are already downstairs. Come on in." He held his arm toward the open door, ushering her into the foyer.

It was warm inside the house. Almost uncomfortably warm. The sort of heat put off by fireplaces in the dead of winter, first chasing away the chill in the air, before making everyone forget there had ever been a chill to begin with. True enough—as Nova walked past the formal parlor, she spied a fire raging inside a tiled fireplace. With sweat already sprouting on the back of her neck, she unzipped her hooded sweatshirt.

"My dads think it makes the place feel cozier," said Adrian, almost apologetically. "It's a lot cooler downstairs. Come on."

She followed him down the narrow staircase into his basement bedroom and froze on the bottom step.

Oscar and Ruby were there—Ruby perched on the sofa and Oscar facing backward on Adrian's desk chair.

But what made Nova hesitate was that Danna was there, too, in the form of hundreds of gold-and-black butterflies that filled every available shelf and table and the narrow sills of the high windows along the south wall.

Nova's mouth ran dry.

Seeing so many of them at once, and not in the blur of battle like Nova always had before, might have been a beautiful sight. Except they weren't moving. Not a beat of wings. Not a twitch of antennae. And though it was impossible to know for sure, Nova had the distinct feeling that all of their tiny bug eyes were fixated on *her*.

"She's been following me around since we found Ace," said Ruby. "Didn't come with me to headquarters, but otherwise . . ." Her worried gaze flitted around at the butterflies.

"Has anyone contacted her dad, to let him know?" asked Adrian.

"I mentioned it to Thunderbird," said Ruby, "and she said she'd have someone reach out and let him know that Danna is okay . . . sort of. I figured she'd go home by now, but maybe she thinks that seeing her stuck like this will make him worry even more?"

"Or maybe she doesn't want to be left out of our exciting detective work," said Oscar. "She's still on the team, even in swarm mode, right?"

"Absolutely," said Adrian. "She did lead us to Ace Anarchy. Maybe she'll have more input to offer . . . however she can."

"Why . . ." Nova paused to clear her throat and dared to take the final step into the room. "Why hasn't she transformed back yet?"

"We figure she can't for some reason," said Adrian. "She needs all of her butterflies to converge. If even one is missing . . . not dead, but, like, trapped somewhere or too far away, then the others will be stuck in this form."

"What I can't figure out," said Ruby, fidgeting with the wire on her wrist, "is why she doesn't take us to that missing butterfly . . . or butterflies, if there is more than one. If she's trapped somewhere, why hasn't she helped us figure out how to help her, like she led us to Ace?"

Oscar shrugged. "Maybe she doesn't know where it is."

"But they all communicate with one another, even when they're in this form," said Adrian. "Like . . . a hive mind sort of thing. It seems unlikely that she wouldn't know where the others are."

Nova sat stiffly beside Ruby, thinking of the night one of Danna's butterflies had been spying on her and the Anarchists inside the catacombs. They had captured it in a pillowcase and held it prisoner, eventually bringing it back to the row house and putting it in a mason jar.

Like a blindfolded hostage, that butterfly wouldn't have been able to see where it was being taken. She supposed it made sense that it still didn't know where it was, and therefore couldn't call the rest of the creatures to it.

Still, she imagined she could feel the disgust emanating from the insects that surrounded her, making the hair stand on end all down her forearms.

Danna may not be able to speak to the others, but she did know the truth. She knew Nova's secret.

It was only a matter of time before she figured out a way to communicate it to the rest of the group.

"I'm glad she's here, at least," said Adrian. He paused then, studying the swarm. "I'm glad *you're* here," he corrected, because it was rude to speak about someone like they weren't even there, though Nova wasn't sure Danna could actually hear in this form. "We'll find a way to help Danna. There must have been a reason she knew about the location of Ace Anarchy's hideout." He drummed his fingers against his thigh. "I don't know this for sure, but I suspect . . . if we find Nightmare and the Anarchists, we might figure out how to help Danna, too."

"Wait, wait, wait," Oscar said. "I sense a transition into actual work coming up, but before we get there . . ." He reached behind himself and pulled out an old heart-shaped tin box. "I brought cookies!" Peeling off the lid, he offered it to Ruby first. Nova could see that the cookies inside were homemade. A few had burnt edges, and others had gooey, underbaked centers, all nestled into a bed of parchment paper.

"Thanks, Oscar," said Ruby, picking one out. She held it up and paused. "Are these . . . ?"

"Lemon-coconut-shortbread cookies with white chocolate centers," Oscar said, his ears turning pink. "Yes. Yes, they are."

Ruby gawked at him. "That's . . . my mom makes . . . these are my favorite!"

"Yeah, I know." Oscar cleared his throat awkwardly and held the tin toward Nova. "I, uh, called your mom for the recipe."

With little appetite, Nova waved away the cookies, while Adrian took three. Ruby continued to stare at Oscar, the forgotten cookie halfway to her mouth. He didn't return the look. Instead, he slammed the lid back onto the tin and nodded at Adrian, as if eager to move on from what might have been the most blatant confession of adoration that Nova had ever witnessed. "Okay, then. Great. Let's do this. Where do we start?"

Adrian shoved the first cookie in his mouth and approached a freestanding whiteboard. Grabbing one side of it, he pushed it away from the wall and swiveled it around so they could see the back side.

Nova's stomach plummeted.

It was a corkboard plastered with notes and diagrams and evidence. A map of Gatlon City covered nearly the entire board, with locations circled where Nightmare had been seen. The buildings where she and the Sentinel had faced off during the parade. Cosmopolis Park with its abandoned fun house. Renegade Headquarters. Various subway tunnel entrances. The Cloven Cross Library was highlighted, too, with notes about the Detonator and the Librarian. And the cathedral, beside which was tacked a recent newspaper article about the capture of Ace Anarchy.

There was a grainy picture of Nightmare tossing the Puppeteer out of his hot-air balloon. A red circle was drawn around her face, with a line connecting it to HQ, and another line drawn to Cosmopolis. Beside the line, in bold letters, Adrian had written: *FACE MASK?*

Another line connected headquarters to Adrian's house, along with the scrawled words: *VITALITY CHARM???*

Another line from the parade to the library. *WEAPONRY?* And in parentheses—*(sharpshooter).*

Another line, from HQ to the cathedral. *ACE ANARCHY HELMET?*

To the side of the map was a series of messy notes and asides.

How was she immune to Agent N and Max? Vitality Charm?? But how did she know about it? How did she GET it?

How did she get the helmet out of the chromium box?

How did she know the helmet wasn't destroyed? / Where it was kept?

Access to Agent N?

Agent N bombs—Fatalia's mist-missiles!

Each of the questions had a line drawn back to Renegade Headquarters.

Nova gulped, hard. Her skin prickled and her legs twitched with the urge to bolt for the door. It felt like a setup, but no one was looking at her.

Ruby stood, brushing cookie crumbs from her fingers, and approached the board. "Okay," she murmured, rocking back on her heels. "What does it all mean?"

Adrian's expression was dark as he inspected the map, too, as if waiting for a new clue to jump out at him and piece it all together. But he had already pieced together enough.

Nova knew what he was going to say before he said it.

Her heart hammered, waiting for the words.

"I do have a theory," he started, speaking slowly, his brow drawn.

"We're listening," said Oscar. In the same moment, a dozen of

Danna's butterflies lifted off Adrian's desk and twirled around the board, before settling on its top.

"For starters," said Adrian, "Nightmare knows too much—about Agent N and Max, maybe even the Vitality Charm—"

"Pause," said Ruby, holding a hand toward him. "What is the Vitality Charm?"

Adrian cleared his throat. "It's . . ." He hesitated again, and Nova could see his thoughts forming as he tried to reason through how best to explain to her this incredible object he'd discovered. "It's an old charm that was found in the artifacts departments. Anyone who's wearing it will be protected from illness, poisons, venom, and even . . . something like Agent N. Or Max."

"You're kidding," said Oscar, cocking his head to one side. "Why haven't we heard about this before?"

"I wanted to tell you, but my dads asked me to keep it a secret until they knew more about the charm and its limitations. They were worried its existence might interfere with the launch of Agent N. And now it's missing."

"Missing?" asked Ruby.

"Simon had it last. He was able to visit Max with it. But we haven't seen it since before Nightmare broke into headquarters."

"So Nightmare stole this thing from the Dread Warden?" said Oscar. "What? Did she, like, pickpocket him?"

Adrian tapped his marker against his palm. "Pops said he left it here at the house, but I don't know. Maybe he forgot, and it was actually at headquarters. Because, listen, all of these things"—he swirled the marker around the board—"were at HQ. The helmet, the Silver Spear, and even those bombs she had. The Vitality Charm, if she did have it . . . maybe it was at headquarters, too. And oh, the mask!" He pointed at a grainy photo of Nightmare, showing the metal mask across the lower half of her face. "Frostbite's team said she was wearing it last night and it was identical to the one she used to wear. I'm convinced that it *is* the mask she used to wear."

Nova sank deeper into the sofa.

"So?" said Oscar.

"So," said Adrian, "her mask was found in the debris at the Cosmopolis fun house. I saw it myself, after the explosion went off that was supposed to have killed her. I talked to Magpie, and she swears it was collected by the cleanup crew and handed over to the artifacts department, but they have no record of it. And Stingray's statement says that Nightmare was in full costume when she attacked him in the security room, even though that was *before* she went to the vault." He pointed to a pieced-together timeline of the HQ break-in along the bottom of the board, where it was indicated that Nightmare had used Stingray's wristband to access the vault's door.

"Which brings up another point," continued Adrian. "Nightmare went out of her way to make sure she hit the security room and disabled all of the surveillance cameras before she went after the helmet. But she wears a mask! Why would she care if she was caught on video footage unless she worried that someone might recognize her."

Nova raised a finger, glad that this, at least, she could make a decent rebuttal against. "If she went into the vault while the cameras were still on, it would have triggered the security team to come after her right away. She would have had to disable the cameras to give herself time to complete the theft before anyone realized what she was doing."

Adrian considered this, then gave a half shrug. "Maybe. But there's also Agent N." He tapped the large board enthusiastically. "I got the report a few hours ago. Those devices they found in the lobby were definitely Fatalia's mist-missiles—gas bombs that were stored in the vault—and Nightmare had definitely reengineered them to release a gaseous form of Agent N, which not only means she had the bombs before she broke in, maybe even weeks before, but she also had a supply of Agent N, which is kept in a secure storeroom behind the laboratories. Either Nightmare broke into that storeroom *before* her attack on HQ the other night, or she was able to get her hands on Agent N some other way."

"But who else has access to it?" said Ruby, stealing another cookie from the tin.

Adrian fixed her with a serious look. *"We do."*

"Whoa," muttered Oscar. "You totally just gave me chills. But what does that mean exactly?"

"We have access to Agent N," said Adrian. "All patrol units. Everyone who's been in training the past few weeks. And the Council, obviously. And everyone who works in the labs."

Oscar rolled the chair forward, pushing off with the balls of his feet. "Go on. I feel like this is about to get really good."

Adrian scratched the back of his head. "It might seem far-fetched, but I have this theory, and it answers so many questions. How she knew about Agent N, and how she was able to steal some before we've even announced it. How she had access to the vault. How she knew about Max, and the team that would be on security detail that night, and the helmet, and all of it. I think . . ." He paused to take in a deep breath. "I think Nightmare has been posing as a Renegade. I think she's a spy."

Nova flinched. She squeezed her eyes shut, only for a second. There it was. The remark that would unravel it all.

Still, she forced a mask of surprise onto her face as her fingertips dug into her thighs. "A spy?" she said, daring to speak, and hoping that the slight quiver in her voice added to her apparent disbelief. "In the Renegades?"

As one, the hundreds of butterflies surrounding them opened their wings in perfect unison, and then closed them again and went back to stillness.

It was as much a confirmation as if Danna had been sitting on the couch between Nova and Ruby, ready to jut her accusatory finger in Nova's direction.

"Yikes," muttered Oscar. "That was weird."

"Danna," said Adrian. "I'm right? Do you know who it is? Or how we can find her?"

And though Nova had been sure that Danna wasn't supposed to be able to hear, let alone comprehend spoken language, in swarm mode, they must have understood well enough. As one, the butterflies lifted into the air, circled once beneath the ceiling, then came to settle.

Directly on Nova.

She squeaked and stiffened as the butterflies and their dainty feet perched on her shoulders, her hair, her arms and knees and toes. Those who couldn't fit on her body surrounded her, taking up residence on the cushions and the back of the couch.

Nova held her breath, suddenly too afraid to move. She wasn't the only one who had gone motionless. Adrian was gawking at her, his mouth hanging open.

The butterflies lingered only a moment before they took to the air again and found their way to the distant corners of the room.

Heart thudding, Nova dared to look at Ruby. Then Oscar. And back to Adrian. They were all watching her . . . not accusatory, not yet. But uncertain, for sure.

Her brain scrambled for words . . . any words, and—"The vault!"

she said, launching to her feet so fast Adrian took a hesitant step back from her. "I think Danna is telling me . . . us . . . that's it. It makes so much sense. So many of the clues pointing toward Nightmare lead to the vault. And I work in the vault!" She forced a grin, as brilliant as she dared. "I can search the records. Talk to Tina and Callum. If Nightmare knew about the mist-missiles and . . . all that other stuff . . . then she must have left some sort of trail. Either in the paperwork or on the security tapes . . ." She pounded a fist into her open palm. "If she's been there anytime in the last six months, I can find out about it. If she is a spy, then I can figure out her identity. I know it."

Adrian relaxed. "You're right. Danna's right. By pinpointing the exact items she used and stole, we should be able to track who it is."

"Also," said Ruby, "we can compare them with the trial records. Probably Nightmare hasn't been in our ranks for long. She might have just joined up at the most recent trials . . . or maybe last year. We can compare what Nova finds with the newest recruits."

Nova's head started to bob as if it were no longer attached to her spine. "Great. Yes. Excellent. I won't let you down."

All the while, her head was throbbing. Panic surging through her veins.

Time was running out. She would be discovered any day, any minute.

How was she possibly going to free Ace before it happened?

CHAPTER FOUR

"HERE'S WHAT WE have," said Nova, clearing mason jars full of honey from their small dining room table. Leroy, Honey, and Phobia stood watching as Nova took the rubber band from a large roll of paper and spread it out across the surface. She replaced a couple of the honey jars at the corners to hold it down flat.

The paper, which she had printed at a twenty-four-hour, low-budget print shop the night before, showed old blueprints of Cragmoor Penitentiary, downloaded from the Renegade database. They were, however, very old blueprints, and Nova knew they weren't accurate. Still, she had been unable to find updated records. If anything, it appeared that the Renegades had intentionally kept records of any penitentiary remodels secure and private . . . perhaps to avoid prison breaks.

"These exterior walls are unchanged," she said, pointing to the outline of the prison cell block and the stone security wall that enclosed it. "Satellite imagery confirms it, as well as the placement of these guard towers and the boat dock. There are still buildings here and here . . ." She pointed to two structures just inside the wall. "But I can't say for sure what they contain. They used to be administration, guard housing, a small medical office, and the cafeteria, but we can't confirm any of that. We do know that prisoners are transferred to terrain vehicles just off the dock and taken up this road onto the island, where they pass through this security checkpoint, manned by Renegades. Let's assume they're heavily armed."

"Possibly," said Leroy. He was leaning against the kitchen counter, sipping from a snifter glass full of brandy. He did not imbibe regularly, but this bottle seemed to be one that he had sequestered for years, and Nova had noticed him emptying it faster than usual these days. "But it's more likely they choose prodigies who have powers that can act as long-distance weaponry, rather than arming them with guns that could potentially be taken and used against them."

"Let's hope so," said Honey. "A few doses of Agent N will solve that problem."

Nova didn't respond. The same thought had occurred to her, but she didn't want to get cocky. After her infiltration of Renegade Headquarters, they knew that Nightmare and the Anarchists had at least some supply of Agent N, and that they'd found a way to weaponize it in gas form. They could be expecting it. She doubted she would get the chance to surprise them with their own substance again.

"And where is Ace in all this?" said Honey. Leaning over the table, she drew a bloodred fingernail along a line of cells inside the block. "Somewhere in here?"

"Doubtful," murmured Phobia. He swirled the blade of his scythe once over his hood, before tipping it forward and touching the point to the blueprint. "They will have him here."

Beneath the blade's edge was a short hallway tucked away in the building behind what may or may not be the cafeteria. Only four tiny cells were printed there, along with the word SOLITARY.

"If that's where they still keep solitary confinement," said Nova. "We know the Renegades have made extensive renovations to the prison, but I can't find any records of what they've done." She pinched the bridge of her nose, feeling a headache coming on. "And as far as current security protocols, cell placements, areas of restricted access . . ." She shrugged. "We can make guesses, but that's all they'll be. Guesses."

"So if we're going to get Ace out of there," said Honey, "we'll be going in blind."

"Exactly."

Honey hummed as she surveyed the blueprints. "I'm beginning to understand the value of our little butterfly friend's ability more and more."

Nova's cheek twitched, though she tried not to let the others see her discomfort. She tended to flinch every time Danna was mentioned. She'd done her best to ignore the glass jar that sat on Honey's vanity in their shared bedroom, with pinprick holes for oxygen punctured into the tin lid, and the occasional cutting of ironweed dropped inside so it wouldn't starve. Nova's guilt over keeping Danna imprisoned was profound. She often wondered if Danna's consciousness was somewhere inside that tiny little insect brain, experiencing what it experienced.

Trapped and suffocating.

But Danna knew too much, and she could not be allowed to escape. As long as they kept the one butterfly separate from the others, she would be unable to re-form into her human self and tell everyone Nova's true identity and the location of the Anarchists.

Nova knew, logically, that she had no other choice. For her own safety and that of the others, she couldn't set Danna free.

But still. Having her own aversion to small, enclosed spaces, she couldn't deny the guilt that pressed in on her to think of the pretty winged butterfly stuck in that jar. Not even kept like a pet. More like—a science experiment.

"It would be helpful to have, well, any sort of idea of what we're walking into," said Leroy, half of his face crinkling with a knowing smile. "Any hope for it, *Insomnia*?"

Insomnia. Her Renegade alias.

"I . . . don't know," she admitted. "I've been trying to come up with a valid reason to go there. To interview Ace, or one of the other prisoners. To conduct some sort of research . . . or . . ." Her shoulders drooped. "I can't think of anything that wouldn't be suspicious. But maybe an opportunity will present itself."

Honey's lip curled. "We don't have time to wait for an opportunity."

Leroy fixed Nova with a concerned frown. "How much longer do you think we have?"

"Before they neutralize Ace? Hard to say. They're still trying to figure out—"

"Not that," he interrupted. "How much longer do we have before they figure out who you are?"

Nova tensed. With that seemingly innocent question, a floodgate of panic surged through her body.

Every wrong turn.

Every arrogant mistake.

Every piece of evidence that had been piling up against her over the past months.

They all blurred in her mind. A thousand missteps flashing through her memory at once.

The time she had put Danna to sleep in the medical wing. How

Winston had seemed to recognize her when he'd been interrogated by Adrian, as had the Librarian's granddaughter, Narcissa Cronin. All the things she had ever taken from the vault. How she had flaunted her shooting skills more than once. How she had left the Renegades' gala early, on the same evening that Nightmare had stolen Ace's helmet.

And, perhaps most condemning of all, how she had helped Max when he was dying.

After seeing the board at Adrian's house and listening to his theory, Nova realized that in some terrible way, she was lucky that Max was in a coma. It might have been in Frostbite's best interest to lie and say that Nightmare had attacked the kid, but when he woke up, would Max tell a different story? Nova wanted him to wake up—of course she did—but she also hoped that his memory of the night would be too befuddled to make sense of.

Because it made no sense that Nightmare would help him, and yet, that's what she'd done. Instead of leaving him for dead, she had tried to stop the bleeding, even going so far as to force Genissa Clark to give him her powers so he could freeze over the wound.

Nova had been through those moments in her head a million times. She knew she should have left Max. She should have grabbed the helmet and run.

But he was *dying*.

She couldn't have just left him. Even now, with all the rationality of hindsight plaguing her, she knew she'd made the right choice.

The truth would come out eventually, and the truth would be her undoing. At this point, any number of truths could be her undoing.

"Perhaps this moment calls for a bit of cold honesty," said Honey, drumming her nails on the table. "I want to rescue our poor Acey as much as anybody, but none of this is very promising. Even if we could get into that prison, the chances of getting him and us *out* again are relatively scarce, and the moment the Renegades realize who Nova is—which, judging from the abject terror on her face, I suspect could happen in the next five minutes—they'll have this place surrounded and we'll be done for." She fluffed her hair as her focus shifted from Nova to Leroy and Phobia and back again. "Has anyone considered maybe that we don't rescue Ace, and instead steal a nice yacht and go live out our days on a tropical island somewhere?"

Phobia made a disgusted sound.

Honey wiggled her fingers at him. "Don't worry, darling. I'm sure we can find one with a cemetery."

"We're not leaving Ace," said Nova.

Honey sighed. "It's time to consider other options."

"Honey has a point," murmured Leroy. "I hate to admit it, but . . ." He gestured at the blueprint. "This isn't giving us enough to even concoct a plan, much less execute one."

"We're *not leaving Ace*," Nova repeated, harsher this time. "He wouldn't leave us."

The others shared uncertain looks and Nova bristled. "Well, he wouldn't leave *me*. And besides. Even if . . ." She swallowed the lump in her throat. "Even if we can't get to Ace in time, that doesn't mean we've lost. He had a vision, and that vision lives on inside us. The hold the Renegades have over this city is weakening every day, as people are becoming aware of their failures and their hypocrisy. Whatever happens with Ace, we need to keep fighting for the world he believed in!"

Nova shut her mouth as tears began to pool in her vision. Feeling infuriatingly melodramatic, she turned her face away, but there were still words left unsaid. Still a deep loathing that burned in her chest.

It wasn't just about Ace's hope for the world—for the freedom and autonomy he felt all prodigies deserved. The right to not be hunted down and killed for what they were, but also the right to use their powers however they wanted, without fear of persecution, even from other prodigies like the Renegades. That was a part of it—it had always been a part of why she fought at Ace's side.

But the deeper reason she hated the Renegades, and had always hated them, was because they had not come to her rescue when she needed them most. They had sworn to protect her family, and they had failed. Her parents were dead. Her little sister, Evie, was dead. Nova would be dead, too, if she hadn't used her powers to put the assassin to sleep. Ace had found her standing over his unconscious body, trying, but unable, to pull the trigger on her family's killer.

All because of the Renegades and their empty promises.

She would not forgive it. And she would not let it happen to anyone else. People believed that the Renegades could save them, but they were wrong. The Renegades made mistakes. They broke their promises. They lied.

And they could not be left to rule the world unchecked.

"All right," Honey said, once their mutual silence had stretched thin. "We'll try it your way, little Nightmare." She tipped her chin toward the blueprint. "But we all know your secrets won't last much longer. We should probably have a contingency plan in place, for when you're discovered."

Leroy nodded. "I've been thinking that, too. If Nova is found out, we'll need to leave this house and destroy as much evidence as possible that we were ever here. And as it so happens, I've been working on just the thing. A cocktail of chemicals that, when combined, will decimate nearly everything they touch. It would at least keep the Renegades from combing through our stuff once we're gone."

"Fine," said Nova. "If necessary, we'll take what we need, destroy everything else, and go into hiding."

A loud thump from the second floor drew their attention to the water-stained ceiling. Nova's body tensed and she felt the rest of her companions go still, except for Phobia, who dissolved into a cloud of inky black smoke and swirled like a hurricane toward the staircase.

Grabbing the nearest weapon—a rather dull knife from the kitchen drawer—Nova charged after him with Leroy and Honey close behind. But when she reached the bedroom that she and Honey shared, she saw only Phobia awaiting her amid the bees and wasps. Honey's creatures were always coming and going through the small window, which was left cracked open to allow them freedom, even when torrential rains soaked the rotting windowsill, as happened more and more as autumn tipped toward winter.

Phobia's cloaked presence felt like a black hole in the center of the room. He was facing Honey's vanity, one skeletal hand idly spinning the blade of his scythe.

Nova's feet paused on the matted carpet. Honey and Leroy crowded beside her.

Nothing on the vanity appeared to have been disturbed, though it was difficult to tell, as the mess of makeup and costume jewelry was generally disheveled. Among them was a mason jar, its lid newly cluttered with bobby pins and a single rhinestone earring. Inside was the monarch butterfly, currently hanging upside down from the lid. Traces of dust from its wings were streaked along the inside of the jar from its attempts to get free, and four yellow wasps were picking their way around the lid, trying to get at the tasty snack inside.

But it wasn't the butterfly or Honey's trinkets that held Nova's attention. It was the mirror, glinting their stunned expressions back at them. Written upon its surface, in black marker and all caps, were the words:

BRING ME THE HELMET
QB'S ROOM—BLACKMIRE
48 HOURS

OR EVERYONE WILL KNOW
WHO YOU REALLY ARE

Nova had barely begun to digest the threat when Leroy moved past her and stuck his head out through the window, scanning the yard and alleyway behind the house. However, even if the perpetrator was out there, lurking in the shadows, Nova doubted Leroy would be able to see them in the darkness.

She read through the words again. She knew that so many Renegades, Adrian among them, had been closing in on her secret for months now. Had one of them finally figured her out? But most Renegades would take the information straight to the Council. She doubted many of them would have the guts to blackmail her for Ace's helmet, even if it was one of the most powerful objects of all time.

Who could it be?

"Well," said Honey, "with Ace gone, it's not like we have much use for the helmet as it is."

Nova scowled at Honey's reflection, cut through with the scrawled words. "We're not giving up the helmet. I risked too much to get it. Besides, we are going to find a way to free Ace, and when we do, he'll need the helmet to get his strength back. I'm not going to watch him waste away to nothing because we gave up the one thing that could restore him."

"I agree," said Leroy, apparently not having seen anything, or anyone, out the window. "But I don't think we should take this as an idle threat. Someone knows your identity, Nova. Not just that—they know where you are. Where we all are."

Nova crossed her arms. "Yeah, but they're a coward, whoever it is. To leave a threatening message and not dare face me in person. Who does that?"

"Cowards can sometimes be the most dangerous of all," said Phobia.

"Phobia's right," said Leroy. "We can't ignore this."

Nova glanced at his face, scarred and disfigured, and thought of the teenage bullies who had dumped acids on him after chemistry class. Cowards, the lot of them. But still dangerous.

Nevertheless, she wasn't about to relinquish the helmet to someone who didn't have the nerve to fight for it themselves, and she didn't have time to be running errands and making deliveries for anonymous stalkers, either.

But she needed more time to figure out how to free Ace from that prison.

Her wall of lies might be ready to collapse on its own, but she wasn't about to let someone take a wrecking ball to it now.

The threat on the glass blurred before her.

48 HOURS
OR EVERYONE WILL KNOW

CHAPTER FIVE

ADRIAN WAS CONTEMPLATING invisibility. As superpowers go, it was one with infinite uses, particularly when one spent a great deal of time sneaking and spying, as he tended to do these days. His dad Simon—the Dread Warden—could turn invisible. So could Max, having absorbed some of Simon's ability when he was a baby, although he could only go invisible for short periods of time. There was one Renegade who had trained in Gatlon City a number of years ago who was *always* invisible, which Adrian had found slightly disconcerting when they'd been around. (To this day, he still wasn't sure of their gender, and their alias, the Wraith, didn't offer any clues.) But they had been sent to a syndicate across the ocean and Adrian hadn't given much thought to them or their power since.

He was giving it plenty of thought now.

Because of all the powers he had given himself using tattoos inked into his body, none of them offered much in the way of stealth. Quite the opposite—the armor that burst forth from the zipper tattooed over his sternum was big and bulky, shiny and reflective. It made him feel invincible when he wore it, but also very, *very* visible.

He couldn't quite picture the sort of tattoo that might allow for full invisibility, though. He figured such a tattoo would have to cover him nearly from head to toe to be effective, but maybe he needed to think outside the box. Maybe he just needed inspiration.

He wondered if Nova would have some ideas, except she didn't know about the Sentinel or the tattoos and he wasn't sure how to go about telling her, or even if he wanted to, especially given the outward loathing she demonstrated for his vigilante alter ego.

But standing on a ledge outside a hospital window, five stories in the air, in broad daylight in his heavy, glinting armor, he decided it was time to start considering other means of sneaking in to see Max. And invisibility would have made it so much easier.

Plastered against the building's side, he angled a small handheld mirror toward the window, following the movements of a nurse as she checked Max's vital signs and noted information onto a tablet. She adjusted something on an IV drip beside the bed, smoothed the blanket across his thin shoulders, signed her initials on a sheet of paper by the door.

Finally she left, leaving the door barely cracked behind her.

The moment she was gone, Adrian crouched and dug his gloved fingertips beneath the window. It opened as easily and silently as it had the last two times.

He stepped inside, cringing at the loud thump of his boots. He pressed a finger to the breastplate, retracting the armor into the pocket beneath his skin. On much quieter feet now, he crossed the room and shut the door the rest of the way. There was no lock, but the movements of the nurses were kept to a tight schedule, and by now he was familiar enough with their methods to know that no one would be back to check on Max for a couple of hours.

And, sadly, the kid couldn't expect many visitors. Having been quarantined inside Renegade HQ for most of his life, he had no friends or acquaintances beyond the Renegades, and there were only two Renegades who could be near Max without him absorbing their powers into himself.

Captain Chromium was one. He was invincible to everything, even the Bandit.

And Adrian was the other—though no one other than Max knew about it.

After he'd discovered the Vitality Charm and what it could do, Adrian had been inspired to design a tattoo that could offer the same measures of protection, even against a power like Max's. And it had worked. He could finally be near his little brother without a glass barrier dividing them.

But until he found a way to explain the tattoos to everyone, especially his dads, he had to keep even this tattoo a secret. And now that the Vitality Charm was missing, he couldn't use that as a foil for visiting the kid.

But there was no way he could stay away completely.

He just had to be careful about it.

With the door shut and the blinds closed, he stepped to the side of the bed and peered down at his little brother. At least, he thought of Max as his brother, and he'd thought of him that way since the first day he'd met the kid. His dads had rescued Max as a baby, after his biological parents—members of the Roaches—had tried to throw him into a river. Max had probably already absorbed their powers by that point, and no doubt the rest of the gang would have threatened expulsion if they didn't get rid of the little bandit before he did any more damage. To a lot of prodigy parents, Max would have been seen as a threat long before he was seen as a child worth loving. For months after, Max had lived with a civilian foster family who cared for him until Hugh and Simon could figure out what to do. From the start, Hugh had felt it was important for him to be kept close, not just because he was a prodigy who deserved to be surrounded by other prodigies, but also because to have him out on his own could make him either a target for the villains or a weapon that they could some-day use against the Renegades.

Which is when they'd started to consider a quarantine.

Construction had begun almost as soon as the Battle for Gatlon was won, and some months later, Adrian had met his foundling baby brother on the other side of a glass wall. He was walking by then, toddling around the wide-open space, exploring the mess of blocks and train sets Hugh kept bringing for him.

Adrian had used a red marker to draw his best shark on the glass wall—not a living creature, but a toy that Max could play with. The drawing was rudimentary and rough, but it had quickly become the kid's favorite toy.

Adrian had loved him immediately.

Pulling a plastic chair beside the bed, Adrian slumped into it and inspected Max's face, almost ten years older than that innocent baby, and about a hundred years wiser. He told himself the kid was less pale than the night before, though it might have been wishful thinking. His breath was as steady as ever. His hair as messy. A faint shade of blue was cast across his eyelids, making his skin appear to be made of rice paper.

He had always been small for his age, and now he looked like he could fade right into the white sheets of the hospital bed.

Adrian tried not to think like that, though. It might have felt like Max had been lying here for weeks, but it wasn't true. Adrian had to forcefully count out the time that had passed.

Three days. Three nights. Some people were in comas for years and managed to pull out of it.

Besides, Hugh had spoken with the doctors, and they claimed that Max was actually improving at a startling rate, especially when one considered how few people would have survived to begin with. The spear had gone clean through his abdomen, just below his rib cage. They partly credited his survival to the ice that had hardened over the wound, stanching the blood both internally and externally—a power he'd absorbed from Frostbite during the battle.

If it had been possible for a healer to tend to him, he might have been back on his feet in a week or two, good as new but for a couple gnarly scars.

He couldn't be tended to by the healers though. In fact, any prodigy remotely associated with the hospital had been instructed to stay away from the room, even the entire wing, where Max was being cared for.

Nevertheless, he had been put under the care of the best civilian doctors the hospital had to offer, and he did seem to be recovering. They were tentatively optimistic.

Those were the words they kept using, that Hugh had parroted back to Adrian and Simon. *Tentatively optimistic.* It was something, but it wasn't enough.

If only Adrian had captured Ace Anarchy sooner. If he'd gotten Max's message. If he'd been just a little faster getting back to headquarters. He could have stopped Nightmare. He could have saved Max.

"Don't worry, kid," he whispered. "I'll find her. I'll make her pay for this."

Then he inhaled deeply and started to tell Max everything he and the team had discussed. His suspicions that Nightmare could be a spy within the Renegades, and the evidence that seemed to confirm the theory. He wished he had a suspect in mind, but the only Renegade who struck him as villainous enough was Genissa Clark, and she couldn't be Nightmare for obvious reasons.

Part of the problem was that powers were public record, and no one in the Renegades had an ability like Nightmare's: to put people to sleep through touch. The closest thing Adrian could find were records of a prodigy who went by Lullaby and had the gift, enviable only to new parents, of singing restless children to sleep with her soothing voice. Lullaby, however, had never been a Renegade, just a prodigy who was a popular babysitter for parents who wanted to stay on patrols.

Which meant that Nightmare was hiding her ability from the rest of them. He thought it was likely that she was posing as one of their civilian contractors. About 10 percent of the Renegade's workforce were not prodigies, including plenty of the lab personnel and administrators.

It made sense, actually, that it would be one of them. They didn't have to pass trials. Though they would have undergone some rudimentary background checks . . .

Still, it seemed like as good a place to start as any.

"Thanks, Max," he said, leaning back in his chair as his words and ideas faded out. "Talking this out with you was actually really helpful."

Though Max couldn't respond, it did comfort Adrian to work out his thoughts this way. Max had often been a sounding board for him, with ideas and perspectives that were mature beyond his years.

Adrian didn't know what he would do without him.

A noise caught his attention and Adrian's head jerked upward. He could hear voices coming toward the room, and one boomed louder than the others.

Hugh Everhart, aka Captain Chromium, aka his dad.

Cursing, Adrian sprang to his feet and shoved the chair back to its place in the corner.

Again. Invisibility. He really had to work on it.

He climbed onto the windowsill and slipped around to the ledge on the outside of the building's facade, a perch that was beginning to feel all too familiar. Except he'd never been out there before when he wasn't wearing the Sentinel's armor. It was shocking how different the sensation was. How vulnerable he felt with the gusts of wind buffeting his skin and the rough stone of the building's wall scratching against his palms. He wasn't afraid of heights, but it was impossible not to imagine what would happen if he fell and his body struck the pavement five stories below.

He dared to glance down and saw, with a small shred of relief, that he would actually land in a flower bed. Not as great as, say, a trampoline, but still better than pavement.

Hugh's booming voice reached him, though it was barely audible over the wind whistling past his ears. Was it his imagination, or had he heard his dad mention the Sentinel?

One side of his mouth twitched down. Adrian shook his wrist, flicking out the marker that he kept inside a pocket of his sleeve. He uncapped it with his teeth and started to sketch onto the building's wall, but the textured stone was too rough for the marker to complete any clean lines, and bits of debris kept sticking to the felted tip. Scowling, he bent forward, ignoring the sheer drop mere inches behind his heels, and drew instead on the thigh of his jeans.

He had learned, over the years of being Sketch, the Renegade who could turn any drawing into reality, that complex, detailed drawings might be impressive, but it was the simple ones that tended to work the best. He could have drawn some sort of high-tech hearing aid with a radio antenna and background-noise dulling capabilities, but why muck around with all that? Instead, he drew an old-fashioned ear trumpet, pointed at one end and open wide at the other to take in sound waves and funnel them toward his ear canal. It was something the elderly might have used hundreds of years ago, and it didn't exactly make him feel too sexy to pull the drawing from the denim fabric and hold it up to his ear.

But it worked. Suddenly, his father's voice was coming through as if he were standing right beside him.

"—a great debt," Hugh was saying, in a calmer tone than when he'd first entered the room, "which is putting us in a hell of a position. You're sure he would have died if the Sentinel hadn't gotten him here so fast?"

"Nothing is certain," said another male voice—Dr. Sutner, Adrian recognized. The civilian doctor who had taken on Max's care when none of their on-staff prodigy healers could get close to him. "He might have pulled through on his own, especially with the ice stanching the bleeding. But . . ." He didn't finish his sentence. He didn't have to.

Adrian felt a tinge of warmth in his chest to know that he had done something right, at least. He had been tempted that night—so very tempted—to go after Nightmare when she had run. But he had chosen Max instead. He had chosen to try to save his little brother rather than exact vengeance on his attacker.

Vengeance could wait.

"Well . . . if I ever meet him, he'll have my gratitude," said Hugh, though there was a heaviness in his words. "Even if he does need to be stopped."

"Stopped, Captain?" said the doctor. "But . . . isn't he working for you?"

"Of course not. He's a vigilante—he hasn't followed our code from day one."

"Right. Yes. The media says that. I'd just assumed . . ." Dr. Sutner trailed off.

"He's not a Renegade. He's not one of us." Hugh's voice took on an edge of resentment. "Maybe he's done some good for us, but . . . it's hard not to criticize his methods. He should have joined the organization, rather than going off on his own. It's given people a lot of ideas about heroics and crime fighting, and that's dangerous when it isn't left in the hands of the professionals. People have been getting hurt, and it's going to get worse."

Adrian wished he could break out his mirror so he'd be able to see his dad's expression, but he couldn't use both the mirror and the ear trumpet. Still, he had a feeling he could tell what his dad was thinking. There had been a lot of talk about the Sentinel's capture of the world's most revered villain. It felt a little unjust, as Oscar, Ruby, and Danna had all helped him do it and should have gotten part of the credit. But after finding out that Adrian was the Sentinel, it had been Ruby's idea to leave the Renegades a note for when they came to get Ace Anarchy. It had read,

> CONSIDER THIS A
> PEACE OFFERING.
> —THE SENTINEL

That way, as Ruby explained, they would know that the Sentinel was on their side. That he wasn't a villain. That they needed to stop hunting him.

Despite her good intentions, though, the note only seemed to have irritated the Council more. People thought that maybe the Sentinel was mocking them by tracking down their worst enemy, an enemy the Renegades had long believed dead. On top of that, the rise in vigilantism had skyrocketed these past months, as news of the Sentinel's victories over criminals had spread. People were beginning to feel like the Renegades and their code weren't enough. There needed to be more drastic measures taken if they were ever going to stop the spread of crime in their city.

It would have been flattering, except not everyone was made to be a superhero, and plenty of good intentions had led to civilians being severely wounded. One ambitious man had nearly been killed while trying to stop a carjacking, and an innocent woman had been shot in the arm when an enthusiastic vigilante had wrongly assumed that she was trying to break into his neighbor's apartment. (In reality, the neighbor had asked her to dog-sit for a few days.)

The more people tried to take matters into their own hands, the more stories like that emerged.

It wasn't that Renegades never made mistakes, but for the first time since Adrian had donned the Sentinel's armor, he was beginning to understand why the Council placed so much importance on their code.

"Your staff knows to keep an eye out for him?" said Hugh, drawing Adrian's attention back to their conversation.

"Just like you asked. There's been no sign. Though . . . if he were to come to the hospital, we probably wouldn't recognize him."

"I know, but I just have a feeling he will . . . It's common heroic behavior, to want to see the people you've rescued. I see it in Renegades all the time, how they want to maintain connections with the ones they've been personally involved in helping. Something tells me the Sentinel will try to see Max again."

"Which begs the question, Captain," said the doctor, sounding a bit hesitant. "How was he able to bring Max all the way here without being affected by the boy's powers?"

Hugh was silent for a long time, though Adrian sensed it was more because he was debating what information to reveal, rather than mulling over the question itself. Finally, he admitted simply, "We don't know. There are a lot of things about him that we don't know. I guess what we do know is that in the course of one night, he managed to capture Ace Anarchy and save my son's life. In spite of everything . . . how dangerous he is, how misguided . . . I can't help but hope that someday I might have a chance to thank him."

CHAPTER SIX

IT WAS NOVA'S first time returning to the weapons and artifacts department since the night she'd stolen Ace's helmet. Her insides were knotted as she rode the elevator up to the warehouse endearingly known as the vault. Her Renegade uniform felt like it was strangling her, the fabric tightening around her limbs, digging into her ribs and throat until she could barely move.

The words on the mirror were etched into her thoughts, and there was a part of her, a big part, that wondered if maybe Honey was right. Maybe it was time to give up. She didn't really think she could save Ace, did she? Especially not before she was discovered. And now to have some unknown jerk stalking and threatening her made her wonder if it was all worth it.

Though she toyed with her own fate often enough, she loathed the idea that someone else now held her fate in their hands. That simply wouldn't do.

She had gone over a lot of scenarios in her mind the night before, most of which ended in her discovering who the blackmailer was and dousing them with one of Leroy's most painful concoctions. Because the idea of giving in to their demands, even if just to placate them temporarily, disgusted her. She was an Anarchist. She was one of the most feared villains of Gatlon City.

She did *not* placate.

And she certainly didn't follow the orders of phantoms who broke into her bedroom and left annoying messages.

But every time her anger ran away with her, she gritted her teeth and reeled it back in. She didn't need retribution right now. She needed time.

The elevator dinged and she squared her shoulders, dragging in a breath until it felt like her lungs would pop.

She was still holding it when the doors opened, revealing the small reception area outside the warehouse—Snapshot's desk, as cluttered as ever, and the desk that was mostly Nova's, as barren as ever.

Snapshot wasn't there, and neither was Wonder Boy, as Nova had taken to calling Callum in her head.

She exhaled and moved toward the desk.

She wasn't ready to see Callum, though she knew she would have to eventually. Not only because they worked together most days, but because she needed to pretend to pry him for information about Nightmare. It would require a careful dance. Letting him know about Adrian's suspicions, leading him to believe that, yes, Nightmare might be a spy in their midst, one who may even have had access to the vault. All while keeping his suspicions away from her.

She wasn't sure she could pull it off. She'd gotten good at lying, but she didn't know if she was *that* good.

Maybe it wouldn't matter today. Maybe she wouldn't see him. Maybe she wouldn't have to look him in the eye and force herself to smile, all the while remembering the moment when he had tried to stop her from taking the helmet and she had been forced to put him to sleep because of it.

She didn't usually feel guilt when she used her power, especially on Renegades, but she did with Callum. He had used his power on her to make Nova see how maybe the world could be different. How maybe her life could be different, if she chose a different path. And the worst thing was knowing that it wasn't Callum putting the thoughts into her mind; it was knowing that they'd been there all along.

And knowing that she wasn't going to do anything about it.

When she had chosen to continue with her plan and take the helmet, it had felt like a betrayal of Callum and all his annoying goodness. It had also felt like a betrayal of some small part of herself. The part of herself that still sometimes dreamed of living a life without vengeance. A life where she and Adrian had a future. Maybe, even, a life of peace.

But that dream, she knew now as strongly as ever, would never be. The truth was closing in around her. Her lies couldn't go on forever. Besides, peace and acceptance wouldn't bring back the family she had lost.

No matter, she told herself, again and again. Taking the helmet was supposed to be the end of this charade. At the time, she was sure that she would never have to face Callum again—or Adrian, for that matter.

But nothing ever went according to plan, and now there were consequences. There were always consequences, and she couldn't stop to think about it. She had to keep moving. Keep going through the motions. Lie. Steal. Betray.

Because that's how she would free Ace.

That's how she would destroy the Renegades.

That's how she would end this ongoing battle in her thoughts. The war between Nightmare and Insomnia. Hero and villain. She had already made her choice.

Nova fell into the chair at her desk and woke up the computer. She opened a memorandum template and quickly typed up the note she'd already planned out in her head. She scanned the text when she was done and decided to add a small typo, because Tina, the director of the artifacts department, was always a little scatterbrained and it seemed more authentic that way.

After printing the page, Nova crossed to the second empty desk and grabbed a pen out of a coffee mug by the keyboard, one with purple ink and a giant purple daisy on its tip. She scrawled a signature across the bottom of the page.

Tina Lawrence

Snapshot

Director

Replacing the pen, she spent a moment riffling through the desk drawers, searching for the stamp Tina sometimes used for official documentation for the weapons and artifacts department.

She had gone through every drawer twice before she gave up with a growl, slamming the final drawer shut. Exhaling, she inspected the clutter on top of the desk more closely, but there was no stamp.

With the paper in one hand, she headed into the filing room. She hadn't taken two steps inside before she spotted the stamp, left behind on a pile of empty manila folders.

"Honestly," she muttered, marching over to the stack and slamming the stamp down on the memo beneath the forged signature. Setting it aside, she folded the sheet into crisp thirds.

"Hey, Nova."

Heart launching into her throat, she cursed and spun around.

Callum started, too, surprised at her overreaction.

"Sweet rot, you scared me!"

"Sorry," he said with a sheepish grin. "I didn't know anyone was in here."

"Right. It's fine." She cleared her throat. "I'm just not used to people sneaking up on me."

It was a bit of an understatement. How had she not heard him come up behind her?

The answer came to her a second later. In the weeks she'd known Callum, she'd never *not* heard him. If he wasn't pushing around a squeaky-wheeled cart laden with artifacts, then he was jabbering away in the incessant way he had, somehow managing to be both charming and obnoxious at the same time.

"I wasn't sure you'd be in today." Callum cocked his head, and she realized he was trying to see the folded letter in her hand.

"Why wouldn't I have come in? I was on the schedule."

He met her gaze and held it for a beat too long before his smile returned. "I must have forgot."

Callum's expression wasn't judgmental, per se, but there was something amiss. Something suspicious.

Something very un-Callum-like.

Nova gripped her own smile like a weapon, already concocting a lie about the letter in her hand.

But he didn't ask about it.

That was stranger than anything. The fact that he *still* wasn't talking.

"Oh!" she said, feigning a gasp. "I heard about your run-in with Nightmare. Are you okay?"

One side of his mouth twitched. "Yeah, yeah. She did her sleep thing on me. You know, I've heard that a lot of people have killer headaches after she's put them to sleep, but I was fine. Felt pretty well rested the next day, actually."

"Oh . . . well, that's good." Nova hoped she sounded confused. "Maybe you're just more resilient than the rest of us."

Or maybe I was being nice.

"I seriously doubt that." His brow furrowed, the grin fading for real this time. "Is it weird to think that maybe she was going easy on me?"

Nova guffawed. It was as fake as she feared it would be. "Nightmare, go easy on someone? That seems out of character."

"Yeah, I know." He squinted, inspecting Nova like he knew something. Her pulse thundered. "I know this sounds weird," he added, "but she seemed familiar."

Nova's eyebrows worked their way toward her hairline. "Funny you should say that," she said, lowering her voice in what she hoped would inspire conspiratorial confidence. "It might not be as weird as you think."

He blinked, and for a moment he looked like a startled rabbit ready to bolt. She knew he suspected her. That he was well aware of why Nightmare would seem familiar.

But she had to convince him otherwise.

"My patrol unit had a meeting yesterday," she said, crossing the room to him. His posture was a study of both curiosity and nerves. He should have been wary of being so close to her. If he really did believe she was Nightmare, then he knew how dangerous she could be. How easily she could put him to sleep again. Though maybe that's what he was hoping she would do.

It would certainly prove his suspicions.

"Adrian has a theory," she went on. "And at first it seemed a little far-fetched, but now I'm not so sure."

Callum's shoulders sank as it became clear that this was not about to become a confession. "What sort of theory?"

"About Nightmare. He's been investigating her for months now, ever since the attack at the parade. He's compiled a shocking amount of information and . . . well." Her voice dropped to a whisper. Callum leaned in closer. "He thinks she might actually *be* a Renegade."

He said nothing. After another strangely silent moment, she saw him become suspicious again. Trying to see right through her.

Finally, he said, simply, "Oh yeah?"

"I wasn't sure at first, but when Adrian started listing all the coincidences . . . like that she knew about the helmet, and had access to Agent N . . . and oh! The mist-missiles? It kind of starts to make sense, right? What if she's a spy?"

His head cocked to one side. "What if she's a spy."

"It would explain a lot."

"Yeah. It would."

"So . . . you think Adrian could be right?"

Callum opened his mouth, but hesitated. Where she had sensed certainty before, she could sense it faltering now. A fault of his own optimism. His belief in humanity.

She realized that Callum didn't want her to be Nightmare. He was searching for a reason to doubt his own suspicions.

It was the crack she needed to find.

"Callum?" she said again. "Do you think she could be a spy?"

"I think it's possible, yeah."

She let herself appear worried. "Then it should be easy to figure out who it is, right?" She gestured toward the front reception area. "We can go through the rental history. Figure out who might have shown interest in those mist-missiles. We could go over some of the security tapes. Whoever she is, she must have left a path. Some clues we can follow. Ruby suggested she could be a recent recruit, but I think it's more likely to be a civilian. Someone who's pretending she doesn't have superpowers at all."

"She's short," said Callum.

Nova's words, whatever rambling thing she was going to say next, evaporated on her tongue. "Excuse me?"

Callum was close to Adrian's height himself, and Nova had never sensed how much he looked down on her, literally, until that moment. But that wasn't unusual. Practically everyone was taller than her. "She's short," he repeated. "Like you."

Her mouth opened. Closed. She tried again. "That's . . . good information. That will help narrow it down. I'll see if we can get more details out of Genissa Clark and her team, too. Compare notes. Um . . . was there anything else you noticed about Nightmare? Anything that could help us . . . pinpoint her . . . ?"

He stared at her. Really *stared*.

And she could feel the words hanging between them. *It's you, it's you, it has to be you.*

But it was eclipsed with doubt, and then a self-conscious grin. "I don't know. It was pretty dark and . . . it all happened really fast. Plus, you know, she has the mask."

"Of course. But if you think of something . . ."

"I'll let you know," he said. "I'll definitely let you know."

"Okay. Great. And I'll mention the height thing to Adrian. I think they keep pretty good health records on all the patrol units, and those might include measurements, so we can start there. Thanks, Callum. That's helpful."

She started to walk away, the sheet of paper crinkling between her fingers.

But just before slipping out the door, she paused and turned back. Her expression softened. "You know, I really am glad you're okay."

◇◇◆◇◇

On the uppermost floor of Renegade Headquarters, standing beneath a massive blown-glass chandelier, beside an enormous painting that captured the falsified death of Ace Anarchy, Nova handed the memo to Prism, the personal receptionist to the Council. Rainbow-colored lights danced over the desk, reflected off Prism's crystal fingers, as she unfolded the paper and read through the note.

She frowned. Not suspicious, but confused. "Snapshot wants you to take the forgery down to the artifacts department?"

"She's worried that having it on public display right now will create unnecessary drama," Nova explained. "Given the theft of the real helmet, people are going to become curious about the forgery. Some might feel that the Council's been lying to them all this time, telling them the helmet was destroyed." *Because they had*, Nova added silently to herself. "Snapshot feels it would be prudent to keep the forgery out of the public eye until the real helmet has been recovered . . . or until the Council has had time to decide the best course of action."

Prism considered this for no more than three seconds before she shrugged. "All right, go ahead, then. The case is unlocked."

CHAPTER SEVEN

NOVA WAS EAGER to put this charade behind her. As soon as she left headquarters with the fake helmet tucked into a plain tote bag, she marched straight for Blackmire Station, one of the defunct stations on the old Gatlon City subway line. She and the Anarchists had lived down there for years following the Day of Triumph, and Nova hadn't realized quite how much she hated it inside the dank, stifling tunnels until after they'd been chased out by Renegades and forced to seek sanctuary inside the decrepit row house on Wallowridge instead.

Though they hadn't left by choice, and they never would have left Ace by himself if they could have helped it, she couldn't deny that the housing situation was an improvement. She wasn't enthusiastic about going back down there now, but the blackmailer's instructions could only mean one thing.

QB'S ROOM—BLACKMIRE

Queen Bee's room, Blackmire station.

Honey, who was known as Queen Bee to most of society, had transformed an old maintenance closet off the main line into her private quarters. It wasn't cozy—nothing in the tunnels could be described as *cozy*—but she had done it up as nice as she could, draping scarves on the walls and bringing in a vintage shaded lamp that cast a pleasant glow over the concrete walls. And there had been her hives. Everywhere, hives, and the constant thrum of the bees who had flown agitatedly up to the surface in search of nectar and pollen every day, only to dutifully, if crankily, return to their queen as the sun was setting.

Nova was on edge as she made her way through the tunnel, the path lit by the beam of her flashlight. Her Renegade-issued boots clopped against the train rails. Rats squeaked, their eyes flashing in the light before they scurried into their holes. Familiar aromas accosted her. The musty air. The rank odor of standing water. The faint scent of decades-old urine. It was met with new smells, too. Sulfur and smoke and the acidic tang of Cyanide's poisons, lingering from the day the Renegades had attacked them.

Beyond the smell of war, and the fact that all their belongings had been confiscated by the Renegades, not much had changed.

Her nerves were tingling as she reached Honey's room. The heavy iron door was parted, but only shadows spilled forth from it.

Nova reached for her shock-wave gun, half expecting a trap. It wouldn't be a surprise if the blackmailer accosted her the moment she stepped into the room, because that's just the sort of thing a nameless villain would do. Her finger slipped over the trigger as she kicked the door open and shone the flashlight into the room.

Empty.

Not only of the blackmailer, but also empty of Honey's things.

Which was unsettling, if not unexpected. Nova knew that all of the belongings the Anarchists couldn't take with them had been packed up and taken to Renegade Headquarters, and were at this moment sitting in a temporary storage room at the back of the artifacts department, waiting to be sorted through. She had seen Honey's dresses there, boxes of jewelry, even the pretty vintage lamp.

The only thing the Renegades had left behind was an old dresser, on which sat a mirror with a chip in one corner and paint peeling off its trim work. The drawers were all missing and it was pulled a few feet away from the wall, no doubt so the Renegades could get behind it in their search for clues and evidence to be held against the Anarchists. They must have figured the dresser itself would be too much work to take back up all those steps. Nova wasn't sure how Honey had managed to get it down here in the first place.

Holstering the gun, she took the fake helmet from the bag. In the dim lighting, the hole in its cranium was almost imperceptible, and no one would be able to tell the faint difference in color, which most people weren't aware of. It was this helmet's lack of luster that had first tipped off Nova to its fraudulence. A lot of prodigy artifacts, including everything her father had ever made, had a unique sheen to them. A luminescence that was hard to detect unless one was looking for it.

Lately, Nova had started looking.

"It's all yours," she muttered to the shadows, setting the helmet down on the vanity. Probably her blackmailer was lurking just around one of the tunnel bends, waiting for her to leave so they could sneak in and claim their prize.

Which was just fine by her. She couldn't get out of there fast enough.

But the moment she stepped back through the door, a body

slammed into her. A hand grasped the back of her neck, shoving her against the gritty wall.

"I knew you'd come back here!" roared her assailant. "I knew——" He cut off quick. "No——?"

She slammed her heel into the arch of his foot and he howled, lurching back from her. The stun gun now in hand, Nova spun around, her finger pressing against the trigger——

"No-va . . ."

She froze. Her arm fell limp at her side. "*Adrian?*"

"I'm sorry," he groaned, sinking down to the ground and crossing his injured foot over his knee. He undid the laces of his tennis shoes. "I thought you were Nightmare."

She gaped at him as he removed his shoe and rubbed his foot where she had stomped on him. "You're not . . ." She glanced back into the room, where the helmet still sat innocently on top of the dresser. Was *Adrian* the blackmailer?

No. That didn't make sense. Did it?

Her thoughts churned and she shook her head, trying to sort them. "What are you doing here?" she asked, holstering the gun.

He flexed his toes, rubbing the arch of his foot as he did. "I've been down here a few times since the raid, seeing if there were any clues left behind. I mean, the cleanup crews are good, but you never know." He started to put his shoe back on. "I'm really sorry for grabbing you like that. I saw the flashlight, and in the dark, you sort of looked . . ."

"It's okay. That's what I get for creeping around dark tunnels, I guess." She nudged the door closed behind her, hoping Adrian wouldn't bother to go inside. She wasn't sure how she would explain what she was doing with the forged helmet down here, of all the random places, or why she was leaving it behind.

"So what are you doing down here?" said Adrian.

"Same thing as you. After our meeting the other day, I've been thinking a lot about whether or not Nightmare could really be posing as one of us. I wondered if maybe there would be something down here that would indicate . . . you know, one way or the other."

Adrian climbed back to his feet. "Actually, there is something the cleanup crew missed."

Her eyebrows lifted. "Oh?"

"Yeah. I'm not sure how much it helps us at this point, but come on. I'll show you."

He pulled a flashlight out of his back pocket and, to Nova's relief, led her away from Honey's room, toward an intersection of the tunnels where *her* train car stood against a wall. There were sheets of paper taped around the tunnel and on the windows of the car, "exhibits" left behind by the Renegades, indicating anything that might have seemed noteworthy at the time.

To her surprise, Adrian didn't head for Nightmare's car, but rather into the adjacent tunnel. The beam of his flashlight danced over a wall of old advertisement posters lined up side by side, each one taller than Nova. Her lungs squeezed when she realized what he'd discovered.

Approaching the last poster, an ad for a thriller novel, Adrian dug his fingers beneath the corner of the frame. The poster swung outward toward them, as it had swung toward Nova hundreds of times when she'd gone to visit Ace.

"Wow," she mused, stepping forward as she pretended to examine it. She shone her flashlight into the narrow tunnel, the sides showing scrapes and scratches where she and the other Anarchists had passed. "Where does it go?"

"To the catacombs under the cathedral," said Adrian.

"Really? That has to be at least a mile away."

"Only about two-thirds of a mile," he said. "The tunnel is a straight shot. It would take a lot longer on the surface. I think this tunnel might have been used after the Battle for Gatlon. It's probably how the Anarchists managed to get away. And how they've been going back and forth, visiting Ace Anarchy and taking him food and supplies." He shook his head. "You know, I came down here weeks ago, when I was trying to find that puppet Winston Pratt wanted? I saw this poster and . . . I had a feeling about it. I was so close to finding it, way back then. We could have found Ace Anarchy."

She forced a small chuckle despite the sourness roiling in her stomach. "Good thing you didn't. To just stumble onto Ace Anarchy like that? You would have . . ." She trailed off, not wanting to hurt Adrian's feelings. But they both knew he wouldn't have stood a chance against Ace, even if Ace was a lot weaker than he'd been ten years ago. At least, she hoped Adrian knew that. He was talented, but not *that* talented. "I'm shocked the Sentinel was able to capture him."

Adrian's mouth twisted into a frown and she could tell he wanted to say something—probably defend his own abilities—but he resisted. "Well," he said finally, "they say Ace Anarchy was pretty weak when they found him. Without the helmet, he's just another telepath."

Now it was her turn to resist the urge to argue. "If you ask me, the Sentinel got lucky."

Adrian grunted, but she didn't think he agreed with her.

"So . . . ," she started, rocking on her feet. "You've gone to the catacombs, then?"

"Just once. But I didn't learn anything that we didn't already know. I've been down here a few times since then, though. I just keep thinking that Nightmare has to show up here again at some point, right?"

She shrugged. "Maybe not. Maybe she knows the Renegades are watching it too closely."

"Maybe." He fit the poster back into place. His expression changed then, the start of a teasing smile appearing at the corners of his lips. Nova immediately tensed. "Nice bracelet, by the way."

She blinked.

Then blinked again.

She reached for her sleeve and tugged it down instinctively, but it was too late to cover the star that was inexplicably set into the prongs of her bracelet—and glowing far too obviously in these dim tunnels.

"I didn't steal it," she said hastily. "At least . . . I didn't mean to steal it. It just kind of . . ."

Adrian chuckled. "I'm not mad. You can have it." He cocked his head, eyes still twinkling behind his glasses. "I realized it was missing after you left, but you didn't say anything, so I thought maybe I shouldn't, either. But the curiosity is killing me." He took her hand and gently pushed up her sleeve, revealing not just the star, but the delicate bracelet that her father had made years ago, the last thing he had ever made. "It fits the setting perfectly. Like it was made for it." Adrian's face was awed.

Nova was more awed by the rush of electricity at his touch. It was hardly the first time he'd touched her, so how did it still affect her this way?

"Did you know it would fit the bracelet? I mean, was the bracelet part of the dream you had?"

"No," she said. "I had no idea it was going to . . ." She peered at the star, not sure how to explain what had happened. "I went back into the room to see it, after you fell asleep. I just wanted to touch it, to see if it would do anything. And it . . . flashed, sort of? And the next thing I knew, it was there, in my bracelet." She grimaced apologetically. "I probably should have told you, it's just . . . it was in your house. It felt a little bit like stealing."

"As far as I'm concerned, that room was made for you," said Adrian. "You're welcome to anything in it. The parrots, the wild-flowers, the noise-canceling headphones . . ."

She flushed, remembering all too well the muted sound of their heartbeats falling into sync as she drifted off to sleep for the first time in ten years. It was quite possibly the most magical moment of her life. There were still times when she wondered if she'd imagined it all, sure that it had been too fantastical, too surreal, to have actually happened.

But Adrian was here, his fingers laced with hers, their toes practically touching, and it *had* happened.

"Well, thank you," she said, inching just a bit closer to him. "I have become a little attached to the star, and . . . it really does seem like it was made for this bracelet."

"I'm glad you like it. It was my first time giving a girl jewelry, which is sort of a big deal, so . . ."

She squinted one eye at him. "You didn't give me jewelry. You gave me a jungle."

He laughed. "That, and almost a full day of blissful sleep."

"Okay, stop fishing for compliments. I admit, you're a pretty good gift giver." She leaned forward, lifting up onto her toes.

"I'm trying," Adrian said, bending down to meet her.

The kiss was everything she remembered. Warmth tingling through her limbs. Shooting stars glinting behind her eyelids. Somehow being so perfectly content, while still yearning for more.

A crash startled them both—something heavy falling to the hard floor. They jumped apart and spun toward the darkened subway tunnels where they had come from.

Nova's pulse raced beneath her skin, and she *knew* that it had been the helmet. Had the blackmailer realized it was a fake? Had they thrown it?

"Just a rat, probably," she said, breathless for more reason than one.

"I don't think that was a rat." Still holding her hand, Adrian started back toward Honey's room.

Nova dug in her heels. The last thing she needed was a run-in with someone who knew her secrets and wouldn't hesitate to give them up, especially to Adrian Everhart himself. "Hold on! What if it's . . . what if it's Nightmare? Or another Anarchist? Shouldn't we call for backup?"

Adrian shot her a baffled look, and even in the dim lighting she could see his confusion. "*You* want to wait for backup?"

He was right. It didn't sound like her at all.

"It's just . . ." She swept her other hand toward him. "You're not wearing your uniform!"

His head shifted to one side, briefly, then he shook it and started dragging her again. "Come on."

She cursed inwardly and followed. She would play dumb. She would deny anything the blackmailer said. If she had to, she would take desperate measures, silencing him or her before anything could be given away.

Or maybe she could knock Adrian out, right now, before he saw them and had a chance to learn anything. She eyed the bare flesh at the back of his neck. She could make up a story—say that it *was* Nightmare in the tunnels, and she jumped out from the shadows and put them both to sleep before Nova could stop her.

Yeah . . . that might work . . .

Her fingers twitched. They were nearly to the maintenance closet where she'd left the helmet. Adrian was rounding the corner. There was no sign of anyone yet, not even the beam of a flashlight or the thud of footsteps running away. Just the scuffle of their own feet along the tracks.

Was the blackmailer still in Honey's room?

The door was still closed, just as Nova had left it. Adrian nudged it open, gripping his marker in one hand. Nova hadn't seen him take it out.

Biting down on her lower lip, she reached for the back of his neck. But something made her stop. A movement in the room. A shadow moving toward them.

Adrian ducked, then flew forward, sending his fist at the attacker.

A crash reverberated through the room. Adrian let out a stream of curses. Nova shone the flashlight toward him.

There was no attacker, no blackmailer. Their assailant had been Adrian's own reflection in the dresser mirror, which had shattered from the punch.

"Okay," he grunted, cradling his hand against his chest, face twisted with pain. "I'm officially done attacking people before I get a good look at them."

"That might be for the best," said Nova, but her words were distracted.

Her attention had snagged on the top of the dresser, where a few chunks of broken mirror had fallen to the surface.

The helmet was gone.

CHAPTER EIGHT

ADRIAN PACED AROUND the waiting room. Simon was sitting at the edge of one of the sofas, his hands clasped and his fingers twitching against his knuckles. They hadn't spoken much since their arrival at the hospital. Hugh had gone ahead to see Max, as the only one who was immune to him. The only one who was *supposed* to be immune to him. Adrian's confession had been on the tip of his tongue ever since.

It was so frustrating to be out here when there was no reason that he couldn't be in the room with Max right now. His tattoo would protect him. All he needed to do was tell his dads about the tattoos, explain that, actually, he was immune to Max's power, too, and he could be back there with his brother.

But the words wouldn't come. There would be too many questions. Explanations he wasn't ready to give.

So instead he paced. Back and forth. Past the fake potted plants. The tables full of fashion and celebrity magazines—one, he noticed, had his dads' faces in a small box on the cover, but Adrian didn't read the headline. Nothing mattered right now except Max.

Sweet rot, why wasn't he back there with him?

It felt like hours before finally, *finally,* Hugh emerged through the swinging double doors, a smile plastered across his face. Hope surged through Adrian's veins. Simon launched to his feet.

"He's going to be okay," said Hugh.

It was all he managed to say before they were embracing one another. Hugh pulled Adrian against him, squeezing tight around his shoulders, and then Simon had his arms around them both. Adrian fought to hold back the tears of relief that threatened to spill over. He ducked away, letting his dads hold each other a moment longer while he gathered himself.

"The doctor says he's been through the worst now," Hugh continued, his voice rough with emotion. "They expect a full recovery, though there will be a scar that I'm sure he'll be proud to show off for the rest of his life. And Max is . . . He's good. Weak still, but good. He's in high spirits. If things weren't in such disarray at headquarters, we could probably take him back by the end of the month."

"Headquarters?" said Adrian, spinning to face them. "He can't go back to headquarters."

"Not anytime soon, obviously," said Hugh, running a hand through his blond hair. "It will take a while to rebuild the quarantine. He'll just have to stay put until then, but I know the staff here is going to keep him comfortable. They say he'll be able to move to a new room in a few days, one that's intended for longer-care patients."

"Hold on," said Adrian. "The quarantine? You're going to rebuild the quarantine?"

Hugh and Simon stared at him, baffled. "Well . . . of course we are," said Simon. "He can't stay at the hospital forever."

Adrian shook his head. "No. You can't!"

"What are you talking about?" said Hugh. "What did you think would happen?"

Adrian stepped back. "I just thought . . ."

What *had* he thought would happen once Max was able to leave the hospital? That he could come home to the mansion? That he could share the basement with Adrian, be brothers for real?

That wasn't possible. Not with Simon living under the same roof.

But to go back to the quarantine?

"This can't be the only option. He hates the quarantine. And now that we don't need him for Agent N—"

"We still need to protect him," said Simon. "He's a threat to prodigies everywhere, which means he can be targeted anytime."

"Or weaponized against us," added Hugh. "And it's dangerous for him to be out in the world. You've seen the trouble we've had to go through just to make sure no prodigy healers accidentally wander past his room while he's here. No. It's safer for him at headquarters, where we can keep an eye on him."

Adrian's heart thumped, as if reminding him of the immunity tattoo inked onto his chest. He swallowed hard. His dads still didn't know about the tattoos. They would ask questions, demand to know more—and all those questions and demands could tread too closely to the truth of his alter ego.

But an idea had been brewing in his thoughts for months now and was becoming increasingly difficult to ignore. What if he could tattoo other prodigies? What if he could give Simon immunity against Max? Not just Simon, but his friends. Nova, Ruby, Oscar, Danna . . .

He didn't know if it would work, but there was a chance. Didn't he owe it to Max to find out?

Just considering it made his pulse drum faster. Because what if his dads discovered his secret? What would they do if they knew he was the Sentinel?

He felt sick to his stomach at his own selfishness, and yet he couldn't bring himself to tell them.

I will, he thought. *If there's no other way to keep Max out of that quarantine, then I'll tell them.*

"It might be safer at headquarters," Adrian admitted, "but it's not better. He's a ten-year-old kid. He deserves to have a life."

Simon sighed, while Hugh started to rub his temple. "I'm sorry this is so upsetting to you, but I don't know what else you expect us to do. And honestly, Adrian, we've already made our decision."

"He's my brother! I deserve to be a part of this conversation. Hell, *he* deserves to be a part of this conversation."

"You're both too young to understand everything at stake here," said Hugh.

"But we're not too young to risk our lives fighting crime every day? Max wasn't too young to be taken into battle against Ace Anarchy when he was *a year old*? You've been controlling him for his entire life, and this is . . . You can't do this to him again."

"We love him, too, you know," said Simon, looking weary. "We're trying to do what's best for him. Do you have any idea how many people want to hurt him? Or use him? This is for his own good."

"Besides, he's still the same Max," added Hugh. "He might seem weak and fragile these days, but he's still . . . dangerous."

Adrian jaw clenched, but he nodded, pretending that he understood.

Slumping into the sofa again, Simon turned to Hugh. "Tell me everything the doctor said. Word for word."

"I'm going for a walk," said Adrian, before Hugh could launch into any medical speak. "I'll see you at home later."

They didn't try to stop him. Adrian pushed his way back out through the swinging doors and left the hospital through a side entrance, as the main sliding glass doors to the ER were still boarded up since the Sentinel had burst through them when he brought in Max.

Within minutes Adrian was springing up to the adjacent rooftop, hurtling over the alleyway toward the fifth floor, and after checking that no one else was inside, sliding open the window to Max's room.

Max was seated up in the adjustable bed, propped against white pillows. When he spotted Adrian climbing in through the window, he yelped and sent a plastic food tray clattering to the floor. "Adrian! What on—"

Adrian shushed him and ducked against the side of the bed, just in case someone in the hallway had heard Max's commotion. He waited three whole breaths before picking up the food tray and piling the fallen dishes of macaroni and cheese, apple slices, and a chocolate brownie back on top of it.

"Sorry. I didn't mean to scare you. But people still don't know about the tattoos so I sort of have to sneak in."

Max inspected the mac and cheese, noting bits of lint from the floor stuck to the yellowish noodles. His nose curled in disgust. He reached for the brownie instead, picked off a mysterious bit of white fuzz, and crammed half of it into his mouth.

It was a testament to his recovery that he could be more interested in eating than giving Adrian the hug he was sure he deserved.

"I'm so happy you're awake," said Adrian, sitting in the chair beside Max's bed. "I thought . . ." He hesitated and changed his statement to: "You really had us scared."

Max used a white cloth napkin that came with the meal to wipe chocolate from the side of his mouth, though there was still some stuck in his front teeth when he grinned at Adrian. "Yeah, the doctor said it was pretty bad there for a while. They say I'm lucky."

"You are. We all are."

Max's expression turned sly. "Naw. The Sentinel rescued me, right? So I guess I have him to thank. You know, if I ever meet the guy in person."

Adrian chuckled. There had been weeks when Max was the only person who knew his secret identity. Since the fight at the catacombs, he'd been forced to tell Ruby and Oscar, too, and he suspected Danna knew as well—though he wouldn't know her feelings on it until they could figure out how to help her transform back into her human shape.

He knew he would have to tell Nova eventually. Oscar and Ruby weren't the most discreet Renegades on the task force, and he wanted to make sure she heard it from him.

"Yeah, well, rumor has it the Sentinel might be a little fond of you, kid." He reached forward and ruffled Max's hair. Having only known what it was like to do that in recent weeks, he was still surprised at how fluffy his hair was. "The team's going to be elated when I tell them the news, and I might have a surprise next time I come to visit."

Max gave him a look that was far more suspicious than excited.

"Okay, I'll just tell you. Guess what we found crawling through the wreckage back at headquarters? I'll give you a hint. It's about this tall"—he pinched his fingers an inch away from each other—"went extinct millions of years ago, and rhymes with . . ." Adrian paused. "Um . . . Burbo."

Max was shaking his head, even as his smile returned. "Those were the worst hints in history. You could have said something like its feet are used both for running and disemboweling prey, but only if the prey is smaller than a mouse. Or, it's likely the only one of its kind to have scales rather than feathers. Or maybe, its babies would be born from eggs, though it never was."

Adrian's eyebrow ticked upward. "Did you just come up with those?"

Shrugging, Max took another bite of the brownie.

"No, seriously, that's really good. Maybe coming up with riddles is another superpower you haven't discovered yet. Except . . . what do you mean by feathers?"

"Dey ad feaders," Max said through his full mouth.

"Velociraptors?"

Max nodded and swallowed. "Don't you know that's where birds come from?"

"Well, yeah, but . . ." Adrian frowned, picturing a miniature velociraptor that was more a cross between a T. rex and a chicken. "Feathers would make him a lot less intimidating, you know? Although, Danna is afraid of birds, so I guess it's all subjective. Still. Feathers. Who knew?"

Max finished off the brownie and inspected his plate, trying to deem what else might be safe to consume. Adrian considered telling him about Danna, that she'd been stuck in swarm mode since the night of the attack and they weren't entirely sure why, but he thought the kid should probably stay focused on his own recovery for now.

"Anyway," he said, "I'll bring Turbo to see you next time I come. I've been taking good care of him. Discovered he really likes turkey jerky."

"I'm not sure he's all that discerning," said Max. "I once saw him try to eat a pencil."

Adrian laughed. "Seriously, I'm so glad you're okay. When I got to headquarters and saw Nightmare crouching over you . . ." He stopped himself. He'd wanted to keep the mood light, but it was impossible not to think of how pale and weak Max had been. And there had been so much blood . . .

Max wiped his fingers on the napkin. "Yeah. It was weird, right? I know I'm lucky to be alive, but I also know that I shouldn't be. Alive, I mean. She should have killed me. It doesn't make sense that she didn't."

"Not for lack of trying," Adrian muttered. "She ran as soon as she saw me. I would have chased after her, except . . . well, you were more important. Obviously."

Max's brow furrowed.

"But I am going to find her," Adrian said, leaning his elbows on his knees. "I swear it. The team and I are already working on a new investigation and we have some really promising leads. I'm going to find Nightmare, and I'll make her pay for this. She'll never be able to hurt you again."

Max's face only became more confused. He blinked at Adrian a few times, then slowly pushed back the tray of food. Leaping to his feet, Adrian took it from him and set it down on the small table beside the bed. "You want some water or something?"

"Adrian . . ."

The tone of Max's voice gave Adrian pause. He looked back down, but Max's focus was on the white cotton blanket over his legs. His fingers dug into the fabric.

"Yeah?" said Adrian, sinking back into the chair. "What's wrong?"

Max licked his lips and for the first time Adrian noticed how dry they were. He would have to mention it to the nursing staff. Maybe get some of that all-natural lip balm they sold at the higher-end drugstores.

"Nightmare didn't try to kill me."

Adrian stared at Max. He was still so pale. Bruises peppered the insides of his arms from where he'd had blood transfers and IV drips. The pale blue hospital gown drooped on his skinny shoulders.

"Max," he said slowly, "she stabbed you in the stomach with a giant chromium spear. The only reason she didn't kill you was because I showed up in time to stop her."

Max shook his head. "Frostbite stabbed me, not Nightmare."

The world seemed to quiet as Adrian tried to make sense of these words. *"Frostbite?"*

Max still wouldn't meet his eyes, and Adrian watched his pupils dance around. He was replaying that night in his mind, seeing the battle, not the blanket. "She had Dad's spear and was charging for Nightmare, but Nightmare ducked. I was standing behind her—I'd gone invisible—and Frostbite hit me, drove it right through me. Nightmare didn't do it."

Adrian's mouth opened, then shut again. His knowledge of what had happened in the headquarters lobby that night began to reshuffle into a new order of events. A new reality.

"But, still. Nightmare didn't exactly—"

"She tried to help me," Max interrupted. His fingers curled into the blanket. "I asked her to take out the spear, and she didn't want to at first because it's not good to remove a weapon, right? But I begged her to, and she did, and when she realized the ice was helping it, she . . . she forced Frostbite to give her power to me. She dragged her closer so I could absorb all of it. She was trying to save me."

Adrian's jaw unhinged as he tried to picture it, but all he could see was Nightmare bent over Max's body. The broken glass, her bloodied hands.

"That . . . doesn't make sense."

"I know." Finally Max dared to look up. His eyes were shimmering.

"Are you sure? You lost a lot of blood. You could have been delirious. Maybe you're confusing what happened—"

"I'm sure. Ask Frostbite."

"Frostbite already . . ." Adrian paused. Frostbite had given an official statement, and she'd declared that Nightmare had been the one to stab the Bandit, as everyone had already assumed. Admitting that she'd actually hit Max by mistake wouldn't have been in her best interest.

And Genissa Clark never did anything that wasn't in her best interest.

Adrian leaned back in his chair, wanting to believe Max, but not fully comprehending what he was telling him. Nightmare was an Anarchist. She had every reason to want to kill Max—the source for Agent N and the catalyst for Ace Anarchy's defeat during the Battle for Gatlon.

What reason could she have had for trying to help him?

Was there perhaps some sinister reason that the Anarchists could have for wanting to keep the Bandit alive? Was it possible they would try to use him for their own benefit?

It wasn't entirely unbelievable, but such a plan was almost too devious for Adrian to wrap his mind around.

"What really doesn't make sense," Max said slowly, "is why she wasn't weakened by me. I saw her put Frostbite to sleep, and that was right after she'd been trying to help me stop the bleeding. She should have been weak, if not entirely neutralized, but she seemed fine. So how . . . ?"

"I don't know this for sure," said Adrian, "but I think she might have the Vitality Charm."

Max's eyes widened in surprise, but the look quickly turned to a frown. "Shame. Her power is one I wouldn't mind having."

Adrian cocked his head. "Really? When would you want to put people to sleep?"

"I just think it could come in handy. You know, like when those scientists come to take more blood samples. It'd be nice to be able to knock them out for a while when I don't feel like cooperating."

Adrian smirked. "You know, you have more rebellion in you than anyone wants to give you credit for."

"Yeah . . ." Max's mouth twitched, barely revealing the dimple in his right cheek. "I get it from my big brother."

CHAPTER NINE

Nova examined the old blueprint of Cragmoor Penitentiary, her hands fisted on her hips, a headache pounding at her temples. Honey and Leroy had wandered off hours ago to get some sleep, and she hadn't seen Phobia all night. She was determined to have this puzzle solved before she saw the others again in the morning.

There was a way to save Ace. There had to be.

And they had the one weapon that just might give them one hell of an advantage, even if it seemed almost wrong to use it.

They had Ace Anarchy's helmet.

Nova's father had created the helmet using the threads of energy he could mold from the air. He had made a weapon that could amplify his brother's abilities. As far as Nova knew, Ace was the only person who had ever worn the helmet.

But Nova had suspicions that the helmet wasn't only for her uncle. There was a possibility it could amplify *any* power—which would explain why the Renegades had been determined to keep it locked away for eternity.

She stretched her spine, wondering how long she'd been standing there without moving. Her attention landed on the coat closet that stood in the narrow hall between the living room and the kitchen. There was something ironic about what might have been the most feared and respected prodigy artifact of all time, now relegated to a mere coat closet in a run-down house on Wallowridge. It deserved so much better.

But their options were limited.

Nova hadn't touched the helmet since she'd stashed it in the closet the night of the break-in. Every day when she got home, she'd open the door, just to check that it was still there, and then promptly close it again.

The sight of it caused an ache in her chest.

But now she forced herself to open the door. The blue-tinged light from the kitchen fell on the helmet, but it couldn't diminish its natural golden glow. It seemed to be watching her through its empty eyeholes. Waiting.

Before she could change her mind, Nova reached for the helmet, cradling it in both hands. The star on her wrist jumped and glowed a little brighter, the bracelet tugging toward the helmet like the two were magnetically drawn to each other.

Exhaling all the air from her lungs, Nova turned the helmet around, shut her eyes, and placed it on her head.

It was too big for her. She could tell that if she were to move even the slightest bit, it would wobble like a broken doll's head. But she didn't move. She just waited. Smelling the slightly metallic scent on the inside. Feeling her own breath against the surface, not unlike when she wore Nightmare's metal face mask.

Nothing happened.

She opened her eyes and gasped, stumbling back against the wall.

The helmet lurched on her head, but she quickly reached up to right it.

The room beyond the helmet was shimmering. Waves of coppery light danced before her, like a golden aurora borealis filling up the dingy living room. It felt as though they were swirling outward—from the helmet, from *her*.

Her eyes began to water. She snatched the helmet from her head.

The lights faded away—not all at once, like a lamp being switched off, but a slow disintegration, as if she were forgetting how to see.

She blinked to clear the remnants from her vision.

Those lights, those beams of energy . . . could they be the same glowing bands she had watched her father conjure from the air so many years ago? As a child, she had assumed he was creating them from nothing, but these were so familiar. Was it possible they were always there, invisible in the ether, waiting for someone with a power like her father's to pull them into reality? To create something brilliant with them?

Stranger still, she knew she had seen those beams of light before, when she had taken the star from the painted room in Adrian's basement. And she hadn't had the helmet then.

She set the helmet back onto her head again. The lights reappeared, as constant and breathtaking as before. Squinting against their brightness, Nova reached out her hand. The star in her bracelet pulsed. Wondering if she might be able to touch the strings of energy, even manipulate them as her father had done, she stretched one finger toward a beam that danced only a couple of feet in front of her.

Her hand passed right through it. The light shimmered, undisturbed. As ephemeral as a shadow.

She tried again and again. But however these shreds of energy might have responded to her father's command, they seemed to be ignoring her completely.

Scowling, she ripped the helmet off again and watched as the vision faded away.

Disappointment clawed at her. Shouldn't she have felt different somehow? Stronger? More powerful? Invincible? That's how Ace had always seemed to her when she was young. After the helmet had been seized, he had practically crumpled from its loss. Shouldn't the helmet's effect on her have been, somehow, *more*?

Nova never slept. Shouldn't the helmet have amplified her boundless, inexhaustible energy?

She could put people to sleep through touch. Shouldn't the helmet have . . . She didn't know. Make it so she could put them to sleep from farther distances? Or . . . even, perhaps, kill them with her touch?

She was surprised at the shudder that overtook her at the thought. That would be an incredible power and certainly could help her break into the prison, but the idea of it repelled more than tempted.

With a huff, she thrust the helmet back into the closet and slammed the door.

A figure stood in the hallway, a welding mask over their face.

Nova yelped and lurched back. Her hand instinctively went for a weapon, but she wasn't wearing her belt.

No matter. She wasn't reliant on weaponry. She *was* a weapon.

She prepared for a fight, but the figure took a step back and held a palm toward her.

"I've taken out an insurance policy on my safety," came a female voice.

Nova hesitated. The voice sounded faintly familiar.

"I have an ally who is expecting my return. If I am not back, unharmed, within the next twenty minutes, they will alert Captain Chromium and the rest of the Renegades of your identity and the location of your secret lair."

Nova's eyes narrowed as she inspected the mask's blank shade. It was reminiscent of the Sentinel's armor, which annoyed her more than it should have. "Secret lair? What is this, a comic book?"

"This isn't a game," the girl said. "I want Ace's helmet, and I want it now!"

"I already gave it to you."

"You gave me a fake, and you're lucky I didn't go straight to the Renegades when I found out. This is your last chance, Nova *Artino*."

"I'm not a delivery service, and I don't respond well to threats." Nova leaped forward and thrust her elbow against the girl's throat, pinning her to the wall. With her other hand, she tore off the welding mask, throwing it to the ground.

She gasped. *"Narcissa?"*

She was thinner than before, with dark blemishes beneath her eyes. Narcissa Cronin, granddaughter of Gene Cronin, the Librarian, who had been killed during the fight at the Cloven Cross Library. Ingrid had shot him in order to protect Nova's identity.

This information clicked into place in Nova's thoughts and so many things began to make sense. Narcissa could travel between mirrors. That's how she had gotten into the bedroom upstairs and Honey's room in the tunnels, both times without being seen, without leaving a trace. That's how she knew Nova's identity.

Narcissa shoved against her, and Nova, weakened by surprise, took a step back. "Narcissa," she said again, still not fully comprehending that this girl, who had always seemed so quiet, so meek, so . . . *unvillainous,* could be the one who had blackmailed her.

"How did you even find me?" said Nova.

A touch of arrogance swept over Narcissa's face. "I knew you were masquerading as a Renegade, so I waited outside their head-quarters and followed you home."

Nova shook her head. "I would have noticed if I was being followed."

"Are you sure?" said Narcissa, almost tauntingly. "Did you check every reflection you passed? There are a lot of mirrors between Renegade HQ and Wallowridge. Once I knew what street you were on, I moved from house to house, vanity to vanity, until I found you. And now that I'm here, you are going to give me that helmet!" Face twisting with anger, Narcissa grabbed a pistol that had been tucked into her waistband.

Instinct and training buckled Nova's knees. She dropped into a crouch, then swung one leg at Narcissa's ankles. The girl cried out and fell backward, landing on her side with a yelp of pain. She tried to clamber back to her feet, but then her spine uncurled and she let out a shrill scream. She dropped the gun and clapped a hand onto her shoulder, barely missing the yellow-spotted wasp as it darted away from her fingertips. It landed on her black sneaker and had just begun to wriggle beneath the cuff of her jeans when Nova barked, "Honey, no! Let her be!"

The wasp paused, its wings beating against the girl's shoelaces.

Nova looked up, panting. Honey stood at the base of the staircase, her hair in massive curlers and a silk robe tied loosely at her waist. Leroy stood behind her, watching with mute interest as Narcissa writhed on the floor. A cloud of bees circled over their heads, their buzzing echoing off the confines of the stairwell.

Nova stooped and grabbed the gun, noting that the safety was still on. Smothering a sigh, she didn't bother to take it off as she aimed the gun at Narcissa's forehead.

Narcissa was in too much pain to notice. Fat tears were sliding down her cheeks as she pressed a hand over the sting on her shoulder.

Nova glanced at Honey. "Can you make the pain stop?"

Honey lifted an eyebrow. "Why should I? She tried to kill you."

"Not very well."

Honey grunted. "One does not have to be competent to be an enemy."

"*Honey.*"

She rolled her eyes. "The burning from the venom will pass in a minute or two, though she'll be sore for a few days. Unless she's allergic. Then she's going to die." Honey curled one finger and the wasp flew back to her. "Do we know her?"

"Sort of." Nova looked down again and saw that Narcissa's long red braid had spilled out from the collar of her shirt. "This is the Librarian's granddaughter. She can travel through mirrors."

"*The* Librarian?" said Honey. "You mean the weapons salesman?"

Narcissa snarled through her pain. "He had a name. And he was more than just an arms dealer. More than the villain everyone says he was!" Her nostrils flared. "He was a good man. A scholar. Someone who cared about his community. And you killed him! Just to save your own skin!"

Nova gulped. She didn't know Narcissa well, but during their few, brief meetings, she'd always liked her. Narcissa had seemed so unassuming. So uninterested in anything related to villains or heroes. She usually had her nose buried in a book and had seemed content to keep it there.

There was none of that now. Narcissa was too thin, too pale, and far too hostile. Clearly, those tender feelings Nova had once had for her were not reciprocated.

"I didn't kill him," said Nova. "The Detonator did."

"Yeah, for *you*." Narcissa used her sleeve to rub the snot from her nose. "But you Anarchists always were selfish. You never care about anyone but yourselves." She pushed herself to her knees, flinching when she put weight on her arm, and tilted her chin up. "It's because of you that my grandfather is dead. The library is gone. You took everything I had!"

"The Detonator did all that!" Nova repeated, louder this time. "I was trying to stop her!"

"If it wasn't for you, she wouldn't have targeted us in the first place. Pretending to be a Renegade. . . . Using my grandfather and his library as pawns in your game. . . . It should have been you! Not him—*you!*"

Clenching her jaw, Nova dropped the gun into Narcissa's lap. The girl startled and began to back away, as if the weapon were a deadly snake. Then she caught herself and wrapped both of her trembling hands around the handle. She did not aim it at Nova again, though her expression still spoke of murder.

"Your grandfather," said Nova, "was one of the most notorious black-market arms dealers in the city. The Renegades finally caught up to him, and Ingrid saw an opportunity to use their sting operation as a trap. None of that is my fault."

Clutching the gun, Narcissa stumbled back to her feet. "The Renegades finally caught up to him? Yeah, because he sold *you* a gun, and you were careless enough to try to assassinate Captain Chromium with it."

"Actually," said Leroy, "he sold the gun to me."

Narcissa spun toward him. "Then you should all be dead! But

here you are, still playing games while more prodigies are suffering! Well, I made a promise that I would bring that helmet back to the Rejects, and that we would use it to restore balance to this world. The balance that's been destroyed by desperate power-seekers like the Anarchists and the Renegades. And I'm not leaving here without it." She planted her feet, and though she'd gone pale, whether from the beesting or her own fears, she stood straight as she faced Nova.

Dismayed, Nova threw her hands into the air. "Who are the Rejects?"

Narcissa's nostrils flared. "Rejected by society for being prodigies. Rejected by the Renegades for not fitting their perfect heroic standards. But together—we are more than just outcasts. We are powerful, and we will tolerate this abuse no more!"

Nova waited. It was clear Narcissa had repeated this speech a time or two.

The weird thing was, it sounded an awful lot like something Ace would have said.

She was about to suggest that maybe Narcissa's hatred was misplaced when the mirror walker continued. "You have a choice," she said, tossing her braid over her shoulder. "Go ahead and kill me, and my people will make sure that your enemies know all your secrets by morning. Or give me the helmet and let me go, and you can live another day, as Nightmare or Insomnia or whoever it is you think you are."

The silence was brief.

"All right, then," said Honey, dragging a pointed nail down the back of a plump bumblebee that was crawling along her pinky finger. "Shall I have the honors?"

Leroy yawned. "I'll warm up the car. Do you think it's best to drop the body into the bay or the river?"

"The river is closer," said Honey. "And I don't really think any-one's going to miss her, despite this talk of Rejects." Her smile became wicked. "I'll call the bluff."

Narcissa's defiance extinguished as her attention darted toward the swarming bees.

It took a lot of venom from even the most dangerous of wasps to kill a person who wasn't allergic to them, but it could be done.

It was an awfully painful way to die.

"*Death*," rasped a voice. "And bees, at least at the moment."

Phobia's form solidified from the shadows, filling up the door-way to the kitchen. There was a bit of moonlight coming through the windows, and a shard of light glinted along the scythe's blade.

"Also spiders, snakes, cockroaches, rats," Phobia went on, rat-tling off what fears he could detect within the recesses of Narcissa's mind. "Scorpions. Public humiliation. Drowning." He chuckled lowly. "Ace Anarchy."

"Great marvels," muttered Leroy. "She's decent at faking cour-age, at least."

"But most profoundly," continued Phobia, and his gritty voice turned mocking, "she has an almost paralyzing fear that she will never experience true love."

"Oh, she's one of *those*." Honey groaned dramatically. "Unfortunately, it seems that fear is going to come to pass."

"Wait," said Nova, lifting a hand. "Narcissa, we're never giv-ing you that helmet, but maybe we can help each other. Your . . . Rejects . . . it sounds like their feud is with the Renegades, not us. You don't have to die for this."

Narcissa fixed her with a cold glare. "You should be worrying about yourself, Nightmare. Are you really prepared for the Renegades to know who you are, after you've worked so hard to keep it concealed?"

Nova's palms were sweating. The answer was no, of course she wasn't ready. She still needed to rescue Ace. She still needed to bring her enemies down.

Then her thoughts went to Adrian. The way he smiled at her. The way he *kissed* her.

It would be over.

She wasn't ready.

"It doesn't matter," Nova said. "They're going to find out soon enough. It's not the bargaining chip you think it is, Narcissa. And we need the helmet. We're going to free Ace Anarchy, and when we do, he will use that helmet to end the Renegades and their tyranny once and for all." She spread her fingers, almost pleadingly. "Why not help us do that?"

They held each other's gaze a long time. Slowly, Narcissa shifted her attention to Phobia. She gulped, then looked back at Honey and Leroy, and finally to Nova again.

Nova could tell that her walls were crumbling. Despite the anger she harbored for the Anarchists and what had happened at the library, she must have seen the logic in Nova's words, because she appeared to be wavering with temptation and uncertainty.

Whatever she would have said, though, was interrupted by the squeal of tires out on the street.

Narcissa's lips curved with relief. "Time's up, Nightmare."

Something struck the front window. The glass shattered. Nova ducked instinctively, even as Narcissa shoved past her.

A huge rock tumbled a few more inches before coming to stop beside the armchair, just as Narcissa's red braid disappeared up the stairwell.

Someone whooped outside. There were celebratory cheers, and

someone yelling, "*Rejects forever! Power to prodigies!*" before tires screeched again and the vehicle peeled down the street.

Cursing, Nova launched herself up the stairs, taking them two at a time. She spotted Narcissa crouched on top of Honey's vanity. One hand was holding the frame of the large mirror, the other gripped a glass mason jar. The gold-and-black butterfly flapped frantically inside.

Nova froze as Narcissa's eyes filled with intrigue. "They've been talking about that Renegade on the news lately. *Monarch*. The one who led her team to the lair of Ace Anarchy." She inclined her head. "Interesting coincidence."

Pulling her arm back, Narcissa threw the jar at the bedroom's far wall.

Nova cried out. At the same moment that Narcissa was vanishing into the surface of the mirror, Nova dove for the jar, but she knew she wouldn't reach it in time. It seemed to move in slow motion as it tumbled through the air.

It smashed into the wall and exploded into dozens of tiny shards.

The butterfly lurched upward, spiraling toward the ceiling. It darted just beyond Nova's grasp and took off toward the window that had been left open for the bees.

Cursing, Nova chased after it. The butterfly dipped downward. Nova lunged, arm outstretched, fingers straining.

The butterfly was flying straight for the window. Bees were clouding in around it, having noticed new prey in their midst.

The butterfly shot through the opening.

Nova dove. One knee on the window's ledge, one hand barely catching the frame to keep from falling, one outstretched hand crushed into a fist.

She hung there, motionless but for her erratic breaths. Though wasps and hornets surrounded her, and some even dared to perch on her knuckles and inspect her squeezing fingers, there were no stings.

Trembling with adrenaline, Nova pulled herself back into the bedroom.

Dazed, Nova looked down to see one hive with a footprint shoved into its papery shell in the center of the room. She'd moved so fast, she hadn't even noticed stepping on it. The bees who had called it home were swarming around, enraged, their buzzing deafeningly loud, but they were not the insects that worried her.

Exhaling, Nova pried open her fingers.

The butterfly's wings were broken. Its hairy, speckled body was still twitching.

Stomach roiling, she dropped the creature to the floor. It was set upon instantly by the waiting bees.

There would be nothing left of it.

She dusted the powder from her hands. Her body was trembling.

This butterfly was dead, and while Danna wouldn't retain the memories of what it had seen, there were hundreds of other butterflies that would be able to re-form now, to tell what they might have uncovered. What else had Danna learned from following Nova, before this one had been captured?

Nova's heart ricocheted inside her chest. She felt hollowed out. Terrified.

She didn't know if Narcissa or Danna would inform the Renegades first, but it didn't really matter. Nova knew one thing for sure.

She was out of time. Danna could become human again at any minute. Maybe she already had.

How long before everyone knew the truth?

"Leroy! Honey!" she yelled, rushing back down to the ground

floor. "I hope that explosive you talked about is ready to go. We need to leave, now."

Leroy and Honey were both standing amid the broken glass in the front room. Leroy was examining the rock that had been thrown through the front window.

Snarling, Honey shook her head. "A plain old rock," she said, aghast. "It's practically amateur hour around here."

"Did you hear me?" said Nova, her voice tinged with panic. "The butterfly is dead. If Monarch hasn't already re-formed, she will soon. I'm not sure how much she knows, but . . ." She trailed off.

"But it's almost certainly enough to incriminate you," said Leroy, dropping the rock. It landed with a heavy thunk on the carpet. "And lead back to all of us. Worst-case scenario, they'll be here in . . . ten minutes?"

"Sooner if they send the nearest patrol unit," said Nova. "Maybe longer if—if the Council makes this a personal priority. But not by much."

Leroy nodded. "I'll set the explosive and be ready to detonate at the first sign of the Renegades approaching. Take only what we need. Don't worry about leaving evidence behind—nothing will be recognizable when I'm done with it."

CHAPTER TEN

T HE LAST TIME Adrian had raced across the rooftops of Gatlon City in the Sentinel's armor, he had been carrying Max, half dead, in his arms. He was only slightly less panicked now. Ruby's message had been so emphatic, and so utterly lacking in explanation. He had immediately responded, desperate to know why she was summoning the team, but there had still not been a response.

So he ran.

Or, jumped.

Some might even say he flew. It was the closest he would ever come, at least until he could figure out how to tattoo wings onto his own back.

The springs tattooed on the soles of his feet propelled him forward, soaring over streets and skyscrapers. He wasn't being particularly discreet, but he'd found that not many people in the city stopped to look up, and if they did, he hoped they might think the glint of his armor was nothing but an illusion in the midday sun.

Even if they did recognize the infamous vigilante, he would be gone long before anyone could think to stop him.

Ruby lived with her family in a three-bedroom apartment in the Shademont neighborhood. To a lot of people in the city, three bedrooms would have seemed spacious, but for Ruby's family it was still crowded quarters, between Ruby and her twin brothers—Sterling and Jade—along with both her parents and her grandmother. Adrian couldn't recall ever hearing Ruby complain about sharing a bedroom with the boys, who would be twelve in a few months, but he had also never questioned why she didn't invite the team to her place to hang out. On the rare occasions when they'd met up at someone's house, it had always been Adrian's.

He was panting by the time he landed on the rooftop of her apartment building, his breaths fogging the inside of his helmet. One last leap, and he landed with a shattering thump in the alleyway below. A stray cat yowled and hissed at him before fleeing around a corner.

He slapped a hand to his chest and the suit retracted, folding in on itself until he could tuck it under the skin over his sternum. He had taken to wearing long-sleeve T-shirts with three buttons at the neck, easy access for the suit, and he fumbled to secure the buttons now as he moved toward the front of the building. His legs always felt a little wobbly after all the jumping, but he ignored them.

He was steady again by the time he reached the Tuckers' apartment on the second floor. The door opened before he could knock. Not Ruby, but her grandmother, a petite woman with streaks of gray in her once-ginger hair. Her hands were curled from arthritis, which Ruby had mentioned as being a result of years in the jewelry trade, using her fingers for the smallest, most detail-driven tasks. Still, she had a poise and strength to her expression that Adrian had admired from the first time he'd met her.

"They're in the children's room," she said, stepping back to let him in. "Last door on the left."

He thanked her and hurried down the hall. The door was cracked open and he could hear voices inside—her brothers yipping excitedly, and Ruby shushing them, sounding frantic.

Adrian opened the door. The twin boys, seated together on the upper mattress of their bunk beds, stopped talking immediately to gawp at him. Oscar was there, too, his legs also dangling from the top bunk, his cane hooked on one of the rungs of the ladder. At first Adrian was surprised that Oscar might have beat him there, until he remembered that Oscar lived not far away, whereas he had to come miles from the hospital.

"The slacker finally shows up," said Oscar, beaming.

That smile helped calm Adrian's racing heart.

He stepped into the room. Ruby sat on the foot of the twin bed that was parallel to the bunks. The only other furniture that fit into the room was a tall dresser and a little desk that had been crammed into the space between the beds.

And there was one other person, lying on Ruby's bedspread.

"Danna!" he yelled, striding the whole two steps it took to reach her side.

She was unconscious, though it was a fitful sleep, her eyelids twitching and small beads of sweat dotting her forehead. She was wearing her Renegade uniform, her blonde dreadlocks spread across the pillow. "Where did she . . . *How?*"

"I don't know," said Ruby. "She's been staying with me ever since we found Ace Anarchy, you know, in swarm mode."

Adrian nodded. The butterflies had become Ruby's shadow since the night Danna had led them to the catacombs where they had discovered Ace Anarchy.

"And I was just sitting here, about to start getting ready for patrols tonight. The butterflies were everywhere, hanging out, like they've been, when out of nowhere they all started to swirl around—you know how she does that cyclone thing?—then she re-formed. She looked *terrible*, all tired and shaky. And kind of spooked. She said, 'Call Adrian, *just* Adrian.' I know she wanted to say more, but then she collapsed."

"She is a master at making a bold entrance," said Oscar.

"Mom thinks she's just hungry," said Sterling—or was it Jade? Adrian hadn't figured out how to tell them apart yet. He would have to ask Ruby if they had a tell.

"Or dehydrated," added the other.

Adrian crouched next to Danna. "She's probably never been in swarm mode for so long. It must take a toll on her body." He gave Danna's hand a squeeze. "Why me? And what is Oscar doing here then?"

Ruby shied away, mildly bashful. "Well, I couldn't *not* call Oscar. But I sent the message to you first."

"Here we go!" said Ruby's mom, bustling into the room with a wooden tray in her hands.

"Yes," said Oscar. "Refreshments!"

Mrs. Tucker cast him a withering look. "These are for Danna. But that's a good point—Jade, Sterling, why don't you go grab some snacks for our guests?"

The boys didn't bother with the ladder, just jumped down to the floor and raced from the room.

Oscar beamed after them. "I love this family."

Ruby's mom set down the tray, which held a bowl of broth, some bread, a large glass of water, and a damp washcloth. "Any change?" she asked, putting the cloth on Danna's brow.

"I'll do that, Mama." Ruby took the washcloth from her and tended to Danna, her face twisted with worry. "Is it weird that she's so . . . twitchy? I mean, people don't usually dream when they pass out like this, do they?"

"I don't know," said Adrian, frowning at the way Danna's chest rose sporadically.

"She's been through an ordeal," said Mrs. Tucker. "But she's a Renegade. She'll pull through. And I must say, I won't miss having our butterfly friends crowding up the apartment anymore. She's always welcome, but it was a little disconcerting." She winked. "I'm going to leave the tray here. You let me know if anything changes."

"Should we take her to HQ?" said Oscar once Mrs. Tucker had gone. "Or the hospital? Or call a healer?"

"Yeah," said Adrian. "The Council will want to know she's back, too."

He started to reach for his wristband, but Ruby stopped him. "I don't know. She said to call you, no one else. It seemed—the way she looked—that seemed really important."

"But why me? What can I do for her?"

Ruby didn't have an answer. Her lips pursed with indecision.

Suddenly Danna dragged in a shuddering gasp. They all turned their attention back to her.

"Danna?" said Ruby, running the cloth over her cheeks. "Can you hear me?"

Danna's eyelids fluttered and slowly opened. Her breaths were still ragged, but they seemed to slow as her gaze darted around the room, alighting first on Ruby, then Adrian, then Oscar. A tiny smile flickered over her face.

"Great skies," she croaked, then cringed as a fit of coughing worked its way up her throat. She grabbed Ruby's arm and tried to pull herself up, but Ruby and Adrian both pressed down on her shoulders.

"It's okay," said Ruby. "You need to calm down. And rest."

The coughing fit passed and Danna collapsed back into the pillow, still wheezing. "I thought I'd never . . ." She cleared her throat again. "It's so good to see you guys through just one set of eyes."

Ruby beamed through her unshed tears. "What happened?"

Danna became serious and she tried to sit up again, shoving Adrian's hand away when again he urged her to relax. "Is anyone else here?" she said, her scratchy voice lowering to a near whisper.

"Just my mom and grandma and brothers," said Ruby. "Actually—I need to tell Mom you're okay. She wanted to—" She started to climb off the bed, but Danna grabbed her wrist.

"Wait," she said. "Shut the door. I need to tell you something."

Ruby blinked at her. "It can wait, Danna. You need to eat and rest and—"

"It *can't* wait."

Adrian went to the door and shut it. "What is it, Danna?"

She fixed her attention on him. "Adrian . . . ," she murmured, and there was a flash of sympathy that made him go still. He saw her grip tighten around Ruby's arm. "Where's Nova?"

Adrian stilled, immediately nervous at the way she said Nova's name, with something akin to fear. "I don't know—home, I guess. Or maybe headquarters." He went back to the bed. Oscar climbed down the ladder, joining them at Danna's side. "Why? Is something wrong? Is she in danger?"

"Adrian," she said again, and it sounded like it hurt her to say it. His chest squeezed. Already he was planning the route in his mind, the quickest way to Nova's house. "I was following her. I thought . . . It's just that she'd been acting weird, suspicious. I needed to know for sure, so I followed her and—"

"Danna, what's going on?" he said, his tone harsher than he intended. "What did you see?"

Danna's face crumpled apologetically. "I'm so sorry, Adrian, but . . . it's her." Her voice was barely a whisper. "Nova is Nightmare."

CHAPTER ELEVEN

THOUGH THEY HAD discussed a contingency plan for what they would do when Nova's secrets were discovered, Nova had hoped they would never have to enact it. She had hoped to leave the Renegades when she was ready, not because they'd finally figured out who she was.

There was no time to dwell on it, though. She had to focus on gathering the things she needed and getting out of this house before the Renegades arrived.

In their shared bedroom, Honey threw open the sash of the window and began screaming at the bees in the room to *fly free, fly free!* The bees followed her command, soaring out the window in a great cloud, where they were joined by the hornets and wasps from the small yard below. Together, they swarmed over the neighbor's house and disappeared. Nova didn't know how or when they would manage to find their queen again, but Honey seemed unconcerned as she grabbed a jewelry box and an armful of dresses and shoved them into a suitcase. There was no saving the nests and hives dotted throughout the room, but no matter. Nova trusted Leroy when he said everything would be destroyed. She doubted there would even be ash left of these papery structures.

While Honey moved on to the cosmetics on her vanity, Nova pulled her duffel bag from where it had sat largely forgotten in the corner for weeks. She had kept few of her belongings from the subway tunnels, so there wasn't much packing to be done. She stuffed her Nightmare costume inside, shoving the metal mask deep into its folds, followed by her heat-seeking throwing stars, the altered mist-missiles, the ink pen with the hidden blow-dart chamber, her shock-wave gun and specially designed wall-scaling gloves, the repurposed bazooka, the binoculars that had taken months to perfect . . .

She paused and scanned the room, even as she heard the growling engine of Leroy's sports car back in the alleyway.

What else was there?

Through the window, she saw Leroy climbing out of the car. He left the driver's side door open for a quick escape and popped the tiny trunk. Phobia was there, too, standing amid the abandoned hives. If he had an expression, Nova couldn't tell what it was beneath the black shadows of his cloak.

"Catch!" she yelled, tossing out the duffel bag.

She didn't really expect either of them to move to catch it, so was surprised when, at the last moment, Phobia spun his scythe and caught the duffel's handles on the hooked blade.

"Here, throw mine down, too," said Honey, shoving the suitcase at her. "I'll start packing Leroy's chemistry things."

Nova tried not to think about the time that was slipping through her fingers. It couldn't have been more than a few minutes before they were gathered behind the sports car, cramming their belongings into the trunk. Nova nestled Ace's helmet inside the plastic bin that held Leroy's beakers and measuring tools before latching the lid.

"Is that everything?" she said, panting. She peered up at their almost-home.

"It's going to have to be," said Leroy, pulling a small device from his pocket. "Learned this trick from Ingrid. There are days when I miss her." He adjusted a dial that might have been foraged from a simple egg timer. "What do you think? Two minutes?"

Even as he said it, the sound of sirens reached them, distant but coming closer.

Nova's stomach sank. Maybe the Renegades were responding to a nearby theft or a kitten stuck in a tree. But she knew better than to hope.

"I suggest thirty seconds," said Honey, slipping into the passenger seat of the car. She scooted toward the center console, making room for Nova.

"Thirty seconds it is," said Leroy, punching a button on the detonation device.

Hair prickling on the back of her neck, Nova moved toward the open car door, but then froze. "Wait—the Vitality Charm. Honey, did you grab the Vitality Charm?"

Honey leaned forward to see Nova beneath the low frame of the car. "You mean that necklace? No. But, Nova, there isn't time—"

She cursed and swiveled toward the house. "Go without me! I'll catch up!"

"Nova!" Leroy yelled, but she ignored him as she sprinted back into the house. Through the kitchen, rounding the stairwell banister, and up the stairs for the last time. The entire place reeked of the chemicals Leroy had doused over the floors and walls only minutes before. The small bomb in the kitchen would be detonated remotely from Leroy's device and the explosion would cause a chain reaction of precisely crafted chemicals igniting one after the other, sending a wave of molten-hot vapor through the structure and, according to Leroy, destroying everything it touched.

Including Nova herself if she didn't hurry.

In the bedroom, she flew to the thin mattress pad on the floor and dug her hand underneath. Her fist wrapped around the chain and she yanked it out. Flying to the window, she leaned out just as the yellow sports car was swerving out of the alleyway onto the road.

Bracing her hands on either side of the window, she climbed up onto the sill and surveyed the small yard. She would aim for the empty hives and nests, which would allow at least a bit of cushion for her tuck-and-roll. With the pendant clutched in her fist, she eyed the area and mentally prepared herself for the jump when she heard pounding from below. A fist beating against the front door.

Her heart leaped into her throat. How much time had passed since Leroy set the device? Ten seconds? Twelve?

The front door splintered as someone kicked it in. Heavy footsteps could be heard clomping in the front room.

"Nova!" someone yelled.

Her breath left her.

Adrian.

"Nova, it's me! We need to talk!"

The bomb. The chemicals.

Nothing will be recognizable when I'm done with it.

An inky wisp drew her attention back to the alley. Phobia appeared where the car had been seconds before.

Still perched inside the window, Nova pulled back her arm and threw the Vitality Charm at him. He caught it easily in one skeletal hand. His hood fluttered, before he vanished again into nothingness.

Nova sprang back into the room and ran for the stairs. She skipped the whole flight of them, landing in the downstairs hallway in a single jump.

Adrian froze beside the coat closet, startled. "Nova—"

"We need to leave," she all but yelled, grabbing his elbow and dragging him toward the destroyed front door. He started to resist, but Nova screamed, "*Now*, Adrian! We need to get out of here, now!"

Maybe it was her tone of voice, or maybe it was simply that he had come here for her and no other reason, but he allowed her to pull him through the door and out onto the sidewalk before he planted his feet and wrapped a hand around her wrist. "Nova, stop! Danna is back and she . . . I'm here to . . ."

"Come *on*," Nova growled, yanking on his arm. He budged, but only allowed her to drag him to the other side of the street before he halted again.

"Nova, stop!" he yelled. "Listen to me! You're—"

The explosion struck them from behind, knocking them both to the ground. Nova's body tumbled a couple times against the concrete, and then she was on her back, her ears ringing and her body feeling like it had just been hit by a bulldozer. All she could see were hazy white dots blocking out the sky, while a deafening static roared between her ears.

She had no idea how long she lay there. How long she was incapacitated, unable to move, unable to think, until the reality of her surroundings slowly, slowly began to take shape again.

The static subsided enough to welcome in the blare of sirens and shouting voices. Her lungs gradually started taking in air, and it tasted like sulfur and ash. When her vision cleared, it was only to see a cloud of black smoke billowing over the neighborhood.

She managed to get a hand beneath her and use the leverage to peel her body from the asphalt. Adrian was only a few feet away, already sitting up and gawking at the house.

Or what remained of the house, which appeared to be little more than the exterior brickwork, and even a good amount of that was scattered in chunks of rubble down the sidewalk. The fire was mostly coming from the adjoining row houses. Nova barely had the wherewithal to be grateful they had both been abandoned.

She turned her head just as Adrian, too, tore his attention from the destroyed house and looked at her, his mouth hanging open, the back of his Renegade uniform streaked with soot.

"Are you okay?" she said. She knew she was probably yelling, and yet she could barely hear her own voice.

He didn't answer. Just kept on staring, like she'd spoken a different language.

Then, to her surprise, he scooted closer and held a hand out to her.

Exhaling, she slipped her palm into his and together they climbed to their feet.

"Adrian . . . I . . ."

Her words caught as Adrian's fingers tightened around hers. His other hand reached for the clasp on the bracelet.

She tried to pull away, even as the bracelet fell from her wrist. Adrian caught it and met her gaze, his expression both distraught and determined.

"What are you doing? Give it back."

She tried to lunge for him, but her body wasn't fully cooperating and her movements were too jerky, too slow. Adrian backed away. Nova tried again, reaching for the bracelet, when she felt cold metal latching around her now-bare wrist.

A cuff. The kind that fully enclosed the entire hand. A cuff intended for prodigies.

For villains.

Her other arm was yanked back behind her and within seconds, that hand had been imprisoned, too. She looked over her shoulder, vitriol rising through her aching chest, but the anger died away when she saw Ruby standing there, and Oscar not far behind. Both of them watching her with that same distress, and the same determination. With Nova handcuffed, Ruby couldn't back away from her fast enough.

"I'm confiscating the bracelet as potential evidence," said Adrian, dragging her attention back to him.

"Evidence?" she said, surprised that her voice even worked. "But that's . . . My father made it. It's all I have. You can't . . . Adrian! Evidence of what?"

"Evidence of your crimes against society and the Renegades." He winced, as though he were in physical pain, when he said, "You're under arrest . . . Nightmare."

CHAPTER TWELVE

B Y THE TIME Tsunami and Torrent had doused the flames on
Wallowridge, the row house was in ruins, along with most of
its neighbors. Ruby had sent a message to Adrian's dads, telling
them about Danna's return and about Nova . . . about *Nightmare.*

Adrian's insides were still in knots and he couldn't help the surge
of denial that eclipsed his thoughts, even now. Even after having said
the words himself. *You're under arrest, Nightmare.* Even having sorted
through all the evidence he'd been storing in his mind, that somehow made it all seem so obvious once the last puzzle piece was put
into place, and yet . . .

Not so obvious.

It had to be Nova. Of course it had to. Who else could have such
inside knowledge of Agent N and the Vitality Charm, the helmet and
HQ security? Who else was so observant, so smart, so determined?

Nova adored Max. Nightmare had tried to save him.

Nightmare loathed the Sentinel. Nova had done little to disguise
similar feelings for the vigilante.

Nova had been at Adrian's house the night the Vitality Charm had gone missing and—sweet rot, *he'd fallen asleep*. He'd been kissing her and then he'd fallen asleep, and he was such a fantastic idiot for not drawing a connection sooner.

Even their superpowers were related. Nova never slept. Nightmare could put others to sleep. There was a harmonious balance that wasn't uncommon in the world of prodigies.

It was so obvious.

And yet.

And yet.

Denial was still there, screaming inside his skull. His fist was wrapped so tight around the bracelet he'd taken from her that the filigree was leaving small indentations in his palm.

Not Nova. It couldn't be Nova. The girl who had rushed into the quarantine to help Max when he hurt himself. The girl who had studied Adrian's art with such awe. The girl who had fallen asleep in his arms.

The girl who had kissed him and he knew—he *knew*—the kiss hadn't meant nothing. It couldn't have just been a lie, a manipulation. No, he had felt it. He had been so sure she felt the same way about him as he did about her.

But then . . . she had put him to sleep.

That had been her. Her power. Her touch.

He groaned, rubbing a hand over his hair as he paced back and forth in front the house's smoldering remains.

Nova . . . no, *Nightmare*. He needed to start thinking of her as Nightmare. She wouldn't even be housed temporarily at headquarters or the medium-security prison that was a few miles outside the city limits, like criminals sometimes were while it was decided the best placement for them. No. She had been taken away in an armored vehicle bound straight for the docks, where a boat would be waiting to take her to Cragmoor Penitentiary.

There was already enough evidence piled up against her, even if, so far, it was all hearsay and circumstantial. Danna's accusation, and a whole lot of coincidences. Too many coincidences.

All they needed now was a single piece of evidence. Real evidence. Ace Anarchy's helmet found amid the wreckage of her home. Or the Vitality Charm or Nightmare's mask and uniform or any number of weapons she'd used over the past years. Or something that would connect her to the other Anarchists. Proof that she was involved with Cyanide or Queen Bee, the Puppeteer or Phobia, or even Ace Anarchy himself.

He found himself wishing that Danna was there. She had intel on the Anarchists that the rest of them could only guess at so far, and her perspective could have been invaluable. But Ruby had insisted that Danna go to headquarters to be checked out by the healers while the rest of them came after Nightmare. It had been the right decision—Danna had been about to collapse again when she told them the truth of Nova's identity—but that didn't change the fact that Adrian wanted his full team on duty right now.

He needed to be surrounded with people he knew he could trust.

With the last of the flames finally doused, Tsunami, along with Torrent and a fire elemental who was immune to burns, made their way into the skeletal remains of the building. Adrian, Ruby, and Oscar were told to wait outside until it was declared safe to enter.

Annoyed, Adrian returned to pacing along the sidewalk, doing his best to ignore his friends' sympathetic stares.

He didn't have to set foot into the remains of the house to know that this had not been a normal explosion or a normal fire. He'd seen the effects that fire had left on the Cloven Cross Library, but this was altogether different. The smell of thick smoke mingled with the acrid sting of chemical compounds. The scorch marks on neighboring brick walls shimmered with a pearlescent-gray sheen and the destruction went far beyond what Adrian would have expected. It wasn't only the flammable materials that had succumbed to the heat and flames—the curtains and floorboards, the upholstered furniture and wood-framed interior walls.

Whatever concoction had been involved with this explosion had caused such an extreme heat wave that even some of the stonework had melted from the blast. The windows had shattered, but some of that broken glass had liquefied into silvery puddles on the pavement, which were just beginning to solidify again as they cooled. Adrian may not have been allowed inside, but from what he could see, there was little left. The roof was gone—mostly disintegrated, he guessed—though there was evidence of some roofing tiles and chimney bricks scattered up and down the street. Nothing remained of the interior walls but a thick cloud of dust and the occasional chunk of plaster. Where the ground floor had been was now an empty crater revealing the basement foundation below.

If there had been any evidence in this house proving Nightmare's identity or her connection to the Anarchists, Adrian wasn't optimistic it was still there.

Their only hope, he thought, would be to find the helmet. He was confident that it could withstand even this trauma. If they found it here in Nova's home, they'd have all the evidence they required.

Nightmare, the villain who had haunted them all these months, would be done for.

And if the helmet wasn't there?

Well, there was still plenty of evidence against her. Even this explosion seemed to prove her guilt. Nightmare must have known that her identity was compromised, and so she or one of her allies had rigged this explosion to keep the Renegades from commandeering any more of their belongings.

It made sense.

But Adrian couldn't quite tear his thoughts away from that moment when Nova had raced down the steps and shoved him out the door. The panic in her expression had been palpable. Her terror as she had dragged him away from the house was undeniable.

She could have been thinking about saving her own life, but . . . Adrian didn't think that was the case. She had been trying to save him, too.

He couldn't make himself believe it was all an act.

What if Nova—no, *Nightmare*—did care for him? Truly cared for him?

It wouldn't matter.

Because she was a villain and an Anarchist. She was his enemy. She had lied to him about everything.

He choked back the bile that was suddenly stinging his throat.

He hated Nightmare. He loathed her to the core of his being.

He repeated these thoughts again and again, hoping that the unsettled twinge in his gut would go away if he just kept reminding himself of the truth.

I hate her. I hate her. I hate her.

"Sketch?"

His head jerked up. Tsunami was standing in the blackened frame of the row house's front door, her white gloves smudged with silvery ash.

"We've deemed it safe for forensics and the cleanup crew to begin inspecting the home. You're welcome to take a look around, too. But . . . as I'm sure you've noticed, there isn't much to see."

Exhaling, he nodded at Ruby and Oscar. Tsunami disappeared back into the house, but Adrian hadn't taken two steps when he felt a hand on his arm.

"You don't have to go in there, you know," said Ruby.

His jaw twitched. "You heard Tsunami. It's safe." There was a definite undercurrent of resentment to his voice, but he didn't care. He *was* resentful. And angry. And hurt.

"That's not what I'm talking about." Ruby tilted her head, sympathy written across her face. "You can leave this to the cleanup crew. It doesn't have to be you."

"Actually, it does have to be me," he rebuked. "I knew her better than anyone. I should have figured out the truth."

"She fooled all of us, Adrian, not just you. She was my friend. She came out to watch my brothers compete in that silly Sidekick Olympics. She danced with Oscar at the gala. She—"

"She kissed me," he interrupted. "She made me think that I . . ." He trailed off, just short of confessing the brutal words that had been clinging to him since the moment he'd found out the truth. *I could be in love with her.*

It wasn't true, though. It wasn't real. It had never been real.

Ruby tensed. "Adrian . . ."

"Besides," he went on, "she didn't fool all of us. Danna figured her out weeks ago."

"Which was still a long time after she joined our team. Remember how Danna brought Nova a care package when she was in the medical wing? And didn't she have dinner at your house, with your dads? Honestly, if she could trick the Council, then—"

"I should have known." Adrian tore his arm away from her. "It's so obvious, isn't it?" He squeezed his eyes shut as memories flooded through him. The library. The carnival. His own basement.

He shivered, and for the first time when he thought of that night, it wasn't a good shiver. "I should have realized it sooner, and everyone is going to know that." It hurt too much to see Ruby's pity, so he turned to Oscar instead. Sadly, Oscar's expression wasn't much better. "It doesn't matter now. We finally know who Nightmare is. She's captured, and so is Ace Anarchy. Good against evil. Renegades win again." He gestured toward the house. "Now let's go see what else we can learn about our enemies."

The moment Adrian stepped through the threshold of the row house, though, he knew they wouldn't be learning much. The house was nothing more than a shell of stone walls, and even their surfaces appeared wilted, like they'd gotten too close to the sun. Tsunami and the others were down in the basement, standing on blackened dirt and ash between the high stone foundation walls, but he could see from their dismay that they were just going through the procedures now. No one really expected this investigation to turn up anything useful.

Adrian took a few steps inside, walking carefully along the narrow foundation wall. He was surprised to see a hallway and powder room to his left with the shreds of scorched wallpaper still visible on the plaster and a towel bar dangling from one screw, until he realized that he was seeing the abandoned neighboring home. The wall that had once separated them was gone.

He took another few steps, though he wasn't sure why he bothered. At some point he became aware that Ruby and Oscar hadn't followed him. They were still standing on the threshold, peering into the hollow space that had once been Nova's home. There was nothing here.

Movement caught his eye and Adrian shifted, peering into the oval mirror that hung over a pedestal sink in the distant parlor room.

The ceramic sink had a large crack running through it and half the mirror appeared to have warped from the chemical explosion, its surface now wavy and distorted. The movement had been Adrian's own reflection caught in its surface.

Or that's what he thought at first, until another face appeared in the reflection. A girl, pale and haunting and almost familiar . . .

He jolted in alarm, but before he could call out, the phantom was gone.

His own eyes stared back at him, wide and unblinking. He rubbed his palm into them, trying to clear the vision.

Great. Not only did he have to suffer through a broken heart and debilitating betrayal, but now he was having hallucinations of Nightmare, too?

Nightmare. He realized how fitting the alias had become.

Teeth clenching, he made his way back to the entryway. "This is pointless," he muttered as he brushed past Ruby and Oscar. "Let's get back to headquarters, see how Danna's doing."

He nearly crashed into a figure on the sidewalk. He drew back, startled. "Oh, sorry, Magpie," he said, taking in the girl's dust mask and perpetual scowl. "I was distracted." He gestured indifferently toward the house. "Should be an easy one. There's not a whole lot left to clean up."

Shoulders hunched, he started to move around her.

"You must feel pretty dumb."

He froze. A mixture of anger and embarrassment welled up in him at Maggie's haughty tone. He wanted a quick retort to come to him, but that desire fizzled fast with the unavoidable truth. "Yep," he muttered. "Among other things."

Magpie leaned against a stair rail. Across the street, two more members of the cleanup crew were milling around a Renegade-issued van, unpacking crates of supplies.

"I never did like her," said Magpie.

He gritted his teeth, recalling the way Nova had bristled every time Magpie was around. "I'm pretty sure the feeling was mutual."

"I *did* like that bracelet, though." Magpie pulled down the dust mask as her gaze fixed on Adrian's tight-closed fist. He recoiled instinctively. "What are you planning on doing with it, anyway?"

He looked down, and with some reluctance peeled open his fingers. Nova's bracelet glinted up at him. The delicate coppery filigree that had encircled her wrist from the day he'd known her, and probably long before. The clasp he'd once fixed himself, before he had any idea who Nova was, what she was.

What she would mean to him.

And there was the star. Glowing faintly, casting its golden light on the dust that speckled the air around him. It was warm to the touch and there had been times since he'd taken it off Nova's wrist that he could have sworn there was a pulse to it, almost as though it were alive.

He wanted to know why Nova had taken it from the statue in his basement. He wanted to know what it was, what it could do, and how it had come to exist at all. It hadn't been in the painting, but it *had* been in Nova's dream, the one he'd done his best to re-create.

It all made his head spin.

More than any of that, though, a deep part of him wanted to get rid of the thing and never see it again. Even holding it now, remembering that night in his handcrafted jungle, Nova breathing softly as she fell asleep in his arms, made his blood run cold.

She was Nightmare. She'd been Nightmare all along.

"I don't know," he finally said, clenching his fist over the bracelet again, cutting off the star's light. "Give it over to Artifacts, I guess."

"You can give it to me," said Magpie, in a tone that was a little too rushed, a little too insistent.

Adrian tensed.

Realizing that she'd moved uncomfortably close, Magpie took a hasty step back. "I mean, to take in to HQ. I'll submit it with the rest of . . . you know, whatever we find here today. Get it cataloged and . . . whatever. I can take care of it for you."

Adrian's fingers tightened. A subtle instinct warned him not to let the bracelet go. There was a meaning to it that he hadn't uncovered yet.

Also, there was something about Magpie's expression. A hint of desperation that unnerved him. A whisper of intuition told him she was lying. Would she really submit it to HQ?

Magpie's hope darkened into a scowl and she held out her hand, palm up. "Come on, Sketch. This is my job, not yours."

He stared down at her hand and found that small argument surprisingly persuasive. She was a part of the cleanup crew. She was a Renegade.

And he loathed the idea of carrying this star around for a moment longer.

"I doubt you'll find anything else to take in," he said. "But I guess that doesn't matter." Smothering his reluctance, he dropped the bracelet into her palm. Her hand snatched it back immediately, as if she was afraid he'd change his mind. "Don't lose it. That bracelet meant something to No—Nightmare. It could be important to our investigation."

Magpie's frown didn't budge. "Do you think I'm new at this?"

She tucked the bracelet into a pouch on the leg of her uniform and marched into the desolate house without another word.

The knot in Adrian's stomach loosened, just a little, to be rid of the thing. The sooner he could forget every blissful moment he'd had in the company of Nova McLain, the better.

CHAPTER THIRTEEN

T HE WAVES OF Harrow Bay crashed against the small boat, sending sprays of water over the edge. Inside the cabin, which was lined with plastic benches bolted to the floor, Nova stared out the condensation-slicked glass, trying to ignore the two guards who stood at either end of the cabin, never once taking their focus from her. Otherwise, she was alone, the only prisoner on this particular ferry ride, heading out to the infamous Cragmoor Penitentiary. She saw it rise out of the thick fog and murky waves like a medieval fortress, surrounded by jagged cliffs and an unforgiving sea. Nova shivered when she saw it, but that could have been the frigid air inside the boat.

As they pulled up to the weathered dock, the chain that connected her cuffs to an iron hook in the floor was released. The guards took her by each elbow, careful not to risk touching any of her skin as they escorted her off the boat. One of them nodded a friendly farewell to the boat captain, who tipped his hat in response. Nova almost laughed for how normal the small interaction seemed, here, on this brutal island, where nothing could possibly be normal.

Two more guards and the prison warden were waiting at the end of the dock. She was shoved into a small motorized vehicle and again had her enclosed hands chained up, this time to a hook on the vehicle's ceiling. No one said much. Some small talk between the warden and the guard who was driving, too quiet for Nova to make out anything over the roaring motor. She welcomed being left alone, though, inspecting the walls of the prison as the car skirted the narrow switchbacks up the cliffside.

As the ground leveled off, she saw the guard towers, manned by Renegades in familiar gray uniforms. Two were carrying guns. The others had no weapons she could see, but she knew that only meant that their superpowers were dangerous enough that weapons would be superfluous.

The wall around the prison was thick stone topped with razor wire. No surprises there. Neither was the gate that opened to let their vehicle through. The main cell block itself was a rectangular structure in the center of the compound, built with only a utilitarian vision in mind. No windows. Only one door, as far as Nova could see, and as far as the blueprints had told her. She had known what to expect, but somehow it still astounded her. The dreary hopelessness of it.

She was not led directly into the cell block, but rather into a smaller building that did have windows, though they were narrow and caked with years of mud flung up by the island's relentless wind. A man at a desk talked briefly to the warden before filling out a line in a register. He turned the page to Nova and asked her to sign in the box.

Feeling numbed to her core, Nova stared at the words on the page while one of the guards opened the cuff on her right hand, freeing her fingers so she could hold the pen. The date and time blurred on the paper, but the name was in sharp relief. Nova McLain. Seeing it gave her a jolt, to know they hadn't yet figured out her real name.

It was followed by a prisoner number, 792, and her alias. *Nightmare.*

Her hand trembled as she took the pen, which was strapped to the desk in case anyone decided to try and stab the administrator with it.

Before they could stop her, she scratched out *Nightmare* and scribbled *Insomnia.*

"Hey!" said the man behind the desk, starting to grab the book away, even as Nova hastily signed her name in the empty box. He and the warden exchanged scowls.

"It's fine," said the warden. "Let's just get this done. You've assigned a cell yet?"

"Got a few options," said the administrator, still looking sour over Nova's small act of rebellion. "She going into solitary like the last one?"

The warden snorted with contempt. "Please. She puts people to *sleep.* It's just about the least threatening ability we've got on this island."

The man behind the counter grunted. "Cell B-26 it is."

Once signed in, Nova was taken to a tiny concrete room and handed a striped jumpsuit. The cuffs were removed fully and Nova rubbed her wrist, not just because of the soreness brought on by the restraints, but to confirm that the emptiness she felt was real. Her bracelet was gone. Adrian really had taken it from her, the last connection she had to her father.

A female guard stood by while she changed, instructing her to put all her belongings in a bin that appeared in a small slot in the wall. It didn't matter. They could burn her clothes and fancy

Renegade-issued boots for all she cared. The one thing that mattered had already been taken.

Well, the one thing besides her freedom. Her family. Her future.

She ground her teeth, chastising herself for thinking it. She hadn't even been there a day. Hadn't even seen her cell. It was too soon to be giving up.

She was just stepping into the jumpsuit when something punctured her in the back, right between her spine and left shoulder blade. She cried out and spun around. The guard was holding a device that looked a bit like Nova's homemade stun gun.

"What was that?" Nova yelled, reaching for the burning spot on her back. She felt something hard embedded into her skin.

"Tracker," said the guard in a bored voice, setting the gun to the side. "Prisoners used to try and escape. Now, we almost welcome it. They don't get far with those, and it can liven things up around here for a day or two."

Nova shoved her arms through the sleeves and did up the buttons. "You could have warned me."

"Oh? And you would have just stood still and said, 'Thank you, ma'am,' when I was done? You'd be the first."

Cuffed again, with the same guards flanking either side, Nova was finally led through the muddy yard and into the cell block. Since Ace had been captured, she had spent a lot of time trying to imagine what it must be like inside Cragmoor Penitentiary, and now she tried to be amused that, after everything, she was being given a VIP tour. She knew the exterior shell of the original building had been relatively untouched, but the interior had been demolished and reconfigured a number of times since they had started housing prodigies. She knew that the prison was constantly being altered and remodeled to contain new superpowers and the many complications they afforded their captors.

But nothing she had read had given much indication as to what the interior of the prison was actually like, and she had pictured tiers of jail cells stretching the length of the building, linked by narrow walkways and high rails.

The reality was nothing like that.

Walking into the cell block, she was greeted by a vast open space stretching from one stone wall to the next. Until her gaze traveled up, to where the ceiling was reinforced with steel beams nearly five stories overhead. The cells, each one a single solitary box, were suspended from the beams by thick cables.

There *was* a narrow walkway, but rather than connecting the cells, it lined the perimeter of the wall around them, where the guards could make their rounds and keep watch on the inmates.

If there were prisoners inside the suspended cells, she couldn't see them from below. The place was silent as death, a silence made more complete by the wind howling against the outside walls, and then their footsteps.

Cell numbers were stenciled with spray paint onto the stone wall, and they paused in front of B-26. Her guard nodded toward a room on the second level, surrounded by black tinted glass. A second later, the grating noise of gears echoed around them, and one of the cells began to descend. Nova watched its slow approach, a part of her wishing that it would just fall and crush her and end this whole ordeal before it even started. Again, she cursed herself for feeling so hopeless. She was an Anarchist. She was Ace Anarchy's niece. She was never hopeless.

But it was hard to convince herself of that now, when the cell hit the floor with a clang and she found herself scanning an enclosure a third the size of her bedroom at the house on Wallowridge, and even that had felt cramped.

One of the guards nudged her in the back. Her lips tightened and she thought about asking if they were going to let her keep the pretty new handcuffs. But her mouth was dry and her heart wasn't in it.

What did a few pounds of chains matter at this point?

The chains clanked as she stepped into the cell. Dark. Cold. Devoid of comfort. It felt a little bit like stepping back into the subway tunnels, but this time, there would be no reprieve from the endless gloom.

Her feet crossed the threshold, and a set of bars slid shut behind her with a reverberating thud. She turned and took in the horizontal metal grate, probably iron. Then a second series of bars, these vertical, slammed down over the first. She gulped. Carbon fiber, she guessed, probably an extra precaution for any inmates who could manipulate metal. Then she heard a hum and saw a faint flicker of red light along the edges of the cell. Her eyebrows lifted. *Lasers, too?*

Sweet rot.

It seemed hilarious, all of a sudden, that Nova had dreamed of breaking into this place. She'd not only dreamed of rescuing Ace from here, she'd actually thought she could succeed. She hadn't known *how*, but failure hadn't seemed like an option.

Now she realized how useless all her plotting had been.

They were never going to rescue Ace.

Just like no one was ever going to rescue her.

As soon as the cell was secured, an internal device on her chains clinked and the cuffs fell from her wrists, landing in a pile at her feet.

The noise of cogs and gears echoed around her and the cell began to rise upward. The guards dropped away below and all she could see beyond the bars was the cell block's exterior wall. Thick stone and mortar.

Though she knew that there were other cells suspended in the air only a few feet away from her own, it made no difference that they were there, or whether or not they were occupied.

She was alone.

She had only ever felt *truly* alone one time in her life—in the moments that followed the murders of her parents and Evie. After she put their killer to sleep, she had stood over his unconscious body, gripping the gun still hot from his own hand, ordering herself to kill him. Kill him. *Kill him.* She had been alone then, and she had known it. No family. No one to take care of her. No one to help her be brave. No one to help her through this.

Until Ace had come and she had remembered—no, she wasn't alone. She still had family. She still had Uncle Ace, and it was all she had, and she had grasped on to that small piece of comfort as tightly as her trembling little fists could.

Now Nova surveyed her cell. Gray walls, made of what material she couldn't guess, but something told her it might be chromium. There was a sleeping pad as thick as a pencil in one corner. A wash-basin against the wall, and a toilet with a small holding tank in the corner. It was so cramped that her feet would be on the mattress pad as she did her business.

Not knowing what else to do, Nova sat down on the mat and tried to think of all the choices she had made that had brought her here. All the mistakes. The failures.

She had tried to assassinate Captain Chromium. She was an Anarchist and a villain. Not long ago, she would have assumed the punishment would be life imprisonment, but she still recalled what the Captain had said the morning after her attack on headquarters.

Soon, the Renegades would be revealing Agent N to the public, and part of their grand presentation would include the "public neutralization of all prodigies who have been heretofore convicted of villainous behavior." Surely, at this point, that would include her, too.

She knew the Renegades had been testing Agent N on Cragmoor inmates, at their our discretion. No judge or jury had approved the permanent removal of their powers. The Renegades had no need of such antiquated practices—they did what served them best. Who cared what happened to a few criminals, anyway? Who cared if they were treated like nothing but disposable lab rats?

Her emotions were a jumble of anger and resentment that clouded what might otherwise have been sorrow.

Nova realized, in the midst of her self-pitying musings, that the fingers of her right hand had wrapped around her left wrist, gripping so tight that the tips of her left fingers were beginning to tingle from lack of circulation. Swallowing, she lowered her head and released her stranglehold. Her skin carried a ring of white where she'd been holding it, thicker than the faint tan line that depicted where the bracelet had sat against her skin for nearly her entire life.

It felt like someone had chopped off a limb, to be without the bracelet. And the star, too, though she'd had it for far less time. Still, the star felt like something *she* had made. Something she had dreamed into existence. With Adrian's help, perhaps, but that didn't change the intense feeling of ownership she had over it. The way it had secured itself, perfectly fit, to the empty prongs of the bracelet had seemed to confirm that it was hers. She hadn't fully realized what a comfort its steady pulsing light had brought her these past weeks, while the rest of her life had been driven into further and further turmoil.

Now they were gone. The bracelet. The star. She hated to think of them in the hands of the Renegades, being examined and inspected. Probably Callum would end up with it at some point. He would write up a description for the database. He and Snapshot would argue over how it should be classified—jewelry, historical artifact, mysterious extraterrestrial matter?

Would they know that the star had been complicit in destroying the chromium box that had once protected Ace's helmet? She shuddered to remember when, in a burst of rage, she had hurled the chromium spear at the box, and in the moment that spear left her hand, the star had let out a wave of light that blinded her, transforming the spear into what seemed like a shard of pure energy.

The next thing she knew, the indestructible box lay at her feet in pieces, and the helmet was free.

It was a mystery that she had only had time to contemplate in the quietest, stillest moments of the past weeks—which had been few and far between. Now, trapped inside her own indestructible box, she found it comforting to have a mystery to contemplate instead of her own crimes and betrayals.

A dream. A star. A painted mural brought to life. Threads of golden energy in the air. The helmet. Her father. The chromium spear. Dozens of artifacts that glowed faintly copper.

They all seemed connected, but how? What did it mean?

Ghosts of her family floated through her thoughts. The smile lines around her father's eyes. Her mother's gentle hands. Evie's dimpled cheeks. And for once, thinking of them didn't make her want to storm through the streets of Gatlon City and tear apart the first so-called superhero she saw.

For once, thinking of them made her nothing but sad.

She had failed them all.

Groaning, she buried her head in her arms, that one word an echo inside her skull.

Failure. Failure. Failure.

She had failed her family. Ace. The other Anarchists.

Even . . . Adrian.

Always at the surface of her thoughts, Adrian.

This time, for the first time in so long, she couldn't even dredge up the memory of his open grin. Or the sensation of his kisses. Or the way his hand held his marker when he drew. Or how he had touched her wrist when they met at the parade. Or—

All that was gone, buried beneath an avalanche of heartache.

Now when she thought of Adrian, she thought only of the way he had looked at her, with the betrayal and disgust and loathing that she had feared for these many months.

She hadn't realized it until that very moment, but it was all too clear now.

She was living her worst nightmare.

CHAPTER FOURTEEN

"Nothing," Adrian muttered to himself, scanning the digital report. "Nothing found in the remains of 9416 Wallowridge can conclusively confirm that any known villains with or without Anarchist affiliations, including alias: Nightmare, recently or otherwise visited or occupied the home." He glanced up at his teammates. "Then it goes on to list everything they did find, which is mostly random stuff that could have been buried under the foundation decades ago. A couple glass bottles, hairpins, leftover wiring. Et cetera, et cetera."

"Doesn't mean anything," said Oscar. "The house was burnt to a crisp. Of course they didn't find anything—there was nothing left to find."

Adrian nodded, but he couldn't shake his disappointment. He believed Danna. He did. There was no denying that in some twisted way, it made sense that Nova was Nightmare, much as he hated to admit it. There were just too many coincidences.

Still. Hard evidence would have gone a long way toward pacifying his lingering doubts. What if they were wrong? What if Danna was mistaken?

But it was only wishful thinking. A burning desire to not be the Renegade who had been smitten by one of their worst enemies. A desperate need for Nova to not be the liar, the spy, the villain she'd suddenly become.

"Do they know what caused the explosion?" said Ruby, peering over Adrian's arm at the screen. They were in the training room in the sublevels beneath headquarters, waiting for another mandatory session on Agent N to begin. But judging from the looks being passed their way from the other teams who were gathered around the mats and firing ranges, no one was talking about Agent N.

Adrian did his best to ignore his fellow superheroes, some with expressions full of pity, others haughtiness and scorn. As if *they* were immune to being duped like he had been, ignoring the fact that Nova McLain had duped them all.

"They've found a number of trace chemical compounds that are almost certainly responsible, but exactly what they are or how they combusted is still under investigation." Adrian scrolled through the document.

"Nova would definitely be capable of creating a bomb," said Oscar.

"Yeah, I know," said Adrian, his brow furrowed. He wasn't sure he had stopped frowning since the moment Nova had been taken into custody. "And unusual chemicals are the trademark of Cyanide's work, too. They could have had this planned for a long time."

"Just waiting for us to figure out that she's a villain," Ruby said with a sigh.

Adrian didn't respond. It was as though he kept willfully forgetting the truth.

She's a villain.

Ruby gasped, startling him. "Danna!"

He and Oscar both turned to see Danna coming down one of the narrow staircases from the catwalk above. She waved at them. Though there were dark circles under her eyes, she still looked worlds better than she had when she'd first retaken her human form. Color had returned to her cheeks and her dreadlocks had been arranged in a loose knot at the nape of her neck. She looked like the old Danna, fierce and confident and ready to get down to business.

"How are you feeling?" said Ruby when she reached them.

Danna stretched her hands gleefully overhead. "Awesome," she said, without a hint of sarcasm. "You have no idea how good it feels to have fingers again."

"So there were no serious injuries?" asked Adrian.

"Nope. I was mostly dehydrated, and being in swarm mode for so long made my symptoms wonky, but nothing a good night's sleep couldn't fix."

"I heard Thunderbird saying you might be given some leave," said Ruby. "They don't want to force you back into the field before you're ready."

Danna snorted. "Yeah, she cornered me this morning to talk about it. Something about unfair labor practices and violations of human rights . . . I don't know, I think they're all in a tizzy over these complaints from Genissa Clark. But there's no way I'm going to sit back now when we're so close to finding the rest of the Anarchists. I want to be a part of this."

"But what if you have to transform again?" said Ruby.

"So?"

"So . . . are you ready for that? So soon after . . ."

In a blink, Danna dissolved, her body replaced with hundreds of fluttering wings. They raced in a circle around the training hall, drawing attention from the other waiting patrol units. After a full lap of the space, the butterflies cycloned and Danna re-formed.

"I'm not afraid of my superpower," she said, arms folded.

Ruby beamed and threw her arms around Danna's neck. "Good. Because this team isn't the same without you." But as soon as she said it, her smile faded and she pulled away, just a bit, casting a nervous glance at Adrian.

He knew she was thinking about Nova. Though she hadn't been a part of their team for nearly as long as Danna had, it still felt like the team wasn't the same without her, either.

But there was no use thinking of that. She had never really been a part of the team at all.

"So?" said Danna, casting her attention between them. "Did they find anything at the house?"

Adrian shook his head and told her about the report. The remains from the fire had provided no evidence that could definitively connect Nova and Nightmare, or indicate where the other Anarchists might be hiding. With Ace Anarchy and Nightmare in custody, the Puppeteer neutralized, and the Detonator dead, that left three known Anarchists still at large: Cyanide, Queen Bee, and Phobia. The Renegades had had scouts posted near the cathedral since the day Ace Anarchy had been captured in hopes that one of his minions might make their way back to the site, and they were conducting routine checks of the subway tunnels throughout the city, but so far there had been no trace of the missing villains.

"Is it possible they left town?" said Oscar. "Like, after Ace was captured, maybe they decided enough is enough?"

"It's too early to determine that," said Adrian. "And if they didn't up and leave after being down in those tunnels all these years, I doubt they'd run away now."

"Unless they finally ran out of options?" said Ruby. "I mean, Queen Bee, Cyanide, and Phobia. None of them are exactly masters of disguise. You would think if they were wandering around the city, someone, somewhere, would have noticed them."

"There are a lot of abandoned buildings in this city," said Adrian. "There are a lot of places to hide."

Danna grunted and gestured at the report on Adrian's screen. "Which means they could be anywhere, and none of this is going to give us any leads."

"Yeah, but right now, it's the best we've got." Adrian's voice lowered. "Unless Ace Anarchy or Nightmare give us something to work with."

"All right, patrols," yelled Blacklight, strolling through the scattered groups in his signature black leather jacket and skintight pants. He was carrying a large plastic crate. "Gather 'round, gather 'round. I know it's been an eventful twenty-four hours, but we do have important business to tend to before I release you all to further your gossip. As you know, our public reveal of Agent N is in less than four weeks. It's to take place at the arena, and media from all over the world will be in attendance. We need to be fully prepared for all patrols to be equipped with the serum before then. As the recent attack on headquarters has understandably left a few of us on edge, we are going to be implementing some new precautions to ensure that Agent N cannot be used against our own."

"Precautions?" said the Wrecking Ball, fisting her hands on her hips. "Like maybe destroying all of the remaining Agent N and never bringing it up again?"

Blacklight cast her a withering look. "Har-har. Nothing so drastic as that. Now, I understand your concerns—we all do, and we were all devastated to lose Frostbite and her team. But this weapon has been an important investment for us, and it remains our best hope at eliminating villains and dangerous prodigies from our city. We were unprepared for an enemy to have access to Agent N, it's true, but we will not be making the same mistake again."

"Investment," scoffed another Renegade, Coyote. "I'm beginning to think Genissa is right—that's all the Council cares about. Their investments."

Adrian frowned at the back of Coyote's head. Though the words had been muffled under his breath, it was clear he'd intended them to be heard. Adrian disagreed, though. The Council cared about them, each of them, and all of the citizens of their city. But at the same time, he wondered if the Council's eagerness was blinding them to the risks of pushing forward with Agent N. With all the attacks from the media and the public's mounting doubts about the Renegades' ability to keep them safe, they were desperate to make it appear that they were still in control.

But at what cost? Did they really believe they could keep their own Renegades safe from Agent N after what had happened to Frostbite's team?

Blacklight set the crate on a table and pulled out a bulky gas mask. "Our friends in tech have made modifications to these masks, and after a series of tests, we can confirm that they will protect a prodigy from Agent N in gas form, which, as you know, was one of the methods Nightmare used to neutralize Frostbite and the others. Effective immediately, all patrol units will be equipped with a gas mask during active duty."

He started tossing the masks into the crowd. The patrols caught them, almost unwillingly. There was distaste written on their faces as they inspected the cumbersome masks.

Blacklight tossed one to Adrian and he quickly understood his peers' irritation. The band meant to wrap around his head was stretchy rubber and the bulbous filter over the mouth was heavy and hideous.

"We're expected to wear these during patrols?" said Shot Blast.

"Only if you feel you're in danger from an enemy who could have access to Agent N."

Ruby raised her hand. "How are we supposed to know who may or may not have access to Agent N? Who knows who Nov—Nightmare could have given those bombs to?"

"Currently," said Blacklight, "we have no reason to suspect that any villains other than Nightmare's own affiliation—the Anarchists—have Agent N."

"Okay, but what about poisoned darts?" asked Zodiac. "That's the method we were going to be using to neutralize our enemies, so how do we know the Anarchists will even keep using Agent N in gas form? How are we supposed to keep ourselves from getting shot with the stuff? Our uniforms aren't going to protect us." She pulled at the stretchy skintight sleeve to emphasize her point.

"That is a concern," said Blacklight, and Adrian could tell he was growing weary of their questions, even if they were valid. "We are discussing the development of full-body armored suits that will replace your current uniforms in the future."

"Armored suits?" said Coyote with a bark. "Like the Sentinel?"

"Not . . . exactly," said Blacklight, with an extra edge to his voice. Adrian had the sense that the uniforms they were plotting were exactly like the one worn by his alter ego.

Oscar elbowed Adrian in the side, smirking with pride. Adrian glared at him.

"How long before those suits are available?" asked Mondo-Man. "Something tells me it won't be before the public reveal."

"And how am I supposed to use my powers if I'm trapped inside a bunch of armor?" added Chameleon.

"I remember that doctor saying Agent N could be ingested, too. What if the villains start poisoning our food with it?"

A barrage of questions started pouring out from all sides of the room. Blacklight's cheeks flushed nearly as red as his beard as he held up his hands, trying to fend them off.

A streak of lightning shot across the high ceiling, crashing into an overhead light. It burst with the impact, cascading sparks, at the same moment a roar of thunder shook the floor beneath them. It was so loud it knocked Adrian back a few steps, leaving him feeling like a giant drum had just been banged inside his skull.

"*Enough!*"

As silence filled the space left by the thunder, they all looked up to see Thunderbird on the catwalk, her face taut with anger. "None of you have the authority to question the Council's decisions in such a disrespectful manner."

Adrian gulped, unable to recall ever seeing Tamaya Rae so livid. And all because a group of Renegades had dared question the Council? Surely they were allowed to do that, right?

Blacklight cleared his throat. "I had this under control. For the record."

"We have more pressing matters to deal with," snapped Thunderbird. "There is a situation in the main lobby. Your presence is requested, immediately." Jaw still tense, she scanned the patrol units. "You are all dismissed."

Without waiting for a response, she swept back down the catwalk, her wings brushing against the railings to either side.

"Right," said Blacklight. "To be continued." Leaving the near-empty crate behind, he rushed after Thunderbird, bounding toward the elevators with as much dignity as he could hold on to.

The patrol units left behind passed mystified glances at one another for a minute, before rushing after the Council members. With a shrug to his teammates, Adrian followed.

CHAPTER FIFTEEN

THE LOBBY WAS still under reconstruction and currently full of broken slabs of stone and caution tape and, it appeared, every on-duty Renegade who was in the building. They had formed a circle around the shattered tile floor, where a long gash could still be seen stretching from the red *R* in the lobby's center to where the quarantine had crashed down from the mezzanine.

The pile of glass and rubble had been cleared away, and steel beams framing the balcony had been put back in place. On the second floor, tucked back from the edge of the walkway, stood a framework of steel spires, like an incomplete birdcage. Beside them, enormous curved glass panels were leaned up against the laboratory walls.

Adrian grimaced to see them there, to imagine what they would become. The thought of putting Max back into that glass prison disgusted him, but he hadn't been able to talk to his dads about it again since Max had woken up.

Raised voices drew his attention back to the crowd—including the sound of Captain Chromium's voice, sounding tense, though Adrian couldn't make out his words.

Danna's swarm fluttered up to watch the proceedings from the upper level, while Oscar and Ruby climbed up onto the curved information desk in order to see above the heads of the crowd. Adrian leaped up beside them.

Standing near the tiled R was the Council—all five of them, hands fisted on hips or crossed over chests. A dozen paces in front of them, backlit from the massive windows at the front of the building, stood Genissa Clark, Trevor Dunn, and Mack Baxter, previously known as Frostbite, Gargoyle, and Aftershock.

Stingray stood beside them, too, his barbed tail twitching back and forth on the floor.

"What's going on?" Adrian asked.

A nearby prodigy shushed him, but Pyrotechnic, on his other side, whispered, "Clark thinks the Council owes her."

"—absolutely ridiculous," said Blacklight, his voice loud enough to carry over the crowd, drawing Adrian's attention back to the Council. "Of course they can't come back on patrols. They aren't prodigies anymore!"

The Dread Warden shot an annoyed glower at Blacklight, but it went ignored as Blacklight waved his arm toward Genissa and the group. "Well, they can't! It's absurd to even consider it!" He took a step forward. "Sorry to say it, but you're acting like a spoiled princess, Miss Clark. Besides, you're the one who said you were done being a superhero. No one here forced you to quit, but we all know it was the right decision. So why don't you go home and start figuring out a more productive use of your time? We have better things to be dealing with."

Captain Chromium settled a hand on Blacklight's shoulder and pulled him back. He muttered something, but it was too quiet for Adrian to hear.

He had no problem, however, hearing Genissa Clark, who seemed thrilled to have an audience. "I've had a change of heart. And now that we're back, you're just going to sweep us under a rug, pretend like we don't even exist? Like we didn't sacrifice our powers in service to this organization. You can't pretend that what happened to us isn't your fault!"

"We're superheroes!" bellowed Blacklight. "What did you expect, that we'd all sit around having tea parties all day?"

"That's enough, Evander," Thunderbird growled.

Huffing, Blacklight crossed his arms, muttering, "Ridiculous."

"We demand retribution for what's happened to us," said Genissa, who had placed herself at the front of her group. She appeared relatively unchanged on the outside—the same flaxen hair, the same cool blue eyes, though her skin did seem to have a mild flush to it that had always been missing before. The coldness of her glare, though, was exactly the same as it had always been. "We joined the Renegades as prodigies, with abilities that belonged to us. But thanks to your carelessness in developing Agent N, and your failure to keep it from our enemies, we're the ones suffering. There is no replacing our lost abilities, but we expect retribution. You owe us!"

"Perhaps we could go somewhere private to discuss this?" said Tsunami, gesturing toward the elevators. "Our offices are—"

"We're fine here," interrupted Genissa. "My peers need to hear what you have to say. After all, any one of them could be next."

"Genissa, we are sorry for what happened to you," said the Dread Warden, "in no small part because we hate to lose you and your team. You were one of our strongest units. But you chose to be a Renegade. You chose the risks that come with this life."

"Actually," said Genissa, smugly settling her hands on her hips, "when we first joined the Renegades, this *risk* didn't exist. Criminals, fine. Villains, no problem. But Agent N exists because *you* created it. How could we possibly have chosen that?"

"Besides," said Trevor Dunn, whose flesh had once fluctuated between compounds of stone but now was covered in patches of pink, flaking skin, "I never signed a contract, signing away my life and powers in service of the Renegades. How about you all? You sign anything?" He gestured around the room, and was met with a lot of uncomfortable frowns.

"Of course not," said Genissa. "A contract would suggest that, if things don't go well, we might actually be entitled to some sort of compensation for the trauma and suffering. But oh no. We're expected to fight for the Renegades, to defend the people of this city, to constantly throw ourselves into dangerous situations all in the name of *heroism*. And we are heroes. Sworn to protect the weak and defend justice. But who is going to defend us? I wouldn't count on it to be *them*." She gestured at the Council. "As soon as they don't need us, they toss us aside, and I'm not going to stand for it." She lifted her arms. "And none of you should, either. The Renegades are nothing without us. We are the heart and muscle of this organization, and they need us, more than we need them. I want the Council to recognize that we aren't disposable trash. We're Renegades! You can't take that away from us, too!"

"Look, Genissa," began the Captain, "we want to treat everyone justly, especially our own. But you can't rejoin the force as patrol units. It wouldn't be safe! I'm sure we can find some other role in the organization that will satisfy you. We don't exactly have procedures in place for this sort of thing. And I'm sorry, but it's not a top priority right now."

"Perhaps it should become one," said Genissa. "And I suggest it becomes a priority fast, because I have my schedule booked full of media interviews this week, and I can either tell them how well the Renegades take care of their own . . . or I can tell them the truth. And with all the effort you've put into this big upcoming reveal of Agent N, well, it would be terrible if the secret got leaked early . . . wouldn't it?"

"Great skies," muttered Blacklight. "You know what—fine! Let's just let them back on the team! Let them get themselves killed if that's what they want!" He shook his head. "Non-prodigy super-heroes. You can't possibly—"

"We're not—" the Captain growled under his breath, but he seemed relatively calm as he fixed his attention on Genissa. "I can't in good conscience allow you to continue risking your lives when you don't have superpowers to defend yourselves with. I'm sorry." He spread his fingers wide. "What else can we offer you?"

This, to Adrian's surprise, seemed to be the magic question. Genissa cast a victorious grin at her teammates.

"Actually," she said slowly, "there is one thing that *might* satisfy our need for . . . well, if not retribution exactly, then at least a bit of retaliation."

The Council shared identical, suspicious scowls, but Genissa pushed on. "There have been rumors that the public revealing of Agent N is to include a public execution as well."

Captain Chromium narrowed his eyes. "That's true. For his crimes against humanity, Ace Anarchy has been sentenced to death."

"Why stop there?" said Genissa. "I would argue that his accomplices deserve the same fate." She lifted her chin, blue eyes glinting. "Nightmare deserves the same fate. Nightmare must die—and I want to be the one to do it."

The words seemed to be sucked into a vacuum. Adrian felt like the ground had sunk beneath him. Like the world narrowed to a pinprick.

Nightmare must die.

He was sure his dads would scoff at the suggestion, but their faces were stoic and unreadable.

It was Blacklight who spoke first. With a quiet chuckle, he said, "Is that all it will take to quit their complaining? Works for me."

Simon shot him a look. "These are lives we're discussing."

"Villains' lives," said Blacklight. "Nightmare doesn't deserve mercy any more than Ace Anarchy does. She *was* the one who neutralized them, so it seems fair to me."

"Think about it," said Genissa. "The people are losing faith in you quickly. Every day we hear people asking if the Renegades are really capable of protecting them, of serving the growing needs of this city. As the Council, you need to show a united front. You can't tolerate any prodigies who refuse to act by the code. And you certainly don't want ex-Renegades like us"—she gestured at Mack and Trevor—"going around telling everyone how weak you really are when it comes to true threats, like Nightmare and the Anarchists."

Adrian's vision clouded, darkening at the edges until all he could see was Genissa Clark's infuriating grin. She was already relishing the idea that she could be the one to end Nightmare's life. She wanted vengeance for her lost powers.

But the Council wouldn't allow that . . . would they?

A hand gripped his elbow—Ruby's, offering support. It snapped Adrian from his thoughts.

It wasn't Nova. It was Nightmare. It was a villain.

But still—*death*? Without a trial? Without any hope for redemption?

"Captain," said Tsunami, "I am not sure this is a wise course of action. The Council needs to discuss—"

"Oh, wow, I hate to interrupt," said Genissa, checking an invisible watch, "but we have to get going! Wouldn't want to miss our interview with the evening news, would we?"

She spun on her heel, but had barely moved before Captain Chromium called out, "We accept."

"No," Adrian whispered, shaking his head. Ruby's hand squeezed tighter around his arm. "They can't let her . . ."

He trailed off as, in the center of the lobby, Genissa Clark pivoted back to the Council with a wicked smirk. "Come again?"

"A double execution will take place at the reveal," said the Captain, his fists clenched as he spoke. "You, Frostbite, may see to the death of Nightmare, who has been our longtime enemy, and a persistent threat to the Renegades and the civilians we have sworn to protect. This execution will be enacted as punishment for her crimes against society and our own."

"Well," said Genissa, flourishing a mocking bow at the Council, "thank you for being so understanding. We'll give your offer due consideration and get back to you."

With a wink, Genissa and her team paraded toward the revolving doors, pushing their way back to the street, where they were immediately swarmed by reporters who had been camped out on the sidewalk ever since the helmet had been stolen.

"Back to work, all of you!" the Captain barked, his voice uncharacteristically irate. The crowd immediately jumped into action, though Adrian doubted many were going to "work." Already he could see the crowd dividing into groups, flocking toward the lounges and training halls to discuss what had just happened.

"Adrian?" said Oscar, poking Adrian's foot with the bottom of his cane. "You all right?"

"Why wouldn't I be?" he said.

A hesitation was followed by Oscar whispering to Ruby, "That's a *no*, right?"

"Excuse me," said Adrian, hopping down from the desk. He shoved his way through the crowd, toward where all five Council members were climbing the newly built stairway to the mezzanine.

"Dad!"

The Captain tensed, and his expression was mildly crumpled as he faced Adrian. "I'm sorry. We didn't have——"

"Capital punishment? Really?" Adrian gaped at each of the Council members in turn.

"And why not?" roared Blacklight. "Do you have any idea how many thousands of people died at the hands of Ace Anarchy and his minions? It's about time we started fighting fire with fire. You show no mercy, you deserve no mercy."

"And how many people has Nightmare killed?" said Adrian. "Other than the Detonator, that is."

"You might recall that she tried to kill *me*," said Hugh.

Adrian felt his face start to burn. "I haven't forgotten," he said lowly. "But she also saved Max."

His fathers both drew back in surprise.

Simon was the first to recover. "Saved Max? She threw a spear at him!"

Adrian vehemently shook his head. He could feel himself edging dangerously close to revealing his own secrets—his dads still didn't know he was able to get close to Max, they didn't know about his tattoos—but he couldn't let Nova continue to take the blame, not for this. "Genissa stabbed him. By accident, while he was invisible. It was Nova . . . Nightmare who tried to help him. She helped him take Genissa's power so he could stanch the bleeding."

Hugh took a step toward Adrian. "That's not what Genissa told us."

"I know. But it's the truth. Talk to Max."

"And how do *you* know this?" asked Simon.

Adrian gulped. "It's a long story," he said, not trying to hide the fact that he was dodging the question. "But if it's true, then maybe we owe her something. Besides, we're still the good guys, aren't we? We don't execute people."

"Exactly," said Thunderbird, the feathers on her wings ruffled. Adrian realized that she was not in agreement on this, and both Tsunami and even the Dread Warden had misgivings written on their faces.

"There are politics in play here that you don't understand," said Hugh, but the fury from before was missing from his voice. "The media and our detractors are trying to divide us at every opportunity. Everything we do is being criticized and questioned. How can we run a city, much less an entire world, if we're busy dealing with every trivial bit of bureaucratic nonsense that comes up?" He ran a hand through his hair. "This solves two problems at once—it pacifies Genissa and her team, and it shows the world that we will act against our enemies swiftly and effectively. We need that right now. And"—he looked around, meeting everyone's gazes—"we need to be united in this decision."

"And why's that, exactly?" said Adrian, feeling venom in his throat. "Do we not want the world to know this is actually a dictatorship?"

Hurt flashed through Hugh's eyes.

Guilt surged through Adrian, but he refused to let it show. He waited for the rebuttal, the argument, but instead, his dad simply shook his head. "This decision doesn't involve you," he said, before turning and walking away. The rest of the Council followed but for Simon, who set a hand on Adrian's shoulder.

Before he could say whatever half-assed comforting thing he

was planning, Adrian shook off the hand and stomped back down the stairs. Blood was rushing through his veins, hot and drumming at the surface of his skin. He was ready for a fight. Wanting one. Or maybe just wanting someone to yell at, needing an excuse to explode. Just once.

But who did he have left to fight?

Nightmare, once thought to be his greatest enemy, was already in prison.

And in a few short weeks, she would be dead.

CHAPTER SIXTEEN

Nova quickly fell into the routine of Cragmoor Penitentiary. In the morning, at what exact time she couldn't say, the prison cells were lowered to the ground floor and, one by one, the bars were opened and the guards on duty shouted at the prisoners to come out of their cells and get in line. They were always shouting, even though Nova had only witnessed the inmates being perfectly compliant. She wondered why no one ever lost their voice.

They were then marched out of the cell block and into what they called the sanitation room, where they were given ninety seconds to shower under cold water and sixty seconds to brush their teeth and comb their hair in front of a trough of sinks. Once a week they were given freshly laundered jumpsuits.

They then had twenty minutes to "stretch their legs" in the yard, though most of the inmates stayed in groups by the wall to avoid the mud. It was almost always raining—a cold, misty drizzle—and even when it wasn't, the wind cut through their jumpsuits like daggers. Nova didn't speak with anyone, not only because the guards were always watching and she had the distinct impression that conversation on the yard was discouraged, but also because, when she did dare to approach another prisoner, they always gave her a scornful look and turned their back on her. It hadn't taken many rejections before Nova decided she was better off keeping to herself anyway. She didn't know where the universal contempt for her originated, whether it was because they thought she might actually have Renegade loyalties, or because they knew she was a villain who had failed to bring down their enemies, and she wasn't sure she cared to find out.

She was getting used to being alone.

After the brief recreation time, they were served their only meal of the day inside a cafeteria where the narrow tables and stools were all bolted to the floor, and the kitchen was kept behind a stone wall, with only a narrow slot through which they could slide out trays of food.

The quality of the food was exactly what Nova had expected. Which was to say, not much worse than what she'd consumed in the subway tunnels most of her life. Most days the meal consisted of a roll of hard bread, an unrecognizable vegetable cooked down to mush, a baked potato, and fish. Nova didn't know what kind of fish, but she guessed it was whatever the cooks could get for cheap. On Sundays, if the prisoner had gone the week without trouble, they were also allowed a sliver of cheese.

Then they were sent back to their cells, roughly two hours after they'd been released, to pass the rest of the day in quiet isolation until lights-out. A few prisoners who had been there long enough to earn some amount of trust were sent to work in the laundry or the kitchen. At first this had seemed like extra punishment, but it didn't take long for Nova to recognize that the long hours of solitude were far worse.

For the first time in her life, Nova's inability to sleep felt far more like a curse than a gift. What she wouldn't have given to spend eight fewer hours every night alone with her spinning thoughts.

And so the days passed by, monotonous and unbearably dull.

Every day, Nova hoped to see some sign of Ace, but he was never in the yard and never in the cafeteria. She assumed he was in solitary confinement, but when she tried to ask one of the other prisoners, the woman looked at her like she was speaking another language and said simply, "Ace Anarchy is dead."

Nova hoped this meant that Ace's capture and confinement were only being kept from the prisoners, not that he had come here . . . and already died.

She couldn't bear that. Not after everything.

With her sanity barely intact, she thought it would be best not to ask anyone else, even if that was only a sign of pathetic self-preservation. She simply couldn't handle any more loss.

On the seventeenth day of her imprisonment, Nova stood at the trough of sinks, her mouth full of baking soda and suds as she brushed her teeth, trying to be as thorough as she could in the time allotted. The muscles in her back where the tracker had been embedded had finally stopped aching.

She was doing her best to appreciate these small things when, for the first time since she'd arrived, there was a disturbance in the routine. The warden stepped into the sanitation room and was speaking quietly with one of the guards.

It was so unusual to break from the pattern that all the inmates froze.

Then the guard's attention cut to *her,* meeting Nova's gaze in the long, dingy mirror.

Nova bent forward and spat. She quickly rinsed her mouth, and the toothbrush was plucked from her hand a second later by the same guard who always took it, because, evidently, a toothbrush was a potential weapon.

For good reason, she supposed. She could definitely do some harm with one if she wanted to.

As she was standing up, her attention caught on a face in the mirror. Not *her* face and not the prisoner beside her.

Her gut lurched. *Narcissa.* She was still behind the glass, watching Nova with an unsettling intensity. She raised a finger to her lips and gave a quick shake of her head.

Then she was gone.

Nova stood blinking at her own startled expression, wondering whether she'd imagined it. Why would Narcissa show herself to Nova here, now? And what did she mean by shushing her like that? What did she think Nova was going to say?

"Seven-nine-two!" barked the guard.

Nova startled and faced him, glaring. "Nova," she said through her teeth. "My name is Nova."

Beside the guard, the warden gave her an appraising look. "You have a visitor . . . Seven-nine-two."

The rest of the inmates studied her, which was more attention than she'd received since the day she arrived. She wondered what the rumors would be. She wondered what it meant to have a visitor in this place. Would they be jealous of her, or were visitors a sign of trouble?

She used the sleeve of her jumpsuit to dry her mouth and, hair still damp from the shower, stepped toward the warden. The guards met her halfway and clamped the familiar cuffs around her hands.

Nova's thoughts were still churning from Narcissa's appearance, and it wasn't until they were halfway across the yard, heading toward a building she hadn't yet been inside, that it occurred to her that her visitor might be Adrian.

Suddenly, her lungs were struggling to hold air.

Her palms began to sweat inside the hard-shelled gloves.

She hoped it would be Adrian.

And, equally, she hoped it wouldn't be him.

Because how could she face him? How could she look him in the eye and lie *again*? Lie more than she already had? Lie in the face of so many truths?

She thought of Narcissa. The finger to her lips. The shake of her head.

The timing was too coincidental—she must have known about Nova's visitor. What had she been trying to tell Nova? To stay quiet? To keep her secrets, even now?

Her thoughts swam. If that was the case, Narcissa needn't have bothered. Nova had determined from the moment she'd been arrested—no, from the moment she'd decided to enter the trials and join the Renegades—that she would never admit to her deceit. She would give them nothing that could be used against her or the Anarchists.

As far as Nova was concerned, she was still Nova Jean McLain, and all she had ever wanted to be was a Renegade.

She knew the lies would come as easily as they always had. She could face Captain Chromium without blinking. She could even stare down her own teammates—Oscar, Ruby, even Danna, despite all she'd done to her—and she could insist on her innocence with trembling lip and pleading eyes. She would shake their resolve, even if she couldn't destroy it entirely.

At least until she knew what they had against her.

But if it was Adrian . . .

Please don't let it be Adrian.

And yet—

Please, please let it be Adrian. Let me see him one more time.

The guards led her to a room on which a circular metal platform stood with a hard-edged chair bolted to its center. An open chasm had been left all around the platform, save only for the narrow plank connecting it to the barred doorway, to keep the prisoners away from the shiny black walls on either side.

Other than Nova and her guards, the room was empty.

The chair appeared wholly uninviting, not only because of the cold metal, but also because of the braces on the arms and the chains around the legs.

She didn't struggle as the guards shoved her into it. They bound her ankles to the chair legs and attached the metal cocoons around her hands to the armrests. Her fingers had just enough room to wriggle inside their confines.

It felt a little bit like being led to her doom, and she wondered whether the visitor thing had been a ruse. Maybe this was where it would happen—already, so soon. It was easy enough to imagine someone appearing in a white lab coat and sticking a syringe full of Agent N into her arm.

The guards disappeared behind her, where she could not see them past the tall back of the chair.

Directly ahead of her, on the other side of the chasm, was a glossy black wall. The base of it disappeared beneath her platform, so she had no idea how far the drop was. There was nothing remarkable about the wall, other than how very sheer and smooth it was. Unscalable, or at least, that was the effect. Not that there would be much point to scaling it. The ceiling, thirty feet overhead, held nothing but a few rows of sickly fluorescent lights.

Then there was a click and the wall before her was no longer just a wall. A portion in front of her, ten feet tall and stretching between the walls of the chamber, lit up, revealing that it was, in fact, a window.

Nova was staring directly into the face of Adrian Everhart.

She shivered, overcome with the mix of relief and dread that surged through her.

She could tell, in the first moment of their eyes connecting, that he had been able to see her from the moment she'd been brought into this room and had time to steel himself. His face was neutral and cold, in a way that didn't fit him at all.

But behind the lenses of his glasses, his eyes revealed what his unyielding features did not.

Disbelief. Hurt. Betrayal.

Hatred.

Nova felt her chin tremble—but it wasn't the act she'd planned. "Adrian . . . ," she whispered.

His only reaction was a brief tightening of his jaw.

There were two more people on the other side of the glass. Adrian's dads, Captain Chromium and the Dread Warden. The three of them together, all wearing their traditional Renegade garb—black cape, blue armor, and that despicable red *R* stitched onto Adrian's uniform—made for an intimidating team. But fear was nowhere near the top of Nova's swirling emotions.

The Dread Warden started to speak, and it startled Nova to realize that she couldn't hear them. Instinct prompted her to lean forward as much as she could in the grasp of the chair, but it made no difference.

Adrian tore his gaze from her and nodded. He spoke. Nova tried to read his lips, but it was no use. Captain Chromium placed a hand on Adrian's shoulder, but it was brief. He gestured toward the back of the room.

Adrian nodded again. Spoke again. Looked briefly at both his fathers. Their features were serious, but kind.

Then the two Council members left, and Adrian was alone inside the room.

Nova's heart thundered, but it might as well have been chained up, too, for how tight her chest felt.

"Adrian?" she said, the name coming out as barely more than a breath.

He flinched, confirming that he *could* hear her.

His Adam's apple bobbed as he reached for a pedestal beside him and pressed a button on a remote.

Nova heard a click, and the chamber became full with both of their silences.

Their eyes bore into each other's, and she didn't know if he was waiting for her to say something, or was trying to build up the courage to speak first.

Before she realized it, she was crying. Tears pooled in her vision and quickly began to slide down her cheeks. She gasped at the sensation of the two warm trails making their way to her jaw, and she wanted to rub them away, but couldn't move. Nova sniffed loudly, hoping she could inhale the tears back into her body, but it was too late.

Adrian moved closer to the window, and he had given up trying to be emotionless. The hurt was written plainly now: in the tension across his brow, in the tightness of his jaw, in the squint of his deep brown eyes against the threat of his own tears.

"How could you do this?" Adrian said, his tone vicious and sharp. The sound of such unbridled anger surprised the tears into a temporary cease-fire.

Nova gaped at him, jaw hanging open, and found that she had no response to give.

Her mind was blank. Empty of everything but the sound of Adrian's disgust.

She remembered everything. Every lie. Every betrayal. The weight of the gun in her hands as she prepared to kill Captain Chromium. Her elation when she reclaimed the helmet. The sight of Danna's butterfly beating against the sides of the mason jar.

Nova gathered herself as one last tear crept down, tracing the path of those before it, and said—with so much conviction that she almost could have believed it herself—"Adrian, I'm innocent."

CHAPTER SEVENTEEN

DRIAN'S SCOFF was so loud and unexpected that it only served to bolster Nova's defiance. She could convince him of her innocence. She had to.

He opened his mouth to speak but Nova pressed on, letting real desperation color her tone. "I mean it, Adrian. I don't know what's going on, but I'm not Nightmare!"

"Danna saw you!" he yelled. "She followed you to those ruins . . . that cathedral. She led us to Ace Anarchy, and she would have led us to you, too, if you hadn't . . ." He hesitated, warring with a brief uncertainty. "If you hadn't done whatever you did to her to keep her from re-forming!"

Nova studied him, her mind racing, devouring and dissecting every word.

Danna had seen her go to the cathedral ruins . . . but not the house?

And they didn't know about keeping the butterfly in a jar, which had to mean Nova was right. That butterfly's memories had been lost when Nova killed it. That butterfly at least—the only one that would have seen Nova and the other Anarchists at the house—couldn't incriminate her.

She swallowed. She could work with that.

She hoped.

"I don't know what Danna thinks she saw," she said, "but it wasn't me. I don't know if I'm being framed, or what, but—"

"Oh, please, Nova," Adrian said. "The inventions? The access to the artifacts department? Knowing about Max and Agent N? I can't believe we didn't figure it out before. Is Nova even your real name?"

"Of course it's my real name! But I'm not Nightmare! I'm not an Anarchist. Adrian, you know me!"

He grimaced. "Yeah. That's what I thought, too."

"Please, just tell me what Danna told you, and I can—"

"You can what? Lie some more? Come up with more outlandish stories about your uncle and his *beekeeping*? Or how about when you were so worried that your uncle wasn't feeling well, you had to leave the gala, conveniently right before Nightmare breaks into headquarters. Or what about how your entire house was destroyed right when we were coming to arrest you! Are you going to tell me that was a coincidence, too?"

"I was designing a new weapon," said Nova, who had had a lot of time to concoct this particular explanation. "I was working with some new chemicals, trying to build an explosive that I thought the patrols could use. But it got out of control and . . . well, you saw. But think about it, Adrian! If I knew you were coming to arrest me, why would I have stayed? Why wouldn't I have run when I had the chance?"

"Because you needed to destroy evidence," said Adrian. "It all makes sense. The only thing that doesn't make sense is . . ."

He hesitated, and Nova's pulse jumped. She waited, sure his next words would have something to do with him, with *them*, but his eyes were burning into her again, quickly dousing any such hope.

She shook her head. "You're searching for evidence that isn't there. Maybe . . . maybe there are some coincidences, but I swear, I'm not—"

"Just drop it, Nova."

"But, Adrian—"

"*Drop it.*"

She pursed her lips together.

Adrian lifted his glasses, pinching the bridge of his nose. "I'm not here for your lies and excuses . . . I'm not even here for a confession. I just . . ." He dropped his hands to his sides. "I need answers. Please, Nova. If you ever . . . If any of it was real, then please . . . just tell me . . . who killed my mom?"

She blinked.

Opened her mouth, but found no words.

If any of it was real . . .

It had been real, she wanted to tell him. It had been more real to her than he could ever know.

But this? His mom? The murder?

She had no answers for him.

"I don't know," she whispered.

His hands balled into fists.

"Adrian, I know you don't believe me right now, but I truly have no idea who killed Lady Indomitable. If I knew, I would have told you a long time ago, but I'm not—"

"Nightmare," he said, spitting the name as if it tasted like sewage. "Tell me who killed her."

"Adrian—"

"Tell me!" he yelled, pounding one hand on the glass.

Nova gasped, pushing back against the chair.

He flattened his palm on the window, as if he wanted nothing more than to snatch Nova out of the chains and shake her. "You know about the note. Nightmare said . . . I heard you say . . ."

Her brow furrowed, but Adrian seemed unable to continue.

"What?" she said, curiosity overtaking her concern. "What are you talking about?"

"'One cannot be brave who has no fear.'"

Adrian fell silent, letting the words fill the cold chamber.

Nova gawked at him for so long, her mouth started to run dry. *One cannot be brave who has no fear?*

What surprised her most, what she had never expected, was that she did, in fact, know those words. She had heard them dozens of times over the past ten years, had even occasionally said them herself.

But what did they have to do with Lady Indomitable? And when had Nightmare *ever* spoken those words around *Adrian*?

Finally, when their silence had become unbearable, Nova licked her lips and said gently, slowly, "I'm sorry, Adrian, but I have no idea what that means."

He seemed to draw inward at this statement. Perhaps he was losing hope that he might get answers today. Perhaps this interrogation was taking more out of him than he would admit.

"Those words were found on a slip of paper left on my mother's body," he said, watching her for a reaction.

Nova had no reason to hide her surprise from him. Why had he never told her this before?

And in that moment, it occurred to Nova that she had lied to Adrian yet again, though unwittingly this time.

Maybe, just maybe, she really did know who murdered his mother.

The thought made her veins feel brittle and cold.

If any of it was real . . .

Sorrow crept over her, wrapping her up like a blanket. Her feelings for him had been real. They were still real.

But . . . evidently, not real enough.

"I'm sorry," she whispered, almost choking on the words, "but I'm not Nightmare. I don't know who killed your mother. I'm so sorry, Adrian. I want to help you, but I—"

"Fine," Adrian snapped, halting her words.

Nova flinched. Tears were gathering again. It was more than she'd cried in years. At this rate, she would end up shedding more tears in this chair than she had since the day her family had been taken from her, but she couldn't help it. Her walls were crumbling. All her years of building protective forces around her heart were under attack. A siege from every twitch of Adrian's jaw, every furrow of his brow, every look of revulsion he shot her way.

And then, suddenly, he changed. His emotions hardened into that same neutrality that had cloaked him at the start. His shoulders pulled back. His chin lifted. He nudged his glasses farther up on the bridge of his nose and peered at her with studied indifference.

Nova shuddered.

"I'd hoped you would tell me the truth, but I'm not just here to ask about my mother. I'm here as a representative of the Renegades, and we have an offer to make you."

Suspicion quickly began to dry up the pools in Nova's eyes. "An offer?"

"You are aware that all villains currently incarcerated here at Cragmoor will be neutralized as a part of our public reveal of Agent N. However, the Council has decided . . ." His head dipped, searching for words or maybe steeling himself for what he already knew he had to say. His voice was steady, but hoarse, as he continued, "The public neutralization will also include a public execution."

Nova's eyebrows jerked upward. "Excuse me?"

"The villains known as Ace Anarchy and his accomplice, Nightmare, are to be executed in a worldwide broadcast, as a consequence for their crimes against society."

Capital punishment? From the *Renegades*? She wasn't sure why it shocked her as much as it did, and yet it was hard to grasp the reality of it. She was still struggling to imagine having her powers stripped from her, and now they were going to kill her?

Adrian's face was almost sympathetic with the recitation complete. "Captain Chromium will execute Ace Anarchy." He hesitated. Clearing his throat, he continued, "Genissa Clark has been assigned the role of executing Nightmare."

Nova studied him, waiting for his words to make sense.

Then she laughed. She couldn't help it.

Genissa Clark? Genissa Clark was going to *execute* her? It was so absurd, so unexpected.

But Adrian's expression turned her abrupt laughter into a stilted cough.

"The Renegades don't execute criminals," she stammered, her breaths quickening. "They've never—"

"They feel . . ." Adrian hesitated. "We feel this is a special circumstance. The Council wants to send a message that our citizens will never again be threatened by Ace Anarchy or his followers."

Nova's gaze traced the sheer, glossy black wall beneath the window, how it faded into the oblivion of shadows. It was fitting, she supposed, that Frostbite would volunteer for such a responsibility. No doubt she was eager to seek vengeance for her lost abilities, and she couldn't very well go after Max.

Nova wasn't afraid of dying. At least, that's what she told herself. It might even be less painful than living with the knowledge of how she'd failed Ace and the others. How she'd betrayed kind, trusting Adrian. How she would never claim vengeance for her parents, for Evie.

She sniffed, once, and lifted her attention back to Adrian. "You said there was an offer?"

Adrian's hands were fisted at his sides again, any signs of pity already gone. "I told my fathers how you saved Max . . . or, helped him, at least, after he was stabbed."

Her lungs expanded. She hadn't realized that Adrian knew Nightmare had done that. Genissa had been happy to let everyone believe it was Nightmare who had stabbed the boy. How could Adrian have figured out the truth?

Unless . . .

"Is he awake?" she stammered. "Max, is he okay?"

Adrian's expression eased, as it always did when he talked about his little brother. "He's out of the coma. He . . . he told me everything that happened. How you tried to stop the bleeding. How you forced Genissa to give up her powers to help him."

She sank against the cold metal chair, overcome with relief.

Then, remembering who she was, who she was supposed to be, she trained her expression to be confused and doubtful again. "Nightmare *helped* him? I thought she was the one who stabbed him. Why would she do that?"

Adrian didn't move for a long minute, and she wondered if that was the first speck of doubt she saw entering his eyes. Then he scoffed, though not as aggressively as before. "The point is, we're . . . grateful." It seemed to pain him to say the word, and he didn't look at her when he did. "My fathers and I. And in return for helping Max, we've agreed to give you a chance to have your execution changed to a life sentence of neutralization and imprisonment."

A sarcastic response filled her mouth. She wasn't entirely sure which option she preferred at the moment.

But she thought of Genissa Clark, who was probably gleeful to act as Nightmare's executioner, and she choked the sarcasm back down.

"Under one condition," he continued. "You tell us where to find Ace Anarchy's helmet, the Vitality Charm, and the rest of the Anarchists. Tell me where they are, and we will spare your life."

She held his gaze and he held hers, as her heart shriveled behind her rib cage. All thoughts left her, leaving the inside of her head cavernous and echoing only with his words.

Sweet, compassionate Adrian Everhart.

Sketch.

A Renegade and, truly now, her enemy.

"Just tell me where they are, Nova. Please. I don't . . ." His face crumpled, and it was as though she were watching him at war with himself. The battle between his loathing for Nightmare, and whatever he had once felt for Nova McLain.

Hatred battling affection.

Fury battling compassion.

Back and forth and back again.

"I don't want to watch them kill you . . . Nova." The whisper was so faint she barely heard it over the speaker that connected them. "Despite everything you've done . . . I don't . . ."

Her pulse skipped with surprising, unwarranted hope.

Not hope that she might escape punishment, but rather, hope that Adrian might still care for her. Even believing that she was Nightmare. She'd been sure, all along, that any feelings Adrian had for her would vanish the moment he knew the truth. Was it possible there was some thorn of endearment still lodged in his heart?

He gave himself a sudden shake. "Because you helped Max," he said again, firmly. "And because, even if you were acting as a spy, you actually did do some good as a Renegade. You killed the Detonator and protected those people at Cosmopolis. You rescued that kid from the fire at the library. Even if it was all an act, it counts for something. So just . . . tell us where you hid the helmet and the Vitality Charm. Tell us what you know about the rest of the Anarchists. That's all you have to do, and you won't have to die."

Even though he was bargaining for her life, and even though Nova knew what her next words would be, that slim flicker of hope was persistent. She had come to know Adrian Everhart well enough to know there was more to this offer than the practical explanations he was giving her. The truth was evident behind the dark frames of his glasses, and it made her chest swell to the point of bursting.

At least a teeny, tiny part of Adrian still cared for her.

It changed nothing. And it changed everything.

Staring into the eyes that had mesmerized her for these past months, Nova was happy, so very happy, that she didn't have to lie to him again.

"Thank you, Adrian," she whispered. "Thank you for at least . . . wanting me to have a chance. You don't know what that means to me. But the truth is, I don't have any idea where the charm is or the helmet or any of the Anarchists. I'm sorry, but I don't know."

His expression fell and, after a long silence, Adrian gave a solemn nod. He started to turn away.

"Adrian?"

He paused, his gaze meeting hers after a short hesitation.

Nova swallowed. "It was real," she whispered. "I hope you know that."

He watched her, unflinching, expressionless. Finally, he said, "I wish I could believe that, Nova. But we both know it's just one more lie."

CHAPTER EIGHTEEN

"WHEN DID YOU start to suspect her?" asked Adrian. His feet were up on Max's hospital bed, a sketchbook in his lap.

He was working on a new tattoo design. A heart surrounded by the impenetrable turrets of a stone tower.

He hadn't figured out exactly what powers the tattoo would imbue, but the entire ordeal with Nova—no, Nightmare—had left him shaken and hollowed out and vulnerable. He'd considered transforming into the Sentinel just to feel the security of the armor on his body. The protection of anonymity. A barrier between him and the world.

"I'm not sure," said Max. He had shredded a tissue to create a nest in the palm of his hand, where Turbo was curled up and sleeping, his tiny breaths wheezing every few seconds. Turbo was sick, and they could both tell. Max seemed to be handling the creature's slow fading with courage, despite the attachment they'd formed.

As for Max himself, he was stronger every day—healing radically fast, perhaps in part thanks to the concoction of superpowers that filled his slight frame. Color had returned to his cheeks. Brightness to his eyes. His hair was as disheveled as ever. "There was a moment at headquarters, when I was still in the quarantine, watching Nightmare fight against Frostbite and the others. It felt so familiar, like I was watching the trials again. And at one point Nightmare looked up, right at me, and I could have sworn . . . but then I ignored it because, you know. It's *Nova*."

"It's Nova," Adrian murmured. The pencil scratched over the paper as he shaded in the details of stonework. He was tempted to add a few arrow slits along the tower's side, like a true medieval castle, but no. He wanted this wall to be impenetrable. No weak spots. No way to get in.

"But then, when I woke up and started thinking about everything that happened, I think a part of me knew. I kept wondering, why would Nightmare protect me? The only thing that made sense was . . . you know, if she was someone I knew. And Nova was the only person . . ."

When he trailed off, Adrian glanced up. Max's mouth twisted to one side as he considered Nova's guilt, Nightmare's secret. Then he gave his head a shake and reached his free hand for the small carton of chocolate milk that one of the nurses had brought along with his dinner earlier. He took a long drink through a short red straw. Setting the carton back on the tray, he leaned his head against the stack of pillows. "They're not really going to kill her, are they?"

Adrian winced and returned his focus to the drawing. "I don't know. Maybe. She won't confess. She won't give us any information. And the Council is convinced that this will show everyone that we have the Anarchists under control. It really freaked people out to know that Ace Anarchy had been alive and in hiding all these years, and they're all wondering if there could be more villains out there, just biding their time, waiting to launch another Age of Anarchy. We need to take a strong stance here, show everyone that we won't have mercy for criminals. At least, that's what the Council's been saying."

"I guess I see their point," said Max, "but . . . it's Nova."

Adrian sighed. "No, Max. It's Nightmare."

Max frowned and whispered, "How do you think Genissa will do it?"

Adrian shuddered. This question had been lingering at the back of his thoughts since Genissa Clark had first made the suggestion that she be allowed to execute Nightmare. He kept seeing her and her team at the shipping yard by the docks, torturing the villain Hawthorn. Literally torturing her. He didn't want to believe the Council would allow anything like that to happen, especially with all the world watching, and yet . . . he wouldn't have believed that they would consider capital punishment at all, especially without a trial, or allow someone like Genissa to have a hand in it.

He didn't know what to believe anymore.

Finally, he answered, "I don't know. But I don't think she suggested it so she could be merciful."

A silence draped over them, filled only by the *scritch* of Adrian's pencil.

After a long moment, Max started feeding himself grapes, one by one, their crunch deafening in the small room. He stared blankly at the wall, chewing like a robot. When the tray was empty and his fingers found nothing but stems, he set to mindlessly stroking one finger along Turbo's back. The creature mewled in its sleep. "What are you working on?"

"New tattoo idea." Adrian angled the sketchbook to show him.

Max studied it for a moment but offered no commentary on the design. Instead, an unexpected glint entered his eye. "That reminds me. I had an idea for a tattoo for you. Can I see your marker?"

Pulling a marker from his pocket, Adrian handed it to him. Max spent a moment considering the marker in his right hand and the dinosaur in his left. Finally, he slipped Turbo and the nest of tissue paper into the space between his knees. The dinosaur woke up and screeched, trying to jab Max's fingers with its needle claws.

"Oh, calm down," Max muttered, fluffing the tissue paper. Still sulking, the dinosaur burrowed around in the shreds a few times, adjusted the thin blanket underneath with its teeth, before lying down and dozing off again.

With both hands now free, Max doodled something onto the tips of his fingers. Adrian leaned forward, but couldn't see what it was. After capping the marker, Max grinned mischievously and snapped.

Tiny sparks burst from his fingertips, flashing white and gold.

Adrian's eyebrows lifted. "You know, I keep forgetting that you stole some of my power."

"I'd say borrowed, but . . ." Max shrugged, then held his hand out to show Adrian the small lightning bolts he had drawn onto his skin. "I can only make sparks, but I figured you could have actual lightning bolts shoot out of your hands. Awesome, right?"

Adrian started to smile, but then the thought of lightning reminded him of Thunderbird, which reminded him of—

His smile dropped away. "Cool idea, except I try to keep the tattoos inconspicuous. Dad and Pops might start to wonder why I have lightning bolts on my hands."

Max wilted. "Good point. Wouldn't be the same coming out of your elbow, though."

"Unfortunately." Adrian thumped the eraser end of the pencil against the paper. "Have you been practicing at all with your new ice manipulation power?"

"Meh. Made a few ice cubes for my drinks. I'm not sure if it's just because I never liked Frostbite, but . . . ice power isn't one that ever interested me. But who knows? Maybe someday I'll take up ice-skating."

Adrian chuckled, amused at the idea of Max gliding around on ice skates. But then he thought of the construction going on back at headquarters, and again, the lighthearted moment vanished.

"Hey, Max . . . has Hugh talked to you about . . . after you leave the hospital?"

"Not really. I know I can't come live with you guys, at least not until that Vitality Charm turns back up, for Simon. And, you know, whenever you're able to break the news to them that you're technically immune to me, too."

Adrian flinched, even though Max hadn't said it in a mean way. Still, he knew it would be easier for him to come see Max if he told their dads the truth about his tattoos and how he was able to imbue himself with this particular invincibility. But he wasn't sure how he could do that without leaving clues about his other tattoos, too. His other powers. And his other identity.

"Remember when you sneaked me up to the thirty-ninth floor at HQ so we could all be together outside of the quarantine?"

Adrian nodded.

"I was thinking, maybe we could, like, remodel that floor into an apartment for me. We could put up big DO NOT ENTER signs, and let everyone know it isn't safe for prodigies to come up and see me. Maybe it could work?"

Max sounded doubtful, though, and Adrian couldn't bring himself to lie and say that, yeah, maybe it could. He knew the Council would never allow Max to roam freely around headquarters. He was too dangerous.

But thinking of the glass walls being mounted into place, forming Max's new prison, turned his stomach.

"What's wrong?"

Adrian jolted from his thoughts. Max was frowning at him.

"You're not telling me something," he said. Not a question.

Adrian swallowed, and it took him a few tries before he managed, "They're rebuilding the quarantine."

Max went still. He didn't seem surprised, exactly. If anything, he appeared only mildly disappointed as he reached for the brownie on the tray. But then he set it down again without taking a bite, and set to scraping the chocolate off his fingers with his teeth instead.

"I wondered" was all he said, when he finally said anything.

"I'm going to talk to them about it," said Adrian, dropping his sketchbook onto the floor and lowering his feet off the bed. He leaned forward, determined. "I mean, I tried once already, but I'll try again. They can't do that to you, Max. They can't keep you locked up forever. You're their son, not a prisoner. And you're a Renegade. After the way you fought to protect the helmet, no one can deny that."

A ghostly smile crossed Max's lips. "I didn't protect the helmet. Nightmare got away with it, and because of me, we lost Frostbite."

"Who cares about Frostbite? We're better off without her."

Max snorted skeptically.

"You're the Bandit. You helped defeat Ace Anarchy."

"I was barely walking when that happened."

"Doesn't matter. The point is they can't lock you away like an animal. It isn't fair, and now that I'm able to be close to you, I can do something about it."

"Sometimes," said Max, fiddling with the cloth napkin that hung over the tray's edge, "I think about being out there, walking around the city. Or being on a patrol team, like you. Stopping bad guys. Being awesome. But then, I think about what would happen if I crossed paths with another prodigy, and before anyone knew what was happening, I was draining their power from them. They wouldn't be doing anything wrong, just . . . being in the wrong place at the wrong time. Being near *me*." He sighed. "And that wouldn't be fair, either."

"We can come up with ways to make sure it doesn't happen. There's got to be somewhere else you can go. Somewhere you won't be surrounded by prodigies."

"You're going to convince the Council of this, are you? To let both their biggest threat and their most powerful weapon go free?"

Adrian blinked. He'd never really thought of Max that way, and wondered if that's really how Max saw himself. A threat. A weapon.

He was just a kid.

He deserved to do normal kid things. He deserved a life.

"I wish you could come home with me," he said. "The mansion's so big . . ."

"But Simon," said Max.

Adrian sighed. *But Simon.*

If only they still had the Vitality Charm. Then Max could live at the mansion and all three of them would be protected from his powers. He could have a family, at last. A real family.

"Ow!" Max suddenly barked, shaking his hand.

The velociraptor had bitten him.

"Honestly, if you want food, I'll get you food," Max grumbled, picking through the leftovers on his tray and finding a couple shreds of ham.

Adrian nudged up his glasses, watching Turbo devour the feast. His movements were slower every day, his coordination clumsier. Someday soon, he would simply stop moving. Stop eating. Stop biting. He wouldn't stop existing, but become like one of those plastic dinosaurs kids got in the coin machines down in the hospital waiting room, the ones that came in clear acrylic eggs.

"Say," Max started, his attention trained almost nervously on the little beast. "Have you ever thought about . . ." He hesitated.

"What?"

He cleared his throat and tried to act nonchalant, wriggling his skinny shoulders back into the pillow. "Do you think the tattoos would work if you gave them to other people? Like . . . could you make Simon immune to me?"

Adrian tapped the end of his pencil against his temple. "It's crossed my mind, but I don't know if it would—"

"I know, I know," interrupted Max. "It might not work on other people. And . . . then you'd have to tell them about the tattoos and that could lead to a lot of questions and . . ."

"I have thought of it, though," said Adrian. "Maybe I could try it on Oscar first. Or Ruby or Danna. I could test it on one of them. And if it works . . ."

Max watched him, and Adrian could see him trying to temper his own hopes. The look flooded him with guilt. Was the secret of the Sentinel worth preserving, if it meant Max would be stuck forever in this sheltered half-life?

"If it works," he continued, more forceful now, "then I'll tell

Hugh and Simon, and offer to give the tattoo to Simon, too. Then you could come home and live with us."

"You don't have to," Max insisted. "I don't want them to figure out who you—"

"No, I *do* have to," Adrian said. "If the tattoo works on other people, then it's a done deal. You're more important than the Sentinel."

Max leaned back again, though he seemed more concerned than excited, as his mind started to race down all the possible outcomes—if the tattoo didn't work, and if it did.

"Okay," he finally agreed. "How long before we know?"

"I'll talk to the team tomorrow, determine who's going to be the guinea pig, and figure out a time to do it. The tattoo needs a few days to heal, and then . . . we'll just have to test it."

"So maybe, like, a week?"

Adrian considered. It seemed optimistic. He needed to be extremely focused when inking the design, otherwise he risked its power being weakened from his distraction.

And focus was something he'd been lacking lately.

But what else could he say? "Sure. A week. Maybe."

Would Max still be in the hospital, or would the quarantine be ready by then? Would he already have been moved back to headquarters? He had a feeling the new quarantine would have strict security measures put on it, much stricter than the first. It might be more difficult to test the tattoo's effectiveness once it was healed.

But an idea was percolating in his thoughts. One that might have been a little foolhardy. An idea his dads would certainly disapprove of.

Which wouldn't be the first time.

"*Now* what?" said Max, eyeing him warily.

Adrian leaned closer. "Why wait around here for the next week? What if we sneaked you out of here instead?"

Max chuckled. "And take me where? A deserted island?"

Scratching behind his ear with the pencil's eraser, Adrian felt a smile creeping across his face. What felt like the first real smile since Danna had told him the truth.

"I have somewhere more hospitable in mind."

CHAPTER NINETEEN

"At what point should I remind you that this is a terrible idea?" whispered Max.

"It'll be fine," said Adrian, leaning against the wall. They were hidden in a small alcove with a hand-washing sink, around the corner from the nurses' station.

Well, Adrian was hidden.

Max was invisible.

Turbo was back in his little carrier, which Max held as to keep it invisible, too.

There were two nurses: a man standing at the desk flipping through a file; and a woman sitting in front of a computer, mindlessly stabbing a plastic fork into a plastic container containing a garden salad. The man would occasionally try to involve the woman in some gossip about one of the doctors on staff, but she seemed utterly uninterested.

Finally, checking something off on a clipboard, the man tucked the file under his arm and wandered down the corridor. Adrian pressed his back against the wall, holding his breath, until he had gone.

"Okay. Remember what to say?"

"This is never going to work" came Max's reply.

"That's the spirit." Adjusting his collar, Adrian approached the desk. "Hi," he said, flashing a brilliant smile.

The woman glanced up. Her eyes widened. "Hi?" she stammered. "Aren't you . . . ?"

"Adrian Everhart." He thrust out a hand, which she took with some surprise.

"Yes!" she said. "I've been helping to care for Max. It's so nice to meet you. Wow, you look just like you do in the magazines."

"I guess I would," he said, with an awkward chuckle.

"I'm so sorry you can't visit Max, given his"—she stumbled over the word—"condition. But I can assure you he's been responding great to the treatment and—"

"Actually, I was hoping I could talk with you a bit about Max and his treatment." He leaned over the counter and lowered his voice. "Privately, if that's all right?"

"Oh. Um." She frowned at the computer, uncertain. "There's always supposed to be someone—"

"Just for a second. It's . . . you know . . . Renegade stuff. And it's important."

A touch of curiosity entered her face. "Of course. Let me just close this out . . ." She logged off the computer, then tucked the fork into the bed of lettuce and stood. Adrian led the way, passing by the alcove where he knew Max was waiting. Adrian flashed a discreet thumbs-up, then paused, facing the nurse. He thought he heard the quiet shuffle of a hospital gown a few feet away from them, but it was hard to tell with the constant thrum and beeps of machinery in the hospital wing.

"So . . . ," Adrian started. "First, I want you to know how impressed my family has been with the care Max has gotten here. It's been apparent how top-notch the staff is, and we just . . . we really appreciate how attentive all you nurses and doctors have been, and the physical therapists and everyone, really. It's clear how much you guys really care for your patients."

The woman flushed. "Well, we do our best."

Adrian smiled at her. "It shows."

He spied movement at the nurses' station. The microphone being lifted from the intercom system.

"And we know how unconventional Max's treatment has been," Adrian continued, trying to keep his attention on the nurse. "I know the prodigy healers who work here shoulder a lot of the responsibility, but your civilian staff has really stepped up to help Max recover, and to ensure he received . . . just . . . the best care possible, even without a prodigy healer."

"Thank you," said the nurse, even as hesitation entered her tone. "But was there something you needed to discuss . . . ?" She started to glance toward the desk.

"Medicine!" said Adrian.

She jumped, startled.

"We, uh . . . we know there's been some shortage of certain pharmaceuticals lately, especially after the theft that was all over the news a while back, and we wanted to check if . . . you're well supplied. With everything that—"

A speaker crackled overhead, followed by a voice erupting through the hall. Max's voice, but lowered in an attempt to sound older, repeating the words that Adrian had coached him on, having heard them a couple of times during his visits.

"Three-two-one! Three-two-one! All available emergency personnel, report to room one-sixteen immediately! We need *all* prodigy healers to report immediately. Repeat, this is a three-two-one alert!"

The nurse cocked her head. "I wonder who that was," she mused. "Must be a new intern."

"That sounded really important," said Adrian, as out of the corner of his eye he saw the microphone replace itself on the intercom. "I'd better let you go. We can discuss this later."

"Oh, that alert only applies to prodigy hea—"

"Keep up the good work!" Adrian clapped her on the arm, then walked past her, past the desk. "See?" he whispered, hoping Max was beside him as he swung into the next corridor. "No healers, no prodigies, no worries. Come on, this way." He headed toward the southern elevator bank.

"Okay, this is sort of fun," Max whispered. "I feel like a spy in one of those old action flicks."

Amusement twitched at Adrian's cheeks, and he wondered if it was cooler to be a spy or a superhero. Maybe they were a little bit of both.

"You would make a pretty awesome spy."

"I know. No one ever suspects the kid."

Adrian chuckled. "That and the whole invisibility thing."

"That goes without saying."

Adrian started at the sound of footsteps barreling toward them. He stepped closer to the wall, holding out his arm to tuck Max behind him—which probably looked like an odd thing to do—but neither of the men in blue scrubs was paying him any attention.

But when they were twenty steps away, the shorter of the two men stumbled unexpectedly, nearly collapsing on top of a cart stacked with near-empty cafeteria trays and paper cups.

His companion froze. "You okay?"

"Yeah. Just feel . . . weird, all of a sudden," said the doctor, pressing a hand over his chest. "Not like a . . . heart attack, exactly, but . . ."

"*Shit, shit, shit,*" Max whispered. "It's me. He's a prodigy. I'm—"

Adrian reached for the air and found Max's upper arm. He dragged Max forward, though the boy struggled weakly, trying to pull Adrian the other direction, away from the doctors. Adrian held firm. Realizing it was useless, Max stopped objecting and they hurried down the hall.

The doctors ignored Adrian, as the taller of the two tried to help his friend to a chair in a small computer alcove.

Before they turned the next corner, Adrian glanced back. The prodigy healer was sitting a bit taller already, nodding at something his peer was telling him.

"*All* the healers will head straight for the first floor!" cried Max, flickering into visibility, presumably so Adrian could see his death glare. "That's what you told me. A three-two-one alert will make sure there are *no* prodigies—"

"Okay, okay," said Adrian, holding up his hands. "So that one was taking his time."

"This is exactly why I shouldn't have let you talk me into this. That guy has lives to save! Patients! Responsibilities! And now—"

"He's fine," said Adrian, heading for the elevator. Max followed after him, still carrying Turbo's cage in both hands. "You were hardly in his vicinity. I'm sure you only got a tiny bit of his power."

"But what if that tiny bit is the difference between a successful heart surgery and a nicked aorta?"

Adrian feigned a confused look. "What's an aorta?"

"It's the big artery that—" Max paused. "You're avoiding the question."

Turbo shrieked angrily.

With a laugh, Adrian jammed his thumb into the up button. "He's fine. And so are you. We shouldn't pass any more prodigy healers."

Max scoffed. "What about prodigy patients? Nurses? Visiting family members? And also—why are we going up? I thought the idea was to leave the hospital."

"I have a plan. And look, I know you've been surrounded by prodigies your whole life, but they aren't all that common outside of headquarters. The chances of us running into any more is really low. Trust me, okay?"

Max scowled, but didn't argue as the elevator arrived and the doors parted.

A nurse started to step out, and Max froze, standing straighter.

"Mr. Everhart? What are you doing here? What's—" She noticed the cage in Max's hands, but Turbo had fallen asleep again and maybe she assumed it was one of those plastic dinosaurs from the machine. Without waiting for an answer, she narrowed her eyes and reached forward, taking Max by the elbow and steering him back toward the hall. "I know you're probably getting restless lying in that bed all day, but we can't just have you wandering around the halls with-out supervision. You understand that, right?" She cast a disapproving frown at Adrian. "I'm sure your friend will understand. Now, come on, I'll walk you . . . both . . ."

Her voice slurred. Her attention was still on Adrian as her eyelids began to droop. Her foot skidded forward another half of a step, and then she started to fall face-first toward the linoleum.

Adrian narrowly caught her, scooping her beneath the armpits as her forehead crashed into his chest.

He gaped at Max, then down at the kid's skinny, pale arms, the insides of his elbows mottled with bruises new and old.

He knew immediately what had happened. Judging from Max's expression, they both did.

"I didn't think you got any power from Nightmare."

"I didn't, either," said Max. "I panicked just now. I didn't really think about it—it just happened. But . . . but Nightmare didn't seem affected by me at all when she . . ." He trailed off, eyes widening. "*Oh.*"

"Oh?"

"The quarantine. I must have gotten it when Nova came into the quarantine."

Adrian swallowed hard. Right. Of course. The night that Nightmare stole the helmet wasn't the first time she'd crossed paths with Max.

It was just one more piece of evidence against her, and though one more reminder of who and what she was shouldn't have hurt, it still did.

He thought again of the tattoo he was planning and imagined putting another stone on the wall around his heart.

"Anyway, good job," said Adrian.

The elevator door started to close and Adrian stopped it with his foot. It opened again with a chime. Spotting an empty gurney against a wall, Adrian lifted the nurse onto it. "I doubt you got much of Nightmare's power, so she probably won't be out for long. Come on."

They got in the elevator just as an obnoxious buzzing started to come from the doors, alerting them that the doors were closing this time, whether they liked it or not.

"I'd go invisible again if I were you."

Max winked out of view as Adrian hit the button for the top floor.

Seconds later, they stepped out into a serene waiting room, the smell of talcum powder wafting toward them and the sounds of a crying baby drifting from a nearby hallway.

"*No,*" Max said emphatically, tugging on Adrian's sleeve. "The maternity ward? Are you nuts? I don't care what you say, there could definitely be a prodigy mom here—or what if there's a baby! I can't—"

"Would you relax?" Adrian whispered back at him, earning an odd look from the nurse sitting behind a reception desk. He smiled and surreptitiously took hold of Max's hospital gown, dragging him forward. "Hi there," he said, leaning his free elbow on the counter beside a visitor check-in sheet. "Is there a way to get up to the roof from this floor?"

Her already-suspicious countenance darkened more. "The roof isn't open to the public," she said, as if this should have gone without saying.

"Oh, I know," he said with a mild chuckle. "I'm Adrian Everhart. My dads are Hugh Everhart and Simon Westwood?"

He was met with instant recognition. Her mouth formed a surprised O.

"Right," he continued. "And, as I'm sure you know, my brother, Max, is a patient here and, well, the other Council members are going to be stopping by periodically to check on how things are going. We're all pretty much one big happy superhero family down there at headquarters, and everyone's really worried about the kid."

A snort came in the direction Max was standing.

"*So,*" Adrian persisted, "Tamaya—er, Thunderbird—is going to be stopping by anytime now so I can give her a full report on Max's condition, and you know Thunderbird, always flying around the rooftops. Never uses the main entrance. It's kind of a superhero thing. I mean, if I had wings—"

Max jabbed Adrian hard in the side and Adrian stifled a grunt. "Which is to say . . . how do we get to the roof from here?"

The nurse led them to a plain door and punched a code into a keypad while Adrian assured her that a Captain Chromium autograph would be no problem. He made a mental note to actually follow through on that promise as he and Max bolted up the steps and pushed their way out onto the hospital roof.

Wind buffeted them from the east. From way up here, Adrian could see the Sentry Bridge, Merchant Tower . . . even the parking garage where he and Nova had staked out surveillance on the hospital when they'd been trying to stop Hawthorn and her gang.

He passed over the helicopter landing pad on the center of the roof, heading for the north wall.

Max, visible now, came to stand beside him, scanning the city rooftops—the water towers, the fire escapes, the windows glinting in the late-afternoon sun. "Did you order a helicopter for us?"

Adrian chuckled wryly. "Nothing that glamorous."

"Then what are we doing on the roof?"

"You wanted to avoid being near prodigies as much as possible, right? Well, like you said, on the streets, you never know who you might pass. But up here, the sky is ours."

Max took a step back, hands held up. "Oooh, no. I realize that you had to carry me like a sack of potatoes when you brought me here, and that's embarrassing enough. You are not becoming my general mode of transportation. Thanks, but no thanks."

"You were half dead. There's nothing embarrassing about that."

"Yeah, well, we'll see how you feel the next time you almost die and *I* have to carry you halfway across town."

"Sounds relaxing. Look, I'm not carrying you anywhere. You don't need me to. Here, let me hold Turbo so you can focus."

"Focus on what?" said Max, even as he handed over the little cage.

"Just watch." Inspecting the closest structure, a squat office building just across the street, Adrian cradled the cage in his arm and crouched. He felt the spring tattoos activate on the soles of his feet. He leaped.

Air whooshed past his ears, and for the briefest of moments, he felt like he was flying.

He struck the next roof, crouching with one hand on the gritty concrete.

Awake again, the velociraptor scratched unhappily at the bars of his confinement, trying to escape. Adrian ignored him. Brushing his fingers off on his pants, he turned back to Max.

The kid looked mystified. Spreading his arms, he yelled across the chasm, "I didn't get that much of your power! I can't do what you do!"

"I know," said Adrian. "But you can do what Ace Anarchy can do."

Max's arms fell. He drew back, confused.

"You have telekinesis," Adrian reminded him. "I know you can levitate. Which means you can *fly*."

Max's jaw worked mutely for a moment, then he shook his head. "I've never done anything more than float a few feet in the air."

Adrian shrugged. "It's the same thing."

"Yeah, except for the twenty-story fall!"

"If you fall, I'll catch you."

Max surveyed the street below, his brows knitted together. He started to rub his arms. He wasn't dressed for the cold weather, much less the intense winds coming off the bay.

"You can do this. You're the Bandit. You're a Renegade."

Shutting his eyes, Max spread his hands, palm up. His feet left the edge of the building, until he was hovering a foot above the rooftop.

A smile stretched across Adrian's face. Like Ace Anarchy's ability, Max's control over telekinesis usually applied only to inanimate objects—not humans or animals. The one exception was to himself. Adrian had known for a while now that Max was capable of levitation, but it was different to see it with his own eyes.

"That's it," Adrian muttered to himself, not wanting to distract him.

An alarm rang out from somewhere inside the hospital.

Max gasped and dropped back to the ground.

"Come on! Now or never!" shouted Adrian.

Max seemed immobilized, frozen by indecision.

Then, to Adrian's horror, he shook his head and started walking back toward the stairwell. Back to the safety of his hospital room. Back to the numbing security of the quarantine.

"Max!"

Then Max turned again and started to run. This time, he didn't hesitate. He launched himself from the edge of the rooftop, arms extended.

Adrian's breath caught and he braced himself, prepared to jump forward and catch his brother at the first sign of danger.

But it wasn't necessary.

Proud laughter tumbled from Adrian's mouth, at the same time Max whooped with joy.

Adrian had been right. The Bandit could fly.

CHAPTER TWENTY

THE PRISON CAFETERIA was eerily silent, as usual. Nothing but sniffles as noses dripped from being out in the freezing wind and the click of plastic cutlery on plastic trays. Nova stood at the back of the line, envying how the pant legs of the jumpsuit in front of her actually fit the wearer. She kept having to roll hers up.

The line shuffled forward.

She shuffled with it.

Her attention switched to the nearest table, where a couple of inmates sat beside each other on the same side, facing the back wall of the cafeteria. To further discourage talking, all seats were on one side of the tables, so all inmates faced the same direction as they ate. Nova eyed their trays, though she wasn't sure why she bothered. She had the menu memorized by now. Roll. Mystery vegetable. Potato. Fish. It must not have been Sunday, because she didn't see anyone with a coveted slice of cheese.

An odd gesture caught her attention. One of the seated inmates tapped the handle of her fork twice against the side of the tray before scooping up some vegetables. A second later, the prisoner beside her used the tines of his fork to scrape against his tray's corner.

Nova didn't know what it meant, but she was sure they were communicating.

Someone grunted behind her, and realizing that the line had moved, she shuffled forward and claimed her own tray.

She sat at her usual place, between the usual peers who, as usual, did not try to speak to her. She scrutinized the room with renewed interest, though. Now that she'd noticed the sly exchange, she started to see more signs of it. At least, what she thought might be a secret language between the inmates. Some gestures were so subtle—a scratch on the nose, a scrape of a shoe, a spoon swirled counter-clockwise over the table—that a lot of it could have been coincidental.

But she was sure that a lot of it wasn't. The inmates had found ways to speak to each other, after all.

She wondered how long she would have to be here before she started to understand it.

"You know the Puppeteer?"

The question was asked so quietly, Nova almost thought she'd imagined it.

She glanced to the side, at a bald man whose skin and eyes were both neon yellow. Between that and the bold stripes of the jumpsuit, it was hard to look at him without squinting.

For his part, he kept his attention resolutely on his food.

Nova dug her fork into the fish, flaking it apart. Just before popping it in her mouth, she muttered simply, "Yeah."

For a long while her neighbor was silent, and she thought that might be the end of the conversation.

But then—"He all right?"

She paused with a chunk of roll half demolished in her mouth. Was Winston all right?

After swallowing, she answered, "Don't know. Haven't seen him in a while." She considered telling him that Winston had been neutralized. That the Renegades had stripped him of his powers. But she didn't know if the inmates here knew about Agent N, and she didn't think she could explain it in muttered half sentences.

Her neighbor kept on scooping food into his mouth.

Nova slowed down her own pace. Usually she ate quickly, so as to gulp down as much of the food as possible without actually tasting it. But it was so nice to speak with someone, to have any human interaction, that she was already dreading when it would end.

"They came for him weeks ago," the man finally said. "Figured he'd be back by now."

Nova thought about that. Where *had* they taken Winston after he'd been neutralized? She supposed it made sense that they wouldn't send him back to Cragmoor—he wasn't a prodigy anymore. Had he been shipped off to that civilian prison upstate? Or a mental health facility? Or was he still at Renegade Headquarters, being subjected to yet more experiments that he hadn't volunteered for?

"He said you fed him to the heroes," the man continued.

It took Nova a moment to realize he was talking about the parade, when she had thrown Winston out of his own hot-air balloon, allowing him to be captured by the Renegades while she saved herself. Her stomach twinged with guilt, and not for the first time.

But when she dared to cast a sideways glance at the stranger, she saw that he was smiling. "Said you never give up. Said that's what he liked about you." His eyes slid sideways, meeting hers. They were so bright, it was a little bit like staring into twin suns.

Nova's shoulders drooped. He had been atrocious, Winston. As the Puppeteer, he had done awful things, things that even the other Anarchists were wary of. And yet she couldn't help the warmth that flooded through her to think of Winston in this cold, brutal place, saying kind things about her, even after what she'd done to him.

A hand suddenly grabbed the back of Nova's head, forcing her face away from the neighbor. "Eyes forward!" the guard barked. "No talking!"

She crushed her teeth. There was a moment when she knew the guard's hand was touching *just* enough of her scalp that she could have driven her power into him. She was almost angry enough to do it, too.

But she resisted. She said nothing, didn't even glare at the guard's back as he walked away. Her knuckles were white as she gripped her spoon, but she wouldn't lash out. She wouldn't give them the satisfaction of getting to punish her for it.

Nova put her fury into her jaw, gnashing her way through another chunk of bread.

She sensed the change more than heard it. The room was quiet enough as it was, and yet, suddenly, the silence was palpable. The chewing, the scrape of cutlery—it was almost as if even the breathing stopped.

Nova raised her head.

The warden was making his way to the back of the room, so that all of the seated inmates would be facing him. He wore a gray suit, identical to the one he'd worn every time she'd seen him.

"Listen up, everyone," barked the warden. "I have an announcement to make and I don't intend to explain this more than once." Coming to a stop at the room's center, he frowned at the inmates, then faced one of the guards. "We're missing one."

"He's being brought in from solitary now," the guard answered.

The warden exhaled, exasperated, but he didn't have to wait long. Moments later, a door opened near the corner of the room, a door Nova had only ever seen closed.

And there was Ace.

He was flanked by two guards, being led slowly into the cafeteria.

Nova stiffened. He was almost unrecognizable. Ace had faded even more since she'd last seen him and no longer resembled himself at all. His skin sagged from his cheekbones. His eyes were deep in their sockets, the skin around them practically translucent. His feet dragged as if he could barely walk and it was clear that he was in pain with every stumbling step.

And yet—the other prisoners did recognize him. At least, many of them seemed to. She could tell not just by their awestruck silence, but by the way those nearest him gave an almost imperceptible nod as he was dragged past, showing their respect for the man who had once led so many of them into a revolution.

The guards, on the other hand, stood at attention with their hands on their weapons or their fingers outstretched, preparing to call on their powers if needed. They were on edge with Ace in the room, watching him like one would watch a tiger who may or may not have been strong enough to break its leash.

Their fear was unwarranted. Couldn't they see that? Ace was sick. He was dying.

The guards led him around the bank of tables toward a solitary table set apart from the others. He was only a few tables away from her when Ace's eyes suddenly flickered with recognition. His gaze met Nova's and went wide. His foot skidded to a stop, startling the guards beside him.

He gaped at her, and Nova could see the realization crashing through him. She was captured. She was a prisoner, just like he was. Sorrow creased his brow, and Nova felt her own hopelessness well up inside her all over again.

She wanted to apologize—for failing him, again. She wanted to tell him how much she still loved him. That she hadn't given up.

Ace started to cough. Not a polite cough spurred on by the frigid weather, but a rough, hacking cough that soon had him bent over and struggling to stand. Nova gasped and rose from her seat, but the little plastic fork was suddenly ripped from her hand. In one motion, it flipped over and the brittle tines pressed into her sleeve, holding it against the table. She scowled and grabbed the fork. The handle snapped in two, leaving the tines still driven through the fabric.

She huffed and raised her eyes to see that she wasn't the only one who had wanted to help Ace. Three of the inmates closest to him had also leaped from their seats. One of them even managed to take hold of Ace's arm to keep him from slumping forward and hitting his head, before the guards started shouting and shoving them back. Ace was pushed against the wall in the hubbub, and he slid down it, one hand digging into his chest as the coughs dwindled to pained wheezing.

More of the inmates were standing now, yelling back at the guards. *Do something. Help him. He needs a doctor.*

One of the guards slammed the palms of his hands together and a wave of pressure pushed outward, bowling over everyone in its path. A number of prisoners fell to the ground. One hit his head on a stool. Though Nova didn't get the brunt of it, the unexpected attack still shoved her back down to her stool.

Only then did the pressure on the fork tines relax. She yanked her arm off the table and plucked them viciously from the fabric.

"What's wrong with you people?" shouted the man beside her, the one who had known Winston. He had not stood up with the others, but she could see the fury written plain across his face. He gestured toward Ace with his spoon. "He's not a threat to you, anyone can see that. He needs help!"

"Yeah?" snapped another guard, even as he bent down to grab Ace's cuffs. He hauled him back to his feet, making a point of not being gentle about it. "He's killed a lot of people. Who came to help them?"

Nova bit down on the inside of her cheek. She was still gripping the broken fork handle and found herself tempted to leap over the table and stab one of those guards in the eye. She didn't even particularly care which one.

But movement caught her attention. What was left of the food on her plate was rearranging itself. The bread crumbs, the potato peel, a few strings of what she had come to determine was probably boiled cabbage. They dragged together and twisted into familiar shapes, spelling out a message.

It read, simply, *Don't.*

She swallowed and looked up.

Ace wasn't watching her. If anything, he kept his focus resolutely away from her the whole time he was being dragged through the cafeteria and forced down onto the stool at the lone table.

The warden clapped his hands, three times, loud and slow. "Always one to make an entrance," he said with a disdainful sneer.

Ace ignored him. He was still breathing hard, half collapsed over his table. The way the nearby guards trained their weapons on him was almost comical.

Until Nova looked down at the word on her plate and remembered that, even in this state, Ace wasn't helpless.

"I've been informed by Renegade Headquarters," said the warden, "that at the end of this month, we will all be going on a little field trip together."

A rustle of interest passed through the inmates, coupled with suspicion.

"During this excursion, we expect total cooperation. You will be shackled together for the duration of the trip. You will all have your hands subdued. We have specially designed masks and blindfolds for those of you with abilities that function beyond the limits of your limbs. Special arrangements will be made for those with uniquely unrestrainable talents." His voice dropped warningly with a glance toward Ace. He might have been glancing at a corpse for all the reaction his words got.

Nova bit the inside of her cheek.

The public reveal of Agent N. The neutralization. Her execution. It was happening, and soon.

"We will be bringing in reinforcements to assist with added security," the warden continued. "If at any time, any one of you so much as blinks in a way we don't like"—he paused dramatically, his glower bearing down on them—"we will not hesitate to kill you where you stand."

No one spoke. No one moved.

"I'll admit," said the warden with a smug smile, "I'm sort of hoping some of you will test that promise." He nodded at the guards and started heading toward the cafeteria exit.

"But where are we going?" one of the inmates asked. "And what for?"

The warden paused, gloating. "You'll see soon enough. I'd hate to spoil the surprise."

He left, and the guards wasted no time in hauling Ace back out of the room. Nova's breaths quickened as she watched him go.

When the door had slammed shut behind them, she sank into her seat, miserable all over again. Lonely and helpless all over again.

Silence hung over the tables as the inmates exchanged baffled, curious looks. A guard barked, "Two minutes! Bring up your trays if you're done, come on now!"

"Might wanna take some more bites," her neighbor muttered. Nova snarled and wanted to tell him she'd lost her appetite. But his yellow eyes dropped to the tray and she realized what he meant. The message was still there.

Still holding her fork handle in a death grip, she pushed the food around until the word was unrecognizable.

A few inmates got up and started stacking their trays, but most stayed put, pretending to finish their meals. Nova noticed more of those minuscule gestures happening, almost in tandem now, while the guards talked distractedly among themselves.

She watched the prisoners sourly, wishing she knew what everyone around her was saying.

"Hey," muttered her neighbor.

"What?" she snapped too loud. A guard glowered their way, before nodding at whatever his peer was saying.

Beside her, the man with the neon eyes took his spoon and tapped the back of it one time on the table next to his tray.

Nova glared. First at the spoon, then at him.

His smile was wide and a little crooked. "Means we're united," he said. "Villains to the end."

CHAPTER TWENTY-ONE

"ARE YOU SURE Ruby's not home?" said Max, keeping so close to Adrian as they made their way down the sidewalk that he kept stepping on the backs of Adrian's heels.

"Of course she's not home. I sent her a message two hours ago," said Adrian. "I wouldn't put her at risk."

"Okay, but . . . what if one of her brothers is secretly a prodigy and no one knows about it yet? Or one of her neighbors? Or—"

"They're not," said Adrian. "Her brothers idolize the Renegades. If they'd shown even a hint of superpowers, they would make sure we all knew about it. As for neighbors, once we have you inside the apartment, you'll be fine. No prodigies are going to come near you, so you won't have to worry about accidentally stealing powers from them, okay?"

Max said nothing, and Adrian could easily picture his doubtful expression.

"Hey, it's going to be all right," said Adrian. He tossed an arm around Max's neck, pulling him to his side. The boy groaned and struggled, but only half-heartedly. "Ruby's family agreed to this. No one wants to see you stuck in a quarantine again. And once I discuss it with Hugh and Simon, I'm sure they'll see reason."

"They're going to be so mad."

"I know. But they'll get over it. And"—Adrian paused in front of a five-story apartment complex with a rugged brick facade—"here we are. The famous Tucker residence."

"Famous how?" said Max, warily eyeing the rows of tall windows, the fire escape, the few balconies that were only wide enough to hold a handful of potted plants.

"Because it's the home of Red Assassin and her twin brother sidekicks. Come on."

Max followed him into the building and up the first flight of stairs. Aged but elegant wallpaper and lit sconces lined the walls of the narrow hallway. Adrian paused in front of Ruby's apartment and was about to knock when the door swung open, revealing two identical boys, only a little older than Max. Their faces were bright with excitement, each of them donning the Renegade uniform costumes their mom and grandma had made them for the Sidekick Olympics.

Adrian had finally thought to ask Ruby how to tell the twins apart, and though it took him a moment to remember, her explanation quickly made sense. Jade's hair was longer and shaggy around the ears, while Sterling kept his cropped a bit shorter. He'd started referring to him as Short Sterling in his head, even though the boys were the same height.

"You made it!" said Jade, while Sterling yelled over his shoulder, "Mom! Grandma! They're here!"

"Come on, come on." Jade waved his hand, ushering them inside.

"This is so cool. Ruby said you stole Ace Anarchy's power? Is that true?"

"And you can levitate?" asked Sterling.

"And turn invisible, like the Dread Warden, right?" added Jade.

"Do you have superstrength like the Captain? If you got shot in the heart, would you die?"

"Dude." Jade smacked his brother on the shoulder. "He was just in the hospital for being stabbed. What do you think?"

"Hey, what's this?" Ignoring his brother, Sterling pointed at the small cage Max was clutching.

"Boys, boys, give them some space!" said their mom, bustling in from a back room. She smiled apologetically at Adrian. "If you couldn't tell, they were a little bit excited when we told them about our new houseguest. You must be Max. Ruby's told us so much about you. It's such a pleasure to finally meet. And lovely to see you again, Adrian."

Max graciously accepted her handshake, but Adrian could tell he was nervous and flustered by the attention from the twins.

"Boys, why don't you show Max to your room so he can get settled in? You can have Ruby's bed, or fight these two mongrels for the top bunk. Dinner will be ready in about twenty minutes. Adrian, are you joining us?"

Adrian grimaced. "I could . . . ," he said, glancing at Max, "but I'm supposed to meet up with the rest of the team to start the next phase of our Anarchist investigation."

"I'll be fine," said Max, still nervous, but doing his best to pretend he wasn't. "Where is Ruby going to stay while I'm here?"

"With Danna," said Mrs. Tucker, "and Oscar's mom said she's welcome there as well if necessary."

"We have plenty of guest rooms at the mayor's mansion, too," said Adrian. "And there's always open dorms at headquarters."

Mrs. Tucker clasped her hands. "She'll be fine. We're all happy to have you here, Max, and you can stay as long as you need to. Jade, Sterling?" She tipped her chin toward the back of the apartment.

"Yeah, come on!" yelled Jade, bounding down the hallway. "Room's this way."

"Is that thing *real*?" said Sterling, who hadn't stopped gawking at Turbo.

"Oh, um, yeah." Max held up the cage for them to see. "He's kind of sick right now, but . . . this is Turbo. He's a velociraptor. Sort of. Adrian made him."

"No way," Sterling murmured. Then—"Jade! You have to see this!"

He chased after his brother. With an awkward chuckle, Max started after him. He hesitated once, turning back to Adrian, a question in his eyes.

"I'll come visit all the time," said Adrian. "If you need anything, just get a message to Ruby and she'll let me know."

Max nodded. "Are you going to tell them where I am?"

By *them*, Adrian knew, he meant Captain Chromium and the Dread Warden.

"Not immediately," he admitted. "I figure I'll clue them in once that quarantine is officially dismantled."

With a faint smile, Max followed the boys. As he disappeared through a doorway, Adrian heard one of them ask, "Is it true they call you the Bandit? That's such an awesome alias. If I were a Renegade, my name would be the Silver Snake, and I would have a forked tongue and venomous fangs. And my brother . . ."

Adrian exhaled, comforted by the boys' easy prattle. Max hadn't had many friends, and none his own age. It was normal that he was shy, but something told Adrian the three of them would hit it off just fine.

"Should I be worried about the wrath of the Council for this?"

He winced and faced Mrs. Tucker. "Probably not as much as I should be."

She squeezed his arm. "It will be fine. Ruby told us all about the quarantine, and the testing to make that . . . serum thing they've been working on."

"That's supposed to be top secret."

She shrugged. "We don't do secrets in our family. My point is, he's just a kid. He doesn't deserve to have all that on his shoulders."

"My feelings exactly."

"I'm sure the Captain and the Dread Warden care about him, just like they care about you. They'll come to understand. And in the meantime, I promise we'll take good care of him."

"Thanks, Mrs. Tucker."

She leaned in and gave him a hug, which Adrian wasn't expecting. "Go on," she said. "Go do hero stuff. And tell that daughter of mine that I expect daily phone calls. Just because she's not living under this roof doesn't mean she's not my responsibility, superpowers or otherwise."

He grinned. "I'll be sure to pass on the message."

◇◇◆◇◇

Adrian hadn't walked three blocks from the apartments when he received a communication over his wristband. His palms became clammy with dread before he even looked down to see who it was from, and he was right.

Bracing himself, he accepted the call.

"Where is he?" barked Captain Chromium. "Adrian, what have you done?"

"So . . . you got the note?" said Adrian, trying to keep his tone light. Not wanting his dads to panic and think that Max had been kidnapped out of the hospital by some covert gang of villains, they had left a note for the hospital staff to find, explaining that Max was with his brother and that the Renegades shouldn't worry about him.

"Yes, we got the note! What's going on? Where is Max?"

"He's somewhere safe," said Adrian. He paused on the sidewalk, leaning up against a light post. "Trust me."

"*Trust* you? What does that even—"

Hugh was cut off, followed by some shuffling on the other side, and then Simon's voice cut in. "Adrian, we do trust you. And we trust Max. But this is serious. We need to know where he is. You of all people should understand how dangerous it is for him to be alone out in the world."

"He's not alone," said Adrian. "No other prodigies will be at risk, and he's comfortable and secure, maybe even happy, which is more than we could ever say about putting him back in that quarantine."

A brief silence followed. Hugh returned, his panic now under better control. "How did you even manage to get him out of the hospital? Did you find the Vitality Charm?"

"No, Dad. But I—" Adrian hesitated and for a moment considered telling them the truth, rather than the story he'd been concocting all day. But no, the time wasn't right. "I borrowed one of the hazmat suits from HQ and put Max into it. The barrier protected me from his powers long enough to get him to where we needed to go."

"A hazmat suit?" said Simon. "And no one noticed a ten-year-old kid wandering down the corridors in a hazmat suit?"

Adrian waited a beat and was met with Simon's subtle gasp, then a groan. "Invisibility. Right. You know, I forget that he has that one, too."

"You did give it to him," said Adrian, "so technically, it's kind of like *you* helped him escape."

"Don't get smart," said Hugh. "And he didn't need to *escape*. He's not a prisoner!"

"Wasn't he?" said Adrian. "Look, I know you guys love him, but I'm not letting you put him back in that quarantine, end of story. For now, he's safe where he is, until we find a more permanent solution."

"No, Adrian, you are going to tell us where he is right this minute, so we can get him back to the hospital and make sure—"

"We'll talk about it later," Adrian interrupted. "For now, I'm late for a team meeting. Okay, guys? Love you, bye!"

The communication band filled with enraged prattle, but was silenced by a press of his thumb. Adrian flinched, wondering whether he was too old to be grounded. When he was a kid and went against their rules, they'd always threaten to take away his comics or video games, but those things didn't hold quite the same sway over him that they used to. What could they take away now that would matter?

He steadied his breathing. It would be all right. Of all the things he'd done in the past few months that could make his dads angry or disappointed with him, whisking Max away to a secret safehouse was hardly the worst of it. A part of him even hoped that, someday, they would acknowledge that he'd done the right thing, for Max and for their family.

If not technically the best thing for the Renegades.

As if the Renegade call center somehow knew Adrian was at that moment breaking more of the Council's rules, his wristband blared with an alarm. He'd almost forgotten that he had patrol duty that night, until he saw the assignment scrolling across the small screen.

Break-in at Dallimore's Dptmt Str, 29th & Merchant, theft in progress, report immediately.

Adrian grinned.

Serving some old-fashioned justice was exactly what he needed.

CHAPTER TWENTY-TWO

"OH, MAN, IT feels good to be heroic!" said Ruby, stretching an arm overhead to work out her muscles. She stood over two cuffed and unconscious burglars who had been caught breaking into a jewelry case in Dallimore's department store.

Adrian couldn't help but agree. It did feel good to be heroic. If nothing else, the arrest had helped take his mind off Max for a while, and Nova, too.

Oscar plopped himself onto a table amid stacks of women's T-shirts in various colors. "And for once, Sketch didn't even have to resort to his *special* abilities." He jutted the end of his cane in Adrian's direction. "Nice to see you keeping it old-school."

Adrian glared, but he knew the teasing was good-natured. "In case you've forgotten, I was defending justice for years before I . . ." He paused and glanced at the burglars, and even though they appeared to be out cold, he still finished lamely, "You know."

Swinging his legs, Oscar surveyed the store, dimly lit by only a handful of the ceiling fluorescents two stories overhead and the display lighting that even now was making the nearby jewelry cases twinkle, including the one that had been smashed to pieces. "Do you think they have any vending machines around here?"

"What? Smokescreen is hungry?" said Ruby, feigning surprise as she wrapped her jewel-tipped wire around her wrist. She had used it to trip the burglars as they sprinted for the emergency exit, and Adrian could see a red line across her hand where the wire had nearly cut into her.

"Hey, I'm a growing superhero," said Oscar. "I need sustenance."

A whorl of butterflies cascaded from the upper balcony, where Danna had been checking to make sure the office safe hadn't been tampered with. "All secure," she said, her body re-forming beside Ruby. "And I didn't see any vending machines, but there's a burger joint two blocks away. We could head there when we're done here."

Oscar offered Danna a fist bump, which she enthusiastically returned.

"All right," said Adrian, punching a code into his wristband. "Store is clear, suspects in custody, awaiting extraction and cleanup."

He grabbed the briefcase of stolen goods and tossed it at Oscar, who unlatched it and started pawing through the assortment of jewelry, laying each piece out on the table so the store could later check it against their records to make sure nothing was missing. "Not a bad haul," said Oscar, holding up a lavaliere necklace with a slender red gemstone dangling from its chain. "Hey, Red Assassin, I think the designers are starting to emulate you."

She grinned and swung her bloodstone like a pendulum. "Aw. I'm a trendsetter! And it's so pretty."

"I guess." Oscar held the necklace up to the light. "Not as pretty as you—yours." Flushing, he hastily diverted his attention back into the briefcase. "Plus, yours is about a thousand time deadlier. Oh, wow, are these earrings?" He pulled out a set of matching chande-lier earrings, each one almost as long as his hand. "These would be like . . . weight lifting for earlobes."

Ruby's cheeks pinkened at his slip. She looked like she wanted to say something, but Oscar seemed determined to move past the compliment that may or may not have been intentional, and so she wrapped her wire back around her wrist and turned to Adrian. "How is Max?"

"Good, I think," said Adrian. "I really can't thank you and your family enough for doing this."

Ruby waved her hand. "I'd do anything for Max. And you should have seen how my brothers went ballistic when they heard that a quote-unquote *real* Renegade would soon be staying with them. Because evidently I don't count." Moving aside a stack of folded shirts, she lifted herself onto the table beside Oscar.

"They were very enthusiastic," said Adrian. "It'll be a big adjust-ment for Max, but good for him, too. He's never had friends his own age before. I just wish—" He caught himself, clamping down on his thoughts before they could escape.

The others watched him, immediately uneasy.

"What?" encouraged Ruby.

"Nothing." He cringed, hating the lie almost as much as he hated the truth. "I was going to say . . . I just wish I could tell Nova about it. I think she'd be really happy to see him free for a change."

The team fell quiet for a long while, until Ruby's small voice asked, "Have you talked to your dads about . . . about the execu-tion? They're not really going to . . . are they?"

Adrian scowled at the floor. "It seems they are. Unless she gives us something useful."

"And she hasn't confessed yet?" Ruby asked.

He shook his head.

"Are you going to go?" said Oscar. "To the . . . you know."

Adrian peered over the frames of his glasses. "It's not just an execution. It's the public unveiling of Agent N. So, yeah. I think I'm pretty much expected to be there."

"Yeah, but . . . people would understand if you decided not to," said Ruby, and though she was trying to be gentle, this conversation was making Adrian's stomach churn with every passing moment.

"Why?" he asked. "She didn't betray me any more than she betrayed you guys, or everyone else for that matter."

The others exchanged looks.

"I mean," said Oscar, "she sort of did. She was, like, your girlfriend."

Adrian's jaw clenched. "I'm done talking about this."

Danna's palm settled on his forearm. He tensed, but didn't pull away.

"I'm really sorry," she said. "We all liked her, you know. It wasn't just you. I can't say that I fully trusted her, but I did like her. I'm just . . . I'm really sorry it was her."

Adrian opened his mouth to reply, though he wasn't sure what he wanted to say. He was sorry, too? It wasn't Danna's fault? It didn't really matter?

He cleared his throat, eager to change the subject. "Ruby, earlier you said you'd do anything for Max. Did you mean that?"

"Anything within reason," she said with suspicion. "Why?"

Adrian squared his shoulders. "You know how I've been giving myself these tattoos so I can——"

He was interrupted by the sound of clapping—slow and methodical clapping that echoed through the department store.

Adrian spun around and spotted a shadowy figure stepping down from a platform of mannequins. The mannequins were wearing ripped jeans and sleek sequined tops, but the figure was dressed entirely in black.

Black boots and pants. Black belt and fingerless gloves.

Black hood.

And a silver mask over the bottom half of her face.

Adrian froze.

He felt his team tense around him. Ruby and Oscar were already off the table, wisps of smoke pooling at Oscar's feet and Ruby's wire pulled taut between her fingers.

"Your sentiments are *so sweet*," said . . . said . . . *Nightmare?*

She stood a hundred paces away, the city lights from outside the window glinting off her metal face mask and the familiar weapons slung across her hips. The black hood overshadowed her face, making it impossible to see her eyes. Adrian blinked, resisting the urge to remove his glasses and clean their lenses.

"You all *liked* her," Nightmare cooed. "You're all so very *sorry* it was her." She tsked a few times. "Well, I hate to be a nonconformist, but to be honest, I wasn't all that sorry. Nova McLain deserves everything she got."

Adrian's mouth was so dry he didn't think he could speak, even if he'd had something to say. Even if the only word resonating in his thoughts wasn't, simply, *Impossible.*

Impossible. Impossible. Impossible.

It wasn't Nova. That much was clear, not only because Nova was imprisoned on an island two miles off the coast, but also because the voice didn't match. Now that he was standing right in front of Nightmare. Now that he could take a moment to compare what he'd only had vague memories of before, the difference was clear.

Still sardonic. Still dry.

But not Nova.

"My compliments on your impressive capture of those two low-lifes," Nightmare said, and it took Adrian a moment to remember the unconscious burglars. "I doubt two non-prodigies were all that difficult to apprehend, but nevertheless, it's nice to witness one of the rare occasions when the Renegades don't show total incompetence."

"Who are you?" said Danna, her voice cutting through the haze in Adrian's thoughts, reminding him where they were, who they were. Renegades. Heroes.

Facing a villain.

The same villain. Always Nightmare. Again and again.

He began to wonder if maybe he was dreaming, but a quick squeeze over his newest tattoo, still sore to the touch, ensured that he was very much awake.

"You know who I am," Nightmare drawled. Then she chuckled, settling a hand on the pouch at her hip from where Adrian had seen her pull those clever throwing stars in battles past. "Oh, wait, I suppose you don't know who I am, because you think that *girl* is me. Thank you, by the way, for finally picking up on all those clues I've been leaving around. It took you long enough to solve the puzzle, but there we are again, back to your famed incompetence. I'll admit, it was more difficult to frame her than I thought it would be, but that's what I get for relying on the observation skills of a bunch of *heroes*. You guys really couldn't be any more oblivious."

"Quit the act," said Danna, taking a step closer. Her body was taut, her hands squeezed into fists, and Adrian could tell she was preparing to swarm. "We know you're not Nightmare. The real Nightmare is in prison, where she belongs."

"Are you sure about that?" Nightmare said, drumming her fingers against the pouch.

Adrian swallowed, hating the confusion muddling his thoughts. Because no . . . no, suddenly, he wasn't sure about anything.

"Nova McLain is Nightmare," Danna said through her teeth. "So who are you?"

"Nova McLain is a Renegade," Nightmare said, her tone dripping with disdain. "*Insomnia*," she spat. "But she wasn't a very good hero, was she? She deserves to be in prison, after she failed to save my grandfather. She deserves for the world to see her as a liar and a fraud. You superheroes are always promising to save people. But did she step in to save my grandfather when the Detonator shot him? No! She watched it happen." Nightmare's stance changed, from relaxed to livid, her hands clenching. "I'll never regret what I've done to her. I needed a decoy and she was just too perfect an opportunity to pass up. Someone had to take the fall for me, when you guys wouldn't get off my back after the parade incident."

"You're lying," said Danna. With a growl, she transformed. The mass of butterflies soared toward Nightmare.

Nightmare cocked her head, the hood shifting so that the light from the jewelry displays illuminated one side of her face, though Adrian couldn't tell if she was surprised or amused.

Then Nightmare took a single step to her left, and disappeared.

Ruby gasped. Maybe they all gasped. Adrian started forward, his heart thundering, as Danna's butterflies formed a cyclone around the column that Nightmare had apparently just walked into.

The mirrored column.

Danna re-formed, one hand pressed against the glass, her face incredulous. "What the hell?"

"And I thought our conversation was going so well."

They spun around. Nightmare reappeared in the doorway to a dressing room, her arms folded as she leaned against the doorjamb.

Adrian traded looks with his team. Though he was feeling no less befuddled than he had the moment Nightmare emerged from that platform of mannequins, he was beginning to realize that standing around gawking at her wasn't going to answer any of his questions—or make the world any safer, for that matter.

"My plan was coming together so well, I'll have you know," Nightmare continued, as if there'd been no interruption. "I want to make it clear that I am not sorry that Nova McLain is in prison. *Good.* No one is searching for Nightmare anymore. *Perfect.* But no, your precious Council couldn't just leave well enough alone, could they? They ruin everything." She sighed heavily. "There are rumors about—and correct me if I'm wrong—but they say the Renegades are soon going to execute Nova McLain. You're going to go ahead and actually kill her!" She put a finger to her jaw, as if in contemplation. "Even though all the evidence you have against her is purely circumstantial? My—that doesn't sound like something the Renegades would do, does it? But that's what I've heard. And at first, I thought, well, even better. With Nova McLain dead, she won't be proclaiming her innocence anymore. And she did fail to save my grandfather, so what goes around comes around . . ."

Grandfather.

At least one piece clicked in Adrian's mind.

The mirror walker. This was the mirror walker they'd seen at the Cloven Cross Library . . . Gene Cronin's granddaughter!

But . . . how could she also be Nightmare?

"However, I am a villain with principles," Nightmare went on, her voice hardening again, "hard as that may be for you to believe.

And as much as I despise that wannabe superhero for her failures, I can't let you imbeciles kill her because you think she's me. I may be a villain, but I'm not a monster." She pushed herself away from the door and spread her hands wide. "So here I am, letting you all in on the big secret. I've fooled the Renegades yet again. *I* am Nightmare. You have the wrong girl."

"And how do we know you're not just an impostor?" yelled Danna, but she refracted into butterflies again before giving the villain a chance to answer.

This time, Adrian moved, too, engaging the springs on his feet to launch him over a series of tables cluttered with handbags and scarves.

Nightmare ducked back into the dressing room.

Danna and Adrian both raced after her, the butterflies mere feet in front of him. The doorway narrowed to a short corridor. To their left, rows of closed dressing room doors. To their right, a triptych of full-length mirrors arranged on a carpeted platform.

Nightmare stood on the platform, leaning against the center mirror. The lights were off and Adrian might have missed her in the darkness, but for the sheen of her mask. Danna must have noticed her at the same time, for the swarm suddenly twisted in her direction.

Nightmare waved.

The butterflies began to converge.

Adrian dove for her even as her body was slipping back through the mirror, its surface rippling outward like the surface of an inky-black pond. Danna's hand grasped at the air, her finger barely catching the edge of Nightmare's hood before she sank into the mirror and the material slipped from Danna's grasp. Adrian's momentum carried him crashing past Danna. He tucked his arm in at the last moment and crashed into the mirror. The glass cracked, a fractured web shooting out from the impact, along with the sting of pain down his arm. He leaped back, cursing and rubbing his shoulder.

Beyond the glass they could still see her, a girl now fractured into a dozen shards. Her hood had been pulled back off her head, setting free a long ginger braid.

Though he couldn't see her mouth, Adrian knew she was smirking at them. She raised two fingers to her mask and pretended to blow them a kiss, before her image faded away and they were left staring at their own reflections.

Reflections that were equal parts furious and mystified.

"What the hell is going on?" said Danna.

"I don't know," Adrian admitted, still examining the spot where Nightmare had been. Nightmare, who could walk through mirrors. Nightmare, who had long red hair. "But I know that girl."

Danna jolted. "What?"

"You weren't with us at the Cloven Cross Library," he said. "When we went to find out if the Librarian was still dealing black-market weapons."

"And?"

"That was his granddaughter. She was working at the library that day." He started walking back toward the doorway, though his skin still prickled from the sensation of being watched. He wondered if Nightmare was still there somewhere behind the glass, waiting to see what they would do next.

He nearly collided with Ruby on his way out, and Oscar wasn't far behind her, though he was moving slower on his cane after their rush to capture the burglars earlier, and Adrian could see he was already winded from the sprint across the department store.

"She's gone again," he told them. "She's traveling through the mirrors."

"Mirrors?" said Oscar. "Like that girl at the library?"

"She *is* the girl from the library," he said. It took Adrian a moment to remember her name. "Narcissa Cronin."

"The Librarian's granddaughter?" barked Ruby. "But she was . . . she's . . . There's no way that girl is Nightmare!"

"Why not?" said Adrian.

His question made them all freeze. Watching one another in the dark, Adrian could see emotions warring on their faces, too.

"But she was so . . . ," Ruby started again, grimacing as she searched for the right word.

"Unvillainous?" suggested Oscar.

"Yes! I mean, we only met her for a minute, but she seemed so shy and . . . and she was reading a romance novel!"

"What's wrong with romance novels?" said Danna.

Ruby huffed. "Nothing! It's just—"

"It's just that villains read only manuals on death and destruction?" said Danna, lifting an eyebrow.

Adrian crossed his arms. "So you admit it might be her?"

Danna gawked at him. "I'm not admitting anything! I just don't think someone's reading preferences automatically rule them out as an enemy."

"She does have villain connections . . . ," mused Oscar. "Including connections to the Anarchists, if her grandpa was selling to them for years. And I guess she does have reason to hate Nova, if she really thinks Nova could have stopped the Detonator that day."

"None of this matters," said Danna, "because she's *not* Nightmare. She's a copycat!"

"How do you know?" asked Adrian.

Danna looked at him, frustrated at first, but maybe a little pityingly, too. Adrian bristled.

"What is Nightmare's superpower?" she asked.

Adrian scowled.

It was Oscar who responded, "Putting people to sleep."

Danna spread her arms, as if this were evidence enough. "Putting people to sleep. *Not* walking through mirrors."

"Yeah . . . ," started Ruby, mindlessly tapping her finger against the point of her bloodstone. "But Adrian has multiple superpowers. So does Max. It's not entirely unheard of."

"You guys, I followed Nova," said Danna. "I *saw* her."

"What exactly did you see?" said Adrian. "You've never told us the details."

She groaned. "There aren't a lot of details to give. I suspected Nova, so I started following her. At some point, she led me to the cathedral, and that's how I knew to take you guys there, but I don't actually remember, because the lepidoptera that was following her is dead."

Once she had finished, a silence descended on them, and Adrian knew he wasn't the only one thinking it. He could see the doubt creeping onto Danna's face, even. Uncertainty. Maybe a twinge of horror.

"It wasn't a trick," she insisted. "She couldn't have—"

"Fooled you," said Oscar. "Fooled *us*."

"Is it possible," said Adrian, slowly, because he didn't want Danna to think he was accusing her of anything, "that while you were following Nova, your . . . lepidoptera . . . got another lead, and followed the real Nightmare to the cathedral?"

"But . . ." Danna shook her head. "No. This is absurd. She's a copycat. An impostor."

"But why?" said Adrian. "Why would Narcissa Cronin pretend to be Nightmare? She wasn't on our radar at all before this, and now it's like she wants us to start hunting for her again?"

Danna cut a sharp glare at him, but he couldn't help it. With every tick of the big clock on the back of the store's wall, his perceptions of Nightmare and Nova and Narcissa Cronin were changing. Melding together, then separating again.

"I don't know," said Danna, "but do we really think she had a change of heart and decided she would put herself on the line just to prevent the death of a Renegade? A Renegade she hates!"

Oscar shrugged. "I wouldn't want the death of an innocent person on my hands, even if I did hate them."

"You're not a villain!" said Danna.

Adrian hardly heard her, though. Oscar's words struck Adrian harder than he'd probably intended. Or, one word in particular. One word Adrian's own mind had been dancing around, refusing to stop and contemplate all it would mean.

Nova was—

No. Nova was not innocent. She couldn't be. Not after everything. He shook his head, trying to rid himself of the thought before it could take hold. There was too much evidence stacked against her, but now, somehow, the evidence that had seemed so damning hours before struck him as . . . what was the word Nightmare had used? *Circumstantial.*

What proof did they really have?

Was it possible they'd been wrong?

Innocent.

If this was true, if they had the wrong Nightmare . . . then Nova was innocent.

But that also meant they'd failed to capture Nightmare, the real Nightmare.

She was still out there, taunting them, taunting *him*. The mystery wasn't solved. She remained at large, a danger to society and the organization and everyone he cared about. This was terrible news. This was a mortifying mistake. This was another black spot on the Renegades' record.

And yet his chest was expanding with every passing moment.

"How can we know for sure?" he whispered, interrupting an argument between Danna and Oscar that he hadn't been listening to. "How can we prove that Nova's not Nightmare, that the real Nightmare is still out there?"

Danna rubbed her forehead. "Let's not get carried away. I know you want this to be real, all of you do, but—"

"Oh, I forgot to mention one more thing."

They all jumped at the clip of Nightmare's voice coming from above them.

"Sweet rot," muttered Oscar, a phrase he'd almost certainly picked up from Nova, which made Adrian's heart ache all over again. Pointing his cane, he yelled, "I wish you'd stop doing that!"

Sitting on the railing of the second floor, not far from the escalator, Nightmare ignored him. "Go ahead and execute Ace Anarchy, if you really think it's going to make a difference, killing a weak, defenseless old man all for the sake of your popularity ratings. You Renegades do what you think is best." She reached for something tucked behind her and held it up. She was met with a collective gasp from Adrian and his team.

Ace Anarchy's helmet.

"Oh, you recognize this?" she chirped. "Then you'll know that we don't need Ace anymore. We already have everything we need to destroy you."

With that, she kicked her legs back to the other side of the railing and walked away. It wasn't long before the drum of her boots was silenced as she vanished into another mirror.

The sound was almost immediately followed by sirens blaring from outside. Adrian was momentarily confused, before he remembered the burglars, the arrest, the extraction crew coming to take the criminals to prison.

He didn't care about any of that.

Hope and clarity swelled inside him.

Nova was innocent.

CHAPTER TWENTY-THREE

|NNOCENT.

She was innocent.

According to the Renegades, Nova Jean McLain was innocent.

Nova's emotions fluctuated every few seconds, from elation to disbelief to the absolute certainty that this was a trap. No one had told her what had been uncovered. What new evidence had been found to prove her sudden innocence. She racked her brain to think what false evidence the Anarchists might have planted to lead the Renegades to this conclusion, but she could think of nothing that made sense. Not after they'd all been so certain of her guilt. Not with the truth hovering over her head that she was, in fact, guilty.

And yet, here she was, being handed a box with her original clothes and boots and told she was free to leave. The same guard who had first embedded the small tracker between her shoulder blades used an even more painful device to extract it. Nova gritted her teeth and didn't complain.

They gave her a thick wad of gauze and a mint.

Was this a trick?

This time, she was left alone to change. Exhaling through her nostrils, she pulled on her clothes, then rapped on the door to let them know she was ready.

Two more guards were posted at the exit, though they ignored her as she was led by. She listened to the bolts clank and the gears rumble inside the massive walls. She watched the gate open and the two Cragmoor guards walked her out into the blustering, frigid sea air. The guards were armed, as always, but this was the first time that Nova had been outside her cell without her hands being cuffed. The guards didn't say much. One of them, a female with inky-black eyes that showed no sign of whites to them, very nearly smiled. "We will escort you all the way to the dock," she said.

She seemed borderline apologetic, though not apologetic enough.

Could it be a trick?

Nova's hands kept twitching to touch the guards and put them to sleep before they could lead her into whatever trap was waiting, but she held back the urge.

Because what if this was real? What if her name had really been cleared?

And if so . . . *how*?

Her skin prickled with gooseflesh, in part spurred by the wind that threw her bangs into her face, but also by the anticipation of an ambush. Maybe her execution was to come early. Maybe they didn't want it to be public after all. She almost expected a bullet in her back at any second, but when she glanced up at the guard towers posted to either side of the gate, she saw their rifles pointing toward the sky. One of them gave her a salute, without expression. The other was focused on the choppy waves of the sea and the hazy fog that hid the distant city skyline from view.

The small island felt like it was a part of another universe entirely, and the sensation chilled Nova to her core.

The small terrain vehicle took her and her entourage back down to the dock, where an armored boat rocked in the turbulent water, where the same captain and set of guards who had delivered Nova to this island now waited to take her back.

And then she saw him.

He was waiting on the dock, a heavy wool coat, a black knit cap, jeans.

Adrian Everhart, looking too good to be true in this dank, dreary place.

In his left hand was a bouquet of flowers—the most vivid sunshine-yellow daisies Nova had ever seen in her life. In his right hand was a tool belt similar to the one Nova had worn over her Renegade uniform.

Nova didn't realize she'd stopped walking until the guard with the black eyes politely cleared her throat. Nova started down the uneven wooden steps, past the jagged black rocks that shone with gathered mist, their surfaces studded with barnacles and kelp.

She came to stand in front of Adrian, her hair becoming damp from the spray, the taste of salt on her tongue.

"Flowers or weaponry?" said Adrian, holding his gifts toward her. "I wasn't sure which would make for a better apology."

Nova's attention dipped to the daisies, then to the belt, before regarding Adrian again. Though his tone had been cheerful, she could see the anxiety underneath.

"I'm assuming your inventions were destroyed in the explosion," he said. "I thought maybe a new tool belt could be a . . . new beginning?"

His hands drooped when Nova still didn't take his offerings. "I'm sorry," he said, with the full weight of a thousand apologies. "I should have believed you. I should have trusted you. I failed you when you needed me to be an advocate, and I know that officially makes me the worst boyfriend in the history of the world, and as much as I want to make it up to you, I will understand if you don't want to have anything to do with me. But if . . . if you can possibly forgive me, then I will do everything I can to make this up to you. I know I can't change what you've been through, but . . . I still care for you, Nova. I never stopped caring for you, and I realize what an incredible jerk I was. I'm mortified when I think of the things that I said to you, the way I treated you in there . . . how I didn't stand up for you, not once, even when you kept insisting you weren't Nightmare. I should have . . ." He grimaced and shook his head. "I should have believed you. I'm so, so sorry." He hesitated, his eyes shining with words still left unspoken.

He was met with silence. Wind gusts. Sea spray.

Finally, he whispered, "Please say something."

Nova swallowed. "Where's my bracelet?"

Adrian's shoulders sank, as if this were the very question he'd been hoping she wouldn't ask.

"It was given to Magpie," he said, and Nova had the distinct impression he was dodging liability. "I'm sure she turned it in at headquarters."

One of Nova's eyebrows shot upward. She was equally sure that the little thief had kept it for herself.

No matter. She could deal with that later.

"Did you draw the flowers?" she asked.

Adrian shook his head. "Bought them with actual money, at an actual florist."

"Hmm." Reaching forward, Nova took the belt from him and snapped it around her hips. "Well, this is the better apology. But . . ." She snatched the flowers away. "I'll take these, too."

He grinned, but it was fleeting. "You'll see there's another gift there," he said, indicating a pouch on the belt. "From the Council, actually."

With a twinge of suspicion, Nova opened the pouch and pulled out . . .

A metal face mask.

Not *her* metal face mask, but one that was similar enough that it immediately set her palms to sweating, and her mind returning to that refrain—*It's a trap!*

She wondered how much Adrian must hate her to have agreed to be part of such a cruel ambush. But his expression stayed sincere and warm.

She trained her focus on the mask again and flipped it over a few times. It was larger than Nightmare's mask, with parallel slits in the front and small filtering chambers that would rest against her cheeks.

"It's a gas mask," said Adrian. "Kind of a crude design, but they didn't want to delay the manufacturing of them. Every patrol unit is being equipped with these going forward, you know, after Nightmare got her hands on Agent N and made those gas bombs."

"Oh," said Nova. "Right." Her fingers were trembling as she tucked the mask back into the pouch. "Thanks?" She stepped around Adrian and headed toward the waiting boat.

No one jumped forward to stop her. There were no weapons directed her way. The captain even tipped his hat as he welcomed her aboard.

As soon as her feet were no longer on the dock, giddy ripples pulsed beneath her skin. Most of Adrian's apology was lost in the tumult of her confused thoughts, but there were phrases that clung to her, loud and clear.

Adrian had never stopped caring for her . . . even when he believed she was Nightmare? She wanted to dig further into that statement, but she resisted, knowing that she didn't deserve his remorse.

And also . . . *boyfriend*? This, too, echoed in her memory as she sat on the first narrow bench, scooting over to the window of the boat and grateful that no guards stepped forward to latch her ankle to the metal rings on the wet floor. She laid the flowers across her lap, their wrapping of butcher paper crinkling against her knees.

Adrian sat beside her, but left a couple of inches between them.

One guard untied the boat from the dock and the other thumped the roof of the boat, indicating they were cleared for departure. The engine rumbled, and within seconds they were pulling away from the rocks and the island and the gray, cold prison that sat foreboding at the top of the cliff, its massive walls and guard towers fading into the pervasive fog.

Nova shivered as she watched it disappear, torn between her joy at Adrian's apology, her relief at being free of that place, but also the knowledge that Ace was still there.

"Here," said Adrian, unbuttoning his coat. Nova watched mutely as he snaked his arms from the sleeves and draped it over her shoulders. Warmth blanketed her, mingling with the spicy scent of aftershave that she hadn't even known she'd memorized until then. It only served to make the moment seem even more unreal.

"How are you feeling?" asked Adrian. "They didn't . . . You weren't hurt in there, were you?"

"No," she answered, sending her focus back to the island, though it quickly became a ghostly outline and nothing more. "But no one's told me anything. What happened? How was I cleared?"

Adrian grimaced. "It was brought to our attention that all the evidence we thought we had against you was . . . circumstantial."

Nova dared to meet his gaze, ignoring how her heart sputtered at the sight of him and how he was once again watching her with affection. The affection she'd been sure she would never see again. She hadn't realized how she'd been starved for a soft look from Adrian, or one of his signature smiles. She hadn't realized how much she'd come to crave his steady presence, his unwavering goodness. She dug her fingers into the fabric of his coat, pulling it tighter around her shoulders.

"It didn't hurt," he continued, somewhat wryly, "that Nightmare herself was the one who brought that to our attention."

Nova started, thinking she must have been too caught up in her emotion to have heard correctly. "Excuse me?"

Adrian started to tell her a story that left her more baffled than before. Nightmare showed up at a department store and proceeded to taunt them about how she had framed Insomnia? Nightmare was . . . she was the *mirror walker*?

Nova's jaw dropped. "You can't be serious."

"I know, it was hard for me to wrap my mind around it at first, too. But the more I've thought about it, the more it makes sense. Of course she would want to frame you, of all people, after what happened between the Detonator and the Librarian. And why she would choose the fun house at the carnival for her hideout spot— it had that hall of mirrors, remember? And also how she got into our house to steal the Vitality Charm without being caught on our surveillance systems, and how she got all that stuff from the artifacts department. Every bathroom has a mirror in it, and every building has bathrooms. That's how she gets around so easily. Plus, she's had access to all those black-market weapons, and a connection to the Anarchists, through her grandfather's business. It all fits together."

Nova gaped at him, feeling mildly insulted.

They thought *Narcissa Cronin* was Nightmare? She'd seen the girl fight, and it wasn't exactly impressive.

"Plus," Adrian added, "she had the helmet."

"The helmet?" said Nova, her mind still reeling. "You mean . . . *the* helmet?"

He nodded. "That confirmed it for everyone when we told the Council. They ordered for you to be released immediately. Everyone is back at headquarters, scrambling to secure it against Nightmare, now that we know what we know. Taking down all the mirrors. I need to go secure the house, too, but I needed to be here for you first. I owed you that much."

He lowered his head sorrowfully, and Nova could sense another stream of apologies brewing. Before he could start, she asked, "What about Danna?"

He sat back against the bench, his hands interlocking in his lap. "She's fully recovered. Doing great."

"I mean . . . what did she say when . . . she was told that she was wrong? That I'm not Nightmare."

Suddenly avoiding her gaze, Adrian looked out toward the water, in the direction they were heading. There was a wall dividing them from the captain at the helm, and the boat's single guard had stayed out on the deck, so they were alone in this tiny room with its freezing-cold metal benches and mildew-covered windows. "She . . . admitted that she might have been mistaken," Adrian finally said, making it easy for Nova to deduce what he wasn't saying.

Danna wasn't convinced. She would still be a threat, but Nova hoped she was a threat that would be at least temporarily nullified.

She had other things to worry about. Like what was she going to do to save Ace, with his execution looming.

And why, for all the diabolical schemes, was Narcissa Cronin pretending to be her?

"Adrian," she said, as the Gatlon skyline began to emerge from the thick mist, "are they still going to execute Ace Anarchy?"

He turned back to her, but this time she was avoiding his eyes, lest he see her horror.

"Yes," he said. "At the reveal of Agent N, after they neutralize the rest of the Cragmoor inmates. The Council is convinced it's the best way to show the world that . . . well, that the Renegades won't tolerate crime and anarchy."

Her jaw tightened. She wondered, not for the first time, if Adrian had any idea how closely related the Council's ideas of crime and anarchy were to her ideas of freedom and self-reliance.

It didn't really matter, though. She had a lot of time to think while she was in her cell at Cragmoor, and she was returning to Gatlon City with new plans. Even some new ideals.

She had begun to dream of a future for herself and the others that was different from any future she'd ever dared to envision before. And though, at the time, she'd believed she wouldn't have any future at all, now she couldn't help but wonder what might be possible.

But first, above all else, she needed to find a way to stop them from killing Ace. She needed to rescue him, as so many years ago he had rescued her.

The blare of a foghorn rumbled over the choppy waves. It was early morning, and the lights of the city were shimmering off the damp air. Orange floodlights shone on the outline of the pier where the boat would soon pull in to the dock. Squinting, Nova could barely make out a number of shadowy forms waiting there, but couldn't tell who they might be. She had a brief fantasy that it would be her family, the closest thing to a family she'd ever had. Honey. Leroy. Phobia.

Well, not Phobia, so much.

Or even Ruby and Oscar. Even Danna, who Nova had found herself liking despite Danna's obvious suspicions. Or Max, she thought. She was startled when her mind even painted Simon Westwood and Hugh Everhart into that picture. A family, waiting to welcome her home. *Any* family.

She sighed, knowing that all of these daydreams were flawed in one way or another. Knowing that future would never come to pass.

A hand, warm and strong, slid over hers, making the paper around the flowers crinkle in the silence. Nova flipped her hand over and laced their fingers together.

"Nova . . ."

"I forgive you," she whispered, smiling at him. "Thank you for not giving up on me."

The lines on his face slowly melted away, softening with relief. She squeezed his hand and he squeezed back, which was when she noticed the lump at the base of his wrist. Nova flipped his hand over and pushed up his sleeve, revealing a thick square bandage on his forearm. "What happened?"

"It's nothing," he said.

A little too quickly.

Nova frowned at him.

Adrian cringed. "I mean, it's sort of something. I'm . . . trying something new. Here." He peeled back one side of the bandage. Where she had expected to see a wound of some sort was . . . a tattoo.

It was fairly recent, by the looks of it. Scabs had formed over the black ink lines, and the skin around it was swollen and red.

Nova took his arm and twisted it toward the grayish light streaming through the window. The tattoo depicted a tower, like a castle turret, sitting atop a hill. The top of a heart could be seen barely visible over the wall, while the grassy slope at the tower's base was littered with fallen arrows.

"Okay . . . ," Nova said, not quite sure what to make of it. "What does it mean?"

"Protection." Adrian sounded a little sheepish as he reaffixed the bandage. "I . . ." He cleared his throat. "I've had this idea, lately, that maybe my power can transfer to tattoos. I mean, it doesn't really matter if I draw with marker or crayon or chalk or paint . . . so why not tattoo ink?"

"You did this yourself?"

"Yes. And I know it might sound a little far-fetched, but . . . I thought I should try it and see what happens."

"Try what, exactly?"

"To see if I can give myself a tattoo that's . . . you know, more than just a tattoo." He lightly pressed his thumb over the bandage, before pulling his sleeve back down. "I thought this one could be useful in a fight. Something that I could use for protection, if I needed it."

Nova stared, not sure if she understood. "So . . . you've tattooed a tower on your arm, in an experimental attempt to . . . do what, again?"

"Well, *if* it works," said Adrian, flashing her a cheeky grin, "it will be sort of like giving myself another superpower. In theory, I'll be able to use it to create a barrier around myself and anyone who's near me, that will deflect attacks from other prodigies."

She leaned against the window. "That's . . . an interesting theory."

He cleared his throat uncomfortably, and Nova had the distinct impression that there was something he wasn't telling her. "I guess we'll see how it goes. It should be healed enough to test out in another day or two."

"You don't seem all that concerned that maybe you've just tattooed a medieval castle on yourself for no real reason."

He chuckled, and he seemed to want to say something, but she could sense his uncertainty. Finally, he answered, "Well, also, tattoos make a guy look tough, don't they?"

She laughed. "Sure they do."

The roar of the engines suddenly quieted. Nova was startled to see that they were already at the dock. The fog had mostly cleared, revealing the buildings along the pier and the skyscrapers beyond. The sun had peeked over the horizon, its beams slashing through the lingering mist.

She clutched her bouquet of flowers and followed Adrian off the boat. She realized with a swell of disappointment that none of the figures she'd seen loitering on the dock had been the so-called families she'd imagined. They were all strangers—a Renegade administrator who asked her to sign a form stating she was returned safely to the mainland following her release, a dockworker who set about mooring the boat, and the media.

A few dozen journalists and photographers were gathered, already snapping pictures of Nova and screaming questions that quickly blurred into nonsense.

Adrian placed a hand on her lower back, steering her past the crowd. "You don't have to talk to them," he murmured in her ear, and Nova wondered just how many newspapers and tabloids would carry this picture in the coming days. Adrian Everhart whispering into the ear of the girl who was previously suspected of being Nightmare herself . . . not to mention the yellow daisies. She flushed, doing her best to ignore the yells behind her—*Nova! Miss McLain! Insomnia!*

"We have a car over there," said Adrian, pointing to a small parking lot, as they made their way past the rows of moored boats, their wooden hulls thumping hollowly against each other in the water.

But just as Adrian was steering Nova toward the lot, an unfamiliar figure stepped out from a waiting taxicab on the other side of the street. "Nova!" he cried, rushing toward her. "Oh, thank heavens!"

Nova froze, frowning not so much at the man, but at the way he'd said her name. Like he knew her.

She scanned his face. He must have been in his late fifties, with salt-and-pepper hair and an unkempt beard. He was dressed in jeans and loafers and a sweater that was tattered and faded and almost certainly not warm enough for the weather.

Nova was sure she'd never seen him before.

She tensed, one hand reaching for the stun gun at her belt, only to remember how she'd tossed all her weapons into the duffel bag and sent it off in the trunk of Leroy's car.

As soon as he reached her, the man grasped Nova's hand affectionately. His skin was leathery, feeling much older than his features suggested. "I'm so relieved," he said. "I thought I'd never see you again!"

To her surprise, there were tears in his gray-blue eyes.

Perhaps reading Nova's bewilderment, Adrian took hold of her elbow, gently tugging her closer to him. "I'm sorry, you are . . . ?"

"Her uncle," said the man, beaming and holding out a hand for Adrian to shake. "You must be Adrian."

Nova stiffened. Her *uncle*?

When Adrian hesitantly accepted the handshake, the man pumped it with enthusiasm. "She's told me so much. Never stops talking about you. It's so great to finally meet you face-to-face. And on such a happy occasion!" His smile grew wider, and before Nova could fully grasp what was happening, he had his arms around her.

Nova's power surged to the surface of her skin, tingling with the temptation to nullify this threat, to knock him out before he could harm her. But he wasn't hurting her, if that was his intention. Rather, he was embracing her like . . .

Well. Like family.

"Uncle?" she tried.

He pulled away, but kept his hands on Nova's shoulders. "I tried to come visit after they took you away, but all our papers were destroyed in the explosion and I had no way to prove who I was. They didn't believe me. And with them thinking you were that . . . that *villain* . . ." He spat the word, his nostrils flaring with disgust. "They had you under so much security, there was no way they would let me get close to you. I'm so sorry. It's been killing me to think of you in there, all alone. I didn't want you to think I'd abandoned you, but I couldn't—"

"It's okay," she stammered. "I'm fine. I'm—" She glanced at Adrian. "I'm free, now."

"I know. I couldn't believe it when I heard, but at the same time, I knew this would all be sorted out. I knew they couldn't go on believing those lies about you forever, not after everything you've done for them." Releasing her shoulders, he returned his focus to Adrian. "I was so proud of her when she went to the trials and got chosen. Being a Renegade's been a lifelong dream of hers."

Adrian smiled, the wariness in his expression slowly fading. "We've been lucky to have her. I can't possibly express how sorry we all are about this mistake. Nova deserved better from us."

"It's all in the past." Reaching out, the man patted Nova on the top of her head, and she couldn't resist snarling and ducking away. "Come on. Let's get you home so you can have a rest. Well . . . not *home*, obviously. The explosion and all. But I've rented us a decent little apartment that'll do until we can figure something out. It's not so bad. We'll make do, just like we always have."

"The Renegades could provide you with temporary housing," Adrian suggested. "It's the least we could do, considering . . ."

"No, no," said the man. "That's very generous, but there are people in this city who need the charity more than we do. Thank you so much, but my Nova and I will be just fine."

He started to guide Nova toward the waiting taxi, but Adrian calling her name made her pause and turn back.

He looked suddenly shy, his breaths fogging the air between them. He seemed to struggle with words he wasn't sure how to say, while Nova waited, her heart tumbling. The world dimmed—the city, the journalists, her false uncle—everything vanishing but for Adrian and his nervous stare boring into her.

"It was always real for me, too," he finally said, his voice barely a whisper. "I hope you know that."

Nova shivered. Before she could talk herself out of it, she thrust the bouquet of flowers at the strange man, then closed the distance between herself and Adrian. She reached her arms around his neck, pulling him to her. Cameras flashed and journalists peppered them with eager, prying questions, but Nova barely noticed them over the sense of fullness that was coursing through her body, from her flushing cheeks to her happily curling toes. All she cared about was conveying in this moment, with this kiss, what she might never have another chance to say.

This was real. In spite of everything, her feelings for Adrian Everhart were real, and she was going to keep this moment pinned inside her heart for the rest of her life. No matter what the future held, she would cherish this kiss, and his words, forever.

Adrian was beaming when she pulled back. Nova allowed herself the luxury of cupping his face in her ice-cold hands and memorizing that smile, those eyes, those elusive, precious dimples.

Then she slipped out of his arms and peeled his coat from her shoulders. Even without it, the heat from the kiss lingered, warming her from the inside out. "Thank you," she said, handing it back to him and hoping he knew she meant for more than just the coat. "I guess I'll see you at headquarters."

Adrian nodded, still grinning. "See you there."

Without meeting the eye of her pretend uncle, Nova took back her flowers and headed across the street to the cab.

She sank into the back seat and waited for the door to shut before rounding on the stranger. "Who are you?"

The man smirked as he started to pick lint from his sweater. "A mighty fine actor, if I do say so myself. Though, perhaps, not as good as you." He shot her a suggestive look.

But Nova didn't care about her red cheeks or erratic pulse or whether or not this man thought the kiss had been an act. "Answer the question."

"If you don't like 'Uncle,' then you can call me Peter. Peter McLain."

Her teeth ground, but the man pressed on.

"And I do believe I just secured the rest of your story. Strangely missing uncle—*found*. That should silence the rest of your doubters, at least for a while. You're welcome."

She gawked at him, simultaneously annoyed and a little impressed. He was right. At some point Adrian and the Renegades would have raised questions about the uncle who had never once come for her after she'd been arrested. The uncle who no one had ever met.

"Okay," she said, "but *who are you?*"

"He's an ally."

Starting, she peered toward the front, as the driver pushed aside the plexiglass window that divided them. She caught his eyes in the rearview mirror, the skin around them mottled and scarred, the eyebrows long ago burned away. Her heart leaped. "Leroy!"

He beamed at her. "Welcome back, little Nightmare."

CHAPTER TWENTY-FOUR

NOVA'S SO-CALLED UNCLE was not staying in a shabby, rented apartment, and neither, it turned out, were the rest of the Anarchists.

Leroy drove them to the Barlow neighborhood and parked on the corner of East 16th and Skrein Avenue. Nova stepped onto the sidewalk and found herself inspecting barred windows that displayed an assortment of goods—a couple of electric guitars, a drill set, a vintage vinyl record player. A faded sign along the top of the building read, in enormous block letters, DAVE'S PAWNSHOP.

Nova took in the street, noting a nightclub closed for the night, a convenience store, and a few empty storefronts with FOR LEASE signs hanging in the windows. Judging from how the signs had yellowed around the edges, occupants hadn't been there since the Age of Anarchy.

Her "uncle" jingled a key chain as he unlocked the door to the pawnshop, also outfitted with impressive metal bars.

"Are you Dave?" Nova asked as he and Leroy ushered her inside.

"Naw, Dave just lets us use the basement," the man answered, bustling through the pawnshop. "For a price, that is. Anything to make a buck, right?"

The overhead lights were off, but a series of glass cases in the store had built-in lighting that cast a dim glow over the merchandise. Watches and costume jewelry in the cases, old cinema posters framed on the walls, shelves along the back stocked with computers, vacuums, and radios. There really wasn't much in the way of household goods that Dave *didn't* seem to have in stock, from practical electronics to pricey luxuries.

Pawnshops had been big business during the Age of Anarchy, when much of the financial system had collapsed and the world's economy was largely replaced with a trade-and-barter system. These businesses had continued to do well even after the Renegades had taken over, as the economy stuttered and stammered to get going again and employment security remained virtually nonexistent. People still needed food, and sometimes the quickest and easiest way to get it was to pawn off your grandma's antique hatpin collection for a fraction of its pre-Anarchy value.

They passed through the shop and into a back room, where utilitarian shelves were lined with more electronics and a random assortment of spare parts. It smelled of grease and must and moth-eaten clothing, which all served to remind Nova of the subway tunnels.

Leroy and the man grabbed a small worktable and together hoisted it off to the side.

A hidden door was cut out of the dingy linoleum flooring, illuminated with yellow light from below.

Grinning in a way that showed off his missing teeth, Leroy gestured for Nova to go first.

She squeezed the bundle of daisies Adrian had given her and, not sure what else to do, tucked them under one arm as she stepped onto the rungs of the ladder. The paper crinkled loudly as she lowered herself into the basement. Her boot had barely touched concrete when arms were wrapping around her and pulling her from the ladder.

"Nightmare, my darling!" Honey cooed, squeezing her from behind. "We've missed you so much!" She spun Nova around so she could cup her face between lacquered nails. Streaks of black eyeliner had dried and caked on her cheeks and she seemed to be covered in more of her bee friends than usual—nine or ten were caught in her blonde hair and Nova spied at least a dozen more wandering around her neck and shoulders. "If I believed in miracles, I would say we've accomplished one. You're free!"

"I'm free," Nova agreed, as Leroy dropped down beside them.

"And oh, flowers! Did Leroy think to bring you those? How thoughtful."

Nova glanced at Leroy. Now that she was back in villain territory, the last thing she wanted to do was confess that, actually, the flowers were from Adrian Everhart.

Leroy winked at her and said nothing.

"I'll find something to put them in," said Honey, taking the bouquet from her. It was immediately set upon by a flurry of enthusiastic honeybees.

The pawnshop's basement was not so much a basement as a bomb shelter, with thick concrete walls and a couple of hallways leading off in various directions. Nova surmised that the shelter must run nearly the full city block. In this central area there were some rickety folding chairs, worn rugs crisscrossing one another across the floor, and crates of food and supplies against one wall.

But what was more surprising to her than learning that her allies had taken up residence in the bomb shelter beneath Dave's Pawnshop was learning that they were not alone.

Nova was greeted by at least thirty faces, almost all of them strangers, who stared back at her, largely expressionless. Nova recognized signs of inherent abilities. A girl a few years her senior had thick auburn hair that floated like seaweed in the air. One man had a growth of fungi covering his right arm. A boy who was probably thirteen or fourteen had gigantic eyes, with pupils shaped like six-pointed stars.

There were more subtle indicators, too. A tattoo of two arrows crossed on a paper scroll—a symbol of the Vandal Cartel, which had been the Librarian's gang years ago. Two young boys dressed in shimmery gold robes, reminiscent of the Harbingers. Nova knew that some of the villain gangs that hadn't been vanquished on the Day of Triumph had gone underground, still existing, still struggling to survive. They had been in hiding, stealing when they had to, fighting for their needs, existing in the shadows—many going through life hiding the fact that they were prodigies, so as not to draw the attention of the Renegades who would surely label them as villains.

But she'd never heard of them banding together into a unified group. Had this been happening without the Anarchists' knowledge all this time?

She spotted Phobia lurking in a back corner, his scythe glinting over the heads of the crowd. Nova gulped. Adrian's words, coursing with anger, came back to her.

One cannot be brave who has no fear . . . Those words were found on a slip of paper left on my mother's body.

How many times had she heard Phobia say that? It was a phrase she had grown up with, one that had struck her as both truthful and encouraging. It was okay to be afraid sometimes, for only then could you choose to be brave.

But the words held a very different meaning for Adrian.

Had Phobia killed Lady Indomitable? Had *he* murdered Adrian's mom?

Nova wondered whether she would ask him if ever given the chance. She wondered how much she really wanted to know.

Turning to Leroy, she asked, "Does someone want to explain to me what's going on?"

But it was not Leroy who answered.

"Maybe we should start with the enormous *thank-you* you owe us."

Nova spun around.

Narcissa Cronin was shoulder to shoulder with the star-eyed boy and an older woman who could have been anybody's grandmother, except she was standing in this dingy room surrounded by villains. Narcissa's arms were crossed and her face showed the same loathing it had the last time they'd crossed paths, when Narcissa had attacked Nova at her house and some unknown allies of hers had thrown a rock through the window.

"We did save your life," said Narcissa, with a sour twist to her lips. It was still odd to see her fuming with anger, when she'd seemed so docile before. It was almost like she was wearing a mask.

Speaking of masks, Nova began to wonder where her costume was. Narcissa must have used it to impersonate Nightmare, but that meant that Leroy and Honey had given it to her willingly.

"Thank you," Nova said, though it sounded a bit mechanical. "But I still don't know what's going on."

"We had to save your life," said Honey, who had found a plastic milk jug for the flowers and set them off in a corner. She put an arm around Nova and smooshed their heads together. "You're our little Nightmare. We just aren't the same without you."

"Yeah, I'd hoped you might try to do something to get me out of there," said Nova, "but who are all these people? What are we doing here?"

"These," said Leroy, "are our new allies." Unlike Nova, he seemed as relaxed as could be, his hands tucked into his pockets, a soft smile on his droopy lips.

Nova pointed at Narcissa. "The last time I saw her, she was trying to kill me."

"I had time to reconsider some things," Narcissa said. "After our conversation, it occurred to me that maybe our objectives aren't so different after all." Her tone suggested this was a painful admission for her to make. "I hate what the Detonator did to my family, to my grandfather and the library. And I did blame you for letting it happen. But then . . . well, you did kill the Detonator, and I figure that is worth something. Plus . . ." She hesitated and glanced at the elderly woman, who gave Narcissa an encouraging nod.

Nova realized with a start that she recognized the woman, though the last time she'd seen her, it had been aboard a tiny, cramped houseboat off the coastal highway. "Millie?"

"Hello again, Miss *McLain*," Millie said, with a mirthful wink. As a psychometrist, Millie had the ability to see into the past of any object she touched, but it was her forgery skills that tended to be more highly valued by the villain gangs. She had, in fact, forged Nova's documents for her application to the Renegades. In some ways, she had created Nova's alter ego, giving her a new name, a new past, a new identity.

"Millie convinced me that the Anarchists could make good allies for us," said Narcissa. "Given your presence in the Renegades, and the way you've managed to get so close to the Council, she thought it would be wise to give you another chance."

"I was rather proud of that new identity I designed for you," said

Millie. "I'd hate to see it all go to waste when we're so close to seeing their organization crumble."

"So you pretended to be me," said Nova, "so they would have to let me go."

Narcissa nodded. "You're welcome."

It had been a risk—a *huge* risk—Nova knew. Narcissa had put herself in a lot of danger to go through with it.

But it had worked. Nova was free.

And now . . .

Now what?

Everyone was watching her, almost expectantly, but Nova was far too weary to figure out what they wanted. What they were waiting for.

She scanned the room. Her attention landed on a skinny, black-haired boy near the back. It took her a moment to place him, before she realized she'd seen him at the Renegade trials. The boy who could make folded origami creatures come to life.

The Renegades had rejected him then. What was he doing here now?

Her pulse skipped. They had rejected him.

The Rejects.

This was the group Narcissa had talked about, the one she'd been trying to steal the helmet for. These were the Rejects.

But . . . she still wasn't entirely sure what that meant.

"All right," Nova said, finishing her perusal of the gathered crowd and determining that she didn't recognize anyone else. "So, who are the rest of you?"

"Isn't it obvious?" said Honey, giggling. "We are the villains of Gatlon City!"

"No, we are not villains," said Narcissa firmly.

Honey snorted and leaned closer to Nova's ear. "She hates it when I say that."

"We are prodigies who have a different agenda than the Renegades," said Narcissa as her cheeks reddened. "We are prodigies who desire to be who we are and what we are, to live the lives we want to live, without fear that the Renegades are going to show up at any minute and intimidate us and push us around, or even neutralize us with that new weapon of theirs, for no other reason than we don't want to be one of them."

"Or that our gangs were at war with them more than a decade ago," added one of the boys in gold.

"Everyone here was either a supplier or a client of my grandfather's," said Narcissa. "When he died, he was holding a book—a ledger, actually. An account of every prodigy and gang he'd had business with over the years. I've spent the last few months searching for the people in that book in hopes of forming new alliances, so we might actually be able to make some change in this city." She hesitated, and for her momentary zeal, started to look a little sheepish. "The Anarchists were in the book, too. Not just the Detonator, but Cyanide and Queen Bee, too. Even you were mentioned once, Nightmare. Given the circumstances, I think Grandpa would have wanted us to work together. The Renegades made it hard, almost impossible, for anyone who had been given the stigma of *villain* to go on with a normal life, and my grandfather suffered for that. We've all suffered. He would have liked to see things change. But it's impossible to make a change when no one will give us a job or lease us an apartment or even see us as normal citizens of this city. When the simple fact that we are prodigies who *aren't* Renegades automatically makes us suspect."

"Makes us suspect, and makes us a target," said the man with the fungi. "Did you know only fifteen percent of the crimes in this city are committed by prodigies? But the Renegades put eighty percent of their task force on hunting down prodigy offenders, and all but ignore the rest. If they really cared about justice and protecting the weak, you'd think they'd give a bit more effort to the actual problem."

"In their eyes, we are the only real problem," said Narcissa. "We take the blame for everything that goes wrong in this city. All so the Renegades can go on pretending to be big and honorable. 'Look, we caught another prodigy, one who robbed a convenience store six years ago! Don't you feel safe now?' It's prejudice, every bit as much as the people who used to stone us for being demons."

"And now they've got this Agent N stuff," boomed a gruff voice. Nova jumped, but couldn't tell where it had come from.

"That's Megaphone," said Narcissa, gesturing toward a group of prodigies that were clustered together, including a man with a grizzly black beard who could not have been more than three feet tall.

"Small body," he said at her surprise, "big voice."

And it was big. Though he wasn't yelling, his voice echoed like a sonic boom through the enclosed space.

"You know about Agent N," said Nova.

"It's been all over the news," said a girl with slitted eyes and a line of reflective scales running down the back of her bald head. "Those three Renegades who lost their powers in a fight against Nightmare. We thought it was something you Anarchists had created—a new weapon to take down the Renegades—but Cyanide told us the truth."

Nova planted her hands on her hips. "They've been developing Agent N for years, intending to use it against prodigies who don't fall in line with their code. Any Renegade who thinks you're misusing your powers will be authorized to neutralize you on sight."

"Let's not fool ourselves," said Millie. "They won't need any new reasons to neutralize almost every person in this room. More than half of us had allegiances to various gangs during the Age of Anarchy, and as Narcissa said so succinctly—it hasn't been easy to cast ourselves in a new light these last ten years. Our past transgressions will be plenty of evidence for the Renegades that we are a threat to society. I half expect them to make a game of it—hunting down their enemies from the Age of Anarchy and getting rid of us, one by one."

Nova didn't respond. She didn't think that was the intention of the Council, but she knew it's what Frostbite and her team would have done once they had access to the serum. There would be others like them, more than willing to abuse this power. Regardless of the Council's intentions, Nova didn't trust them to defend the rights of prodigies who had once been gang members, or those who still had to fight and steal in order to make their way in an unforgiving world.

Her chest felt hollow as she met the gazes of those around her. She felt a heavy sympathy for this crowd of misfits, who could never be superheroes, but who didn't deserve to be called villains, either. What chance had they been given to live the lives they wanted? Under the Renegades' rule, they were still guilty. Still oppressed. Still a threat to be exterminated at the slightest misstep.

She could see their exhaustion, though it was coupled with resilience. They had survived until now, but they were done with simply surviving. They were ready to take matters into their own hands, and they believed she could help them. They believed the Anarchists could help them.

It would be war all over again. Heroes versus villains. A new struggle for dominance.

Nova had believed she was ready for this. They were finally at the precipice she'd been climbing toward all her life.

But it felt different now, staring into the uncertain future. What if the lines weren't so clearly drawn? What if she wasn't either a hero or a villain? What if she was both?

"So we're all here because we want things to change?" she said.

"And because, for the first time in ten years, we have a chance," said Leroy. "The Renegades are weaker now than at any time since the Battle for Gatlon. The people are losing faith in them. Their resources are spread too thin. They are trying to be too many things, but don't have the workforce or the infrastructure necessary to make good on their promises. This is a perfect time to strike."

Nova shuddered, wondering why his words felt so distant and impossible to her, even while the strangers in her midst were nodding fiercely in agreement. Yes, the Renegades' popularity had suffered lately, but they were still powerful. It would be naïve to think they weren't.

"What's your plan?" she said, turning to Narcissa. "You've got us all here. What now?"

Narcissa shrank a bit under the attention.

"Our plan," Leroy said for her, "was to get you back. Now that we've accomplished this goal, it's time to set our sights on the next one."

Nova laughed. "So there is no plan."

"These things don't happen overnight," said Millie.

"Besides," said Honey, "Ace was always our visionary before, and lately . . ." She gave Nova a pointed look, and her meaning was clear. Lately, Nova had been the new visionary of their small group.

Nova exhaled slowly. "I . . . might have an idea. Something I thought about a lot while I was in prison. Something that might get us all what we need and want. Freedom. Autonomy. Control over our own lives for once."

"Death to the Renegades?" said Honey, licking some of the honey from her lips.

Nova winced. She bit her tongue, unable to say the truth to this crowd of Rejects and Anarchists, who had been lied to and toyed with too many times.

But if she could make things go her way, then she would avoid another war entirely. She'd never imagined herself thinking it, but . . . if all went right, then the Renegades would be spared.

"I need more time to work things out," she said, avoiding Honey's and Leroy's gazes, "but for starters . . . we need to get Ace back. He's the real visionary, not me, and we're not moving forward without him."

It was almost indiscernible—*almost*. The ripple of fear and discomfort that coursed through the crowd.

Even villains were afraid of Ace Anarchy.

"We're really sorry that you've lost your leader," said Narcissa, "but Ace Anarchy isn't our concern. We need to do something about this Agent N. We need to find a way that we can start living our lives without being afraid all the time."

"We need to take down the Renegades!" someone yelled from the back.

Nova shook her head. "You risked everything to bring me here, and now I'm asking you to trust me. Ace Anarchy is our best hope for success."

"You say that," growled the star-eyed boy, "but you've had Ace Anarchy at your side for ten years, and none of us even knew about it. We thought he was dead. So what good has he done for anyone?"

"He's been sick," said Nova. "His helmet was taken from him during the Battle for Gatlon, and it weakened him. But we have the helmet back now . . ." She hesitated. "We *do* have the helmet, right?"

"Of course," said Leroy. "Phobia's been guarding it night and day."

She swallowed and pretended that this didn't bother her. Phobia was still an Anarchist, she reminded herself. She had never thought of him as a friend, but he was still her ally.

Even if he had killed Adrian's mom.

"Have no fear," rasped Phobia's sullen voice. Nova spun, startled to find him suddenly only a few feet away from her. The blade of his scythe was arced through Ace's helmet, hooked through the neck hole and jutting up through the eye socket. "To most prodigies, this helmet would be more burden than gift."

Nova wasn't quite sure how she felt about the helmet, which was perhaps her father's greatest achievement. She would not call the power that it wielded a burden, and yet there was a weighted dread that settled in her stomach as she started to reach for it. She took hold of the helmet and slid it off the blade. The metal was warm to the touch, still casting off that familiar glow as she cradled it in her hands.

"Ace would fight for any of us," she said. "He *did* fight for us. Everything he's ever done has been to make life better for prodigies. We can't leave him in that place. We can't let them execute him."

"It's impossible," someone muttered, though Nova couldn't tell who. It didn't matter. She could see the thought mirrored on every face surrounding her.

"It's not impossible," she insisted. "This morning, I was a prisoner in Cragmoor Penitentiary and had only three allies in the outside world." She gestured at Honey, Leroy, and Phobia. "And now here I am. Here we all are. If you're serious about wanting to change things, then this isn't up for debate. Ace has done more to further the cause of prodigies in this world than any human alive, and we're not going to abandon him. Besides, he's my uncle. He rescued me when I needed him. I'm going to rescue him now, or I'm going to die trying."

"Well, at least one of those scenarios seems likely," muttered Narcissa. "You'll definitely die trying to break into Cragmoor."

Nova glared, even as anticipation began to pulse through her veins. That familiar hum of adrenaline when she was making a plan, working through the logistics, figuring out what she was truly capable of. "We're not going to attack the prison. We're going to stop the execution."

A stout man who was old enough to be Nova's grandfather barked a laugh. "Well, jolly good, then! Tha'll be easier. No worries that the entire Renegade crew'll be about."

"You're right; there will be a lot of Renegades there," said Nova. "But the Renegades tend to get cocky when they're in big groups. They let their guard down. And while they might be expecting Nightmare to make an attempt to save Ace"—she glanced at Narcissa—"they won't be expecting all of us. But I need some time to think. And I'll need to go back to headquarters. There are a few things—"

"That's it?" said Narcissa. "We risk everything to get you out of prison and you're just going to rattle off some vague hopes about rescuing Ace Anarchy and risking our lives to do it? This is about more than Ace Anarchy, more than the Anarchists."

"I know it is," said Nova. "But I need time to figure this out. You'll have to trust me."

"We trust you," said Leroy. "You are the one who stole back Ace's helmet, from the Renegades' own vault, no less."

"Oh!" said Honey. "Speaking of things stolen from the Renegades, do you think you'll be needing this back?" She reached for her collar and pulled a black medallion from the bust of her dress. The Vitality Charm.

Nova felt a surge of apprehension as she scrutinized the design impressed into the black iron. Though it had protected her from Agent N, a part of her had hoped she would never have need of it again.

She said nothing, though, as she slipped the chain over her neck and tucked the charm beneath her shirt.

"Let's reconvene in a few hours," she said. "I'll need to know what each of you can do, to see if your abilities might be useful as I develop a plan."

"Your old fears have returned, little Nightmare," Phobia added, his voice low, but not low enough. "They are stronger now than ever before. A nearly petrifying fear of failing . . . *again*."

Nova peered into the bottomless pool of shadows beneath Phobia's hood. His attempts to psychoanalyze her usually filled her with irritation. It felt like a violation of her privacy, for him to be poking around in her head that way, searching for her deepest fears, uncovering her best-kept secrets.

But it didn't seem to matter so much this time. She was afraid to fail again. She was afraid to let everyone down—not just Ace and the Anarchists and this unexpected new group of allies, but also Adrian and the friends she'd made at the Renegades.

Yes, *friends*. The word was foreign and almost unbelievable, but she had faced the truth in that prison cell. The realization was too stark and painful to ignore. She had fallen in love with these people, who had taken her in and trusted her. And yet she betrayed them. To know that they would go on despising her for the rest of their lives left her feeling almost as hollowed out as the knowledge that Ace would never again look at her with beaming pride.

"Yeah, I am afraid that I'm going to fail again," she said, still peering into the nothingness of Phobia's face. "But one cannot be brave who has no fear."

CHAPTER TWENTY-FIVE

THERE HAD BEEN many times since Adrian and his dads first moved into the old mayor's mansion that Adrian had the nagging thought that it was far more space than the three of them needed. Not only because there was a formal parlor, formal dining room, and four guest rooms that had yet to welcome a single guest, but also because three grown men simply had no use for seven—count them—seven bathrooms.

Each one, of course, came equipped with a mirror. And that wasn't even considering the mirrors in closets or the one hung over the fireplace mantel in the parlor, and probably some he hadn't even thought of yet. It seemed reflections were everywhere he looked these days.

Adrian unscrewed the mirrored medicine cabinet from the wall of the third bathroom on the main floor, thinking for the umpteenth time that he hadn't given enough credit to Narcissa Cronin's power when he first met her at Cloven Cross Library. Sure, traveling through mirrors had seemed like a neat party trick, but now he was beginning to fully appreciate what a useful ability it could be.

There were mirrors *everywhere.*

It was almost like having a skeleton key to nearly any door in the world.

It drove him nuts every time he stopped to think about it. He had been in the same room with Nightmare that day at the library. She had been *right in front of him,* and he had been completely oblivious. It made him sick to think how she must have been laughing behind his back.

Realizing what a tedious job it was going to be to get rid of all the mirrors in the house, he'd been tempted to simply smash them to bits, or maybe just drape them with heavy cloths. But he didn't think his dads would be too happy coming home to a house full of glass shards, and he didn't know enough about Nightmare's mirror-walking ability to know if a heavy cloth would be enough to keep her out.

And so, they had to be taken down.

The final screw fell into his palm and he pried the cabinet from the wall. He hadn't bothered to remove the toiletries inside and he heard them sliding and crashing into one another as he carried it down the hall, down the steps, and into his basement bedroom. Past his bed and TV, past the desk where he had spent hours sketching in notebooks and, more recently, giving himself tattoos, and into the room that had once been deemed his art studio.

The room that had of late been converted into a living jungle.

He hadn't entered the room in the days since Nova's arrest. It held too many memories that were soured by his belief that Nova was his most loathed enemy. Memories of her head tucked against his shoulder, her face tranquil in sleep. Memories of her surprise when she saw the mural Adrian had painted on these walls, then watching her unspeakable awe as he brought the trees and vines and exotic flowers to life.

Since that night, the jungle had begun to fade, just as Turbo was. Adrian's power didn't include immortality. His creations would wilt and die, just like things in real life. Faster, actually, than things in real life. Now, when he entered this room, the one-time aromas of perfumed flowers had been replaced with the smell of decay and rot. The vibrant colors of the flowers faded to grays and browns, their silky petals drooping and papery crisp. The vines that hung from overhead tree branches became brittle to the touch, and a number of them broken, disintegrating on the mossy ground that was, itself, dying to reveal the plain concrete floor underneath.

Only the statue that stood at the far end of the room appeared untouched—but then, it had never been alive to begin with.

Adrian set the mirror against the wall with the others that he had already removed. He figured that if Nightmare did come through one of them, she'd be so confused by the dying flora that she'd think she took a wrong turn in mirrorland, or however that worked.

As an added precaution, he set up a couple of booby traps through-out the room that would alert him to an intruder—including a net that would fall down from the tree canopy and trap her inside. He really hoped she would set that one off. It would serve her right, he thought, remembering the bazooka-like gun she'd once used to trap him, as the Sentinel, inside a similar net.

Just thinking of their battle at the parade set his teeth on edge. Nightmare had embarrassed him enough times. Though he was happy—overjoyed, really—that Nova wasn't the villain after all, he was more frustrated than ever to know that the real Nightmare continued to be one step ahead of him.

"Okay," he muttered, surveying the mirrors and the traps he'd set. "Five down. Just thirteen more to go."

He was passing through the foyer when the creak of a floorboard overhead made him freeze.

Hot adrenaline rushed through his veins as he listened for any more signs of life in the old mansion, but there was only silence. Pulling his marker from his back pocket, he crept toward the staircase, his heartbeat suddenly the loudest thing in the house.

With a faint memory of his mom once scolding him for scribbling with his crayons on the wall of their apartment, he took his marker and started to draw a quick weapon on the white wainscoting. Not a gun—he'd always been a terrible shot. Instead, he drew what vaguely resembled a fireplace poker, with a vicious spike at each end. He exhaled as he pulled the weapon from the wall, clutching it in one hand and keeping his marker at the ready in the other. Hopefully it would keep him from having to resort to his Sentinel powers. The last thing he wanted to do was release a fireball inside his own house.

He started up the steps, knowing where to place his feet to prevent the stairs from creaking as he ascended. Pausing just shy of the landing, he scanned the hallway to the right, but all he could see were shadows and closed doors.

The double doors to his dads' room were parted, and unable to remember if they'd been open before, he slipped inside. There was a sweater thrown over the back of a chair. Some books and newspapers left on a nightstand. Knowing there was a full-length mirror in the walk-in closet, Adrian prepared himself to see his own reflection moving among the suits and boots and capes, but the sight still made him jump. He doubted he would ever look at a mirror the same way again.

Nothing seemed out of place.

He shut the closet door, then drew a small bell to hang around its door handle, so that if Nightmare came in through that mirror and tried to open the door, he would know immediately. He did the same on the door to the master bathroom, not yet having removed the mirrors above the double sinks, then stopped again to listen.

Silence.

He was beginning to think that maybe he'd only imagined the noise before when there was a thud from the hallway.

Gripping the poker, he raced out of the master suite and noticed the light spilling out from beneath the door to the office. He was sure it had been dark before.

Pulse racing, he inched toward the door and wrapped his hand around the knob.

He braced himself.

Then he threw the door open, weapon at the ready.

His attention landed on the large window behind the desk. The sash had been thrown open and the curtains were fluttering from the nighttime air. The sound of rain outside was suddenly deafening. With a curse, he crossed to the window, searching the lawn for signs of movement, scanning the side of the house for the shadow of a girl who was quite adept at scaling buildings.

Footsteps sounded behind him, barely heard over the downpour.

He spun around just as the figure, dressed in her signature black, darted into the hallway.

"Hey!"

Adrian chased after her. She ran into the master bedroom, slamming the door shut between them. Growling, he shoved it open, preparing to throw the weapon, javelin style, at the same time the tattoo on his right arm began to glow molten white, readying an energy beam to incapacitate her.

The bell chimed as Nightmare, a dozen steps ahead of him, yanked open the closet door. She held what appeared to be a bundle of files tucked under one arm. She didn't look back as she sprinted forward.

It took Adrian a split second to decide—energy beam or spear?

He could kill her. He could end her now.

The second passed. He lifted his right arm, fist squeezed tight, and aimed.

A piece of paper fluttered from her hold as she launched herself through the mirror at the back of the closet, in the same moment the beam of light blazed from the diode that had risen up from his flesh.

The beam struck the glass. It shattered, the impact sending shards flying across the carpet, into the clothes on the racks, some no doubt landing inside his dads' neatly organized shoes.

Adrian cursed and, for good measure, threw the poker, too. It hit the backing of the mirror, puncturing a hole through it and sticking there.

"Dammit, dammit, dammit," he muttered, letting the laser diode sink back into his skin as he ran both hands over his hair. Stomping into the closet, glad to be wearing shoes as bits of glass crunched beneath him, he wrapped his hand around the weapon, but then thought better of it. This would at least explain how the glass had broken.

Huffing, he stooped and picked up the piece of paper Nightmare had dropped, wondering what could have brought her snooping through their house again. He expected blueprints of headquarters or research findings on Agent N or a list of home addresses of all the Renegades currently active in the organization.

Just the thought of the mirror walker knowing where his friends lived made him shudder.

But when he flipped the paper over, he was surprised to see that it wasn't any of those things.

It was a drawing.

He squinted at the illustration, done in a combination of markers and crayon. It was one of his childhood conceptions of the monster who had, for years, haunted his nightmares. His mom had told him that one way to combat bad dreams was to draw them out—that doing so could teach your brain that they were only figments of your imagination, and nothing to be afraid of.

He had drawn the monster more times than he could count, and it had never made the nightmares any less real.

Crushing the drawing in his fist, he retraced his steps back to the office to see if he could figure out what else Nightmare had taken. Surely this drawing was a fluke—something she just happened to grab along with whatever prize she had really come for.

But all the drawers in the desk and filing cabinet were closed. The stacks of papers neat and tidy. Nothing pulled from the bookshelves.

Nothing, that is, except a single box that usually lived tucked away in the corner of the bottom shelf, but now sat on the carpet. Adrian knelt beside it and began rummaging through the papers that remained, all drawings from his childhood that his dads had cared enough to save.

Why would Nightmare care about these?

He reached the bottom of the box, and a thought struck him.

A terrible thought.

His palms grew sweaty as he flipped through the papers again, hoping he was mistaken. Hoping maybe they were kept somewhere else, that they'd never been in this box to begin with.

But no—they were gone.

Nightmare had taken his comics. The three issues of *Rebel Z* he'd made as a kid, about a boy who develops superpowers after a mad scientist tampers with him, and later uses those powers to transform himself into a powerful hero.

The Sentinel.

Adrian sat back on his heels, massaging his forehead. She *knew*. He couldn't begin to guess how she knew, but she would have evidence enough in the pages of those comics. Enough to try to blackmail him, or out his secret to the world.

In the midst of the dread that clawed its way into Adrian's thoughts, something else occurred to him.

Standing, he considered the open door to the office. She must have been hiding behind it. He must have passed right by her when he'd rushed to the window.

Close enough to touch.

His gaffe was so obvious in hindsight that thinking of his vulnerability made him slightly nauseous. In all the times he'd fought against Nightmare, never once could he recall her missing an opportunity to disarm her opponent, to get the upper hand.

And this time, she'd definitely had an opportunity to render him unconscious.

So then . . . why hadn't Nightmare taken it?

CHAPTER TWENTY-SIX

BEFORE SHE WAS arrested, Nova had felt like every time she stepped into Renegade Headquarters, she could be walking to her doom. Surely they had figured her out by now. Surely this time they would be waiting to put her in chains.

And so it was with the most peculiar lightness that she pushed past the revolving glass doors the day after she was released from Cragmoor Penitentiary. Somehow, the worst had happened. She was found out. She was arrested and sent to prison. Her secrets were revealed. And yet, she emerged unscathed.

Her lies felt more secure now than they ever had. With not only an alibi but a scapegoat—Narcissa Cronin, having assumed the role of her alter ego—Nova felt like the weight of paranoia and constant suspicion was lifted from her.

For the first time in a long while, she almost felt like she belonged at HQ. Like she had earned the right to be there.

"Insomnia!" yelled Sampson Cartwright, the non-prodigy greeter who ran the information desk. He waved as Nova strolled by. "Glad to have you back!"

She smiled and returned the wave a little self-consciously, though she knew that Sampson was one of the most genuine people on the staff. It warmed her to think that maybe some people here, other than Adrian and the team, might actually have missed her.

She was met with a mix of emotions on the faces of Renegades and staff as she made her way to the elevators. Some watched her with open suspicion, not ready to believe in her innocence. Others sent her a look that was somewhere between a friendly grin and a grimace, laced with guilt for her false arrest. A few patrol units she barely knew offered her enthusiastic high fives. Others warily avoided making eye contact.

Nova was nearly to the elevators when she heard her name being shouted across the lobby. She turned to see Ruby bounding toward her.

"I'm so sorry!" Ruby yelled, yanking Nova into an embrace. "I'm so, so, so, so sorry!" Pulling back, she gripped Nova's shoulders, and Nova couldn't tell if her eyes were glossy from unshed tears or mere jubilation. "I'm so incredibly happy you're not Nightmare, but I also feel like a terrible human being for having believed otherwise. We should have at least let you explain before . . . Well, I'm just really sorry."

"It's okay," said Nova. And she meant it. Ruby had believed that she was the notorious villain who once fought against them on the rooftops over the parade. She couldn't exactly be offended. "It's all in the past. I'm back now."

"And we are overjoyed," said Oscar, appearing beside them and holding up a fist, which Nova happily bumped. "I've got to admit,

I've grown rather fond of you and your no-nonsense, badass ways. And I'm really sorry, too, by the way."

"No more apologies. It's fine. Anyone would have done the same in your position."

Nova's attention caught on the third member of their group. Though Danna had followed Ruby and Oscar, she stayed back a few steps, her arms crossed, her jaw set.

Clearly not about to apologize.

Nova had prepared herself for this, though. Of everyone she would have to persuade of her innocence, she knew Danna would be among the most difficult. Her accusation had landed Nova in jail in the first place. Nova still wasn't sure what Danna had seen; she knew only that her testimony must have been shaky enough to allow for doubt once Narcissa showed up in Nightmare's mask, helmet in hand.

And so, despite Danna's cool demeanor, Nova beamed at her, as wide and chipper as she could. "Danna, we were so worried about you. Being stuck in swarm mode for that long . . . I know it must have taken a toll on you, but I'm really glad to see you're okay."

Danna's expression thawed . . . but only a little, and only on the surface. The look in her eyes remained speculative. "Thanks. I'm glad there aren't any hard feelings."

"None at all. I'm still not sure I understand how Nightmare managed to frame me like that, but the way I see it, you were as much a victim as I was. I just hope we can work together to bring her down, for real this time."

Something flickered across Danna's face, and though Nova couldn't be sure, she thought it might be a hint of uncertainty. An ongoing question. Could she really have been wrong about Nova after all?

Whatever she saw there, it would be left uninterpreted, as Oscar thumped his cane on the tile floor. "Hear, hear to that! We are going to *destroy* Nightmare. But first . . ." He grinned at Ruby, and in unison they both shouted, "Pizza!"

"You have to come with us," said Oscar. "It's a celebratory yay-our-newest-recruit-isn't-a-murderous-villain-after-all meal."

Nova's gut tightened at the insult. "Actually, I—"

"Don't worry, Adrian will be there, too," said Ruby, winking impishly as she took Nova's elbow. "He was going to visit Max for a bit and then meet us there."

At the mention of Max, Nova's thoughts catapulted over themselves. Max. *Max.* She'd been so bewildered when she'd been released from the prison, so full of disbelief and so eager to find a way to ensure Ace's freedom, too, that she'd completely forgotten about Max.

"How is he?" she said, refusing to budge when Ruby tried to lead her toward the exit. "Last I heard he was recovering, but—"

"Oh, you don't know!" bubbled Ruby. "He's out of the coma and doing great! In fact, Adrian had the brilliant idea to let him stay—"

"*In the hospital*," Danna practically shouted, startling them all. "For a little while longer. To make sure he has a full recovery before they move him anywhere else." She shot a glare at Ruby and Oscar, one that wasn't particularly subtle.

"Um . . . okay . . . ," said Ruby, cocking her head at Danna.

"And they're rebuilding the quarantine," Danna added, jutting her thumb toward the busy construction zone at the far end of the lobby. "But they're going to make it nicer, bigger . . . make sure he's extra comfortable this time."

Nova's mouth went dry as she took in the glass walls that were waiting to be finished on the mezzanine. "I didn't think they would rebuild the quarantine."

"Yeah, well, Max is safer here," Danna said. "You know. From all the people who would hurt him. Like Nightmare and the Anarchists."

Oscar cleared his throat. "Yeah, so, there's a basket of garlic bread sticks calling my name from three blocks away . . . Are we going?"

"You guys go ahead," said Nova.

"Oh, Nova, no!" said Ruby. "You have to come! I'm sure they'll give you the day off after what you've been through."

"Next time, I promise," Nova insisted. Extricating her arm from Ruby's grip, she walked backward, waving good-bye. "Have fun. Tell Adrian I said hi."

"He's going to be devastated!" Oscar called after her. "If his heartbroken tears fall on my chicken pesto deluxe, I'm blaming you! I don't like salty pizza!"

"Noted," said Nova, offering him a salute.

Her three teammates sulked grumpily toward the main entrance. Nova started to turn around when she crashed into an unexpected wall. Or—a chest that felt like a wall.

She tilted her head back to be met with the rosy cheeks and pearly smile of Captain Chromium.

"Oops, sorry, Nova."

"Uh . . . hi," she stammered, not sure what she should call him. Captain Chromium or just Captain? Adrian's dad? Mr. Everhart?

She was saved from making a decision when Hugh clasped her right hand and gave it a solid handshake. "I asked Sampson to let me know when you came in. I wanted to be one of the first to welcome you back to the team."

"Oh. Thanks."

"And," he said, releasing both her hand and the dazzling grin. His brow creased with regret. "I wanted to offer you a formal apology for this abysmal misunderstanding. I'm ashamed to think how we treated you, as one of our own, when your loyalty and dedication has been so unwavering. It's just . . ." He shook his head. "All this turmoil that's been going on lately, you know? The parade, Cosmopolis Park, the attack on headquarters, Ace Anarchy . . . sometimes I feel like we're jumping through hoops set on fire, and every one of them is a little bit smaller. If we don't keep ahead of all the threats and dangers, then one of these days, the whole thing will go up in flames."

Nova narrowed her eyes, not entirely sure this was a good analogy, and also wondering whether the Captain was aware of the insensitivity of the statement, given what had become of the house on Wallowridge.

But no—she could tell he was oblivious.

And so she chuckled understandingly. "Well, good thing you're invincible, at least."

"Yeah," he said, with a small shrug. "I might be, but there are people I care about that don't have that luxury, and I'm just doing what I can to protect them. I hope you understand that we did what we had to do, given the circumstances."

The circumstances, she thought. Those circumstances being that they had been prepared to execute her, without so much as a proper trial. Because they were the Council, and their word was law. Because they were Renegades, and the Renegades could be judge, jury, and executioner, if that's what they felt was required for the protection of the people. The *normal* people. Not villains. Not prodigies who could be dangerous. Protection of their rights didn't matter.

But Nova didn't say any of that. She just kept smiling, jaw clenched. "Of course."

"Good. Because you are a part of the Renegade family now, and it's important to me and all the Council that everyone here feels like they're being treated fairly. That they are a part of this team."

Suddenly, it became clear to Nova that this wasn't just an apology.

Hugh Everhart was worried. Given the drama with Genissa Clark, which continued to shake their sterling reputation, he was afraid that Nova, too, would go to the media and begin exposing the mistreatment within their ranks.

He was trying to head her off at the pass.

In that moment, Nova felt almost giddy to realize she had stolen another small piece of power away from the Council. They had built their organization on a shaky foundation, and she could put one more fatal crack into it.

Lucky for Captain Chromium and the Council, she wasn't planning to go to the media with her story of unjust imprisonment. She had other plans for the future.

But that didn't mean she couldn't use this conversation to her advantage. What if she could make the change she needed right here, right now?

"I don't blame you and the Council for what happened," she said. "You were given information and you had to act on it. I understand why you did what you did."

Before Hugh Everhart could appear too relieved, Nova added, "But I was surprised by the whole execution thing."

His gaze darted away. "Yes . . . it's unfortunate that we . . . Well, I hate to think what you went through. But I am so glad it's all worked out."

"Yes," she said slowly, "it worked out for me, thankfully. But I have to admit that I'd always wanted to believe the Renegades were, well, above capital punishment. To end someone's life, giving them no possible chance for restitution, and to do it without even offering a fair trial, it seems—how do I say this?—a little villainous."

To her surprise, the Captain chuckled, as if the idea of the Council doing something even remotely villainous was too absurd to consider. "To be fair, we did believe you were Nightmare, and Nightmare *did* try to kill me."

She bristled. "I'm aware of that, but . . . don't you think she would at least deserve another chance?"

His eyebrows shot up.

Realizing that she was edging too close to an unspoken hope, she immediately withdrew. "Or, maybe not Nightmare, specifically. But think about it. I was in that prison—wrongfully, yes—but it still gave me time to think about my life and my choices, and to decide that, if I ever got out of there, I would do things differently. The Renegades have to be willing to look beyond the mistakes of the past and understand that people can change. And I'm not just talking about the execution, either. I know you'll never forgive Ace Anarchy for what he did, and maybe you'll never forgive Nightmare, either, but there are dozens of prodigies on that island, some who have been there for more than a decade. And yet—we have no systems in place to see if they really are as dangerous as we think they are. To see if they deserve the punishment they're receiving. Maybe some of them want to become useful citizens in this world; maybe some of them deserve that. But you want to strip their powers from them, without even giving them a chance to explain why they did the things they did or how they've changed in the years since. Many of them are still being persecuted for crimes they committed in the Age of Anarchy . . . I mean, didn't you do anything during that time that you're not proud of?"

Though the Captain seemed confused by most of her speech, at this, an understanding dawned on his features. "We did what we had to do to stop the villain gangs, to bring order and peace. We would do it again if we had to."

"Even if that meant doing things that you wouldn't allow today as part of the Code Authority?"

His lips pinched, and she knew he couldn't deny it.

"Maybe some of those prisoners did things that were . . . justified, in some way. Maybe they stole things because there were no jobs back then. Maybe they fought against authority because authority abused and ostracized people like them. Maybe they would choose differently now, if we only gave them a chance."

"Nova . . . ," he began, and before another word was uttered, Nova felt her frustration rise, knowing what he was going to say. "I can tell you're passionate about this, but . . . you have to understand that the people in that prison aren't like you. You were innocent. You shouldn't have been there in the first place. While *they* are criminals and villains, practically savages some of them."

"How do you know? How many of them have you talked to recently? Or for that matter, how many of them ever received a fair trial?"

He sighed and glanced around. Nova realized that, standing not far from the elevator bank, they'd begun to draw a crowd. Renegades loitering nearby, pretending to be engrossed in the daily newspaper or something on their wristbands.

"What are you suggesting?" he said, his voice lowered. "That we postpone the Agent N reveal until we can . . . what, interview them? Or should we devote our resources to gathering evidence from ten years ago, all so we can prove what we already know? They are villains."

"I'm not a villain," Nova said, almost believing it herself. "But that wasn't going to stop you from executing me."

Hugh flinched.

"And no," she continued, "I'm not suggesting you postpone the reveal for a while, I'm suggesting you postpone it indefinitely. In fact, I think you should destroy Agent N."

He took a surprised step back.

"All of it," she said more forcefully. "Along with any possibility that it could ever be re-created."

Hugh's astonishment faded into understanding. "If this is about what happened to Frostbite and her team, it's important for everyone to know that we are working to ensure the safety of all Renegades—"

"That's not what I'm talking about," said Nova. "This isn't about the patrol units or figuring out how to defend ourselves more efficiently or any of that. The world doesn't revolve around the Renegades!" She spread her fingers wide, surprised at how important this suddenly seemed. She hadn't come to headquarters expecting to have this conversation, but these thoughts had been tumbling and growing inside her mind from the moment Agent N had first been shown to her. From the moment she'd watched it change Winston Pratt forever. From the moment the implications of such a weapon had become clear. "Isn't it our responsibility to bridge the gaps between people? To recognize that we all have to live in this world together? We need to start seeing other prodigies not as villains, but as . . . well, as other human beings, who maybe aren't so different from us after all. I want to believe that we can close this divide between us, but . . . Agent N isn't the answer."

Hugh was silent for a long time. Longer than Nova had ever heard him be silent, she realized as she tried to read his inscrutable thoughts.

"I know this is coming from a place of good intentions," he finally said, his voice having taken on a new edge. "I don't expect you to understand the challenges facing our world or the difficult decisions we've had to make, but I can assure you that none of our decisions have been made lightly."

"I know that, but—"

"Everything the Council has done these past years has been in service to the people of this world who need our help, for protection and for justice. I'm afraid this isn't up for debate, Nova. Our decision regarding Agent N, and the fate of those villains, has already been decided. And our decision is final."

CHAPTER TWENTY-SEVEN

Normally, it was easy for Nova to shake off the disappointment she so often felt in the Renegades and the Council. They had disappointed her so many times, beginning when she was just six years old, a child full of conviction that the Renegades would come. A child who had been wrong.

It shouldn't have been any different this time. She and the Renegades would never share the same principles. Her faith in the Council would never be restored.

She felt foolish to have thought, even for a moment, that things could be different.

She felt extra foolish for the sting of rejection that followed her into the elevator and up to the artifacts warehouse. She didn't have time to dwell on Captain Chromium's decision, even if she knew he was wrong. She shouldn't have let herself care so much.

If anyone was going to help the prodigies of this world—the prodigies who didn't fit into a perfect mold of what a superhero should be—it wasn't going to be the Renegade Council.

She stepped out of the elevators into a reception space that was unchanged since she'd been gone—two desks, one messy, one stark. A clipboard with a form for tracking equipment rentals from the vault.

Trying to clear her thoughts, she sat down and searched the database for the Hollow Glass. According to the records, it had not been rented out to a Renegade in years, and was currently available in the vault.

She hoped it was a good sign.

Changing the parameters, she searched for *star* next. Then *jewel*, *gem*, and *bracelet*. Each term called up a substantial list of possibilities, but judging from the descriptions, none of them were *her* bracelet.

She wasn't particularly surprised, but frustrated all the same.

After a moment's consideration, she closed the artifacts database and instead pulled up the Renegade directory. Magpie was easy to find.

```
Margaret White. Alias: Magpie. Ability: Asset
     perception, subcategory: telekinesis.
```

"Asset perception," Nova muttered. She guessed that was Renegade speak for "someone who can locate valuable things," which seemed to be the gist of Magpie's ability, as far as she could tell.

She jumped to the residence information and frowned.

```
Current residence: Unknown
Previous residence: Gatlon City Prodigy
              Children's Home
```

She was familiar enough with the institution, which was supposed to be an orphanage, though had also become a dumping ground for kids abandoned by families who wanted nothing to do with their superpowered offspring.

An addendum at the bottom of her profile went on to list a series of petty crimes—mostly small thefts and pickpocketing—for which Magpie had repeatedly received no punishment, it seemed, beyond a stern talking-to.

None of it was at all helpful in getting Nova her bracelet back.

She was scowling at the screen, drumming her fingers against her cheek, when the elevator chimed and Callum arrived. Already smiling, because he was *always* smiling. And in the second that passed before he noticed her, Nova braced herself to see that smile fall. She knew he had suspected that she was Nightmare after he had tried to stop her from stealing the helmet. She wouldn't have been surprised if he, like Danna, maintained that air of suspicion. And for reasons she couldn't quite explain, Callum's opinion of her meant—well, a lot. Maybe because he was the sort of person who was always willing to give the benefit of the doubt. He saw the good in everyone, regardless of whether they deserved it.

She wanted him to see the good in her.

Spotting her, Callum froze, one foot still in the elevator.

Nova, too, went still.

Then—

"Insomnia! You're back!" He bolted forward and swung himself around the end of the desk. Before Nova fully realized what was happening, he had pulled her out of the rolling chair and enveloped her in a strangling embrace, one that she might have thought was an attack if she hadn't known Callum so well.

"I didn't want to believe it," he said, pulling away. "I mean, I *did* believe it, because—did you know you and Nightmare are almost exactly the same height?" He placed one hand about head level with

Nova. "Uncanny, but not a reason to assume the worst of someone. I'm sorry. But in my defense"—he gave her a mischievous look—"a part of me thought it would actually be kind of cool to be working side by side with an Anarchist. I mean—the difference in perspective, right? What are the odds of that, really? Anyway. I'm glad you're back. I've come to think of you as, like, my artifacts-obsessed kindred spirit."

She laughed. Not only in relief that Callum didn't despise her, but also at the idea that she was as obsessed over the objects in the vault as he was. She was relatively sure that no one could be as obsessed as he was. "Thanks," she said. "I'm ready to get back to work and put all this behind me."

"Great plan!" He clapped his hands. "Let's return to our previously scheduled awesome lives." He grabbed a clipboard from the desk. "It's been slow around here, what with everyone focusing on rebuilding the lobby and the upcoming Agent N announcement. Do you want to take the desk for a bit, or would you rather handle the restocking? It's not much . . . just seven or eight items, if I remember right."

"I can restock. I don't really feel like sitting behind a desk right now. I did plenty of sitting around at Cragmoor."

"Aw, man, I bet that was awful," said Callum, his expression going distant. The moment of solemnity was short-lived, and then he was grinning again. "But that place has some wicked history. Kind of cool that you got to see it up and close and personal, right? If those walls could talk." He shook his head. "I'd love to visit it someday. Fascinating."

Chuckling, Nova took the clipboard from him. "No, you really wouldn't."

She started to head toward the vault, but paused. "Hey, Callum?

You wouldn't happen to know where I could find Magpie, would you?"

"That troublemaker?" He pondered the question. "Well. I guess I'd check to see if the cleanup crews have been called out for anything today. Barring that . . . maybe the lounges?"

Nova nodded. "Thanks, I'll give that a shot."

She passed through the filing room, half expecting to see Tina—or Snapshot, the official keeper of the vault—but the room was empty. Stepping into the enormous warehouse, full of row upon row of towering shelving units, each stocked with famous, and some not-so-famous, prodigy-related artifacts, Nova exhaled a long, slow breath.

Squaring her shoulders, she grabbed the cart containing a handful of recently cleaned objects, set the clipboard on top of it, and started pushing it down the main aisle. She returned the first two objects to their places among the collection—the Wandering Map and Tarot's fortune-making deck of cards—but as she made her way to the back armory for the next two items, she took a detour through the section of prodigy-made tools and weaponry.

She spotted Turmoil's Sound Deadener sitting on its shelf and recalled renting it out to Genissa Clark what felt like ages ago, though she'd never found out what Frostbite wanted it for.

Not far from the Deadener was the spot where Fatalia's mist-missiles had been. The label remained on the shelf, but the missiles themselves were gone. Nova had taken them when she and Leroy were converting the stolen samples of Agent N into a chemical weapon, and with some minor tweaking, the missiles had provided the exact casing they'd needed. Nova had used two in her fight against Genissa Clark and her team. The remaining four had been stowed away with Leroy's stuff at the house, and were now stored safely beneath Dave's Pawnshop.

On the other side of the Sound Deadener was the object Nova had come for. She felt some of the tension leave her body at the sight of it. After Adrian had told her that all mirrors were being systematically removed from headquarters to prevent any more break-ins from the mirror walker, she'd worried that this, too, would have been moved to a more secure location.

It seemed the Renegades had neglected to inventory their warehouse of powerful artifacts. Though to be fair, the object almost didn't even resemble a mirror. Nova picked it off the shelf—a large oval surface, as long as her arm, was framed in simple pewter, making the whole thing unexpectedly heavy for its size. Tilting it up, Nova peered into her reflection. The surface was dark and distorted, so that her face appeared like a phantom of herself.

The Hollow Glass, reported to reflect the shape of one's soul when peered into under the light of an equinox moon.

Whatever that meant.

Nova had a much more mundane use in mind for it.

It wasn't as big as a dressing room mirror, or the large mirror she had once seen Narcissa walk through at the library, but Narcissa had a small frame and lithe limbs (though she was at least three inches taller than Nova herself, which would surprise Callum if he ever crossed paths with her impostor).

She thought it would be big enough.

It would have to be big enough.

Wondering if this could be her last act of subterfuge while wearing the guise of a Renegade, Nova slipped the mirror onto the bottom shelf of the cart and wheeled it back toward the front.

◇◇◆◇◇

Less than an hour later, Nova tracked Magpie down at a nearby construction site. She'd learned, talking to a few folks in the HQ call center, that on days when there were no crime scenes to investigate, the cleanup crews were often sent to local community rebuilding projects. Though Gatlon City had changed significantly in the past ten years, it still maintained scars from the Age of Anarchy, with plenty of neighborhoods suffering from run-down buildings that were as unsafe as they were unattractive, half-demolished structures, city parks left overgrown and untended, and on and on. Today's project was an abandoned school that the Renegades had hopes of renovating into a community recreation center.

Nova couldn't help wondering, as she approached the building with its pile of discarded rubble outside and broken windows and missing roof tiles, why such a job had fallen into the hands of the Renegades. Weren't there civilian tradesmen who could use the work? Carpenters who could frame walls and install windows just as well as a prodigy could?

Ducking past the line of orange safety cones, Nova stepped into the overhang of the building. Seeing her gray-and-red uniform, most of the workers ignored her, going about their business.

It only took a few minutes to find Magpie in a back room. She was sifting through a pile of debris, using her limited telekinetic powers to separate anything that could be deemed reusable, from an intact light fixture to a tangle of copper wiring.

She looked immensely bored.

Until she glanced up and spotted Nova. She started and the copper wiring tumbled back into the rubble.

Then she was sneering, which was exactly what Nova had expected.

Callum, always cheerful. Magpie, always cantankerous.

"You have something that belongs to me," said Nova, crossing the room. She held out her hand. "I'd like it back."

Magpie stepped away, and made the subtlest of movements—one hand briefly pressing against the side cargo pocket of her pants. She covered it up quickly, though, by fisting her hands on her hips. "I don't know what you're talking about."

Nova raised an eyebrow and considered putting the girl to sleep and moving on with her day. She really didn't have time for this. But that, she knew, could come with all sorts of negative consequences.

Instead, she exhaled through her nostrils and said, "My bracelet. Now."

"I don't have your junky bracelet," said Magpie, which was about the most incriminating thing she could have said, given that she'd tried to steal the bracelet once already, and had practically drooled over the star when she'd seen it at the gala. They both knew Magpie didn't think it was *junky*.

"I know Adrian gave it to you," said Nova. "You were supposed to hand it over to Artifacts, but I just checked, and it's not there."

Magpie shrugged and changed positions, tightly crossing her arms. "Maybe Callum forgot to record it."

Nova ground her teeth until her jaw started to ache.

Magpie held her glare, unflinching.

"Fine," Nova finally said. "I guess I'll check again."

"You do that." Magpie relaxed, just a bit, which is when Nova lunged for her.

She grabbed Magpie's arm and spun her around, twisting the arm up behind her back. Magpie cried out—more in surprise than pain, though Nova wasn't trying to be particularly gentle. "Let me go!"

Ignoring her struggles, Nova plunged her hand into the pocket

Magpie had indicated earlier. Her fist closed around a couple of loose objects. She shoved Magpie away and opened her palm.

She could have danced with elation to see her bracelet again, undamaged, the star as bright as ever.

The second object in her palm was a little more unconventional. She would expect the little crook to carry around coins or swiped jewelry or even something useful, like lockpicking tools, but not . . .

"Is this a bullet?" said Nova, holding it up between pinched fingers. It was heavy for its size, its once-silver sheen dulled from time.

"Give it back!" Magpie yelled, her face flushed. She jumped for the bullet, but Nova easily swung it out of her reach.

"Why on earth do you have——"

Magpie spread her fingers. The bullet was torn from Nova's grip and sent soaring into her palm. She wrapped it in a tight fist, clutching it to her chest. "None of your business!" she spat, face full of venom.

Nova snorted. "And you tried to call *my* bracelet junky? When you carry around a——"

"It's not junk!" Magpie screeched. She was really worked up now, her face flushed red, her small hands clenched and shaking. "This bullet gave me my powers! Without it, I . . . I wouldn't . . ." She released a frustrated growl, before repeating, "It's none of your business!"

Nova cocked her head to the side. "A bullet gave you your powers?"

Before Magpie could respond, someone knocked at the door that had been left open. They both jumped to see the cleanup supervisor watching them with concern. "Everything okay in here?"

Nova glared at Magpie. Neither of them spoke for a long moment.

Finally, Nova huffed and began securing her bracelet to her wrist, using the same latch that Adrian had once drawn for her. "Yep," she said, breezing past Magpie, who flinched away so their shoulders wouldn't touch. "Everything is just as it's supposed to be."

CHAPTER TWENTY-EIGHT

"**S**o . . . NIGHTMARE SNEAKED into the house and stole some comic books?" said Max, his expression more than a little skeptical.

"My *Rebel Z* comics," Adrian clarified. "I drew them when I was about your age."

"I don't remember you drawing any comics."

"I never showed them to you. Don't worry, you didn't miss much. And I only made three issues."

Since Max hadn't been able to venture out into the world, Adrian had made it a priority as the kid's big brother to bring the world to him as much as possible. That responsibility included supplying Max with plenty of popular movies, books, and video games, along with Adrian's personal favorite, comics. Max had pretty much learned to read on Adrian's comics collection, but Adrian had never felt that *Rebel Z* was good enough to be shared with anyone.

"Why did you stop drawing them?"

Adrian picked up a stray soccer ball that had rolled against Ruby's dresser. "I don't know. I got to the part where the main character transformed himself into the badass superhero and . . . just started to lose interest. I hadn't really thought past that in terms of the storyline, and it started to feel like actual work." He chucked the ball against the wall, where it bounced back and landed squarely in a clothes hamper.

He and Max were both sitting on the floor of the small bedroom, and it felt weird to be there, knowing this was supposed to be Ruby's space—and it *was* Ruby's space, at least on this side of the room, where there were *Super Scouts* graphic novels on the shelf beneath the window, a hand-painted dartboard behind the door, and a poster of sarcastic emoticons beside the bed. The opposite side of the room, with the bunk beds and bins full of action figures, obviously belonged to the twins.

The room was supposed to be Max's now, too, but he hadn't brought any belongings with him—no favorite books, no witty artwork, nothing to suggest he was the new resident in the space that smelled of popcorn and Ruby's strawberry-scented shampoo. He wondered how long it would take for Max to establish a home here and hoped he wouldn't ever find out. He wanted a permanent home for Max, and as grateful as he was to the Tucker family for welcoming the kid with open arms, he knew that this wasn't where he really belonged.

"The thing is," said Adrian, leaning his head against the bed's quilt, "those comics were the inspiration for the Sentinel. The character pretty much *becomes* the Sentinel by that third issue, and I modeled my armor off what I drew back then."

"And you think that's why Nightmare wanted them? To blackmail you or something?"

"Maybe. Or just to have the evidence to tell the world who I am."

Max frowned, apparently unconvinced. "But how did she know about them in the first place? How many people did you show that comic to?"

"Not many. I mean, Dad and Pops have seen them, but it's been so long, I don't think they remember them all that well. And . . ." He trailed off, considering. He had no memory of showing the comics to anyone else. "I think that's it."

"What about Ruby or the rest of the team?"

"No, I never showed it to them. I hadn't looked at those comics in years. I have no idea how Nightmare knew about them."

"You never showed them to Nova?" said Max, lining up a collection of small figurines on the carpet.

"No. I would definitely remember showing them to Nova."

Max hummed, but Adrian couldn't interpret the sound.

"What?"

"I don't know," said Max, adjusting one of the toys to stand straighter. "You never mentioned them to her?"

Adrian opened his mouth, but hesitated. In fact, his dads had said something about *Rebel Z* that time Nova had joined them for dinner, but . . . it had been just a random comment, nothing that would lead someone to be interested in the comics, much less suspect they held the identity of the Sentinel within their pages.

Besides . . .

"Nova's not Nightmare."

"I know," said Max, but his tone said otherwise.

"Max, she's *not*. She was in prison when—"

"The Librarian's granddaughter showed up in the department store, and she had the helmet, yeah, yeah, yeah." Max flicked one of the figures in the head, sending it toppling onto the carpet, before meeting Adrian's eye. "But it doesn't really make sense."

"It makes perfect sense," Adrian insisted. "I've spent a lot of time thinking about it, and with all the mirrors and her access to—"

"Not that. It doesn't make sense why she would help *me*." Max swiped his hand across the toys, knocking them over in one fell swoop, so that he could start all over again. This time arranging them as opposing army lines preparing to face off in battle. Heroes on one side, villains on the other. "I've never met the Librarian's granddaughter. Why would she risk herself to help me like she did?"

Adrian pondered this, watching as the figures were slowly pitted against one another. "Maybe she had a connection to the Roaches. Maybe she knew your biological parents or something."

Max scoffed. "The parents who tried to kill me? In that case, you'd think she'd be more than willing to finish the job. And also, it doesn't explain how I ended up with her power. If she really did steal the Vitality Charm, then she was protected from me—fine. But then how did I put that nurse to sleep?"

"Well . . . again, maybe you had some interaction with her when you were a baby. Her grandfather probably sold arms to the Roaches, so you could have come in contact with her."

Max shook his head. "If I'd been able to put people to sleep my whole life, I think I would have known about it."

"Maybe not, though," said Adrian. "You haven't exactly had a lot of human contact."

Max grunted. "I would have known."

Adrian looked away. He didn't want to doubt Max, but . . . he knew there had to be some explanation, some piece to the puzzle they didn't have.

Because Nova wasn't Nightmare. Nova was innocent.

"Anyway," he said, studying the spot over the dresser where a mirror had recently hung, its silhouette crisply outlined by the faded paint color around it. "I hope it wasn't too much trouble to have all the mirrors taken down. I'm sure Nightmare still has the Vitality Charm, which makes you vulnerable until we can find her and get it back."

"The Tuckers didn't seem to mind about the mirrors. They're pretty easygoing about stuff. Did I tell you that Turbo got into Mrs. Tucker's desk and shredded apart a bunch of her old photos and postcards? She tried to pass it off as no big deal, but I felt horrible."

Adrian grimaced. "Well, it's not your fault. I'm the one who created him."

"I know. Maybe next time you can make, like, a sloth. Or a platypus."

Laughing, Adrian glanced around the bedroom, which was about 50 percent toys, 40 percent dirty clothes, and 10 percent bedding. He wondered how Max or the twins ever managed to find anything, but he figured he'd probably been just as messy at their age. No wonder his dads never dared venture into his basement unless they absolutely had to. "Where is Turbo, anyway?"

Pressing his lips, Max pointed to the top drawer of the dresser, which was pulled open a few inches. "Sleeping."

Adrian stood and peered inside. The creature was curled up on top of a wad of T-shirts. Adrian slipped his hand inside and scooped Turbo into his palm, then slid down next to Max again. They both spent a moment watching the little dinosaur, who had not stirred at Adrian's touch. That was unusual in itself. Plus, his coloring was off—more ash-gray than before—and his breaths so shallow Adrian almost couldn't feel them against his skin.

"He doesn't look so good," Adrian murmured.

"I know," said Max. "It's been like that since yesterday. I tried to feed him last night and all he ate was two little bacon crumbles. He usually loves bacon." He gently took Turbo out of Adrian's hand. "I knew it would happen eventually. But . . . I'm gonna miss him."

"I can draw you another one?"

Max shook his head. "Don't do that. He's irreplaceable."

Adrian didn't argue. He knew the feeling.

Cradling Turbo in one palm, Max returned his focus to the arranged battle scene, appraising the figures like a warlord preparing his strategy. But when he looked up at Adrian, there was stark worry in his face. "About Nightmare and the mirrors . . ."

"Yeah?"

"I'm putting the Tuckers in danger by being here, aren't I?"

There was no point in denying it. Max's presence would always come with heightened danger. Instead, Adrian said, "You would have been putting the hospital staff in danger, too."

"But I could go back to headquarters."

"You're not going back to headquarters."

"But . . . wouldn't I be safer there, too? At least until you find Nightmare?"

Adrian drew his knees closer, draping his arms around them. "Do you want to go back?"

It took Max a long moment to answer. "I like living here, but . . . I don't want to hurt anyone else."

A sharp pain jabbed Adrian's chest. He knew Max carried a lot of guilt over the superpowers he'd stolen in his short lifetime, and he knew no amount of justifying it would make the kid feel any better. It wasn't his fault, he couldn't have helped it, and besides—he'd stopped Ace Anarchy, which was worth a lot more than a few powers stolen from time to time.

As if reading his thoughts, Max added, "I've been having night-mares about Ace Anarchy." He picked up one of the action figures, a muscled, gray-clad man in a cape and helmet that might have been loosely modeled after the infamous villain. "I keep dreaming that he comes after me, but this time, instead of him getting weaker when he gets close to me, it's the opposite. I get weaker, while he gets stronger and stronger."

"Just dreams," said Adrian. Reaching forward, he plucked the doll from Max's hand and held it up. "I met Ace Anarchy, remember? He doesn't look anything like this. He's not that scary anymore, just a frail, cranky old man. And, in a few days—"

"He'll be dead," Max murmured.

Adrian tossed the figure into the middle of the battle. It landed facedown in the carpet.

Defeated.

Max stared at it a long moment, then picked it up and set it back into the line of combatants. "So," he said, his tone more upbeat, though Adrian sensed some strain. "What are you going to do about the missing comics?"

"I'm not sure. Maybe it's time I come clean, though. Tell every-one the truth."

Max turned to him, surprised. "Really?"

"I don't know. I don't feel like I'm ready, but it also makes me sick to my stomach to think of Nightmare holding this secret over me. Whatever she's planning, if I outed myself first, it would take away her ammunition. And besides, with everyone so focused on Ace Anarchy and the Agent N publicity and Genissa Clark's threats and now the ongoing search for Nightmare and the rest of the Anarchists . . . maybe the whole Sentinel thing won't seem like such a big deal? It could kind of blow over, you know?"

Max's cheeks twitched with a stifled laugh. "Sure. The vigilante who's been embarrassing the Renegades for months and defying the Code Authority every few minutes turns out to be none other than Adrian Everhart himself." He nodded sagely. "That will hardly cause a stir."

"Thanks for the encouragement."

Max's crooked grin returned, for real this time. "On the bright side . . . at least no one thinks your girlfriend happens to be one of the world's most wanted villains anymore."

Adrian's pulse skipped to hear Max referring to Nova as his girlfriend. Coming from someone else made it sound so . . . *official*. "True," he said. "That does make things easier."

Thinking of Nova made him even more determined to fix whatever he had ruined when he hadn't believed in her innocence. The way she'd kissed him on the pier seemed to suggest that she'd already forgiven him, but he didn't want to take any chances. He never wanted to lose her again.

His thoughts were interrupted by a tiny, shrill screech. Adrian started, but Max, used to the noise, lifted his palm and examined Turbo. "About time you woke up, little dude. Are you hungry?"

The velociraptor unhinged its jaws in what might have been a yawn, then untucked its back legs. It took a few awkward attempts to climb to its feet. Max sighed. "Yeah, you don't feel so great. I know. I'm sorry."

Turbo stood, watching Max with its black eyes. It made another sound—this one a pathetic mewl—and slowly reached forward one little claw, stretching the tiny needle-like talon forward until it barely tapped the end of Max's nose.

Then, like watching a wind-up toy as it finally wound down, the little dinosaur grew still.

Neither Max nor Adrian spoke for a long time. Adrian wanted to say something to comfort Max as he stared at the creature, now as motionless as one of the plastic figurines, but he didn't know what to say.

Finally, Max let out a long, slow exhale. "I'm glad you made him. He was a fierce little dude."

"Yes, he was."

A small, impish smile sparked over Max's face. He set the dinosaur, frozen in its final stance, in the middle of the battlefield. "And he is going to make one hell of a supervillain."

CHAPTER TWENTY-NINE

"I DON'T KNOW if I can travel through a magic mirror."

Nova considered Narcissa with disbelief. "That might have been good information to have yesterday."

Narcissa shot her an exasperated look of her own. "Well, maybe you should have told me what you were planning! I know you Anarchists are all 'every man for himself,' but I would have thought spending so much time with the Renegades would have made you more of a team player."

Nova opened her mouth to rebuke the idea that she could learn anything useful from the Renegades, but she stopped herself. In truth, Narcissa might have had a point. Exhaling, she asked instead, "Do you really think it won't work?"

Narcissa screwed her lips to one side, pondering the question. "I mean, it probably will? But I guess it depends on what sort of . . . enchantment, or whatever, it has on it." She shrugged. "Do we have any other options?"

Nova blew a lock of her bangs out of her face. "Not really, so let's assume for now it's going to work. I stashed the mirror here, in a pile of construction equipment." She drew an X on the blueprint that showed the floor layout for the headquarters' ground and mezzanine floors, including early plans for the laboratories near the quarantine. "Once you're in, you'll go down this corridor, then left through these doors, and the storerooms are on your right. I don't know which storeroom, so you might have to check them all. And I also don't know who they have on night duty these days, but you can bet they'll be watching this floor closely, so you have to be quick once you're in."

Narcissa appeared thoroughly unimpressed. "And here I was hoping to get some quality reading time while I was there."

Ignoring her, Nova added, "And don't forget to bring the mirror with you in case you need a quick exit."

"You can stop with the obvious. I've been doing this my whole life."

"Fine."

"What if the storerooms are locked?"

"They will be." Nova reached for the pile of folders beside them and shuffled through until she emerged with a white ID card—the same she'd once nicked off an unconscious administrator outside the Renegade security room. "This should get you access."

"Should?" Narcissa said dryly, pocketing the card. "What if it doesn't?"

"How good are you at picking locks?"

Narcissa's eyebrows rose in dismay.

"Kidding. If this doesn't work, then just get out of there and come back here. We'll switch to plan B."

"What's plan B?"

"I'm not sure yet."

"Comforting," Narcissa deadpanned.

"You're the one who got me out of jail. You wanted me to help with strategy, so that's what I'm doing."

"Yeah, but I figured we'd be plotting the ultimate downfall of the Renegades, something that would take months, maybe even years. I didn't think we'd give ourselves less than a week to rescue the most infamous supervillain of all time."

"I like to aim high."

Narcissa laughed, but there wasn't much humor in it.

"I'll talk to Cyanide and check on how the decoy is coming. Be ready to move on this tonight—headquarters tends to be emptiest between three and four a.m."

"Yeah, yeah. I'll be ready," said Narcissa. "But look, I need to be honest with you. I think trying to stop the execution and rescue Ace Anarchy is a terrible idea and I know a lot of the Rejects think so, too. Maybe you can persuade some of them to join you in this crusade, but I won't be one of them, and I'm not going to push anyone else into it, either."

"What are you talking about? You just said—!" Nova pointed at the blueprint.

"Yeah, I'll do this," said Narcissa. "But not for you and not for Ace Anarchy. I'm doing it for all the prodigies who have been oppressed by the Renegades. This will be a huge blow to them and their dominance, and I'm all for that. This is what my grandfather would have wanted me to do. But I'm not going to the arena with you, and I don't know how many of the others will go voluntarily, either. We're doing this so we can live better lives, lives with peace and freedom.

But people are going to die if you do this, and that's not a risk we're all willing to take. Not for Ace Anarchy, at least."

Nova crossed her arms. "So much for teamwork. Don't you realize how much Ace Anarchy has done for us? For all of us?"

"Yeah, I do realize what he did. But he also drove everyone into a war! And I know you care about him, but . . . I'm not sure I agree that we need him to take down the Renegades. We can do this without him. And if you and the Anarchists don't make it back . . . then we'll do it without you, too. You are handing us a pretty awesome weapon here."

Nova glared at the blueprint. It felt like a betrayal, but she'd known Narcissa for such a short time, she wasn't sure why it surprised her.

"Fine." Nova started to roll up the blueprint. "You wouldn't be much use at the arena, anyway, but I do need to know who's with us so I can work it into my strategy. And make sure you don't leave any Agent N behind when you're leaving that storeroom."

"Of course."

One of the Harbingers appeared in the hall, his gold robes rustling around his legs. "Cyanide asked me to tell you the substance decoy is just about . . . ow!" He clapped a hand to his arm and spun around.

Nova jumped to her feet, already tensed for an attack. But it was only Leroy standing behind the boy, a small needle in his hand. He grinned sheepishly. "Apologies. I only had to be sure—"

Before he could finish, the Harbinger boy let out a groan and collapsed against the wall.

"So very sorry," Leroy said again.

Honey appeared, coming to see what had caused the yelp. She

seemed mildly intrigued as she took in the unconscious boy. "What's wrong with him?"

"He'll be fine. Should wear off in ten minutes. Twenty at the most." Leroy held up the needle, showing Nova. "Good news. The paralysis poison is ready. I'm going to call it *Agent P.*"

Nova grimaced. "For the sake of fostering good will, let's try to find willing volunteers next time you need to test something, all right? But . . . nice work."

"Thank you."

"That still doesn't solve the problem of how we're going to simultaneously inject hundreds of Renegades with it," continued Nova. This dilemma had been cause for much discussion since she first broached the possibility of rescuing Ace. Originally they planned to dose the Renegades with a gaseous anesthesia pumped in through the venting system, except, thanks to Nightmare's Agent N bombs, most of the Renegades would now be outfitted with gas masks.

"Don't worry," said Honey. "Leroy and I are working on a few options. You stay focused on getting to Ace and making sure the Agent N reveal falls through. We'll take care of the rest." She draped an arm over Leroy's shoulder and steered him back toward his makeshift laboratory in the basement's far corner.

Nova watched them go, her gut tight with apprehension. There were so many things that could go wrong.

But there wasn't time to dwell on any of them.

"All right," she said, turning back to Narcissa, who was still staring dumbfounded at the unconscious Harbinger. "Did you find what I asked for at the mansion?"

Narcissa blinked at Nova for a few seconds, before giving herself a shake. "Yes, I did. Right where you said they'd be." Narcissa pulled a satchel from behind her and set it on the table. Reaching inside, she produced a thick stack of papers, many yellowed with age and crinkled at the corners, some tears fixed messily with clear tape. "At first I thought this was just a part of your infatuation with the Everhart guy, but now . . . I get it."

Nova tensed. "You read them?"

"Of course I read them." Narcissa flipped through a few pages, then stopped on a child's drawing of a shadowy monster with narrow white eyes. "It's just a blob at first, but as he got older, and his art got better . . ." She kept flipping. The papers were more organized than when Nova had seen them the first time, stuck in a forgotten box on a forgotten shelf. Narcissa must have put them in roughly chronological order, and the result was striking. She stared as, page after page, Adrian's phantom took shape.

At the bottom of the stack were the three issues of *Rebel Z*, the comic Adrian had started in his younger years. Nova had flipped hastily through the first one when she'd been sneaking around the office, but Narcissa took her time now, turning page by page. In the story, a homeless street kid who looked an awful lot like a young Adrian was abducted by an evil scientist. He, along with twenty-five other children, were subjected to cruel testing. Narcissa stopped on a page showing one of the other kids strapped to a medical table, screaming in agony as the doctor and his assistants applied some sort of high-tech probes to his skull and chest.

Narcissa turned another page, and Nova's breath caught.

The boy on the table appeared dead, and rising up from his parted blue lips was a monster—the same shadowy figure that had plagued Adrian's artwork for so many years. But it was no longer vague and obscure. Now its edges were outlined in crisp black.

A hooded cloak hovered over the boy's body, bending down as if to see into the boy's dead eyes.

A skeletal finger stretched out from billowing sleeves.

A weapon was clutched in its opposite hand, glinting faintly in the doctor's laboratory.

A scythe.

"It could be coincidence," Nova whispered.

"I thought that, too," said Narcissa, lowering her voice. "So I asked Honey about him. Most of the Anarchists had followed Ace for decades; some had been with him since before the start of the Age of Anarchy, even. But Phobia just appeared out of nowhere a year or so before the Day of Triumph and told Ace that it was his purpose to bring terror to their mutual enemies. As far as Honey knows, he's never told anyone his real name or who he was before he became Phobia." She shivered. "The timeline works. Adrian Everhart would have been . . . what? Five or six when he first started drawing this . . . thing." She pulled some of the older drawings from the stack. "His skills weren't there yet, but it seems safe to say that he was drawing Phobia . . . even back then."

Nova massaged her temple. She had half expected this. Thoughts of Phobia and Lady Indomitable had plagued her in her prison cell almost as much as thoughts of Adrian himself. It was a puzzle that had quickly resolved itself once Adrian told her about the card found on his mother's body. *One cannot be brave who has no fear.*

Phobia's power was to prey on his enemy's deepest fears, and Adrian himself had told Nova that the greatest fear of his childhood had been that someday his mother would leave and never come back.

She'd hoped she was wrong. But now . . .

"He created Phobia," she whispered, taking the child's drawing from Narcissa and inspecting it with mounting dread. She was startled to find her vision misting as she tried to imagine what Adrian would feel if he knew the truth. "He created the monster that killed his mother."

"Nova . . ." Narcissa reached forward and took the drawing back. "Adrian Everhart is a Renegade. He's not on our side."

Nova straightened, blinking back any signs of approaching tears. "I know that."

"Yeah, but . . ." Narcissa frowned doubtfully. Hell, she looked borderline *sorry* for Nova.

Scowling, Nova gathered up the papers and shoved them back in the bag. "Thanks for getting these. I need to talk to Millie and—"

"Whoa, whoa, there was something else I wanted to show you." Narcissa grabbed the *Rebel Z* comics before Nova could put them away. "Have you read these?"

"I don't have time."

"But there's something—"

"Later," Nova snapped. Then, feeling guilty, she forced a smile. She wasn't mad at Narcissa; she was mad at this whole impossible situation.

Adrian Everhart was her enemy.

Phobia was her ally.

So why did it feel like her heart was breaking, to know how much pain it would cause Adrian to ever learn the truth of their connection?

"I'm sorry," she said. "You can show me later, okay? I just . . . I really need to talk to Millie about some stuff. It's important."

Fingers tapping on the comic's cover, Narcissa slowly nodded. "Sure, it can wait. It doesn't change much at this point anyway."

◇◇◆◇◇

Nova had a long list in her head of everything she needed to do and everyone she needed to talk to in order to make sure all was going according to plan—the plan that was still forming by the minute. Especially now that she knew not all of Narcissa's Rejects would be willing to pull their weight as she'd been led to believe.

But she wanted to talk to Millie first. She hoped the psychometrist might offer answers that Nova doubted she'd find anywhere else.

The basement beneath the pawnshop was divided into a series of large rooms, where a few members of their fledgling alliance had staked out a corner here or set up a cot for themselves there. There was one toilet and a shower with running water that never truly got warm, and so it was only the prodigies who were wanted by the Renegades who spent much time in the underground hideout. Many of the others still had their own homes to return to, though Nova had insisted they meet at particular times to hash out the details of her burgeoning plan.

Of the prodigies who were more permanent fixtures in the shelter, Millie had been given her own space, sharing a converted closet with the power generator that rumbled and cranked incessantly. When Nova arrived at the room, she saw Millie sitting cross-legged on an old sofa cushion, cradling a teacup in the palms of both hands. Her eyes were closed almost blissfully, but one popped open in annoyance when Nova knocked at the plywood door.

"Could you look at something for me?" said Nova, stepping into the room before Millie could shoo her away.

Grunting, Millie peered down into the cup, which Nova realized was empty. "I'm busy."

"This is important."

"You young people think everything is important."

Nova tensed, annoyed at the idea that *her* problems might be trivial. "If we fail, Ace Anarchy is going to die. Or am I the only one who cares about that?"

Millie hummed, unflustered, as she turned the teacup upside down, examining it. "Eighteenth-century bone porcelain. Gilt edging. Hand-painted botanical motif." She rubbed her thumb over a red imprint on the bottom. "Clear backstamp. Back when pretty things were valued more highly than they are today, this would have sold for upward of two thousand dollars."

Though Nova was irritated at Millie's willful ignorance of her statement, at this, her eyebrows rose in mute surprise. She studied the teacup more carefully now, but to her, it continued to look like an antique, useful only for holding tea.

With a crooked grin, Millie set the teacup on her table. "At least, that's what it wants you to believe. Alas, it's a fake. A quality replica, but still an impostor. It's interesting, don't you think, how an impostor, no matter how good it is, can never be as highly valued as the original." Her expression turned faintly mocking. "I suppose you know something about that, don't you, Young Renegade?"

"I suppose I do," Nova muttered. "Is that from the pawnshop?"

"Was brought in to be pawned yesterday morning. Dave's been hiring me to do appraisal work for years. People bring in a lot of random stuff to sell, and it can be hard to sort the gold out of the dung heap. Luckily, that's where I excel."

"Coming here was your idea?"

She shrugged. "Miss Cronin tracked me down at my boat and told me what she was planning, trying to bring together the old cohorts of her grandfather's. I liked the idea—it's been getting harder and harder to conduct business, with the Renegades always breathing down everybody's neck. But we weren't all going to fit on my little houseboat, so I suggested Dave's place. The Ghouls and a few of the other gangs used to have meetings down here."

"What about your boat?" Nova asked. "Aren't you worried about leaving it unprotected while you're here?"

"It'll be fine," said Millie, her eyes sparking. "Leroy helped me set up some defenses. If anyone tries to steal my treasures, they'll have regrets." Setting the cup on the floor, she folded her hands on her lap and turned her full attention to Nova. "What is it you wanted me to look at?"

Nova shut the door behind her. Stepping across the room, she unlatched the bracelet, her fingers fumbling with the clasp Adrian had once drawn for her. The chain slid from her skin. The star brightened momentarily before returning to its faint glimmer.

"I want to know more about this," she said, holding it out to Millie. "When I stole the helmet, my bracelet reacted to it, almost like the two were magnetized. And the"—she stumbled on the word *star*, instead saying—"jewel had some sort of reaction, too. It helped me break into the chromium box that the helmet was being kept in. I feel like they're connected somehow."

Millie's face as she stared at the bracelet was akin to a curator admiring a fine piece of art, and yet she didn't reach out to take it. "I haven't touched the helmet, so I may not see any shared history, if that's what you're hoping for."

"I can have Phobia bring you the helmet, if you need it," said Nova. "I've been thinking maybe we should all try it on, anyway, to see how it affects our powers. It's supposed to amplify any prodigy ability, which could be useful. And we're going to need every advantage we can get."

Millie guffawed. "You go right ahead, but I've seen enough hardship in my life." Standing, she paced to a small table littered with a mishmash of dishes. She selected a chipped ceramic coffee mug, but rather than coffee, she grabbed a green bottle and filled the cup with red wine, nearly to the brim. "The destruction wrought from a thousand relics, the tragedies of too many family keepsakes to count." She sat down again, cradling the mug in both hands, and took a sip, eyeing Nova. "I don't need to see what that helmet has seen."

Nova tried not to think too much about the early days of the Age of Anarchy. The sacrifices that Ace had made in service to his vision. The people who had been killed, the devastation wrought on this city and the world as other prodigies followed his example.

She supposed she couldn't blame Millie for not wanting to think about those things, either.

"Can you look at this, at least?" she said, holding out the bracelet again. "What is it? What is it made out of? Anything you can tell me might help."

Millie squinted, but still her hands stayed around the mug. "That pretty bauble was not there the last time I saw this bracelet." Her mouth quirked teasingly. "I'd almost forgotten about the boy I'd seen then, the one who fixed the clasp. Now that I recall his face . . ."

"I know," said Nova, feeling heat rise up her neck. "It was Adrian Everhart, but I didn't know it at the time. That's just a coincidence."

Millie chuckled. "Once you've seen as much history as I have, you won't believe in coincidences anymore." She took another drink of wine, this one almost a gulp, like she was fortifying herself.

She sighed and set the mug on the floor beside her chair.

Finally, she held out her palm.

With a twinge of nervousness, Nova dropped the bracelet into her hand.

Millie jolted upright. She glanced at Nova with surprise. It was a brief look, and without explanation, she cupped her other hand over the star and shut her eyes.

Nova watched with mounting curiosity as Millie's features went through a series of transformations. Sometimes her brows would rocket upward, other times they would furrow deeply. Sometimes her lips would move as if she were speaking to herself, and sometimes she would laugh inexplicably or clench her teeth with concern.

Nova said nothing through it all. After the first minute, she pulled a rickety wooden chair from the room's corner and sank down onto it, fingers drumming on her thighs.

Five full minutes passed before Millie's eyes popped open, slightly unfocused. She seemed to be waking from a bewildering dream as she scanned the room.

"Well," she said. "That answers one question at least."

Nova leaned forward.

"You sense a connection between this bracelet and your uncle's helmet because they are *deeply* connected. They were crafted from the same raw material, taken from the same source."

Nova peered at Millie's hands, still clasped around the star, shielding it from view. "And that material is what, exactly?"

Millie giggled. "The stuff of stars," she whispered, almost mockingly, and Nova realized that she must have seen some of Nova's conversation with Adrian as they discussed the impossible star in his jungle.

She bristled. She knew it wasn't a star. Stars were suns, billions of light-years away.

This was a fancy marble.

But what was she supposed to call it?

"You seem skeptical," said Millie. Cradling the bracelet in one hand, she bent down and picked up her wine with the other. "Tell me, Miss Artino. Are you familiar with the Monteith Theory of Prodigy Origin?"

Nova's skepticism grew. "Let me think. Is that the one that says all prodigies are descendants of ancient gods? Or that we came here aboard alien spaceships? Or, no, no, that's the one that has something to do with radioactive sludge, right?"

"Actually, Dr. Stephan Monteith was an astrophysicist who speculated that all prodigy abilities are the result of our physical systems reacting to a cocktail of biological chemicals and the stardust that lies dormant in our physical makeup."

Nova snorted. "Stardust. Right. I'll go with the sludge, myself."

"Don't be so quick to judge. I have traced the history of several prodigy artifacts back to the very star from which their mystical abilities seem to have originated." Millie leaned forward. "Consider that every chemical in our world is formed from stars that long ago exploded. From the salt in our oceans to the cobalt in that teacup's paint."

"You can't be named *Nova* and not know about supernovas," Nova said, growing weary of this conversation. "Are you going to tell me about the bracelet or—"

"I am, if you care to listen."

Nova bit the inside of her mouth.

"According to Monteith," Millie continued, pausing to take another sip before going on, "the particles from one particularly powerful supernova reached our solar system many centuries ago. They came to our planet—an invisible invasion—settled upon our dirt and in our oceans, and took up space in the very air we breathe. These particles, this *energy*, would become the substance that your father could detect in our world. This raw energy is everywhere, but only visible to a lucky few."

Finally something Nova could relate to. "The energy my father could see," she said, scooting to the edge of her seat. "I saw it, too. Or, I think I did. When the star first attached itself to the bracelet. And again, once, when I put the helmet on. Like, beams of light, all around me."

"Now, consider," said Millie, "that this energy isn't simply in the air. It is inside us. Every human being on this planet has trace amounts from this supernova inside of them, and that raw energy contains the potential for great power, but only if it's awakened by a chemical reaction. That was Monteith's theory. Everyone has the potential to become a prodigy, but for those who are not born with this inherent power already awakened, their powers will only reveal themselves in the face of great trauma. Monteith believed the chemicals released into the bloodstream during extreme duress create the conditions necessary to awaken our latent abilities."

"Ooookay," said Nova, trying to disguise her disbelief. "So a big star exploded, its tiny little particles crashed down to earth, and now we all have the potential to be superheroes? Sure. Great." She pointed at Millie's clasped hands. "What does this have to do with my bracelet? Are you telling me that *this* is the central core of that star that exploded or something?"

"Of course not. I'm only pointing out that your father gathered and used that raw energy, which is possibly the most powerful substance in our galaxy. He made the helmet, among other things, and he made this magnificent gem as well." She opened her hands to reveal Nova's bracelet.

Nova frowned. "No, no. My dad made the bracelet, but the gem was made by—"

"Adrian Everhart? Oh, I *saw*."

Nova flushed self-consciously.

"The mural was remarkable, but no. How do I explain this?"

Millie rubbed her thumb over the star. "As one of his final acts while still alive, your father made this bracelet, yes?"

"Right."

"Well, the setting was not left empty because he ran out of time to complete it. In fact, he had already created the gem that was intended to fill the setting some months before, and hid it where he did not think anyone would ever find it." Leaning forward, Millie pressed a finger against Nova's heart. "He hid it inside of you."

Nova blinked, once again sensing that she was being teased. "Excuse me?"

"I mean, not actually right *here*," said Millie, tapping Nova's chest again. "That just seemed more dramatic than the truth. It was actually stored at the base of your amygdala. Not as romantic, that, but . . . ah well. I'm sure your father had his reasons."

Nova held up a hand. "You saw all this?"

With a chuckle, Millie held out the bracelet. Nova took it from her, cradling it in her fingers. "You came to me for answers, didn't you?"

Nova rubbed her thumb over the surface of the star. It brightened at her touch.

"But . . . why? What did my father make it for? And why hide it inside of me?"

"We can only guess." Millie rubbed her cheek, stretching her thin, pale skin with each press of her thin, pale fingers. Then she took another large draft of wine. "Perhaps it was intended to be a weapon, like the helmet."

Nova chewed the inside of her cheek. It was possible. Her family had never had enough food when she was growing up, and with Evie getting bigger, things had been more desperate than ever. Another weapon crafted by David Artino would have been incredibly valuable. He could have sold it to the highest bidder.

But that didn't seem right.

A faint memory came to Nova. The day her parents had been murdered, her father had said to her that he hoped the bracelet would put right some of the injuries he'd caused the world.

Still, what did that mean?

Nova's fingers felt cold as she clasped the bracelet back onto her wrist, remembering the power the star had exhibited, imbuing the chromium spear with added strength. With the help of the star, she had destroyed an otherwise indestructible box.

If the star was supposed to be a weapon, what if her father had been making it *for* Ace, to be used against the Renegades? The Renegades had promised to protect her family from the Roaches, but a part of her had always wondered why her parents hadn't gone to Ace and the Anarchists for protection instead. Maybe, even back then, her family knew that the Renegades couldn't be trusted. Perhaps her father had made a weapon that was even stronger than the helmet.

A weapon that was strong enough to defeat even the invincible Captain Chromium.

CHAPTER THIRTY

ADRIAN HAD BARELY seen Nova since she'd been released from Cragmoor. His guilt over not believing her grew stronger every day, mingling with the fear that he might have ruined everything. He wanted things to go back to the way they'd been the night she fell asleep at his house. They had been comfortable in each other's presence. He felt like he could tell her anything, and like he'd earned the same trust from her. He'd begun to think that he might even be falling in love with her.

But things had changed, and he knew it was his fault.

Nova hadn't joined them for patrol duties the past few nights, and he couldn't blame her after what they'd put her through. They crossed paths a couple of times at headquarters, but their conversations were stilted and awkward. Adrian had more daydreams of telling her about the Sentinel than he could count, wondering whether maybe sharing his greatest secret might show her, in some way, how much he really did trust her.

But then he recalled the loathing with which she spoke the Sentinel's name and knew the time wasn't right.

There hadn't been any more sightings of Nightmare since she'd taken his drawings, which added to Adrian's anxiety. He was sure she was plotting her next strike.

With Ace Anarchy's execution only hours away, he suspected that strike would come sooner than later. He wanted to believe Nightmare wouldn't be arrogant enough to attack an event in which almost every Renegade in the city would be present, but then, she'd never shied from taking big risks before.

Adrian made his way down the concrete stands of the arena, the same venue where the trials were held every year. The seats weren't nearly as crowded now. Members of the media had been invited to witness the reveal of the Renegades' new weapon, as well as the execution of Ace Anarchy, but these proceedings would not be open to the general public.

Adrian had never been in the stands of the arena, only down on the field. It was a completely different perspective—the buzz of energy from the crowd making the hair on his arms stand on end, the elevated view of the field making him feel more like a bystander than a participant. Which, he supposed, he was.

He was a Renegade, but he had no role to play in the reveal of Agent N. The neutralization of dozens of known villains. The execution of Ace Anarchy.

His fathers, on the other hand, would be in the spotlight, as always. He saw Simon on the field already, standing alongside Tsunami as they talked to a crowd of journalists.

Spotting Oscar and Danna in the front row, Adrian hurried down the rest of the steps to join them. "Hey," he said, claiming a seat. "Ruby's not here yet?"

"Not yet," said Oscar. He glanced back up into the stands, as if searching for her, then leaned conspiratorially toward Adrian. "Before she gets here, can I ask your opinion on something?"

"What, my opinion wasn't good enough?" said Danna, stretching her arms and lacing her fingers behind her head.

Oscar shrugged. "I'm just trying to be thorough."

"It's not poetry, is it?" asked Adrian.

"Even better. Check it out." Oscar made pistols of his hands, aiming toward the empty air beyond the edge of the stands. A stream of smoke shot from his left finger, forming a pale gray heart a few feet in front of them. It was followed by a cupid's arrow from his right finger that shot straight through the heart. The image lasted only a few seconds before the smoke began to dissipate into the air.

"Then I thought I could follow it up with words, something like—*Hey, Ruby . . . I really like you! Like, so much that even thinking of doing this makes me want to spew my breakfast tacos all over these seats.*"

"Inspired," Danna muttered as the Renegades in the next row cast Oscar concerned looks.

Oscar sighed. "It's honest, at least. I did read somewhere that honesty is a keystone of a healthy relationship."

Adrian scratched the back of his neck.

"Anyway," Oscar continued, "I'm still working on it. I thought it'd be reminiscent of those old airplanes that used to do skywriting over sports events, you know? So, what do you think? About the general idea, not the spewing part."

Adrian glanced at Danna in time to see her roll her eyes. "Is this something you were thinking of trying out *today*?"

"Yeah, maybe," said Oscar, rubbing his hands together. "I'd make the heart a lot bigger, put it somewhere over by the megascreen so everyone can see it. I did check with the Council to see if I could put a message up on the screen before the whole Agent N thing goes down, but they denied the request. Thunderbird—*not* a romantic."

"Oscar," said Adrian. "They're going to drain the powers of some of society's most dangerous villains and then execute someone."

Oscar studied him, expressionless, for a long moment. "So you think it might be in bad taste?"

"Just a little."

"Told you so," said Danna.

Glowering, Oscar sank down into the plastic seat. "Do you have any idea how hard it's been finding the right time to make a dramatic proclamation? It's like someone's always getting arrested or un-arrested or we're apprehending a criminal or taking down a villain. . . . When is a guy supposed to make his move in the midst of all of that?"

"You could try *not* making a dramatic proclamation," suggested Danna. "Just ask her out. It's not that big of a deal."

Oscar groaned. "Not a big deal? I'm trying to tell the girl of my dreams that she's, you know . . . the girl of my dreams! That's the biggest deal of my life!" He shook his head, his brow creased with anxiety. "And I'm worried I'll screw it up."

"What the heck, Adrian?" yelled Ruby, suddenly barreling down the stairs.

Oscar tensed and smacked Danna and Adrian with a hasty *shush*, as if they were preparing to give him away. Danna smacked and shushed him back.

"Hey, Ruby," said Adrian, standing so she could get past him to her seat. "What's up?"

"The concession stands are closed," she said, gesturing toward the back of the arena. "Every last one of them. Who's in charge of this shindig?"

"Proof that you two are made for each other," muttered Danna.

Ruby glanced at her. "Huh?"

"Nothing," said Danna, shaking her head. "This isn't a sporting event. Let's all show a bit of respect."

Ruby huffed. "There is no occasion that doesn't warrant the sale of stale popcorn and licorice ropes. It's practically a basic human right."

"Protest," said Oscar, nodding stoically.

Flopping into her chair, Ruby crossed her arms. "Where's Nova?"

Adrian winced, though he tried not to let it show. "I don't think she's coming."

He tried to ignore Danna's arched eyebrow. He knew she still harbored doubts about Nova's innocence, and it was beginning to irk him. They had seen Nightmare, and it wasn't Nova. Why couldn't she accept that?

"Why not?" said Ruby, surprised.

He pushed up his glasses. "She's always been against Agent N, and I think having spent some time at Cragmoor made her *really* against it. My dad told me she made a pretty passionate plea for them to call off the neutralization. She thinks the criminals should be given a chance at rehabilitation instead."

"Imagine that," said Danna.

Adrian shot her a look, which she ignored.

"I guess I can understand," said Ruby, disappointed. "I've hardly seen Nova since she came back. I'm worried she might be mad at us. . . ."

"Don't be," said Adrian. "I think she's just trying to work through a lot right now. You know, the explosion, Cragmoor, being reunited with her uncle . . . just give her some time."

"Of course," said Ruby, though she didn't seem to find much comfort in Adrian's words. He couldn't blame her. He'd been telling himself the same thing lately. He would give Nova the space she needed. He would be patient. And when she needed him, he would be there for her.

But it was easier said than done. The truth was, he missed her. He missed her more now than he had even when she'd been in prison. At least, then, he'd been able to tell himself it was for the better.

"Oh, look, there's Genissa," said Oscar, pointing. "As cheerful as ever."

Genissa Clark was on the field, an impressive crossbow strapped across her back. She was talking to Captain Chromium. Even from up in the stands, Adrian could tell that they were both frustrated with each other.

"Is that a cooler?" said Danna, indicating the box at Genissa's feet.

"It is," said Oscar. "Damn her. She probably thought to bring sandwiches."

"I don't think it's sandwiches," said Adrian. "I heard she was planning to execute Nightmare with an icicle, thinking it would have some sort of poetic justice. I bet she brought one with her."

Ruby made a disgusted noise. "That would have been so . . ."

"Unnecessary. And messy," said Oscar.

"And overdramatic," added Danna.

"Would you prefer an old-fashioned hanging?" said Adrian, his insides churning to think of how narrowly Nova had evaded this fate. "Or burning at the stake, like they used to kill prodigies?"

"*No*," said Ruby. "I would prefer . . . I don't know. Isn't there a way to put someone to sleep first so they don't feel anything?"

Adrian peered down the line of his friends and knew they were all thinking the same thing. Putting people to sleep was Nightmare's specialty, her attack of choice. Never before had it occurred to him that it could also be an act of mercy.

"How is your dad going to, you know . . . ," Oscar started, "do in Ace Anarchy?"

Adrian watched Hugh for a second, still arguing with Genissa. "I'm not sure what he has planned. But . . . I think right now Genissa is trying to be the one to do it. She's been threatening them all week, ever since Nova was released, saying that she at least deserves some glory if she can't have revenge. Otherwise, she's still saying she'll ruin the Renegades by going to the media with her laundry list of complaints."

Danna grunted. "That girl has a strange sense of glory."

"People have been talking, though," said Oscar. "I'd never really thought of it before, but . . . it is strange, isn't it? That no one has ever stopped to consider what might be best for us and not just the organization? I mean, we all chose this life. We're willing to risk a lot for the cause. But . . ." He trailed off.

"But shouldn't we have a little bit more say over what that cause is?" suggested Ruby. "And what, exactly, we're risking?"

He sighed. "I hate to sound like I'm with Genissa, but it's made me think."

"You don't just sound like Genissa," said Danna, slightly teasing. "You almost sound like an Anarchist."

Oscar wrinkled his nose. "Now, that's just uncalled for."

"I think they're starting," said Ruby, drawing their attention back down to the field. A long stage had been erected, stretching nearly the full length of the field, and seven chairs were set up in a line at its center beside a narrow podium. The media had been sent to the box at the forefront of the audience. Adrian wasn't sure where Genissa had gone. As the Council approached their seats, the crowd began to quiet.

The Council—Captain Chromium, the Dread Warden, Tsunami,

Blacklight, and Thunderbird—was joined by Dr. Hogan, one of the lead researchers and developers for Agent N. And . . .

Adrian leaned forward, squinting. They were just far enough away that he felt like his eyes must be playing tricks. "Is that the Puppeteer?"

"Sweet skies, I think it is," murmured Ruby. "But . . . he looks so different."

The last time Adrian had seen Winston Pratt, his skin had been ghastly pale, almost as pale as when permanent makeup had been painted on his face, complete with rosy cheeks and black lines on his jaw reminiscent of a ventriloquist dummy. Those physical markings of his alias and superpower had faded when he'd been injected with a dose of Agent N. In less than a minute, his power—which was the eerie ability to morph children into brainwashed puppets—had been stripped away. The Puppeteer was no more.

Adrian had seen Winston a couple of times since that day, having questioned him about Nightmare and the other Anarchists. But in those meetings, Winston had been dispirited and weak, a shell of his former self. That was not the man standing onstage now. His back was straight. Healthful color had returned to his complexion.

He was *smiling*.

And not a cruel, preparing-to-manipulate-a-six-year-old smile, but something genuine and unexpectedly warm.

It rendered him almost unrecognizable.

As the others took their seats, Captain Chromium approached the microphone. He spent a moment welcoming the crowd and the media who had gathered for their important announcement, conveying how the purpose of the Renegades was and had always been to ensure the safety of their citizens, while working to improve the quality of life for both prodigies and non-prodigies around the world. He talked about his enthusiasm for the new asset they were about to reveal and the pride he felt having been a part of its development. How he foresaw the potential of this tool to be, literally, world-changing.

As the audience clapped politely, the Captain stepped back and welcomed Dr. Hogan to the microphone.

Her speech was almost exactly the same as when she had first introduced the concept of Agent N to the Renegade patrol units. *Agent N offers a nonviolent solution with instantaneous results . . . It is completely safe to be used around non-prodigy civilians . . . This will provide a humanitarian consequence for prodigies who defy regulations . . .*

Adrian kept his attention on the media gathered in their box. Their surprise and interest. Their pens scribbling across small notepads. Their cameras zoomed in on the doctor's face.

He wondered what the news would soon be reporting. The Council hoped this would replace the rumors that the Renegades had become incompetent and ineffective. Agent N was their big chance to show the world what they had been putting their efforts into all these years. This was their chance to demonstrate how they intended to deal with wayward prodigies going forward. This was their chance to show that villainy would not be tolerated. Not so long as they were in charge.

And Adrian wanted to believe it. His marker was in his hand, though he didn't remember taking it out, and he found his fingers fiddling with it unconsciously. He wasn't nervous so much as . . . unsettled.

He remembered watching as Frostbite and her team bullied the Anarchists, trying to force them to incriminate themselves, whether or not they'd actually been involved in the attack on the parade. He'd seen them torture Hawthorn, ultimately murdering her and framing the Sentinel for the brutal attack.

The Anarchists and Hawthorn were villains. Perhaps they deserved no sympathy.

But in those moments, Adrian had been forced to question who the true villains were.

If Frostbite's team could get away with it, he knew that more Renegades could, too. Who would stop them? Who would even try?

"Shortly, we will have a demonstration of what Agent N can do," the doctor said, "so that you can see its effectiveness with your own eyes, and witness both how swift and how merciful a weapon it is. But first, we wish to invite one of our greatest success stories to offer his own opinion on the serum and its life-changing effects. Please join me in bringing to the microphone none other than a former villain and associate of Ace Anarchy himself. You will know him by the name of the Puppeteer, but today he is known only as Mr. Winston Pratt."

There was applause, though it was stilted and unsure. Murmurs flooded the crowd as Winston stood and took his place before the microphone. It all felt so surreal. The day he'd been neutralized, he had used a young Renegade to try to attack Dr. Hogan. He had been led from the stage in shackles.

What had changed to now make him appear so relaxed, so . . . *jovial*?

"My gratitude, Dr. Hogan," Winston said, bending toward the microphone that had been lowered for the doctor and left far too short for his willowy build. "I *am* grateful. Not only for the ways in which the direction of my life has changed—thanks to Agent N and the team of doctors and therapists who have been working with me—I am also grateful for this chance to tell my story."

He smiled again, but it was more bashful now. Adrian could tell he was nervous. He spent a moment awkwardly adjusting the microphone, then cleared his throat and took a set of index cards from his pocket. "I have known many . . . villains . . . over the years. I was an Anarchist for more than half my life, starting at only fourteen years old. I joined Ace Anarchy's cause after running away from home." Pausing, he tapped the edges of the cards on the podium. Inhaled deeply, and continued, "Often, when a new member joined us, we would talk about our 'origin stories.' It's a popular topic among us prodigies—both heroes and villains, I think. I gave little thought to it at the time, but . . . it's become clear to me that our stories all had something in common. With the exception of those of us who were born with our abilities, the rest of us became prodigies after . . . well, some great trauma. Though we spoke of our origins with pride, in reality, these times were often . . . horrific. And painful. Perhaps the fact that we survived them made our pride greater, but I . . . I never thought to ask my companions, or . . . even myself . . . whether we would have been better off to have never undergone such trauma in the first place."

Adrian's brow creased. He glanced at his teammates. Danna, like him, had been born with her gift. But Oscar had become a prodigy after nearly dying in a fire, and Ruby gained her powers after being viciously attacked by a member of the Jackals gang.

In fact, every origin story he knew was rooted in trauma of one sort or another.

"As for me," Winston continued, his tone growing weary, "I never shared my real story. Not with the Anarchists, not with anyone, for all those years. The story of how I became the Puppeteer brought me no pride. Only shame and anger." Gone was the easy smile of minutes before. He hesitated, and looked out at someone in the audience. Following his gaze, Adrian recognized the counselor who had been working with Winston after his neutralization. She gave an encouraging nod.

Stooping down, Winston opened a bag at his feet. The journalists near the front tensed, perhaps expecting him to pull out a bomb or gun.

But it was only a doll. Adrian recognized Hettie, Winston's childhood doll that he had once traded to the ex-villain for information regarding Nightmare.

"This is Hettie," said Winston, holding the doll up for everyone to see. "My father made Hettie for me for my seventh birthday. A part of me thought I might be too old for dolls, but . . . there was something about this one. I loved it immediately." He paused, a shadow eclipsing his expression. "A few months later, my parents were out one night, and I was being watched by a neighbor. A . . . longtime family friend who often babysat me. He took an interest in Hettie . . . suggested we play a game . . ." Winston paused and Adrian could feel his own chest tightening in the horrible silence that followed. Finally, Winston gave his head a shake and set the doll on the podium, as if unable to look at it. The doll's shiny black eyes peered emptily into the crowd. "I didn't understand it then, but the game became a foil for him to . . . to . . . molest me. For the first time. It . . . would not be the last."

There were gasps in the crowd. Hands pressed over speechless mouths. Looks of pity and horror. From the corner of his eye, Adrian saw Ruby squeeze Oscar's arm.

"I had never felt so powerless. So ashamed, and confused." Winston was scrutinizing the doll as he told his tale. "I would not know that I had become a prodigy until weeks later when, at school, my anger boiled over, and I lashed out at a kid who was a grade older than I was, who had taken the last slice of pizza in the cafeteria. Before I understood what I was doing, I had my strings around him. I made him . . ." He paused, clearing his throat. "I made him bash his own face into the tray. It broke his nose."

A long silence followed this statement.

"My powers began to change after that," Winston continued. "They changed me inside and out. Since that day, I have hurt more children than I could count. Not in the way that I was hurt, but as victims, powerless under my control. I don't tell you this story because I want your pity. I also don't mean to justify the things I've done, or to make excuses for the role I played as an Anarchist and . . . a villain." He uncurled his spine, no longer bending over the microphone. "I tell you this because many prodigies will insist that their powers are a gift. I believed this, too. My powers were my identity. They were the source of my strength, my control. I didn't know until recently, until after my powers were neutralized by Agent N, that they were none of these things. They were a burden. A curse. They kept me in the head of a victim for all those years, and they turned *me* into a monster, too. I know that I will never be free of the trauma I experienced or the memories of all the awful things I've done. But thanks to Agent N, I feel . . . for the first time, I feel like there might be a path forward. For the first time, I feel like I'm beginning to heal. To speak on my own behalf and maybe, someday, on the behalf of kids who were like me. I am so sorry for the hurt I've caused. I may never be able to make amends to the many children I used as puppets, but I do hope to make amends in as many ways as I can. I can't say that other prodigies who are neutralized will feel the same way, but as for me, I am not sorry to be free of my powers." He took Hettie and set the doll down on the floorboards of the stage, then held out a hand toward Captain Chromium.

The Captain stood and lifted the tall chromium pike that had been leaning up against his chair. The Silver Spear. He handed it to Winston.

Winston stood back, gripping the pike in both hands. "I am no longer a victim!" he yelled. With that, he swung the pike down. The flat end crashed into the doll. It shattered from the impact—its head caved in, one arm flew off the stage, a leg skidded off beneath Tsunami's chair. Winston hit it again—two times, three.

He finally stopped after the sixth time, rendering the doll little more than broken pieces and battered clothing. Panting from the exertion, Winston handed the spear back to the Captain, then he craned his head one more time to the microphone. "But even more important than that," he said, his voice full of emotion, "I am no longer a villain."

CHAPTER THIRTY-ONE

EVEN ABOVE THE buffeting wind, Nova could hear the crowd inside the arena erupt over her earpiece. She flinched from the noise—a thunderstorm of applause.

She used the moment to catch her breath. She wasn't exhausted from scaling the exterior wall of the arena. Rather, she felt like she'd hardly breathed during Winston's speech. She was supposed to be focusing on the job ahead, but instead she was caught up in his story. Her throat was dry. Her heart felt like it was strapped into a vise. She wondered how it was possible to live beneath the same roof—or, in the same subway tunnels—with a person for ten years and still know so very little about them.

As the cacophony within the arena quieted, Nova heard Phobia's voice rattling in her ear.

"*Traitor.*"

She flinched. Though she knew Phobia was talking about Winston, it felt like an accusation of her and her sympathy, too.

She didn't respond.

"Let him choose weakness and mediocrity if that's what he wishes," said Honey. "We need to focus on getting our Acey back."

"Precisely," said Leroy. "Nightmare, what's your status?"

Shaking away the lingering feeling of heartbreak, Nova double-checked the reading on her laser measurer. "Almost in position," she said, marking the exterior outline of her entry point. Precision was important. Cut the entry point too far afield and she'd end up with a hundred-foot free fall, right into the waiting arms of the Renegades. "Thirty more seconds," she said, her own voice muffled behind the metal face mask.

"No rush," said Leroy. "They're just now bringing out the prisoners."

Honey sighed heavily. "And knowing Captain Chromium, he'll be droning on for at least another twenty minutes before anything exciting happens."

Nova hoped the Captain was feeling particularly verbose.

Calculations complete, she hooked the laser measurer back to her belt and retrieved the diamond-bladed electric saw. She waited until the Captain's booming voice filled her earpiece, being fed to the group by Cipher, one of Narcissa's allies who was unknown to the Renegades and had no trouble getting entry to the event, along with sixteen others from their growing group, after Millie concocted fake media passes for them. They would be positioned around the arena, waiting to help Nova and the Anarchists complete their mission.

Nova's objective was simple.

Get the helmet to Ace.

The curved roof of the arena vibrated beneath her knees, both from the buzz of her saw and the thundering speakers inside. She paused each time the Captain did, trying to sync the noise she was making to the times his speech grew particularly impassioned.

With one hand gripping the suction cup she'd attached to the roof, she finished the last cut. She gave a hard tug and the piece of roofing popped upward. She slid it away from the hole.

Exactly eight feet below her hung a platform for one of the lighting and sound system operators. She could see only the top of the woman's head, covered in large headphones, her attention on the huge spotlight she was aiming toward the field below.

The beam of light was following the line of prisoners that were being led out from what had once been the arena's locker rooms, where Nova had waited for her turn at the trials. The prisoners all wore the glaring black-and-white jumpsuits from Cragmoor prison. Their ankles were bound in shackles, each shackle chained to the next prisoner in line. Their hands were fully enclosed in chromium cuffs. A number of armed guards walked beside them, most of whom Nova recognized from Cragmoor, their weapons targeted at the more dangerous of the prodigies in the line.

Ace came last, and even from so high above, Nova could sense the buzz in the crowd as he appeared. His complexion was ghastly white, with deep purple bruises beneath his eyes. The skin hung from his bones as though it could slough off at any moment. He was broken and defeated, his back bent and his head heavy as he was led in on the chain of prisoners. A mockery of the prodigy he had once been. He was not a threat. He was not to be feared, not anymore.

Nova's teeth ground, hating to see him reduced to this.

"Everyone at their stations," she said, tightening the straps on her backpack. She abandoned the saw on the rooftop, not wanting the added weight. Bracing her arms on either side of the hole, she slipped her legs inside, dangled for a moment, then dropped.

She landed with a thud behind the lighting operator. The woman startled, but before she could turn, Nova's fingers were on the back of her neck and she collapsed into Nova's arms. Nova laid her down on the platform. "I'm in."

She checked that the spotlight was still positioned on the stage. It was one of four such spotlights, each one currently targeting Captain Chromium, who was at the podium again while the inmates stood shoulder to shoulder down the length of the field.

Knowing that the other three operators would likely be the first to notice their absent peer, Nova ducked back toward the scaffolding that connected the platforms around the perimeter of the roofline and started making her way toward the next operator.

She mostly ignored the Captain's droning voice, but a handful of words still filtered into Nova's consciousness as she crept through the shadows.

Villains . . . neutralized . . . execution.

She reached the second operator and felled him as easily as the first. Two down . . .

Below, the Captain was listing Ace's many crimes against humanity, justifying their choice to end his life in this public manner. "Before we proceed," he said, "I would extend a dignity that this villain never offered to any of his victims. Please, escort Ace Anarchy to the stage."

At the end of the line, Ace's shackles were unlocked from his neighbor's. The guards prodded him, urging him toward the steps and onto the platform. He fixed his attention on the Captain, who waited for him at the podium. The loathing between the two men was palpable.

The arena hushed. Nova slowed so that her footsteps would make no sound as she made her way to the third platform with as much stealth as possible.

Once Ace stood before the Council, Captain Chromium spoke

again into the microphone. "At this time, I ask my longtime rival, this enemy of humanity, Alec James Artino, if you would like to express any final words."

He stepped back, offering the microphone to Ace.

Nova swallowed. She wanted to stop and watch, to listen, but she knew there was no time for that.

She reached the third platform, and put to sleep the woman she found there.

One more to go.

Below her, the arena was quiet. Her thoughts shifted to Winston, who was still on the stage, now only feet from Ace. She wondered if the two of them had made eye contact as Ace was brought up to the podium. She wondered if Ace had heard Winston's story. Would he, like Phobia, see Winston as a traitor, or would he feel the same sympathy that Nova had?

She thought also of Adrian, who she knew was somewhere down in that crowd. She wondered if she would ever see him again, knowing that—if all went according to the plan—the answer would likely be no.

She wondered if she would regret not finding a way to say one last good-bye.

Ace approached the podium. It felt like the whole arena had gone still. Even Nova had to remind herself to keep breathing as she crept along the walkway.

His voice, when he spoke, was brittle and dry from disuse. "As I stand before you . . . ," he said, his words barely a croak. Nova flinched to think of him as he once was, powerful and strong, a true visionary. Now he was little more than a relic, a memory from a foregone era. "Knowing that my time left on this earth is short, I am faced with an excruciating truth. I once destroyed a world order in which prodigies were condemned and persecuted by those who feared us, those who could not appreciate our potential. And now . . ." He faced the Captain. "Now we are condemned and persecuted by our own." He lifted his chin. "Alec James Artino is already dead, but Anarchy will live on. It will persist in the hearts of all prodigies who refuse to bow before this dictatorship. Our fight is not over, and we will not rest until there is freedom and autonomy for all our brethren. Until we no longer need to fear for our well-being, not from those who fear us, not from those who hate us, and not from those who envy us. The Renegades *will* fall, and we will rise again!"

The fourth operator was reaching for his walkie-talkie, probably confused as to why the other three lights had fallen motionless, when Nova's fingers reached out from the shadows and brushed the back of his hand. She caught him as she had the others, then released a long exhale.

Phase one complete.

Down below, Ace was being led back onto the field, while a parade of men and women in lab coats marched out to join the prisoners, each one holding a syringe.

The spectacle of it was too surreal. It felt more like a choreographed stage production, like it had all been planned with more consideration for the pictures that would later appear on the fronts of newspapers than for the dignity of those involved.

Nova examined the trusses that held the light fixtures and speaker boxes, a complicated maze of metal scaffolding crisscrossing the ceiling of the arena. She pulled herself onto the railing surrounding the spotlight's platform, reached for the nearest overhead truss, and hauled herself up the rigging.

Blacklight had the honor of signaling for the neutralization. All of the inmates were to be neutralized simultaneously, and so he began by counting down from ten. Nova did her best to ignore what was happening below, focusing instead on putting one hand in front of the other as she crawled toward the center of the building.

She did pause, though, when Blacklight reached number one. She peered down through the metal bars.

She could only see the tops of their heads—the prisoners, the lab technicians, the Council. Winston and Ace. She couldn't see any of their expressions. She was too far away to tell if any of the prisoners flinched as the needles were plunged into their arms.

A second passed. Then two. Ten seconds. Twenty.

Even from her bird's-eye view, Nova could tell when the technicians began to stir uncomfortably. She saw the Council shifting in their seats, trading looks with one another. She noticed Dr. Hogan checking her wristwatch.

The arena was quiet enough that she heard one of the journalists cough from their box.

Not all prodigies had physical characteristics that indicated their powers, but plenty did. Not just Nova's yellow-skinned friend, but also Colosso, who was more than ten feet tall, and Billie Goat, who had vicious pointed horns growing from the top of her head, and the Scrawl, who regularly had blue-black ink overflow from her lips and stain the front of her jumpsuit. By now, all of those characteristics should have been fading away. By now, those villains should have been reduced to average humans.

But, as the Renegades were beginning to realize, that wasn't happening.

Even the inmates were squirming uncomfortably, unsure if they were supposed to feel something different.

CHAPTER THIRTY-TWO

T HE AUDIENCE'S ATTENTION shifted from the row of prisoners on
the field—who had apparently *not* been neutralized—to the
paper bird fluttering over their heads. Adrian stared, his brow
pinched with suspicion, as the bird made a full circle over the stands
before dipping down and hovering in front of Captain Chromium.
He snatched it from the air, crumpling its wings in one fist. His vis-
age was already dark as he unfolded the square of paper. There must
have been something written on the inside, because his scowl deepened before he crushed it again and threw it onto the stage. He was
about to speak when a voice boomed throughout the arena.

"Ladies and gentlemen, prodigies and prisoners, superheroes and
scientists . . ."

The voice did not seem to be coming from the overhead speakers. If anything, it seemed to be coming from everywhere at once.

"We do apologize for the delay in today's Renegade-sponsored
programming," the voice continued, with an edge of sarcasm. "While

your honorable Council members sort through these technical diffi-
culties, we hope you'll enjoy this free entertainment, compliments
of . . . *the Crane*."

Adrian frowned at his team, who were all sharing the same baffled look.

"The Crane?" said Ruby. "Wasn't he at the trials?"

"The origami guy?" said Oscar.

Adrian saw them then. *Everyone* saw them—hundreds, perhaps
thousands, of paper cranes in the most beautiful array of pastel and
jewel tones soaring into the arena. Adrian leaped to his feet. He wasn't
alone, as the stands all around him erupted with concern.

But only a *little* concern, Adrian noted.

They were just paper cranes.

"They're coming in through the air vents," said Danna. She was
gripping the railing, her knuckles white.

"Could it be a diversion?" asked Ruby.

Adrian didn't respond. He had no answers, but he had a feeling
that Nightmare and the Anarchists had something to do with this.

He loosened his collar, making easier access to the zipper tattoo.

The cranes spread throughout the audience, hovering inches over
their heads. One was caught by Fiona Lindala, or Peregrine, who was
standing in the next row with her beloved bird of prey perched on
her shoulder. Adrian watched as she unfolded the paper, the falcon's
head bobbing curiously. All around him, Renegades were doing the
same. Snatching the paper birds from the air. Unfolding them to
uncover their secrets.

Fiona cried out in surprise, drawing Adrian's attention back to
her. Her eyes were wide, though perhaps in more surprise than pain.
She dropped the crane, but it left behind another creature.

A chubby, fuzzy, black-and-yellow bumblebee sitting on her palm.

Adrian had barely registered the sight before the peregrine shot forward and caught the bee in its beak.

"It stung me," Fiona said to no one in particular, picking the stinger out of her palm.

Then there were more. More bees, almost adorable in their plumpness, leaving the protection of the paper cranes and buzzing toward the nearest Renegades.

"Queen Bee," said Adrian, swatting one away. All around, he could hear disgruntled gasps, though the sounds were more of annoyance or surprise than anything else. It wasn't fun to be stung by a bumblebee, but compared to daily life as a Renegade, it wasn't exactly petrifying, either.

Danna's face was contorted in disbelief. "Why bumblebees? Why not hornets or wasps or . . . ?"

Adrian yelped in surprise and clapped a hand to the back of his neck. His fingers came away cradling the furry body of a bumblebee. He tossed it to the ground and reached back, rubbing where it had stung him.

Around them, people were crushing the bees in fists and under boots, tearing the beautiful paper cranes into shreds. Baffled. Confused.

Until a sickening wail began to rise up around them.

It started with Peregrine, who was gaping, horrified, into her companion's intelligent eyes. "No," she cried, stretching one finger to stroke the bird's wing. But the bird ducked away. It walked down the length of her outstretched arm, staring at her like it wasn't sure whether or not she was edible. "Pern, please, it's me."

The peregrine shifted its head away, its talons digging into her forearm. Then it spread its massive wings and leaped into the air, soaring over the stands. Fiona cried out, reaching, but she had no hope of catching it. Her eyes filled with tears. "I can't sense him anymore," she stammered. "He doesn't understand . . . what's happening?" She looked around, searching nearby faces for answers. "My power. It's gone."

Realization struck Adrian like a gunshot. He scanned the audience, as all around, expressions morphed into panic. Renegades inspecting their outstretched hands as they felt their powers drain away. As scales sloughed off of baby-soft human skin, as sixth-sense antennas retracted beneath human hair. A girl made of smoldering black embers watched as her skin mutated into plain human flesh. A boy with horns on his back cried out as the horns snapped off and were left like discarded nail clippings on the ground. Sparks extinguished. Energy evaporated. Shadows dispersed.

The voice returned, echoing and amused. "If you're one of the unlucky Renegades who have just received a tiny sting, we urge you to remain calm. You're bound to experience some slight discomfort, maybe a bit of queasiness, but in just a few moments you'll be back to normal. Completely, utterly normal."

"Agent N," said Adrian. "The stingers have Agent N on them."

Oscar cursed and squished a bumblebee beneath the butt of his cane, even though Adrian was pretty sure it was already dead.

"The syringes must have had a decoy," said Adrian. "The Anarchists switched it out somehow."

"Adrian," said Danna. "Your powers?"

He shook his head. "My tattoo should protect me. But something tells me this isn't the worst of it. Come on, I need to find a place to transform."

"We're coming with you," she said.

He slipped from the row, preparing to dash up the stairs to the back of the arena, but he was stopped by a voice, meek and trembling.

"Guys?"

He turned back. Danna and Oscar paused, too, all of them staring at Ruby.

Her face was pale, her eyes watering and round. In her right palm, she held a dead bumblebee.

In her left was the red stone that always hung from the wire at her wrist.

Adrian's heart sank. "Ruby . . . no . . ."

They all watched as the stone began to melt, dissolving into a sticky, bloody mess over her fingers, dripping down to the concrete floor below.

Ruby swallowed and tried to put on a brave face, despite her shock. "My brothers," she whispered, "are going to be so disappointed."

◇◇◆◇◇

Nova was halfway across the first lighting truss when she realized what was happening. She gripped the edges of the cold steel, peering down at the audience as their cries went from bewildered to horrified.

She pressed a hand to her earpiece, hoping that maybe she was wrong. Maybe she was misinterpreting the situation, unable to see clearly from so far away.

"What is going on down there?"

Honey's voice crackled. "Can't you tell? We're finally winning."

Nova's hands felt clammy, but she was perched too precariously to wipe them off. Her jaw throbbed behind the mask. "Tell me that's not Agent N . . . It was supposed to be Leroy's poison! You were just supposed to paralyze them for a few minutes!"

"Stay calm, Nightmare," said Leroy. "We need you to stay focused on your prerogative."

"How am I supposed to stay focused when you change the plan in the middle of it?" She realized that she was practically yelling but knew that no one would hear her above the chaos below. She found herself scanning the stands for signs of Adrian and the others, but the seats were too crowded, too jumbled with identical Renegade uniforms.

"It was my idea," said Honey, sounding very proud of this fact. "Why would we leave our enemies momentarily paralyzed when we could neutralize them forever? It's nothing they wouldn't have done to us."

"But that's not what we agreed on!"

"Because you wouldn't have agreed!" Honey snapped back. "Because you've gone too soft for these superheroes. But they deserve what they're getting, and you know it!"

Nova strangled the steel bars. How many bees had Honey unleashed? How many Renegades would no longer be prodigies?

And why did this fill her with fury when, not long ago, she would have been delighted by it? Would have even encouraged the plan herself?

"They were supposed to be *paralyzed*," she repeated. "Do you know how much more difficult you just made this for me?"

"You're resourceful. You'll figure it out," said Honey. "I did what was best for the Anarchists, what's best for *us*. No more playing both sides, Nightmare. It's time to choose whose side you're really on."

Nova flinched. Below, Renegades were spilling onto the field. Most of the bees had already been killed, and it was impossible to tell how many superheroes had been stung. Half? More?

While the Council barked orders, trying to whisk away the civilian journalists into the sublevels for safety, while simultaneously setting up a defensive perimeter, a second wave of bees surged in through the air vents. This time Honey didn't bother with the disguise of the paper cranes. The swarm fanned out, hundreds of tiny black specks from Nova's perspective, diving into the crowd.

Amid the chaos, Nova's focus landed on Ace. He stood almost serenely in front of the platform, his wrists and legs still shackled.

She felt the weight of the backpack pressing down on her.

Though anger continued to surge through her veins, she tucked her chin and kept moving.

Adrian cursed when he saw a fresh swarm of bees flooding the arena. Captain Chromium's voice boomed through the speakers, urging Renegades to protect the members of the media whose panicked cries were mixing with the loud buzz of the incoming insects, while trying to organize others into some sort of counterattack. No enemies had yet shown their face, though—only the bees, and they were so small and quick, most Renegade superpowers were useless against them.

"I know this goes without saying," said Adrian, "but Oscar, Danna . . . try not to get stung."

"Real sensitive, Sketch," Ruby said. Her face was still stricken, but Adrian could tell she was trying not to show how devastated she was at the loss of her powers.

"I have a better idea than just not getting stung," Oscar growled. His expression had a rarely uncovered ferocity as he lifted both hands and began to flood the stands and the arena with sweet-smelling smoke.

"What are you doing?" said Adrian. The smoke quickly changed from a fine mist to a thick fog. It wasn't long before Adrian could barely see his own hands, much less his companions beside him—or the bees that he could hear buzzing nearby. "Smokescreen, is this supposed to be helpful?"

"They're bees," came Oscar's voice. "Smoke tranquilizes them."

Adrian tried to blink back the smoke as it stung his eyes, but soon his annoyance dimmed. True enough, the buzzing noise grew quieter as the smoke filled the arena.

"Okay, good thinking," he admitted, even as he heard a number of their colleagues starting to cough.

The smoke offered one other benefit. Now concealed, Adrian reached for the zipper tattooed over his sternum. With a hiss and a series of clanks, the Sentinel's armored suit unfolded from the non-existent pocket beneath his skin, extending over his arms, down his chest and back, enclosing his arms and legs, and finally pulling up over his head. The visor came last, dropping down over his face.

"Oh dear, that's not very *bee*-friendly, my smoky friend," came the thunderous voice again. "I suppose that means we'll have to resort to plan *B* . . ." He cackled.

What followed was pure pandemonium. With everyone disoriented by the smoke, it was impossible to tell what was happening through-out the arena, but Adrian could sense from the yelling and grunting that it wasn't good. He saw flashes of light from the field below, and caught a glimpse of Thunderbird's wings churning through the smog. He felt the boom of an explosion under his feet. Danna dissolved into butterflies and swept toward the field. Slowly, the fog thinned. Bees were crawling across the backs of chairs and along the rails, but they seemed disinclined to attack anymore. Something soared past Adrian's helmet—an arrow? A spear? To his left, he heard the ricocheting clang of metal. To his right what sounded like the roar of a feral beast.

One thing was clear: They were under attack; and it wasn't just bees anymore.

Adrian waited until the mist had cleared enough that he could see vague shapes on the arena floor so he wouldn't crush anyone beneath his weight. As he prepared to launch himself toward the stage, movement above made him pause.

He squinted at the shadow making its way across the scaffolding near the high, arched ceiling. He waited until he was absolutely certain of what he was seeing.

His gauntlets clenched into fists.

Nightmare.

CHAPTER THIRTY-THREE

Nova was nearly to the center of the arena's lighting system when the truss she was on trembled from a jolting impact. She cried out as the scaffolding rocked beneath her.

Taking hold of a steel safety cable, she glanced over her shoulder. "Oh, you've got to be kidding me."

The Sentinel was perched precariously on the scaffolding, his armored hands holding the bars of the truss as he tried to get his footing. He lifted his head, and despite not being able to see his face, Nova could practically feel his hatred hit her like a wave.

She pulled herself to her feet, using the cable for balance. Her other hand hovered near her belt.

"Didn't expect to see you here today," she said. "What are you doing, crashing a Renegade party?"

"Could ask you the same thing," he said as he tried to stand. But the scaffolding swayed from his weight and he quickly returned to a crouch. "Except, I think I know. And it's not going to work."

"So far, so good," she spat.

Maintaining a hold with his left hand, the Sentinel raised his right fist. The gauntlet began to glow white-hot.

She sneered. "Not this time, toy soldier." She pulled a gun from its holster on her hip—one she'd designed for precisely this moment.

They both took aim.

They fired.

The Sentinel's concussion beam struck Nova in the left elbow. She stumbled back and for a moment there was empty air beneath her, before her flailing hand caught hold of the safety cable again. She dangled from the rafters, her right hand on the cable, one knee looped over the thick bars.

She exhaled in relief.

The Sentinel was not so lucky. The projectile struck him square in the chest, magnetizing itself to his suit, before releasing a powerful electroshock. Nova, dazed from her own hit, barely registered his yelp of pain. Then he was falling.

She heard the impact as he landed on the field below, along with startled cries from those around him.

Nova grunted. Her left arm had gone numb from the blast. She cursed, sweat beading on her neck as she struggled to haul herself up one-handed.

"That jerk," she muttered, with a few curses, before she finally had both knees securely planted on the truss again. A quick survey of the scene below showed her the Sentinel's prone body splayed out on the ground. She wondered briefly if the shock had killed him. She hadn't had time to test its effectiveness.

No matter. It was clear that she had lost the element of surprise. Multiple sets of eyes turned her way. Thunderbird's burning glare fixed on Nova. She prepared to launch herself into the air, a lightning bolt crackling in her fist, when Cyanide appeared from the fog and jabbed something into her back. Thunderbird howled in pain and swiveled to face him. Within seconds, the bolt in her hand sputtered, flashing brightly, just once, before dissolving in the air.

She dove at Cyanide with all the fury of an enraged thunderstorm.

Nova tore her attention away, searching for Ace. No longer standing stoically beside the platform, he had slumped to his knees, his head bowed and one hand clutching his heart. Debris was scattered around his feet in a perfect circle, and Nova could tell he'd been using what little ability he still had to protect himself from flying objects and shrapnel.

His powers were enough, just enough, to keep him safe amid the carnage. But his strength wouldn't last. She could only guess at what it had cost him to deflect whatever weapons and projectiles had been flung his way since the onset of the battle.

It was only a matter of time before he was targeted, despite his frailness and the shackles.

Nova had hoped to lower herself as close to him as possible, but as she considered the trusses stretching out before her, she knew it would take her too long to traverse the rest of the way with her injured arm. She'd be faster on her feet, even if there were more obstacles below.

Adjusting the backpack, she fumbled for the clip at her belt and hooked it around the safety cable. Her lips contorted as she measured the distance. She'd never rappelled one-handed before and she didn't relish the opportunity to try it now.

Opening a pouch on her tool belt, she wriggled out one of her gloves and used her teeth to pull it onto her hand. She shook loose the nylon rope, watching it cascade to the ground, then secured her ankles around it. Her hand took hold, she sucked in a deep breath, and dropped.

The rope hissed between her boots. Despite the protective glove, she could feel the friction burning hot in her palm. Her left arm began to tingle.

A few seconds later, she let go, landing in a crouch in the midst of a battlefield. She peeled off the glove and shoved it back into the pouch, then started in Ace's direction. She weaved through the melees and wrestling matches, the glinting weapons and projectiles and blasts and screams. She saw Locksmith moving down the line of prisoners as sneakily as he could, undoing their shackles one by one. She saw Leroy pinned to the ground by a dark-haired woman who was trying her best to strangle him, even while he pressed his acid-oozing fingers into her face. His expression was wild and manic, almost as if he was enjoying the brawl, and it occurred to Nova with a shock of surprise that it was *Thunderbird* who had him by the throat. Thunderbird . . . without wings.

He had neutralized a member of the Council.

A whip lashed around Nova's ankle, yanking her to the ground. She grunted from the impact. A second later she was being dragged through the dirt. She flipped onto her back, facing the Renegade—Whiplash—with a snarl. She snatched a throwing star from her belt and hurled it at her attacker. Whiplash yelped as it caught her in the arm and dropped the handle of her whip. Her distraction gave Nova enough time to untangle her leg, and a second later she leaped for the woman, who bared her teeth and lifted her hands to meet Nova's attack.

Her bare hands.

Big mistake.

The moment their skin met, Whiplash's eyes widened in realization, half a second before they rolled back into her head and she collapsed into the dirt.

Checking the security of the backpack, Nova started running. Though her attention was focused on getting to Ace, she couldn't help scanning the faces of Renegades as she bolted past, wondering if Adrian was near. But the only member of her team that she saw was the occasional glimpse of a monarch butterfly weaving in and out of the thrum.

When she spotted Ace again, she was startled to see him watching her. He was still bent over his knees, panting. His eyes carried an unfamiliar desperation. A pleading.

"I'm coming," she whispered, as much to herself as to her uncle. "I won't fail you. Not this time."

Nova ducked out of the way of a barbed tail—*Stingray?*—then launched herself over a suspicious puddle of inky-black goo. Her feet touched the ground again, just in time for an enormous wave to crash into her, knocking her onto her side. The water eddied way, leaving her spluttering as the dirt floor thickened into sticky mud. She cursed Tsunami and climbed back to her feet, preparing to fight, but the Councilwoman was already fending off an attack from one of the freed prisoners.

Arm tingling as sensation returned to her muscles, Nova pushed the sopping-wet bangs back from her face and readjusted the weighted hood over her face. Between the mud and the drenched clothes, it felt like every step toward Ace was becoming more and more of a struggle.

She had just caught her breath when her own name pierced her ears.

"Nova! NO!"

She spun in time to see Winston Pratt throwing himself at her.

Nova reeled back, bracing herself for a fight.

But Winston didn't attack her. Instead, he gasped and stumbled to one knee, gaping up at her in shock.

It took Nova too long to understand what was happening. It took her too long to notice the stain of red spreading across the front of his shirt. It took her too long to see the clear glass shard jutting from his chest, slicked with blood.

Distantly, she heard someone cursing. She looked past Winston and saw Genissa Clark gripping a crossbow. She dug out another projectile from a small cooler at her feet and loaded it onto the crossbow's track. Not glass, Nova realized. *Ice.*

Genissa's face was red with fury, her teeth gnashing as she lined up the sights with Nova's heart.

Nova dove to the ground. The icicle whizzed past and shattered on something behind her. Nova pushed herself up and lunged at Genissa. The girl had another icicle in hand, but no time to nock it into the crossbow before Nova tackled her. They fell to the ground. Genissa swung the icicle, trying to stab Nova with the tip, but Nova grabbed her wrist and pinned it to the ground.

Nova's body was aflame with anger. Her blood pumped with adrenaline as she replayed Winston's panicked voice shouting her name.

In that moment, she wanted nothing more than to murder Genissa Clark.

Instead, she screamed, as loud as she could, the contempt tearing at her throat—*"You are so lucky I don't have time for this!"* Then she pressed a hand to Genissa's forehead and released her power like a sledgehammer into the girl's skull. Genissa's head dropped limply to the dirt, her lips parted, her pale skin coated in dust and muck.

Panting, Nova ripped herself away. Mere seconds had passed

since she heard Winston call her name, and he had not moved. He was still kneeling in the dirt, his back to her, the white shard of ice prominent against the red stain on his clothes.

"Winston."

She collapsed beside him, a hand on his shoulder. He met her gaze, and she could see him already losing the fight to stay with her. His skin was as pale now as when he had been the Puppeteer. "It's okay," she whispered. "It's okay. I can't take out the ice just yet, because . . . the bleeding . . ." She sniffed and scanned the arena, wondering if there had been any Renegade healers in the audience. She knew none of the Anarchists' new allies had healing abilities, but if they really saw Winston as one of *them* now, then maybe the Renegades would take care of him. "I'm going to find someone. Just hang in there—"

"Nightmare," he said, with a bit of a cough. He sagged, sitting back on his heels, grimacing at the movement. "I'm sorry. I . . . called you Nova . . . before."

"It's okay. I don't think anyone's paying attention. Can you walk? We have to get—"

"Nightmare . . ." He took her hand, and she realized he was crying. In that moment, she realized that she was, too. "We were friends, weren't we?" He coughed. A bit of blood sprayed across his bottom lip. "I know I wasn't always . . . a good friend . . . but I . . . I liked having you around, back then. When you were little. It was nice to be . . . a kid . . . again."

Her breaths started to come in erratic gulps. "Of course. Of course we were friends."

He smiled, but it was laced with pain. His eyes were losing focus. "I wanted to tell you . . ." He coughed. The ice in his chest jostled with each movement. "I'm no longer sure . . . I was meant to be . . . a villain." His gaze softened affectionately as he squeezed her hand. She wasn't sure when he'd started holding it. "I'm not sure you are, either. Maybe . . . none of us . . ."

A nearby explosion made Nova jump. She threw her arms wide, as if to protect Winston from the blast. A dozen steps away, a cloud of smoke was spreading outward, sending Rejects and prisoners and Renegades alike scrambling to cover their faces.

"Winston, I need to get to Ace. And then I'll get you out of here, okay?" She faced him again. "Ace and I will . . ."

Her words faded away, settling with the smoke and dust.

Winston had slumped forward, barely supported by Nova's arm and the ice that kept his chest from collapsing on itself.

He was already dead.

CHAPTER THIRTY-FOUR

Nova stumbled to her feet, feeling like her insides had been raked out with a fork. She spun in a dazed circle, expecting another attack on her life to come at any second, from any direction. She saw no sign of Leroy or Thunderbird. She saw Honey in the stands, having barged in when the fighting ensued, the cloud of wasps and hornets surrounding her so dense that her body resembled a living hive. She caught sight of Phobia at the same moment that his body transformed into a writhing pit of venomous snakes that darted at a group of Renegades, driving them apart. The prisoners, having been freed of their shackles, had joined the fight. She saw allies and enemies, doing their best to survive. Doing their best to maim and kill.

She saw a lot of blood. A lot of terror. A lot of fallen bodies.

Pulse running hot, she looked up, blinking dust from her eyes.

Ace.

If she could just get to Ace, she could put a stop to this.

She reached for the strap of the backpack and froze.

It was gone.

She reeled around, searching, frantic. *There.* Not far from Genissa Clark's unconscious body. She raced toward it, then dropped, skidding through the dirt as her hand grasped the handles.

She immediately knew that something was wrong.

"*No.* No, no, no!"

The zipper was partially undone, and though she already knew the truth, her hands worked on autopilot, yanking it down the rest of the way.

Revealing an empty receptacle inside.

Nova threw the bag to the ground and searched out Ace, hoping that maybe he'd used whatever power he had left to call the helmet to himself. But no—when she spotted her uncle, he was half collapsed over the edge of the platform, his breaths coming in ragged gulps of air. The helmet was nowhere in sight. A thousand possibilities flashed through her mind, each more terrible than the last, as she desperately scanned the arena. She wanted to believe that maybe it had fallen out during the fight, maybe it had rolled beneath a chair or gotten buried in the mud or—

"Looking for this?"

Her head jerked up.

Magpie was standing in the front row of the stands, holding Ace Anarchy's helmet.

"You really should keep a closer eye on your things."

Growling, Nova ran for her, already calculating the best way to scale the short wall up to the audience seats. Magpie didn't wait for her to catch up. She bolted up the steps, taking them two at a time.

She had a head start, but Nova was faster. She had just hurtled herself over the railing when Magpie reached the top of the first level. Instead of running to the exit, though, Magpie sprinted down a row of seats, yelling, "*Catch!*"

Nova's heart galloped, as she imagined Magpie giving the helmet to Captain Chromium or the Dread Warden or even Adrian or—or—

Magpie threw it as hard as she could. Nova's gaze traced its arc over the bleachers, one hand gripping the rail she'd just vaulted over, her mouth dry.

A pair of hands clumsily caught the helmet.

Nova blinked, dismayed. She stumbled. *Callum?*

He appeared equally bewildered, almost frightened, as he looked from Magpie to Nova. He was practically alone in the stands, most of the Renegades having made their way to the field to join the fight. He surveyed the helmet that was suddenly in his possession, not with a hungry greed, like some might have. Not with revulsion for its history, either.

He just looked like Callum. Awestruck and giddy.

"What are you waiting for?" Magpie screeched at him. "Put it on!"

Pressing her lips, Nova started moving down the nearest row of seats. Callum was an easy enough target. She just had to get close enough to put him to sleep. Wouldn't be the first time.

Callum lifted the helmet and dropped it on top of his head.

It made him look like a kid playing dress-up.

Snarling, Nova catapulted into the next row. Callum was not a formidable opponent. She would get the helmet and she would complete her mission.

But she hadn't gone a dozen steps when she was struck by a thought so staggering, so brilliant, that it made her stumble over her own feet. Her knee smacked the hard plastic arm of one of the seats, but she barely felt the stitch of pain, because . . .

She was still alive.

She laughed, a little startled by the realization. How many attempts on her life had been made in just the past fifteen minutes? And yet, she had survived them all. She was still standing, still breathing, and . . .

What was more, she wasn't the only one.

Frozen in place, Nova peered out across the arena floor and felt as though she was seeing it clearly for the first time. Yes, there had been death. Not only Winston—*Winston, who sacrificed himself for me*—but others, too, heroes and villains alike. There was havoc. There was ruin.

But amid all that, there was still hope. Hope that things could change. Hope that this wasn't the end.

Nova's lungs squeezed. She had been a recipient of Callum's wonder-inducing superpower enough times to know that what she was feeling was a byproduct of his ability. But she also knew her thoughts were the truth or, at the least, what she believed to be true.

There was still hope that things could be different. That things could be better.

She was not the only one who had been frozen under the weight of this realization. All around her, people were exchanging speech-less looks. There was a clarity in their expressions, born out of the stillness of the moment.

Despite all odds, she still had this one precious life. She still had a chance to do things differently. Which meant they *all* could do things differently. They could choose a different future, a different fate. Together, they could end this senseless destruction. They could choose to rebuild, to create, rather than tear down and destroy. Isn't that what Callum had been trying to tell her all along?

She realized that Callum was watching her from behind the face of Ace's helmet, and she knew, beyond a doubt, that he recognized her. He saw her. He knew her.

And still, somehow, he did not look at her like she was the enemy. What would have seemed impossible moments before now seemed not only possible, but inevitable.

Life was full of second chances.

◇◇◆◇◇

Not two minutes ago, Adrian had woken up, flat on his back in the Sentinel's armor, feeling like he'd been struck by lightning, then run over by a truck. He didn't know what Nightmare had shot at him, but he hoped he never came in contact with one again. In the first few moments after opening his eyes, he'd been confused, hurt, and somewhat shocked that he hadn't been trampled where he lay. The arena was a disaster. The fight showed no sign of letting up, not until one side was completely demolished.

He staggered to his feet, hoping that the tingling vibrations in his limbs would fade with movement, and started scanning for signs of Nightmare. All his old fury returned, and he swore that this was the last time she would defeat him in a one-on-one fight.

Many times, he had sworn to himself that he would find Nightmare and he would destroy her.

This time, he meant it.

Or, he had.

In the two minutes since then, the battle had fallen into an unexpected cease-fire. Adrian looked around, awestruck not by the mayhem, but by the mere fact that everyone here was willing to fight with such conviction for their own cause. How could they all feel so compelled to risk everything for what they believed? He saw his dads amid the chaos—Simon helping Zodiac to safety; it seemed she might have a broken leg—while Hugh was uncharacteristically still, beaming up at the stands with actual tears in his bright blue eyes.

Adrian was overjoyed to see them both. Knowing that the loss was devastating, but also knowing that it could have been worse.

He saw a group of men and women wearing the Cragmoor prisoner's uniform and recalled Nova's plea to give them a chance for rehabilitation. He thought of his mother, who had died defending the people of the city she loved. He thought of his dads, who had worked tirelessly these past years to rebuild their fallen society.

Was it possible that the lines that had divided them for so long could be approached with a bit more understanding, blurred with a bit more empathy, even erased altogether with just a bit more compromise?

He was so startled by the thought that he actually started to laugh. He kept searching the crowd, wanting to find his friends and ask them if they, too, felt that they'd been going about things all wrong, all this time.

He didn't see Oscar, Ruby, or Danna in the confusion—but his attention did fall on Nightmare.

She was in the stands, gripping the back of one of the seats, scanning the arena with apparent awe. Until her gaze latched on to him.

Logically, he knew it could have all been in his own head. His practical thoughts fought to stay in control, reminding him that there was no real way for him to know what Nightmare was thinking. But, somehow, he felt like there was an understanding that passed between them in that moment.

I have fought to protect the people I care about. I have fought to defend my beliefs.

I see now that you have, too.

Are we really so different?

Nothing had changed.

And yet, everything had changed. Two minutes ago, he would have killed her. But in the light of this wonderful clarity, nothing but a truce would suffice.

Nothing but a chance for peace, for compassion, for—

A shadowy form gathered at the edge of his vision. Adrian cocked his head, feeling the disturbance in this stunning new reality like a knife slashing through tissue paper.

Phobia appeared in the stands, standing behind a boy who was, inexplicably, wearing Ace Anarchy's helmet. The boy didn't seem to notice Phobia towering over him.

It was as though it were happening in slow motion. One moment, Adrian's thoughts were full of wonder and possibilities and truth. Of second chances and hope.

The next—they were nothing but horror.

"No!"

His scream made Nightmare shift to see what had caught his attention.

Phobia swung his scythe. The blade punctured the boy's abdomen, slicing from his navel to his breastbone.

The world stilled. The air left Adrian's lungs and refused to return.

He heard a scream, and thought it might have been Nightmare.

As the boy collapsed, Phobia withdrew the blade, sending blood splattering across the stands.

He took hold of the helmet with one skeletal hand and lifted it off the boy's head.

Callum Treadwell. Wonder.

"One cannot be awed who has no soul," Phobia said, and it

seemed almost as though there were humor in his brittle voice. "Just as one cannot be brave who has no fear."

Adrian blinked. He was still in shock at the senselessness of it. Dazed not only by the sight of Callum's lifeless body slumped over a seat, but by the jumble of worldviews crashing through his thoughts.

Heroes and villains. Friends and foes. And those words . . . that phrase . . .

One cannot be brave . . .

A sour taste filled Adrian's mouth. He gaped at Phobia and felt the injustice of Callum's death surge through him as the words that had haunted him for nearly his whole life burrowed into his skull.

Phobia.

It was Phobia.

And now, standing over Callum's body, Phobia held Ace Anarchy's helmet. He lifted his voice so all would hear him, even as the spell of wonder evaporated from their minds.

"You have all fought bravely," he said. "And now . . . it is time for you to know fear."

Then he was a phantom, an inky, transient monster soaring like a bird of prey over their heads, his cloak like darkness. He dropped into the center of the arena, making no noise as he stepped across the platform and lifted the helmet overhead.

The helmet left his grip, hovering in the air for a moment, before settling onto Ace Anarchy's shoulders.

Ace Anarchy lifted his head.

The shackles on his wrists sprang loudly apart and fell to the dirt.

"Master of Anarchy," Phobia rasped. "Rise again, and let us watch them fall."

CHAPTER THIRTY-FIVE

THE MOMENT THAT Ace Anarchy was in possession of his helmet, everything changed. He did not stand so much as float upward, his spine straightening and his hands flexing, as if he were regaining feeling in his extremities.

The arena began to tremble. Wood splintered and metal groaned. Seats were yanked up from where they had been bolted in the stands and sent soaring toward the Renegades who still had enough strength to fight, pinning many of them in place. The steel trusses that held the light fixtures were torn from their structures, dropping onto Ace's enemies, curling around them into makeshift cages.

Adrian felt like he was watching the scene unfold from somewhere outside of himself. None of it felt real—not the armor heavy on his skin, not the blood dripping down the bleachers, not Ace Anarchy suddenly, impossibly, returned to power.

Sensing that they would soon lose this fight if they didn't stop him, the remaining Renegades shifted their attention to Ace. It might have left them open to attacks from the Anarchists and

Cragmoor prisoners, except they, too, seemed dazed by the quick turn of events. How swiftly their worldviews had been altered and tested in the space of only a few minutes.

First, Callum Treadwell, and now this.

On the field, Blacklight threw a blinding strobe into Ace Anarchy's face. The villain instinctively ducked his head, putting the briefest pause on his assault on the arena.

It was enough time for the Captain to hurl his chromium pike. The weapon speared through the air, glinting in the spotlights still aimed at the stage.

Ace flew upward. The pike missed him by mere inches. He snarled at the Captain, and then with a wicked grin and a flick of his wrist, he lifted the chains that had held the Cragmoor prisoners off the ground and sent them flying at Blacklight.

One chain wrapped around Blacklight's torso, locking his arms at his sides. Another chain swept around his head, gagging his mouth.

"No!" Adrian screamed, his voice mingling with a hundred others.

But it was not enough.

Ace flicked his fingers.

The chains yanked in opposite directions, snapping Blacklight's neck.

Cold sweat dripped down the back of Adrian's neck as the arena filled with screams. He heard his dad yelling—*Evander!*

Fury roared inside Adrian. He called the laser diode up on the forearm of his suit. Every part of him that had been filled with wonder when Callum had taken over the helmet was now filled with rage. White sparks flashed in his vision as his gauntlet began to glow.

He was not the only one spurred on by Blacklight's murder. On the field, Tsunami released a guttural scream and sent a tidal wave crashing toward the villain, but Ace merely flicked his wrist and the entire platform on which he'd been shackled flipped onto its side, creating a barrier between him and the water. The wave broke and crashed away from him, flooding half of the arena. Ace's fingers twitched, tossing the platform at Tsunami. She cried out and raised her arms to defend herself as the makeshift stage crashed on top of her, burying her beneath its weight.

In that moment, Ace roared with pain, one arm jerking back, but striking only air.

Adrian held his fist toward the villain, but hesitated. Ace spun, allowing Adrian to see a knife buried to the hilt in his back, near his left kidney. Adrian had not seen anyone throw it, which meant . . . the Dread Warden had just stabbed him.

Adrian gulped. He was so far away. An attempt to hit Ace would put his invisible dad at risk.

He didn't have time to make the decision. From the stands on the opposite side of the field, Queen Bee screeched at the sight of the blood soaking into Ace Anarchy's prison uniform. She threw her arms forward, and every wasp flew in Ace's direction, searching for the invisible assailant. They found him easily, the black cloud of their thick, buzzing bodies forming the silhouette of the Dread Warden. Adrian heard his cry of pain. Simon flickered in and out of view a couple of times, before becoming fully visible as he collapsed to his knees, curled into a ball in an attempt to defend himself from the painful venom of the insects' stings.

Adrian adjusted his aim and fired.

The concussion beam struck Queen Bee in the chest, probably the best shot he'd ever had from such a distance. She fell backward, landing awkwardly across a row of plastic chairs.

The swarm shifted away from the Dread Warden, flying back to protect their fallen queen.

But Ace was waiting. The knife had pulled itself from his back and as soon as the distance between him and the Dread Warden was clear, he sent the weapon straight for his enemy's throat.

Another flutter of motion replaced the swarm of bees—golden butterflies, converging in front of the Dread Warden. Danna blocked the knife with her forearm, knocking it from the air.

"Nice try," she hissed.

Ace cocked his head. "I remember you. Last we saw each other, I believe I had you trapped in a *pillowcase.*"

Whatever counterattacks either of them were planning were interrupted by a new volley of attacks aimed at Ace, drawing his attention away from Danna and the Dread Warden. No one dared attack him with more weapons, seeing how easily he deflected them and turned them on their own, and so he was pummeled instead by sandstorms, streams of acid rain, even deafening sound waves. Ace blocked what onslaught he could, using everything at his disposal to put a series of barriers around himself—chairs, doors, the podium, cinder blocks torn out of the walls, sheets of metal dragged down from the ceiling. Adrian himself sent a series of fireballs and concussion beams into the melee, but none of them made it through Ace's defenses.

All the while, Ace's eyes were shining, as if this were a game he'd come to miss.

Until a bolt of black smoke struck him directly in the face, sending Ace into a frenzy of coughs and wiping the grin away. Pride swelled inside Adrian. He was sure it had come from Oscar somewhere in the chaos.

Danna morphed again into the monarch swarm. The Dread Warden was on his feet, still visible, and trying to stumble out of the path of destruction, but his movements were jerky and he kept slipping on the uneven, muddy ground.

Adrian crouched and leaped, landing with a hard thump in the squelching mud. He ran the rest of the way toward his dad, skidding beside him as Simon stumbled and fell hard onto one knee. This close, Adrian could see the marks of dozens of stings he'd received on his face, hands, and throat, everywhere his uniform didn't cover. Swelling splotches marked with raised white welts.

"Are you okay?" Adrian said.

Simon looked up at him, surprised. Seconds later, Hugh dropped down on Simon's other side, breathing hard from his sprint. His steely eyes glanced at the Sentinel, but darted immediately to his husband, while the ground rumbled and walls cracked around them. "Simon, what happened? What's wrong?"

"At least one of those hornets must have had Agent N," said Simon. He seemed almost apologetic as he met Hugh's gaze. "I've been neutralized."

Hugh set his jaw, and Adrian knew that he'd been expecting this response.

The air left Adrian's lungs. The Dread Warden—a member of the Council, an original Renegade—now a normal human, just like that.

"We need to get you out of here," said Hugh, putting an arm around Simon. "Can you stand?"

Simon ignored the question and the offer of help. "Have you seen Adrian?"

Adrian flinched at the worry that passed between his fathers. As Hugh shook his head, Adrian had to bite his tongue to hold in the truth.

"We'll find him," said Hugh as he helped Simon to his feet.

"He's strong. He has to be fine." He said it almost like a threat to the universe.

Adrian grimaced.

Simon nearly crumpled as soon as he put weight on his legs. "I'm okay," he said, waving a hand at Hugh's concern. "It's just . . . my whole body feels like it's burning up from the inside out. Whatever venom those wasps have—" He groaned.

"Here, let me take him," said Adrian.

Hugh frowned.

"You need to stop Ace Anarchy," Adrian added, knowing that he was lucky to not have drawn the villain's attention so far. He remembered how Ace had easily taken control of the Sentinel's armor in the catacombs, and that was without his helmet. If he tried to engage Ace Anarchy now, he would be more a liability than an asset.

Hugh's expression eased just a fraction. "Thank you."

"Don't get killed," Simon muttered.

Hugh almost smiled. "I'd like to see him try." Then he was gone.

Only once they were alone did Simon sigh. "I wouldn't."

"He'll be okay. Come on. Put your weight on me."

Simon leaned into Adrian, and together they started for the nearest exit, a concrete tunnel leading toward the arena's administration offices. Despite his pain and the distress of losing his powers, Simon kept looking around, squinting through the smoke and dust.

Adrian knew he was searching for *him*.

They were halfway to the tunnel when Simon tripped over the outstretched leg of a fallen prisoner—dead or unconscious, Adrian couldn't tell. Simon grunted in pain as his shoulder bashed into the ground.

Adrian stooped beside him, trying to help him back up, while keeping one eye on the fight at the center of the field. The ground around Ace was littered with debris and fallen bodies. Many Renegades were seeking cover in the stands, but it was futile when Ace could so easily tear those seats apart. Captain Chromium reached his fallen pike.

Simon gripped Adrian's forearms and pulled himself to his feet again, but they both stood, entranced and hopeful, as Captain Chromium began charging toward Ace Anarchy.

"Come on, Hugh," Simon whispered.

Hugh picked up speed. Adrian gripped Simon's elbow as he watched his dad close the distance to his longtime foe.

He was twenty feet away.

Ace's back was turned. The attacks from the Renegades were less frequent as more and more were trapped beneath piles of rubble and furniture, but they hadn't given up. Ace had pulled down so much of the arena's roof that there was a wide hole above them, open to the cold, cloudy night sky. The edges of its domed shape were beginning to cave in without proper support, yet he continued to rip out chunks of sheet metal and I-beams, deflecting a bolt of electricity, blocking a stream of molten lava, sending a group of Renegades scattering for cover as he shot a volley of steel pipes after them.

Captain Chromium was twelve feet away. Ten. *Eight*—

A set of shackles reared up from the busted platform underfoot, latching on to the Captain's ankles. He fell forward, sprawling across the ground. The pike speared into the dirt only a few feet away from where Ace stood.

"*No!*" Adrian and Simon yelled simultaneously. Simon made to move toward Hugh, but Adrian gripped his arm, holding him back.

As Ace Anarchy faced his archenemy, two more shackles lifted from the rubble and clamped around the Captain's wrists, chaining them together.

"Use your impressive strength to break free of those, *Captain*." Someone from the stands sent a ball of crackling energy toward Ace. He listed his head and the arena's enormous display screen fell to the ground, absorbing the blast. "Or have you lost your edge in the ten years since we last met?"

"Go," Adrian hissed. "I'll help him." He released Simon and faced Ace Anarchy, though fear was pounding inside his skull. *One cannot be brave who has no fear.*

His fists tightened.

"No offense," said Simon, "but I don't think that tin-can suit of yours is going to protect you against him."

"Yeah, Pops, I know. But trust me. I've got this."

There was a pause, before Simon asked, "What did you say?"

Exhaling, Adrian pressed a hand to his chest.

The armor began to retract.

◇◇◆◇◇

Nova had stopped trying to revive Callum. She had known it was futile from the beginning, but she'd spent countless minutes trying to stanch the bleeding coming from his abdomen. It was hopeless. She doubted even the most talented of prodigy healers could have closed up a wound like this.

Finally, she stumbled away from his body. No tears came, but she could hardly breathe. She looked around. She'd almost forgotten where she was. The arena was barely recognizable from the place where she had once fought the Gargoyle and earned a place among her enemies.

Death and destruction.

Isn't that what Ace was known for?

Isn't that precisely what Callum had so desperately wished to prevent?

There were so many bodies, heroes and villains alike. She spotted a fair number of Renegades hiding behind crumbled walls and overturned chairs, occasionally daring to reveal themselves to throw another attack at Ace, but nothing was working. They were no match for him. They hadn't been ten years ago, and it was as if no time had passed. The sick, frail uncle she and the others had cared for this past decade was gone in a blink, replaced with the villain the world remembered.

Nova wasn't sure that *she* remembered this villain. Who was he?

Either way, the battle had become his show now. She saw Honey on the opposite side of the arena, up in the stands, bent over a couple of chairs as her bees climbed across her body. It reminded Nova of maggots on a corpse, and she shuddered, hoping Queen Bee wasn't dead.

Phobia was harder to find, until she noticed the inky-black boa constrictor wriggling its way toward the wingless Tamaya Rae, and remembered that the Councilwoman was supposed to be afraid of snakes. Her gut curdled and Nova was surprised at the sympathy that surged through her. She had no love for Thunderbird, and yet . . . hadn't she suffered enough?

Dragging her attention away, she spotted Leroy against the short wall that surrounded the field, along with a group of Cragmoor inmates. The lot of them were covered in blood and dirt, watching Ace Anarchy with equal parts awe and uncertainty and, in Leroy's case, an eager grin.

With her allies accounted for, Nova dared to search for Adrian.

She hadn't seen him once throughout this whole ordeal. Maybe he'd stayed home in silent protest of Agent N and the execution. Was it too much to hope?

She did occasionally catch glimpses of Danna's butterflies in the cacophony. And yes—there—Ruby and Oscar were together up in one of the commentator booths that lined the top of the stands. The glass window had been smashed, and Oscar was shooting darts of smoke at Ace, for what it was worth. She wondered why Ruby hadn't joined the brawl on the field. It wasn't like her to sit out a fight. Either way, Nova was relieved to see them both alive.

But where was Adrian?

She stumbled away from Callum's body, her legs heavy as lead.

Ace was going to destroy them all if she didn't stop this. He had his helmet now. They had succeeded.

They could leave.

Why hadn't they left?

At the end of the aisle, she nearly tripped on a small form that was curled up against the last plastic seat. Nova froze.

Magpie didn't raise her head, though she no doubt knew that Nova was there. That *Nightmare* was there. She had her knees pulled to her chest, her arms wrapped tightly around them. Her face was coated in dust and streaked with tears.

Nova didn't know what to do. Magpie was a Renegade, an enemy. She'd never even liked the girl to begin with.

But still, something inside Nova refused to let her just walk away.

"He annoyed the hell out of me," Magpie said with a hiccup. Nova was surprised that she was speaking at all, and at that, not making sassy commentary for once. She sniffed. "But still . . . I thought, if he had the helmet, we might be able to win. He was obnoxious as hell, but he was always . . . more heroic than any of us. He didn't deserve . . ." Magpie grimaced. "It's my fault. I shouldn't have given him the helmet."

Nova swiped the sweat from her forehead, no doubt leaving traces of blood in its wake. "It's Phobia's fault."

Sniffling again, Magpie turned her head to Nightmare, her eyes full of loathing. "It's your fault, too."

Nova swallowed, hard. "I know."

She reached forward. Magpie started to pull away, but it was too late. Nova's fingers brushed her forehead and the kid sank down onto the steps, asleep.

Nova staggered down the rest of the stairs and over the rail. She was too weary for a graceful landing, and instead collapsed when she hit the muck-covered field. She forced herself to stand and keep going.

She noticed *him* then. The Sentinel, standing in front of the Dread Warden, who was remarkably visible for once. Visible, with his face covered in swollen welts. Ace was speaking again, taunting Captain Chromium, who had shackles binding his wrists and ankles.

Nova could still stop this. Everything had spun out of control so quickly. This had not been what she'd planned, what she'd wanted.

She needed to get to Ace.

"Ace," she started, but it was barely a croak. How many times tonight had she screamed? In anger, in heartbreak, in denial. "Ace . . ."

The Sentinel put himself between Ace Anarchy and the Dread Warden, acting like a protective shield. Nova shook her head. He was an idiot if he didn't realize how vulnerable that suit would be to a telekinetic like Ace.

Except . . . it was the Sentinel who captured him in the first place . . .

Then, the Sentinel pressed a hand to his chest, and the armored plates started to condense, the suit folding in on itself. It was like watching an origami doll as it got smaller and smaller, then disappeared altogether into the chest of a human boy.

Nova froze.

The world faded, a tunnel around her vision. Like peering through narrow binoculars, bringing the world into sharp focus, yet being unable to comprehend what she was seeing.

The boy . . .

The Sentinel . . .

It was *Adrian*.

Even as she stared, trying to comprehend, her uncle was lifting a thousand weapons from the debris, surrounding Adrian and his dad with everything from abandoned blades to splintered wooden beams.

"No . . ." Her voice broke.

Ace didn't hear.

She staggered forward. She couldn't quite align the identity of Adrian with the Sentinel, but she could see that Ace intended to kill him. There would be no surviving the attack of so many weapons at once.

She couldn't watch it. Not him, too. *Anyone* but Adrian—

"Ace!" she cried. "Ace, wait!"

He didn't wait.

With the twitch of a finger, he sent the amassed shrapnel flying at Adrian.

Nova screamed.

Adrian thrust out his left hand.

Something erupted from his palm, expanding outward, encapsulating him and Simon before Nova's scream had broken.

The spears, the daggers, the broken pieces of concrete, all struck it with deadly force and ricocheted harmlessly away.

Nova's scream stammered and fell silent. In shock. In utter disbelief.

What *was* it?

A wall of sorts. A protective barrier made of invisible bricks, each held together with glowing copper-colored mortar. It stood like a circular tower around Adrian and his father. A medieval turret, imbued with some sort of force field . . .

How had he done it?

For that matter, how did he do any of the things the Sentinel could do? He was Adrian. He was *Sketch*.

Ace, too, seemed surprised. He inspected Adrian through the shimmering wall that divided them. "You are full of tricks," he mused. "But don't get cocky. I've yet to meet a wall I couldn't bring down."

"The tattoo?" Nova murmured, remembering the tattoo he'd given himself on his inner wrist. The castle turret. *In theory, I'll be able to use it to create a barrier around myself and anyone who's near me. . . .*

She tore her gaze away from Adrian and stumbled toward her uncle. "Ace," she panted, grabbing his arm. He startled, as if he'd forgotten there was anyone here but his enemies. "We need to leave."

Through the slitted hole of the helmet, he considered her. "Leave? Things are just getting interesting."

"*Ace*," she said, more insistent now. "You have your freedom. You have your helmet. We all sacrificed a lot for that. We need to take care of our injured. We need to regroup."

He snorted derisively. "We need to finish what we've started." With a roar, Ace reached one hand toward the sky, then pulled his fist back down.

Steel beams erupted from the walls. Concrete blocks blew up from the floor. A cyclone of stone, wood, plaster, and glass spun through the arena, crashing into the iridescent barrier. Adrian was motionless, his expression hinting at only the slightest bit of fear as his barrier was pummeled from every side, as Ace Anarchy did his best to destroy the wall.

But Adrian's wall held.

"Ace!" Nightmare yelled, her voice barely carrying over the storm he'd created. "Stop! *Uncle Ace, please!*"

The chaos shuddered, slowed, and finally stilled. Ace's expression was still full of vitriol, his face contorted with loathing. "If this is about *him*——"

"It's about *us*," she said, only half lying. "Your allies and friends. Your family. Look around. We've done enough today. Now, we need to take care of our own."

Ace did look around, and Nova could only guess what he was seeing. The ravages of battle, the destruction he and his helmet had wrought, the bodies—so many bodies . . .

A loud hiss sent a shiver along her spine. Nova spun to see the boa constrictor rising up, its eerie white eyes meeting hers. Then the snake's body melted into a sludgy liquid and Phobia emerged once more, his cloak shimmering briefly like snakeskin before solidifying around his body. The hood wavered from his raspy breaths, his nonexistent mouth.

Nova could feel his accusations before he spoke, and she didn't want to hear them. She didn't want Ace to hear them.

The truth.

She was terrified that Ace Anarchy would win this fight.

She lifted a hand toward Phobia, her lips curving into a snarl. "Not now," she said, before fixing her attention back on her uncle.

"Ace, please. We came here for you, and we succeeded. Remember your purpose. A world without persecution. A society with free will. We can achieve that. But not here. Not like this."

As quickly as the fit of anger had come, Ace morphed back into a picture of quiet temperament. Muscles relaxing. Fingers spreading wide.

Everything still caught in his frozen cyclone came crashing down. Their allies slowly appeared from the rubble, emerging from their hiding places. Not only the Anarchists and the Rejects, but the prisoners, too.

Ace scanned them mutely, then allowed his gaze to linger a moment longer on Captain Chromium, the Dread Warden, and Adrian. There was a promise in his silence. A promise, and a threat.

Nova tried not to think about it.

Ace turned to the Cragmoor inmates, those still standing amid the chaos, and stretched out his fingers. The group of them grimaced and bent over simultaneously, their faces tight with pain. Nova winced, sure that Ace was hurting them, though she couldn't imagine why.

And then one of the inmates—the same who had sat beside her in the cafeteria—reached for the collar of his jumpsuit and tore apart the flimsy fabric.

A small device clattered to the ground at his feet.

The tracker that had been buried in his skin, now slick with blood and covered with dust.

Ace released himself of the device, too, pulling it out of his skin and down his sleeve before dropping it into the dirt and crushing it beneath his heel.

Ace lured a wide concrete slab into their midst and stepped up onto it, gesturing for the others to follow. Nova felt a twinge of relief to see Honey alive, though bedraggled and stumbling, leaning on Leroy's shoulders as they both limped toward Ace. Others followed—the Rejects, the inmates—gathering at Ace's side in the midst of the battlefield. All except Phobia, who dissolved into a wisp of black smoke without another word.

Their dead were left behind, including Winston Pratt. Nova cast a sorrowful last look at his body and Callum's, as Ace raised his palms and the concrete lifted into the air. It drifted slowly, smoothly over the arena's field.

Kneeling to keep her balance, Nova forced herself to face Adrian, He was still standing, brave and defiant behind the shimmering wall that divided them. The wall that he had built to protect himself from her and her allies.

She was overcome with more emotions than she could name as their eyes met across the distance.

Then the villains cleared the destroyed roof of the arena and were gone.

CHAPTER THIRTY-SIX

THEY DID NOT soar for long, though from the serenity and strength in Ace's eyes, Nova believed he could have kept them in the air for a year if he'd wanted. He was not tired. He was not unsure.

Leroy was guiding Ace, and their time spent weightless after leaving the arena was too short. Nova wasn't ready to face whatever was going to come next.

She was still reeling from the truth of what she had witnessed. Her brain kept replaying those last moments in the arena over and over again. The Sentinel was Adrian. Adrian was the Sentinel.

A hundred other realizations struck her in fast succession. The Sentinel's uncanny ability to gain new powers each time she faced off against him. Adrian thinking he could use tattoos to increase his own abilities. How the Sentinel always seemed nearby when she and the rest of the team were there. How she'd never seen the two of them at the same place, at the same time. How the Sentinel had seemed murderous when he'd found her over Max's unconscious body. How he'd once rescued her as the Cloven Cross Library burned around them.

Adrian. The Sentinel.

The Sentinel. Adrian.

She felt like the biggest fool in history for not having seen it sooner.

Adrian Everhart. Who had fixed her bracelet. Brought her childhood dream to life. Made it possible to have one night in which she could sleep, for once feeling safe and protected.

He was her enemy. He was the one who had been hunting her all this time. He was the one who had captured Ace. *Adrian.*

Her stomach grew tighter and wormier until she was sure she would be sick.

Ace changed their trajectory, lowering them toward the ground where Leroy indicated.

Nova choked back the sour bile that had filled her mouth. She would not think about it. Not Adrian. Not the Sentinel. Not Winston. Not Callum. Not those who had died, nor the hundreds of Renegades who were now powerless.

Not the fact that even the Anarchists had lied to her.

She had done what she'd set out to accomplish that day, and she would allow herself this moment to be proud. Though she had hoped for far less devastation, on *both* sides, what was done was done and there was no going back. She tried to find solace in knowing that the Anarchists were together again. Ace had his helmet. The Renegades could no longer threaten them with Agent N.

Things were not what she'd hoped, but at least she had not failed.

This was a good day.

Ace had set them down in the street outside Dave's Pawnshop. A man smoking a cigarette near the side alley stood gawking at their ragtag group, with their muddied jumpsuits, blood-soaked clothes,

Ace and his helmet. The man's mouth hung agape as the cigarette burned, forgotten, down to his fingers.

Ace twitched, and the cigarette dropped to the ground, extinguishing itself in a puddle of standing water beneath the nearest street lamp.

The man let out a wail, shaky and terrified, then turned and ran. Soon the sound of his pounding footsteps fleeing down the alley was the only noise they could hear. That, and the electric zaps of the fluorescent CLOSED sign illuminated in the pawnshop window.

One of the Rejects cleared his throat and said, quietly, "So, that was Dave."

No one else spoke for a long while. No one moved toward the store. Everyone seemed to be waiting for Ace to make the first move. When Nova dared to look at Ace, though, she could see disgust in the eyes behind the helmet.

Finally, Leroy explained, "There is room in the sublevels for us all. It isn't much, but . . ."

"We are not staying here," said Ace. "We will not be sent into hiding and secrecy like rats, not again. Not this time."

He lifted his hand and the barred door of the pawnshop blew outward toward them, snapping the hinges, destroying the locks and bolts. A bell clattered but was quickly silenced as the door landed with a bang on the sidewalk.

The noise was so jarring and unexpected, the whole group jumped—except Ace, who strolled through the opening as if nothing had happened. "There are more allies here?" he said, scanning the shelves of electrics and household appliances, the cases of costume jewelry. "Inform them we've arrived, and it is time to leave."

One of the Rejects started heading for the backroom, but it was unnecessary. Summoned by the commotion, it was mere seconds before Narcissa burst out into the store, brandishing a handgun.

She drew up short when she saw them, and Millie crashed into her from behind. Narcissa barely caught a nearby shelf. Soon, they were all there, fanning out around the cases, gaping slack-jawed at Ace Anarchy. His prison uniform covered in rips and blood. His skinny wrists bruised from shackles. But fearsome in the recognizable helmet, his posture erect and an undeniable sense of power that seemed to shimmer in the air around him, as if the world itself were electrified by his presence.

Ace allowed them to stare. Allowed them to catch their breaths. Allowed them to come to terms with his return.

Then, without introduction, he said, "I understand that you chose not to join the fight this evening. You opted to protect your own self-interests, rather than join my comrades in an attempt to secure my freedom. You chose your life over mine."

Even in the dim lighting, Nova saw Narcissa going pale. Fear flashed through the expressions of the Rejects who had stayed away from the arena that night.

Nova opened her mouth, prepared to come to their defense. Ace should know that they had helped, even if they had not fought. But before she could speak, Ace started to laugh. A low, amused sound.

"You are Anarchists now. As such, you are permitted to *always* choose your life over anyone else's. I commend you. And—I forgive you."

No one moved. No one else dared to laugh, or even look relieved.

Ace waved his arm, as if shooing them away. "Get your belongings and any useful supplies. You have two minutes."

Turning away, Ace gestured to a rack of clothing against the far wall. A long military jacket peeled off its hanger and flew to him, securing itself around his shoulders and covering the disgusting jumpsuit. As the gold buttons did up themselves, Ace marched back toward the street, as if he couldn't stand to be surrounded by such mediocre junk for a second longer.

The villains exchanged looks, their bodies tense in the shadowed room. Some looks were elated and hopeful. Others were filled with doubt, even dread.

But there was no discussion. No questions asked. No stories told.

They got to work.

◇◇◆◇◇

When the group descended from the sky a second time, their destination seemed, to Nova, no more hospitable than the pawnshop.

Ace had brought them back to the wasteland, where his cathedral had stood more than ten years before. The moment their feet touched the ground, Narcissa, clutching a backpack of hastily gathered belongings, shuddered in relief and collapsed against a toppled column.

Much of the northeast side of the cathedral was still standing: the library, the chapter house, the main chapel. Even the bell tower was there, though most of the roof and the south wall had crumbled, leaving some of the huge bronze bells visible through the stone ruins. Otherwise, the cathedral was not much more than a pile of rubble. The nave, the choir, so much exquisite architecture, destroyed in the cataclysm between heroes and villains.

Already Nova could sense the dismay from her companions. The pawnshop may not have been much, but it had provided shelter and security. Ace couldn't expect them to stay here.

But Ace's countenance was altogether different as he stood before the ruins, taking in the abandoned bell tower with the faint light of dusk glinting off the helmet. Nova began to wonder if Uncle Ace, when he wasn't downtrodden and suffering, might actually have a taste for the grandiose.

Ace stepped forward, clearing a path in the rubble with a twitch of his fingers. He paused a few steps away from where the main entrance had once stood, where worshipers would have entered the nave through a pair of vast, ornately carved wooden doors. "I am proud of you all," he said, facing them. "Prodigies the world over will be encouraged by our victory tonight."

Leroy lifted a hand in Nova's direction. "Our little Nightmare deserves most of the credit. She planned it all." He winked at her. "Everything will change now. You will see, Nova. Nothing shall be in vain."

Nova frowned, memories of the fight flashing through her thoughts. Callum. Winston. *Adrian.*

She didn't want credit for everything that had happened, and she certainly hadn't planned it all. By using Agent N, Leroy and Honey had double-crossed her. Perhaps the decision had resulted in some sort of victory, but Nova couldn't help feeling that she'd lost as much as she'd won.

Phobia stood off from their group, gripping his scythe in one hand as he peered toward the city buildings beyond the wasteland. "There will be a delectably exorbitant quantity of fear today," he said, his voice being carried on the evening breeze. "Panic. Desperation." His cloak fluttered as he craned his head toward Ace. "Retaliation. It will not be long before they come for us."

"So they shall." Ace sounded almost excited by the prospect. "And we will be ready to meet them when they do. I will not fall to the Renegades again." He flicked his fingers through the air and the rubble trembled at their feet. Rivulets of dust slid down the sides of fallen arches. Colorful shards of stained glass glinted beneath the setting sun.

"Oh, Ace," Honey swooned. Nova realized with a start that Honey was crying. Already her dark mascara had made pathways down her cheeks. She sank to her knees at Ace's side and grabbed his hand, nuzzling her face against it. "It is so very good to have you back. To see you as you were."

She went to kiss Ace's fingers, but he pulled his hand from her grip. "Stand up," he said, almost sharply.

Honey started, blinking up at him, but Ace was already making his way over the foundation of where the nave had stood. Stone and crumbled benches parted before him.

"You are a queen, Honey Harper," he said, lifting his hands to either side. The crumbled stone blew upward and stayed, hovering, in the air. A million pieces of debris, waiting.

Narcissa gasped and dove off the column as it, too, began to rise. As it *all* began to rise.

It felt like the threat of an earthquake beneath their feet.

"You must never kneel," Ace continued. "Not to me. Not to any-one. Not one of us shall ever kneel again."

He spun in a slow circle, studying the bits of wreckage that now filled the air. Nova remembered this look from her childhood. Ace had always seen the world differently—like a series of building blocks that he could learn the secrets to, if only he cared to inspect them a little closer.

His confidence was disarming.

He was finally whole again.

"My friends," he said, his voice filled with tenderness. "My dream was never to be a king lording over his subjects. I never wished to rule. But history has shown me my mistakes. If hubris is the great flaw of our enemies, then apathy was mine. I did not do enough to guide humanity down the path toward true freedom. I was too passive. Content to let free will run its course, I stayed in the shadows while others claimed control. But now my fate is clear. This is not the day that I become a king." He raised his hands toward the brightening sky. "Today is the day we become gods."

The sun glinted off the wall of the cathedral, its beams striking Ace and setting his figure aglow. He was dazzling. Golden and unstoppable.

While they watched, motionless, Ace did what Nova had never seen him do before.

For once, he did not destroy.

He created.

He rebuilt.

It was like watching a cataclysm in reverse. Great cracks in the cathedral's foundation fused together. The stone walls reassembled themselves, piece by piece. The towering columns stood like soldiers, while the vaulted beams of the ceiling perched high above. Glass shards melted together, forming a gallery of windows along each breathtaking wall. Splinters of raw wood were knit into pews and choir seats and polished handrails. Not a piece was missing from the west face's facade—every spire, every gargoyle, every Gothic arch, every watchful saint.

When the rumbling of the earth fell quiet, Ace could no longer be seen, having enclosed himself within the opulent building. The rest of them stood outside the doors to the nave, their ornate carvings exactly as Nova remembered from her childhood—wheat fields and lambs and serenity.

No one moved. Nova's eyes stung from the dust that had been

kicked up in the reconstruction, but she hardly dared blink, lest this was all an illusion.

So often she had heard tales of the ruin Ace Anarchy had wrought on the city. In the early days of his revolution, he had collapsed whole bridges, torn down entire neighborhoods. He had been full of fury and passion. He had wanted to see this cruel world burned to the ground.

But the helmet and Ace's power could be used for other purposes, too.

What a marvel.

What a gift.

With her heartbeat thundering, Nova found herself clapping a hand over the star on her wrist. It was made of the same material, created by her father's hands, just as the helmet had been. She knew it was powerful, but could it be capable of something so miraculous?

Phobia moved first. With the blade of his scythe aloft, he drifted toward the grand entrance. The doors blew back as he approached, and Nova couldn't tell if it was Phobia who had controlled them or Ace.

Stirred into action, she followed, still half in a daze. The others filed in at her side.

She couldn't withhold a gasp as she stepped into the nave. It was precisely as she remembered. She felt like she was that same child, stricken and afraid, who had walked into this space all those years ago, having just had her life torn to shreds. Despite her sorrow, her breath had caught even then. She had not been immune to the magnificence that surrounded her. Every little detail of the cathedral had amazed her, and it amazed her still, staring up, up, up, at the vaulted ceiling.

Only one thing was missing.

Ace.

"Where did he go?" whispered Honey, and the tremor in her voice suggested to Nova that none of the Anarchists had ever seen Ace do anything like this before.

Suddenly, the peal of ringing bells echoed around them.

They exchanged glances. Narcissa and many of the Rejects appeared more than a little hesitant, while a number of the rescued Cragmoor inmates hovered together at the door, wary and guarded.

Narcissa was as pale as the white stone walls.

Nova had to remind herself that she had nothing to fear. None of them did. Not from Ace, at least. And so she started toward the bell tower, walking a path that felt like walking through a long-forgotten memory.

Not knowing what else to do, the others followed.

A number of their allies were panting by the time they reached the top of the staircase that spiraled up to the bell tower. Ace stood at one of the open-air windows, studying the city beyond the waste-land. Renegade Headquarters could be seen rising up from the skyline.

The bells had stopped ringing.

It was almost as though Ace *wanted* the Renegades to come find him. Was he so eager for another fight? Nova's nerves were frazzled. There was so much they had to discuss, and soon, before this went much farther.

Today is the day we become gods.

No.

Nova didn't want to be a god. She had a much different plan in mind, one that had been seeded during her time in Cragmoor prison, and one that felt more necessary now than ever before.

"Ace," she started, "they're going to know exactly where we

went." She gestured at the others, hoping for their support. "Should we talk about what to do from here? Make a plan?" She cleared her throat before adding. "I . . . have some ideas."

Ace turned, beaming at her. "You have always been full of ideas, my little Nightmare. I owe you so much. You have returned to me my strength, my power. You have laid the foundation for our ultimate victory. You have secured for us the Renegades' own weapon, ensuring not only our survival, but their demise."

Ace began to walk the perimeter of the bell tower. Though it was newly reconstructed, the wooden boards beneath his feet creaked exactly as they had when Nova was a child. He let his focus linger on the city skyline as he passed each window—eight in all, each hung with a bell of its own, though none as enormous as the two gigantic bells that hung in the tower's center. The steeple over their heads was a labyrinth of crisscrossing support beams, pulleys, and ropes. Nova could hardly believe that she was standing here, again, after all these years. That it could be so unchanged.

"I have been granted a great gift these past ten years," said Ace. "Rarely are we given the opportunity to ponder our failures and prepare ourselves for a new path. For this, I shall always be grateful for the Renegades and what they did. To me. To *us*." He dragged his fingers along the stone windowsills. "I now have a clarity of purpose that eluded me before. I was not prepared to usher our world into the society I envisioned. But that has changed. I believe in a man's freedom to craft his own life, to make his own choices, without the meddling of a higher power. Without the interference of arbitrary laws. Without the forced imposition of someone else's principles, all under the guise of providing for a *greater good*."

He scoffed. For as long as Nova could remember, this had been one of Ace's most hated phrases. That vague, altogether subjective notion of a so-called greater good. What did it even mean, he had often asked. Who got to decide what constituted that greater good, and what was worthy of the sacrifice in its favor?

"What is anarchy but our right to have our own thoughts, and to speak them? To have our own desires, and to use our own resources to obtain them? To not have to live in fear that everything we have worked so hard to procure will be taken from us against our will? *And yet . . .*" He sighed, and his voice grew quiet. "I must concede that it is not human nature to allow anarchy to prevail. A new ruling order will always rise up and claim power. In the past, I allowed other gangs and their leaders to become that ruling order."

He surveyed the prodigies around them, many who had fought alongside them at the arena. Nova wondered how many of them he recognized as gang members from years past.

"So long as we were no longer faced with persecution, and those that I loved were well cared for"—his gaze settled briefly on Nova—"then I did not bother myself with how the city was run, or who was profiting and who was suffering as a result. I did not wish to become the ruling elite I have always despised. I did not believe it was my place to choose the winners and losers of this world, as previous tyrants had chosen. But we must have a vision going forward. My friends. My companions. This time, I do have a vision."

Ace lifted his arms. "When a society collapses, a new master will rise up to replace the old. This time, we will be that master. We will be the new ruling order. If humanity is so determined to have a king to follow and a god to worship, then we will be those kings. We will be those gods." His voice rang through the tower. "But first, we must destroy the Renegades and everything they have built."

Nova's skin tingled. She knew she should be happy to see him so spirited. This was what she wanted, too, she reminded herself. No

Renegades. No Council. No villain gangs. Only the Anarchists—invincible to all the world.

With no superheroes to save the day, society would correct itself. No one would lie around waiting for handouts, expecting to be rescued. People would accept their own responsibilities. Defend their own families. And when someone mistreated another human being, their punishment would come from society itself, not some clueless government.

This was what she had fought for.

But not anymore. She had a vision of her own and, for the first time, it did not align with Ace and his ideals. Not entirely.

And so, she raised her voice and declared, simply, "*No.*"

CHAPTER THIRTY-SEVEN

ADRIAN STOOD SHIVERING for a long time, listening to the groans of compromised steel beams and the trickles of broken plaster. The villains were gone.

The arena was in shambles. The Renegades were in shambles.

But he had faced Ace Anarchy a second time and survived, *again*. That was no small feat.

"Adrian . . ."

Simon's voice from behind him was subdued, and it brought back a shock of memories that had been buried in the storm Ace Anarchy had created.

With a strained gulp, Adrian closed his fist. The clear, shimmering tower dissolved into the air like the remnants of sparklers raining down on them.

Thinking of sparklers made him think of Evander.

He shuddered as he turned to face Simon, braced for disappointment, maybe even anger. His identity as the Sentinel was revealed.

He'd had no choice, and yet, he wasn't sure he was ready for the fallout.

But Simon appeared more relieved than anything as he climbed painfully to his feet. They stared at each other, catching their breaths. Some of the swelling on Simon's face and arms was starting to go down, the pain gradually receding from his eyes.

Simon held out his arms.

Adrian exhaled and fell into the embrace. Simon flinched and Adrian quickly loosened his grip. "Sorry."

"It's okay," said Simon. "We're all right." Pulling away, he looked around. "We need to take stock of the injured, prioritize the wounds for any healers who weren't neutralized, get everyone else to the hospital. I need to check on Tsunami—"

"I'll get her. You help Dad get those shackles off."

Adrian ran toward the collapsed wooden stage, upturned and splintered so that it resembled a pile of old lumber more than the platform it had been only hours before. He started pulling the debris away, and soon was joined by others—those who were still strong enough to help. Behind him, he could hear Simon shouting orders, urging the Renegades to help the wounded and start gathering their dead.

Adrian had cleared away half the wooden planks before he finally spotted Tsunami's white boot. "Please, oh, please," he murmured, moving faster to reach her. Soon they had uncovered her body. Her eyes were closed and a stream of dark, drying blood covered half of her face, the result of a deep gash to her head.

Adrian fell beside her, searching for a pulse.

At first, he couldn't be sure if he was mistaking his own thrumming heartbeat for hers. But—no, there it was, faint but steady.

"She's alive!" he cried, even as someone was pressing a cloth to the wound on her head. Others started clearing a path so she could be taken to where a handful of healers were setting up to tend to the wounded.

Adrian scooped Kasumi into his arms. She felt fragile, but he had known her long enough to know her small form was deceptive. She was strong. She would make it through this.

Once he had handed her off to the healers, Adrian made his way through the wreckage, searching for more survivors. Dust coated the inside of his lungs. Smoke stung his eyes. The ground was littered with dead bees and bits of plaster, melted plastics and scorch marks, puddles of filthy water and broken glass.

He started to take stock of their losses, though the sight of so many casualties made him feel like he was being pulled apart, bit by bit. Adrian didn't know all of his peers well, but he knew enough to have an idea of which of them still lived with their parents, and who had children of their own. Who had been challenged at the trials and who had chosen to work in administration rather than be sent out on patrols. He knew they all believed in their purpose—to seek justice, to protect the weak, to defend the innocent.

He saw Genissa Clark's body sprawled against a wall. And in the stands, stubborn Magpie slumped onto the stairs. He saw Winston Pratt in a pool of blood, and Callum Treadwell—*Callum*—who had almost managed to end the slaughter when he had the helmet. Who, for just a moment, had shown them a different path.

He saw Evander Wade. Blacklight. Adrian had idolized him when he was growing up, convinced that he was by far the coolest of the Renegades' founding members. He had seemed so carefree, so suave, so quick with a joke.

Now he was dead.

Thunderbird had been neutralized. He spotted her tending to the injured, and almost didn't recognize her, not only because she no longer had the black wings folded at her back, but also because her face was swollen and burned where Cyanide had touched her. She had always been intimidating, not only with the massive wings, but also with the bolts of lightning she could conjure with a snap of her fingers. Though Captain Chromium often received the credit for being the most powerful of the group, Adrian had often suspected that Thunderbird was actually the strongest—she just wasn't the type to flaunt it. That argument could never be made again.

Simon was also forever changed. The Dread Warden was gone. Simon Westwood would never again be invisible, would never vanish in the blink of an eye.

But at least, Adrian thought, he would be able to visit with Max now, for as long as he wished.

It was a small consolation, but consolation nonetheless.

If Tsunami was all right, she and Captain Chromium would be the last of the Council with their abilities intact. It was a harrowing thought.

The damage wrought upon the Renegades that night was inconceivable. Not only in lives, but in superpowers, too. How many had been stung by those bees? How many superheroes had been lost?

He sought out his dads. Hugh had managed to free himself using the chromium pike to break apart the shackles, and he was now working to clear the rubbish away, searching for anyone else who might have been caught beneath a crashed wall or fallen truss.

Adrian was heading toward them when something crinkled beneath his boot. He paused and looked down. It was a square of pink-and-gold origami paper, still showing the creases where it had been folded into the delicate crane. Adrian recognized it as the crane that had flown directly to Captain Chromium, before everything had dissolved into chaos.

He picked it up and flipped over the paper, reading the message printed there.

Everyone has a nightmare.

Welcome to yours.

Jaw clenching, he shredded the paper in half, then fourths, tearing it apart until it was nothing but confetti fluttering to the mud.

"Adrian?"

He jolted and was relieved to see his friends tromping toward him through the debris.

Adrian beamed, overwhelmed with joy to see them all alive. He met them halfway, accepting a tight hug from Ruby, a clap on the back from Oscar. He wrapped an arm around Danna's shoulders, each of them leaning into each other, sweaty, stricken, and exhausted.

With a groan, Oscar collapsed onto a bench that had once been in the upper stands, but was now on the field, sunk halfway in mud. He started massaging the joints of his legs, which Adrian had never seen him do in public, no matter now tough a fight had been. This battle had pushed them all to their limits.

"Ruby, how are your . . . wounds?" said Adrian, not sure how to distinguish between old wounds and new. Ruby had taken off the gray uniform jacket, revealing a plain tank top and the bandages that she had always kept wrapped over her arm and shoulders. She had never stopped bleeding, not since the attack that had first awoken her powers years ago, but this was the first time Adrian had seen those bandages soaked through with actual blood.

"No more crystals," she said, and he couldn't tell if her tone was sad or simply truthful. "Now they won't stop bleeding. I'm fine, though. I'll talk to one of the healers after they take care of the people who really need help."

"Here," said Adrian, taking out his marker. "I can stitch them up for you."

Ruby hesitated, but then nodded. Danna helped unwrap the wounds, revealing the deep gashes that had been there, unhealed, for years.

"Do they hurt?" Oscar asked as Adrian wiped away what blood he could and started drawing stitches onto her skin.

"They've always hurt," Ruby said quietly, watching, expressionless.

Oscar started in surprise. This was news to Adrian, too, who had never once heard Ruby complain about her injuries. She had always focused more on the results. The bloodstones she had weaponized, the superhero she had become.

"That will do for now," said Adrian. "Keep you from losing too much blood before the healers can get to you, at least."

Ruby tenderly touched the black lines that had become black thread holding her wounds shut. "Thanks, Sketch," she whispered. Her lip began to tremble, but she hastily covered it up with a brilliant smile. "I don't know how I'm going to tell the twins. Being a superhero was the only thing that kept me even remotely relevant in their eyes." She chuckled, but it sounded forced.

"That is definitely not true," said Oscar.

She cut him a sideways glance. "You've met my brothers, right?"

"Yes, which is how I know they idolize you, and not just because you're a Renegade or because you bleed rubies." Oscar gestured at Ruby, sweeping one hand from her dyed black-and-white pigtails to the toes of her muck-covered boots. "It's because you're, like, the coolest big sister any kid could ask for. You can hit a target with a dagger from fifty feet away. You're proficient at three different kinds of martial arts. You know how to use a *grappling hook*."

"Oh." Ruby sighed longingly. "I'm going to miss my grappling hook."

"I will get you another grappling hook," said Oscar, reaching over to take her hand. "You're still Red Assassin. You're still a totally kickass superhero." He must have noticed the way Ruby's eyes had started to shine, because he went on, growing more emphatic with each word. "You're still the coolest person I've ever met, except for maybe Captain Chromium, but that's not really a fair comparison."

She chuckled. "Oscar . . ."

"And you're beyond relevant. You're, like, the thing that other things try to be relevant *to*. And you're fierce and loyal and crazy adorable when you're playing Battle to the Death, and I'll even admit, okay, it's not easy to say this, but you're right. You beat me in that last game, fair and square, even though I—"

"Oscar, stop!" she said, laughing outright now. "I get it. Thank you."

He paused and cleared his throat. "Right. Yeah. Sorry. Just saying." He hesitated, his focus landing on their entwined hands. He gulped. "Just . . . one more thing?"

Ruby faked an exasperated eye roll. "Oh, if you insist."

Oscar lifted his head. "You're the girl of my dreams."

Ruby's head swiveled toward him, the nonchalant smile evaporating.

"With or without superpowers," Oscar added, holding her gaze.

Color bloomed in Ruby's cheeks. Fresh tears started to gather in her eyes until, without much warning, she grabbed the front of Oscar's uniform and kissed him.

Adrian's eyebrows shot upward and he spun away, meeting Danna's amused gaze for half a second before they both spent some time inspecting the damaged roof overhead.

"Adrian?"

Adrian spun around to find himself face-to-face with both of his dads. Their features, at first, were unreadable. Weary. Cautious. A little relieved, a little disappointed, but not *angry* as far as he could tell.

They must have been done organizing the others, making sure aid was offered to those who needed it and cleanup of the arena was underway. It was time to focus on other matters.

Evidently, he was up first.

He swallowed. "I'm sorry I didn't tell you."

Hugh's mouth thinned and there was the anger Adrian had expected. But it was short-lived. He wilted and stepped forward, pulling Adrian into a tight hug.

Adrian held him back. "Thanks, Dad. I'm okay."

"That's the most important thing," said Hugh. "*You* are the most important thing." He pulled away, stoic again. "You still owe us a lot of explanations, though. Not just how, but why. You've broken a lot of rules, and taken advantage of our trust. But . . ." He sighed heavily. "Today, at least, I'm glad you did what you did. You were very brave, and . . . you saved a lot of people."

Adrian flinched, feeling like he hadn't saved enough. "We're superheroes," he murmured. "That's what we do."

"First order of business," interrupted Simon. "You need to tell us where Max is. It's likely Ace Anarchy will try to target him. We need to keep him safe, and we can't do that if we don't know where he is."

Adrian nodded. "He's staying with Ruby's family."

"I can go," said Ruby, standing beside him. "I'll get him, take him wherever you want me to."

Simon frowned. "What about . . . ?" He hesitated, taking in the stitches along her arm. Understanding swept over his features. "Ah. I'm sorry, Ruby."

She shrugged, and Adrian realized that she was still holding Oscar's hand. "These wounds aren't what made me a superhero."

"You're right, they weren't," said Hugh. His attention swept around the arena, at all the neutralized prodigies. "I hope you're not the only one who feels that way."

"What are we going to do?" said Danna, still limping as she joined them. "We only have a fraction of the prodigies we had before. How are we going to defeat Ace Anarchy now?"

"We only have a fraction here in Gatlon City," said Simon, "but we've already started reaching out to the international syndicates. They're sending reinforcements. All available Renegades will be arriving in the next twenty-four hours to help us move against the Anarchists."

"But we don't even know where they went," said Adrian.

"Actually," said Hugh, rather darkly, "we know exactly where they went."

"Ace Anarchy was never known for subtlety," added Simon. "He's returned to his cathedral."

Adrian stared at him, recalling the ruins where he and his team had fought Phobia. "The cathedral? Why would he want to go back there?"

"Maybe he's sentimental?" Oscar suggested.

Simon shook his head. "It's brilliant, actually. He's familiar with the landscape, the location, its strengths and weaknesses. Plus, with the wasteland, it's impossible to take the cathedral by surprise. They'll see an attack coming long before we get there."

"But . . . it's nothing but a pile of rubble and a bell tower," said Adrian.

"Not anymore. He's rebuilt it," said Hugh. "You were too young to remember the extent of Ace Anarchy's abilities, but it isn't terribly surprising to us. Some of the news media caught footage of the cathedral being . . . pieced back together."

Adrian's jaw dropped. He had heard a lot of stories of Ace Anarchy using his powers to tear buildings down, but he'd never known the telekinetic could also put them back up.

Adrian scanned the arena. So much violence. So many casualties. While they were waiting for help to arrive from the international syndicates, Ace Anarchy would be developing his own strategy to destroy the Renegades once and for all.

Could they afford to wait?

Hugh playfully smacked his arm. "Don't look so helpless. I'm still invincible, you know. We're not beat yet."

Adrian glared at him. "And you're going to stop him single-handedly?"

"If I have to. I've done it before."

"No, you didn't. You . . ." Adrian trailed off, not wanting to remind them all of what was *actually* their greatest weapon. Not Captain Chromium. Not even Agent N.

Their greatest weapon was Max, had always been Max.

But Adrian didn't want Max anywhere near Ace Anarchy.

"You had help," he finished lamely.

"He still has help," Danna said. "Those villains haven't defeated us yet. I'm ready for another round."

Adrian bit the inside of his cheek, considering. She was right. They were beat down, but not defeated.

Ace would be expecting them to realign their forces before making a move. He would expect a full-scale attack on the cathedral, because that's how the Renegades operated—with flashy attacks and extravagant displays of their strength. Whereas the Anarchists had adapted to be stealthy and secretive. They used the element of surprise, and that's how they had bested the Renegades this time. That's how Nightmare kept beating them.

Maybe he could win at her own game.

He faced his dads. They were already discussing counterattacks and battle maneuvers when he interrupted them.

"How much Agent N do you think they have left?"

Hugh shook his head. "It's impossible to say for sure, but from the amount we had in storage, and what was used here today . . ." He frowned, pondering the question, then shook his head. "I can't imagine it's much."

"Let's hope so," said Adrian. "If we're going to attempt a counterattack, it would be nice if they didn't have any more of that stuff at their disposal."

"It would," said Hugh, "but we can't know for sure. It wouldn't have required much to arm those bees with it. But I can talk to the lab, see if they can pull together an estimate for us."

"And do we have any left for ourselves?" asked Adrian.

It seemed to take a moment for his question to register. Finally, Simon said, "They replaced our supply with some sort of decoy."

"Yeah, I know, but there must be some left, somewhere?"

"I have some."

He bristled at the sound of Genissa Clark's haughty voice, though he did his best to hide his dislike as he faced her. She looked terrible, her skin practically translucent, with garish purple spots beneath her eyes. She was clutching her head, as if it would roll right off her shoulders if her hand wasn't there to support it. He was surprised to see her at all. He'd half expected her to be dead, but she must have only been unconscious.

Nightmare's doing?

"I took some with me when we went after Hawthorn," she said, unholstering a gun from her hip. "I still have one dart left."

Adrian wanted to appear grateful, but he was already trying to figure out what he would say when Genissa insisted she be allowed to join him on the risky mission he was considering.

To his surprise, she held the gun out to him, handle first.

"You can have it," she said, almost angrily. "I'm done playing heroes and villains. For real this time. The Renegades aren't worth this."

He took the gun and watched as she tried to saunter away, though her movements were stiff and jerky. Adrian opened the projectile chamber and saw the lone dart inside, swirling with green liquid.

"Uh-oh," said Oscar. "I sense some serious vigilante recklessness coming on."

Adrian glared at him, wishing he hadn't chosen that moment to remind his dads that they were still supposed to be upset with him.

"The only way we're going to defeat Ace Anarchy is if we can either get that helmet back or neutralize him," he said.

"To do that," said Hugh, "we need to get into the cathedral. And like I said, with that wasteland—"

"They'll see us coming," said Adrian. "But I know another way in."

CHAPTER THIRTY-EIGHT

A SILENCE DESCENDED on the cathedral tower, almost as loud in Nova's ears as the bells had been before. Her rebellion echoed among the bronze and timber, that single, simple proclamation. *No.*

Ace, his arms still outstretched from his grand speech, slowly turned toward her. It felt different now to see him with the helmet on, his strength and vitality so quickly restored, after years of watching his body deteriorate day after day.

She'd always assumed the change would be for the better, but now, seeing the unfamiliar coldness in his gaze, she felt a shiver of apprehension down her spine.

"Little Nightmare?"

Nova stepped forward from the group. "I share your beliefs, Uncle, and your conviction. But I disagree with the path you would put us on to achieve our goals. I know that for years we've been talking about destroying the Renegades. I understand that you believe we can only establish a society that works if we first dismantle the society that operates under our enemies. But you're wrong. We don't need to fight. We don't need to destroy. We need to *leave*."

Ace's expression tightened, but Nova plowed ahead.

She had to make them understand.

"We don't have to stay in Gatlon. There's nothing keeping us here. Let the Renegades have their city. We can go somewhere else. Establish our own community, under our own rules, our own principles." Her nerves thrummed as she spoke, knowing that she did, actually, have something that might keep her here in Gatlon.

But Adrian was only a dream. Had only ever been a dream. Someday, he would know the truth. Someday, everything would fall apart.

Better that day was today.

"The Renegades are no longer relegated to Gatlon City," said Phobia, his voice dry and annoyed, as if this should have been obvious. "Their influence has spread across the world. They have syndicates in nearly every country."

"In the major metropolises, yes," said Nova. "I'm not suggesting we trade one city for another. That would just lead to the same conflicts we've faced here. I'm saying we start fresh. Find a place that's entirely our own." She inspected the faces that were watching her with surprise—some tinted by curiosity, others a faint hint of suspicion. "We are prodigies, and with Ace Anarchy leading us . . ." She faced her uncle. "We can build the society we've dreamed of. Literally build it from the ground up. Look what you did here. In a matter of minutes you turned a pile of rubble into *this*." She gestured at the bell tower around them. "We could walk out into any wilderness and transform it into the home we deserve."

Ace watched her, calculating. But the fact that he hadn't silenced her gave her courage.

"Look," she said, more emphatically now as she moved to stand in the center of the room, on the old wooden floorboards beneath the central bells. They amplified her voice as she spoke. "We talk a lot about personal responsibility. Maybe it's time we took responsibility for our role in what this city has become. I don't like the way the Renegades are running things, but as Ace just reminded us, things weren't great when we were in charge, either. We helped make a mess of this city, and despite all their failings, I . . . I'm convinced that the Renegades really are trying to make things better. We may not agree with their methods, but this is the way the world is now. If we don't like it, then maybe instead of trying to tear it down, we should lead by example. Build something new, something better. If we form a community outside of the Renegades' control, show how we are capable of governing ourselves for a change, then . . . maybe that's how we change this world. And if it doesn't change the world, then who cares? Maybe this isn't our problem to solve. At least the war will be over."

Honey spoke first, her voice ireful and her arms crossed tightly over her chest. "This is that boy talking, isn't it? I knew it. He's brainwashed you."

"I'm not brainwashed!" said Nova, heat flaring across her cheeks.

"You want to run away," Honey snapped back. "You want to give up. Now, when we might actually have a chance of beating them!"

"I'm saying that maybe we don't *have* to beat them. That's the problem, isn't it? It's always *us* and *them*. Heroes or villains. Prodigies or civilians. The powerful and the powerless. I'm saying that I want a chance at a better life. For all of us, and anyone who wants to follow us. I want a life where we aren't the villains anymore!" Her voice rose, with determination, but also with fear that they wouldn't understand. "We can go anywhere. Be free anywhere. Why settle for this?"

Finally, a flicker of emotion in Ace's eyes, still shadowed by the structure of the helmet.

It wasn't understanding, though. If anything, he seemed hurt.

"Settle?" he said. "Settle, for Gatlon?" He moved toward her. "This is our city. Our home. I will not *settle* for anything less. I will not cower before the enemies who stole it from me."

Nova's shoulders sank. She shook her head. "We wouldn't be—"

"Enough."

She reared back, the harshness of his voice like a blow.

"If we are the villains to their heroes, so be it. We will give them reason enough to fear us." He paced around the tower, somehow regal in his stolen double-breasted coat. "We will not run. We will not hide. We will stay and fight. And this time, we will win. This city will be ours!"

A roar of approval rang through the tower.

Nova shuddered. As the others pressed forward, she felt almost invisible. Her tongue had become gummy in her mouth.

She had been so confident that, once Ace was free, the others would agree with her. Leaving made sense. She had expected relief—that they could have their freedom without sacrificing more lives, without another battle.

Had she not been compelling enough? Had she not conveyed the power of her ideas?

How was it possible, with the world now open to them, that they would rather stay here and fight?

"We were not prepared when the Renegades surrounded us at the Battle for Gatlon ten years ago," said Ace, approaching one of the open windows. "We will not make the same mistakes again."

He lifted his hands, fingers outstretched toward the horizon. The wasteland beyond the cathedral stretched for acres in each direction, enclosed within a puny chain-link fence. A ring of torn-up pavement, the debris of crumbled buildings, crushed and overturned cars.

Those ruins began to tremble.

The others moved forward, gathering behind Ace.

Nova was still trying to form her thoughts into words, still thinking of how she could persuade Ace and the others to choose differently, when bits of debris began to rise anew from the wasteland. Plywood and unhinged doors. Metal sheeting and steel beams. The side torn from a bus, still papered with a faded advertisement. Bricks and stonework, appliances and roof shingles, broken glass, rebar and copper pipes, old street signs and a plastic slide from a child's playground, ladders and porcelain bathtubs and traffic lights . . .

Countless bits of raw materials emerging from the wreckage. They began to fuse together at the edge of the wasteland. Bit by bit. Piece by piece.

Ace was building a wall.

Nova walked away from the others, to the opposite side of the tower. Here, too, the mess of materials was interlocking. Unlike the shimmering, near-transparent barricade that Adrian had used to protect himself at the arena, this wall was as thick and impenetrable as it was dark and unruly. It surrounded the cathedral in every direction, growing higher and higher, until it eclipsed even the great bell tower where they stood. Higher still, until it towered over the cathedral's sharply pitched roof. Higher still, until the jumbled structure arced inward, knitting together overhead. It blocked out the city below. Blocked out the sky.

When Ace was finished, they were trapped beneath a dome of sharp edges and rust.

It felt like being in the tunnels again.

It felt like the opposite of freedom.

"There," said Ace. "That will slow them down."

Nova gulped, thinking of all the Renegades she'd come to know. Could Adrian get past this wall? Could *the Sentinel*?

What about Max, with his telekinesis and the ability to manipulate metals?

Or Captain Chromium, with his unbreakable weapons?

She gnawed at her lower lip, remembering how many of the Renegades were no longer prodigies. Their powers had been drained from them.

Like they would have done to you, she remembered.

It did not diminish the sour taste in her mouth.

"Still, it will not hold them forever."

Ace peered around at their group, fierce and hungry. "You have fought valiantly tonight, but we must prepare for the next battle." He focused on Leroy and Honey. "You were able to use the Agent N substance to great effect. Do we have any left?"

Leroy shook his head. "What we took from the Renegades' storehouse is almost entirely used up. We have only a few of the gas-release devices Nova designed, and less than half a container of the liquid."

"Good enough," said Ace. "With any luck, we will finally be able to determine that age-old mystery . . . is Captain Chromium truly as invincible as he seems?" Grinning wickedly, he swept an arm around the room. "Fellow Anarchists, find accommodations and rest until further notice. I would like a moment alone with my niece."

Nova tensed. A few of the villains cast her looks that were gloating and smug. Others seemed nervous on her behalf. Leroy smiled comfortingly and winked, the movement awkwardly drawing up the paralyzed left side of his face.

Nova smiled back.

It was only Ace.

Within a matter of minutes, the bell tower had emptied out, the drum of footsteps on the lower staircase growing more distant by the second.

Only one of the villains lingered behind. To Nova's surprise, it was Narcissa, her expression full of concern. Though she had taken a leadership role among the Rejects before, she had been loitering at the back of the group since they'd arrived at the cathedral. Her fear in the face of Ace Anarchy was palpable, and the look she was giving Nova suggested a hesitation to leave her alone with him. There was something almost kind in her expression. Something almost protective.

Nova's spirits lifted, just barely, to think that perhaps the mirror walker no longer hated her.

"Is there something you would like to say, Mirror Walker?" Ace asked.

Narcissa opened her mouth, but hesitated. Her voice trembled when she finally spoke. "I agree with Nightmare," she said, barely above a whisper. "I think we should leave Gatlon."

Ace studied her, and Narcissa slowly shrank under the look.

"There is a mirror in the chapter house," Ace said. "I do not keep prisoners. You are free to go as you please."

Narcissa gulped.

"But if you stay, I will expect your cooperation in our efforts to destroy our enemies. I will not tolerate betrayal."

She paled. Her gaze clashed once more with Nova's, briefly, before she, too, disappeared down the ladder.

The wooden door clapped shut behind her. The air inside the belfry became uncannily still, with no breeze from the outside world able to make it through Ace's barrier. The tower smelled of old iron and the dirt that had been stirred up after so long.

Nova waited for Ace to speak. Already she missed being able to read his expressions. The wrinkles of his cheeks. The furrow of his brow. He felt more closed off from her now than he had the whole time he'd been hiding in the catacombs, and she was surprised to find that she already missed the man she had come to know—even if that man had been shattered and weak. At least she had never been afraid of him, but now, she couldn't keep herself from feeling a jolt of apprehension as he fixed his attention on her.

"I cannot fault you for wanting more than the life I've been able to give you," he said. "I cannot even fault you for being drawn to the lies that the Renegades have tried to sell to the world. It is a beautiful story they tell, one of righteousness and courage and justice. But it is only a story." Ace put his hands on a windowsill, though there was nothing to see now but their own dark cage, rough and pieced together from the unwanted remains of a long-ago war. "Your father had a faith in the Renegades that I could never understand. I offered to protect you and your family. I would have had my companions guarding your apartment day and night. But he didn't want my help. He insisted that the Renegades would protect you. I thought he was foolish, but it was not my place to interfere. David wanted to make his own choices, to find his own path through those dark times." His head lowered. "It is my greatest regret to this day. I wish I had been there for you. For David. For your mother and sister."

"It wasn't your fault," whispered Nova.

It was the Roaches and the assassin they hired.

It was the Renegades and their false promises.

She shut her eyes and the memory was there, as painful as it had ever been. Gunshots ricocheting in her skull. Blood splattered on their front door. Evie's cries, silenced forever.

"But, Ace," she whispered, feeling like her heart was being ripped into pieces, "is this really the way to avenge them? All these years, it's all I've wanted, to see the Renegades brought to their knees after they failed us. But . . . this hatred, it's destroying us, too. It's destroying *me*. Is this what my parents would have wanted?"

Ace's features filled with remorse. "It isn't about vengeance, little Nightmare. We cannot bring them back, but we can honor their deaths by preventing the same tragedy from happening to other families. We can keep the Renegades from spreading their falsehoods any longer. We can show the world who they really are. Not heroes, but false idols. Impostors. Liars."

Nova moved closer to Ace. "They're not all bad," she insisted. "They're not all good, either, but . . . I believe now that most of them want to help the people of this world, even if they're confused on how to do it. They're not just the power-hungry bullies we've thought. They're *not* all liars."

"Like Adrian Everhart?"

She froze.

To her surprise, Ace reached for his helmet and lifted it from his head. Setting it on the sill, he turned toward Nova. He did not seem angry. If anything, there was compassion scrawled across his features. "He lied to you, too. I think you know that now."

A shiver ripped through her. The Sentinel.

"He was the one who found me inside the catacombs—he and those friends of his." His eyes crinkled sympathetically at the corners. "They know his identity, too. But they didn't tell you, did they?"

Pulling her hand away, Nova paced along the wall of the tower. Ruby and Oscar knew the truth? And Danna, too? For how long?

They were a team. She'd thought they trusted one another. She'd thought Adrian felt things for her that went beyond camaraderie, beyond even friendship. She knew it was hypocritical for her to be angry at his keeping this secret when she kept so many of her own, but it still stung, to think that her entire unit had known and not told her.

"You cannot trust them, Nova. You are not one of them, much as you might wish otherwise."

She kept her back to him, hoping he couldn't tell how this information hurt her.

"You are one of us. You are a part of *this* family." A hand settled on her shoulder. "If you want to leave, I will open a path for you. I will not keep you here if you do not wish to be a part of our revolution anymore. You have already done so much for our cause, and for that, you will always have my gratitude and respect. But, Nova . . ." His voice dropped. "You know what the Renegades will try to do to us when they make it past these barriers, including Adrian Everhart. I hope you will choose to stay and fight. I hope you have not been so taken with their promises that you can no longer see what's been driving us forward all these years. Stand beside your family, Nova. Stand with us, and fight for our future, not theirs."

He patted her shoulder once, gently, then let his hand fall away. She heard him picking up the helmet and moving toward the trapdoor.

And she heard the gunshots.

And she heard Evie crying.

And she heard Captain Chromium's steady voice: *We did what we had to do to stop the villain gangs, to bring order and peace. We would do it again if we had to.*

"Ace?"

The bell tower fell silent, but she knew he was still there. Her hand was trembling as she wrapped it around her bracelet and turned to face him. He watched her. Always patient. Always waiting.

The star pulsed against her skin.

"I found something," she said. "Something my father made before he died."

His chin lifted, interest piqued.

"I think . . . I think he might have created it as a weapon to destroy Captain Chromium."

CHAPTER THIRTY-NINE

THE LAST TIME Adrian had stood in front of the creepy poster inside these creepy subway tunnels, Nova had been at his side. Until now, she was the only person he'd told about the tunnel that connected the subway to the catacombs, and he would have given just about anything to have her there at his side again.

He would have preferred to be kissing her again, rather than getting ready to risk his life to ensure the defeat of Ace Anarchy, but he would have been content just to have her there. She was a fierce ally, a strong fighter, and her skills would have put his mind at ease as they prepared to sneak into the cathedral.

That, and he wouldn't have been devoting a corner of his brain to worrying about her.

He hadn't heard from Nova since before the attack on the arena, despite numerous attempts to contact her via their wristbands. Surely she had heard the news—everyone in Gatlon City knew about what had happened by now. But she had never shown up at the arena, and as far as he knew, no one had heard from her at headquarters, either.

He would have gone to her in person and told her about their plan to sneak into the cathedral while Captain Chromium led the Renegades in a diversionary assault up above, hoping that she would join them. Except . . . he didn't know where she was. The house on Wallowridge was gone, and he had no idea where this apartment was that she and her uncle were staying at.

The more he thought about it, the more his fingers twitched with nervous anxiety.

What if something had happened to her?

He knew he needed to stop thinking about it, though. One crisis at a time, he told himself, and for now, that crisis was stopping Ace Anarchy and protecting the world as they knew it.

He reached for the corner of the poster and swung it outward, revealing the narrow tunnel beyond.

Oscar whistled. Danna remained silent.

The three of them were alone this time, and it felt off balance to be without Nova, who had become a reliable fixture in their group, and Ruby, who had gone to keep watch over Max until they could be sure that Ace Anarchy couldn't come after him. Though Ruby's family had been instructed to remove all the mirrors from their house, he still worried that Nightmare might have other ways to figure out Max's location. The last thing he wanted to do was underestimate her or any of the Anarchists.

Captain Chromium had wanted to come with them. Actually, he'd at first insisted that he go alone into the cathedral to face off against Ace and the others by himself. But his leadership was needed at headquarters, organizing the Renegades who had been pouring in from outside syndicates and preparing them for the counterattack that would soon be underway. Only after Adrian had reminded his dads that his team had already fought Ace Anarchy and won, and only after he'd given them a number of demonstrations of his Sentinel abilities, proving that he had, in fact, made himself into one of the most powerful prodigies of all time, and only after he pointed out that this plan required stealth, which was not a skill that Captain Chromium possessed, did Hugh and Simon reluctantly agree to let his team attempt this raid. They knew, as Adrian did, that taking Ace Anarchy by surprise was their best chance to neutralize him. To steal back the helmet. To defeat him, once and for all.

"I'll check that the coast is clear," said Danna. She transformed and the swarm disappeared into the shadows, their wings catching on the beam of Adrian's flashlight.

Leaning on his cane, Oscar peered over at Adrian. "We are going to survive this, right?"

Adrian swallowed. "Of course. We're Renegades."

Oscar nodded. Neither of them bothered to point out that a lot of Renegades had not survived the battle at the arena.

"Good," said Oscar, a little wistful. "Because I really want to see Ruby again after this."

Adrian completely understood. He really wanted to see Nova again after this, too. There were far too many things left unsaid.

They waited in silence for what felt like an eternity but was probably only a few minutes. Finally Danna returned, or two of her butterflies did, dancing briefly around their heads before fluttering back through the passageway.

With his marker in one hand and the flashlight in the other, Adrian followed.

The catacombs were exactly as they had left them after the

fight against Ace Anarchy. Bones and skulls littered the stone floor, making it nearly impossible to walk without disturbing the silence. Marble statues lay in pieces, sarcophagi were overturned, giant cracks ran through the church's thick foundation.

They made their way, as stealthily as they could, through the catacomb's chambers and up the narrow stone staircase. Before, this stairway had opened out onto the wasteland, surrounded by nothing but ruins and destruction. But now, as Adrian neared the uppermost landing, there was no light filtering down from an open sky. Only more shadows, and their footsteps echoing off thick stone walls.

Adrian's breath caught as they stepped out into a small circular chamber. A second staircase continued upward, but two doorways opened on either side, each one flanked by statues of hooded figures. He had known from secondhand reports that Ace had rebuilt the cathedral, but he'd been picturing a jumbled structure. Broken stone and timbers barely held together with old mortar and rusted nails. He had expected something flimsy and precarious, ready to collapse at the slightest blow.

But the chamber around them seemed as ancient and solid as if it had stood there undisturbed for hundreds of years. The thick stone walls perfectly fitted together, with no sign that they'd recently been strewn across the wasteland. It was as if the Battle for Gatlon had never happened.

He cast an uncomfortable look at Oscar. The fact that Oscar hadn't said anything was proof enough of his own surprise. In fact, the cathedral was as silent as the tombs below. Adrian knew the silence wouldn't last. Soon, Captain Chromium and every Renegade who could still fight, including those who had arrived from outside syndicates, would attack the wasteland barrier with all the force they had. Adrian hoped this would create enough of a diversion and lead most, if not all, of the villains outside the cathedral while he, Oscar, and Danna attempted to find and neutralize Ace Anarchy.

But finding him might be a problem.

A few of Danna's butterflies flitted toward the nave, the vast, central area of the church, so Adrian crept after her, listening for any signs of the villains.

As he paced beneath a gigantic stained-glass window that stretched all the way to the vaulted ceiling, Adrian was astounded to think that all this had been mere rubble before. How was a single prodigy capable of this, in such a short amount of time?

He moved toward the central aisle, set with wooden pews and iron candelabras and vast stone pillars on either side.

His gaze traveled down the long, wide aisle.

He froze.

There—at the far end of the nave, what felt like a mile away, dwarfed by the vast ceilings and monumental windows—stood Ace Anarchy. Waiting for them, his helmet glinting in the light of a hundred candles lit along the sides of the choir.

He was not alone. More than a dozen villains were at his sides.

And, a few steps in front of the altar, stood Nova.

Adrian's blood ran cold. When had the villains found her? How long had she been a prisoner here, a hostage?

His vision sparked red, and before he knew what he was doing, Adrian was charging down the aisle. His right forearm began to glow. A ball of fire swirled around his left fist.

Danna screamed. "Sketch—*no!*"

Seconds later, a monarch butterfly danced in front of his face. Adrian batted it away.

The cyclone of wings appeared in front of him, then Danna herself, hands upheld. "Adrian, stop!"

Something hit the ground at Danna's feet. Green vapor burst from the capsule. This, more than Danna's plea, made Adrian skid to a halt. Danna gasped and swarmed again, her butterflies swirling upward. They were halfway to the vaulted ceilings when they began to converge.

Adrian stared, horrified, as the cloud of gold-and-black wings re-formed. Then they were Danna, and she was falling, forty feet from the ground. Her scream ricocheted through the nave.

Allowing his flame to smolder and vanish, Adrian leaped. He caught her midair and landed just beyond where the gaseous vapor was dissipating. The air smelled suddenly of sharp chemicals, burning the back of his throat.

Danna coughed and rolled out of his arms, landing crouched on one knee. "No," she murmured, pressing a hand to her heart. *"No."*

A bolt of black smoke blurred past them. Adrian lifted his head in time to see the smoke arrow strike Ace Anarchy in the face. He reeled back, coughing into his elbow. Another bolt followed, then another, as fast as Oscar could send them, each one striking one of the villains gathered at the far end of the nave.

Then Oscar cried out.

Adrian looked back to see that Oscar's cane had been ripped from his hand. It took on a life of its own, striking the backs of Oscar's knees, knocking him hard to the ground.

"Smokescreen, cover me!" Adrian yelled.

Oscar raised one hand to block another blow from the possessed cane, while his other palm extended toward Adrian. A drift of thick white fog started to roll down the aisle, filling up the pews, when Oscar yelped in pain and swatted at the back of his neck.

Oscar inspected his hand, something small and black clinging to his fingers.

Queen Bee cackled. "Serves you right for that little trick you played at the arena!"

Oscar met Adrian's gaze. His expression was ferocious, but Adrian could still see the torment behind it. The bee must have had Agent N, just like the ones at the arena.

The last of the fog faded away.

Adrian ground his teeth. His fists tightened.

Danna grabbed his arm. "Adrian, think. It's a trap."

He tore his arm away and started to run again. Having been so close to the mist-missile and the cloud of Agent N, they probably thought he'd been neutralized, too.

They were wrong.

Nova hadn't moved. She watched him charging for her, her face pale, a fear like he'd never seen before brimming in her eyes.

"Let her go!" he yelled, as another flame burst forth from his palm. Adrian prepared to lurch forward, to attack, to tear Ace Anarchy and his cohorts apart, if they'd done anything to hurt her—

He didn't see the net until it was too late. Until his foot had crossed some invisible mark and, as one, the knot of ropes engulfed him. He stumbled and rolled a few times, entangling himself more.

Choking for air, he tried to rebound to his feet, but one leg was caught. He felt like a wild animal, ensnared in a hunter's trap, and Danna's words came back to him, further igniting his anger.

Igniting.

Recalling the first time he'd been caught in ropes like these, he snarled and clenched his left fist around the nearest rope. He summoned his flame, letting it burn as hot as it could.

The fire was an inferno, nearly engulfing Adrian's entire body, by the time he realized that it wasn't working. The ropes grew sticky, but they did not burn.

"Fire-resistant coating," said Cyanide, drawing Adrian's attention back to the villains. "We do try to learn from past mistakes."

With sweat dripping down the back of his neck, Adrian maneuvered his right arm so he had a clear shot through the net. His skin lit up. He targeted Ace Anarchy, standing not far from Nova, and fired.

A series of pews flew up onto their sides, forming a wall between Adrian and the villains. The pews crashed back down to the floor, their splintered wooden seats leaving just enough space between them that there remained a narrow aisle down the nave's center.

"Great marvels," said Queen Bee. Stepping forward, she linked her elbow with Nova's. Adrian tensed, panic surging through every nerve. "If you want her so much, here—you can have her."

With a saccharine smile, Queen Bee shoved Nova forward. She stumbled down the few steps onto the long, narrow path that distinguished the choir from the nave. She caught herself and hesitated.

"Nova," said Adrian, his voice thick with despair, his arms straining against the ropes. "Are you okay?"

She stared at him, swallowing hard.

She said nothing as she started down the aisle. She appeared tormented and unsure. He had *never* seen Nova, confident, brave Nova, look like that before.

But as she came closer, he noticed something else, too.

She was not tied up, like he would assume a Renegade prisoner would be.

She was not wearing her Renegade uniform, or even her usual civilian clothes, but rather a black jacket and a utility belt that seemed eerily familiar.

Adrian's stomach gave a lurch. He would have backed away, but he was stuck, peering at her through the ropes that were as constricting as his own rib cage.

"She's done well, hasn't she?" said Ace Anarchy, speaking for the first time. His voice carried a lilt of amusement, but Adrian barely heard him over the truth and disbelief that had gone to war inside his head. "Your plan was a clever one, sneaking in through the catacombs. It might even have worked, if you hadn't already told my niece that you knew about the escape tunnel. Now that you're here, we'll have to make sure that entrance is blocked off, so no one else thinks to follow in your footsteps." He gestured to a couple of the villains. "Bind the others and secure them in the treasury for now. Take the Everhart boy to the east chapel and await further instructions."

Ace Anarchy's orders barely registered.

Nova was nearly to Adrian now. The fear he'd seen before was fading away, being replaced by her signature determination. Her jaw tense, her shoulders set.

Had he only imagined the torment before? The regret? The doubt?

"Nova," he breathed, nearly coughing on the word as his own jumble of emotions stuck in his throat. "Who are you?"

She crouched so they were eye to eye. They were as close now as when they'd danced at the gala. As close as when he'd put noise-canceling headphones on her ears so she could finally sleep. As close as when they'd kissed in the subway tunnels, just outside the hidden passage to the catacombs.

The last shreds of denial shriveled up inside him. The truth won. Suddenly, he knew.

When Danna had first accused Nova of being his worst enemy, the villain he had been hunting for months, he had been angry. Mortified. At times, even disgusted.

Now, all that was left was a deep, devastating sense of loss.

His shoulders fell under the weight of the ropes that bound him.

Nova reached for Adrian's hand, placing two fingers against his knuckle. He flinched at the touch and thought, just for a moment, he might have seen hurt flash through Nova's eyes. But it was his imagination, because a second later her expression had hardened into something cold and impenetrable.

"Everyone has a nightmare," she said. "I guess I'm yours."

That was the last he remembered before darkness claimed him.

CHAPTER FORTY

"WELL, ISN'T THAT clever," said Queen Bee, inspecting the bottom of Adrian's bare foot. He did his best to ignore her. He'd been trying to ignore the whole lot of them, the ever-revolving door of Anarchists and villains, even as they'd attempted increasingly obnoxious tactics to get a reaction from him.

His eyes stayed resolutely on Nova whenever she was in the room.

Her eyes stayed resolutely away.

"Springs," said Queen Bee, trailing a sharp fingernail down the sole of Adrian's foot. He did his best to stifle a twitch. "To jump farther. Isn't that clever, sweetie?"

He was pretty sure *sweetie*, in this case, was Nova, but it was hard to tell, as Nova seemed as determined to ignore Queen Bee as he was.

Having Honey Harper inspect the soles of his feet was the last in a long line of indignities Adrian had endured since his capture. He did not know what had become of Oscar and Danna, or where he was inside the cathedral. When he had come to, he was inside a small circular chapel. In comparison to the magnificence of the nave, the chapel felt like an afterthought, so dreary and insignificant that Adrian wondered if the saint it was named for might have done something that annoyed the architect in charge of honoring him. Besides a smooth black altar and a series of narrow stained-glass windows, it felt barren. Echoing stone walls, hard stone floors. The atmosphere wasn't much improved by its moody dimness, either. Adrian had no way of knowing what time it was, as no sunlight, or moonlight for that matter, could permeate the structure Ace had erected over the cathedral, leaving them shrouded in constant darkness. Their only light came from a small gas lantern in the corner that sent their shadows flickering and shifting across the walls.

Adrian was tied up with his back against the frigid altar. One of the villains had cut away the sleeves and collar from his shirt, revealing the tattoos on his arms and chest.

Nova frequently came in and out of the chapel, dressed in full battle regalia. Her belt was strapped with two different guns, ropes, darts and ammunition, gloves, flares, a hunting knife, and those awful throwing stars Nightmare had always been so fond of. But for some reason, she had left off the metal mask, and though Adrian knew he shouldn't assign this any significance, he couldn't help it.

Without the mask, he still didn't see her as Nightmare. He could only see Nova.

Nova, who had betrayed him a hundred different ways. But still Nova.

He had tried to ask her where Oscar and Danna had been taken, if they were okay, but she seemed determined to stay silent. He wasn't sure if she was there to keep him from trying to escape, or just to make sure he wasn't being mistreated.

Perhaps the worst part was that Phobia came and went, too. It had taken Adrian a while to notice him at first, watching silently from a corner. The room was so dark, and he held so still, that at times the villain seemed more like a figment of Adrian's imagination.

He was real, though. He was very real, and every time Adrian noticed him, a chill swept down his spine. Phobia's cruel words, spoken as he stood over Callum's body, echoed back to Adrian again and again.

One cannot be awed who has no soul, just as one cannot be brave who has no fear . . .

It was him. Adrian knew it now, had known it the moment Phobia said those hateful words. The note left on her body. The unbridled terror on her face.

Phobia had killed Adrian's mother.

Adrian sneered, baring his teeth at the villain, whose only response was to spin the scythe in a steady circle over his head.

The news reports had said that Lady Indomitable had plummeted to her death from a seven-story building. There were no other wounds, no injuries that weren't direct results of the fall. Whatever Phobia had done to her, whatever he had shown her, it had frightened her enough that, for a moment, she'd forgotten she could fly. She had been petrified. Scared, literally, to death.

What didn't make sense was how Nova could possibly be on the side of that *thing*.

But he knew he shouldn't be surprised. His mother had been a Renegade. Nova was an Anarchist. What did Nova care that Lady Indomitable had been murdered more than ten years ago? One less superhero to deal with.

He was grateful when Phobia finally left, vanishing from the room as silently as he'd come.

Cyanide, too, disappeared some time ago, muttering about an experiment, and Adrian hadn't seen the mirror walker since they'd arrived. A handful of others had come and gone. A few of them he recognized from past Renegade trials—prodigies who, like the Crane, had not been accepted into the Renegades. A few of them he was sure had been wanted for various crimes around the city, frequently hunted by patrol units. It made him wish he'd done more as the Sentinel to track down known criminals and see them apprehended.

"Have I missed any?" asked Queen Bee, shining a flashlight over Adrian's arms, twisting his wrists against the bindings. "Let's see . . . that's the fire, the castle wall thing, the jumping, the suit, the . . . what is this?" She dug a fingernail into his right forearm. "Oh, right, the laser thing." Her expression switched from jovial to vicious. "I recall that one intimately."

Adrian glowered back. "You were trying to kill my father," he said, breaking his own vow of silence.

She clucked at him. "Your father shouldn't have stabbed my Acey."

"Ace was going to kill us all!" He shot a look at Nova, half expecting her to offer an opinion, maybe even an argument in his defense, but she stayed silent. Her back was to them, standing just inside the chapel's arched doorway, staring out into a corridor lined with statues.

Queen Bee blew a raspberry with her ultra-glossy lips. "He was not going to kill *us all*," she said. "Just you. And everyone you care about." She winked, as if this were all a joke. A hornet was crawling up her earlobe, but she didn't seem to notice. "Now then, Nightmare, dear, which one do you think we should start with?"

Nova moved almost imperceptibly toward her. "Which what?"

"The tattoos. We can't let him keep them, after the trouble they've caused."

Nova shifted again, studying Honey more intently, though her gaze never strayed toward Adrian. "What are you talking about?"

Honey sighed dramatically. "We have to cut them out." She parted the thigh-high slit in her sequined dress and pulled a stiletto knife from her stocking.

Adrian tensed.

"You're not serious," said Nova.

Honey smirked. "What did you expect?" She tapped the tip of the knife against the immunity tattoo over Adrian's heart. He gulped. "He's immune to Agent N, so we can't just inject him and be done with it. And we can't risk him getting loose and ruining everything. So the tattoos have to go." She planted a hand on her hip. "If you're squeamish about it, you can busy yourself finding me some bandages." She batted her lashes at Adrian. "We're not savages, after all."

He ignored her, focusing on Nova instead. He couldn't tell whether or not Queen Bee was just trying to intimidate him, but regardless, he hoped his silent pleading might have an impact on Nova.

If only she would *look* at him.

"I think . . . this one goes first," said Honey, pressing the edge of the blade against his right forearm, where the energy beam cannon was drawn. "It'll be my little revenge. Besides, we wouldn't want you to get worked up and blow a hole in our roof. We just finished remodeling."

She angled the knife, its point breaking the skin.

Adrian pressed his head back against the altar, his teeth clenched. In the doorway, Nova had crossed her arms tightly over her chest. Her focus was glued to the blade as it cut into his flesh.

Adrian inhaled sharply.

The pain burned, but he'd suffered worse.

Then Honey paused and pulled the knife out. "Unless you'd like to do it?" she said, holding the handle toward Nova. "His powers have brought you a lot more headache than they ever brought me."

Setting her jaw, Nova turned away, back toward the corridor. From her stiff posture, Adrian could tell she was uncomfortable with this, but she didn't move to defend him.

"Suit yourself," Honey said.

The knife dug into his arm again. He screwed up his face, refusing to so much as grunt as she sliced away the top layers of skin.

Once she had finished carving out the tattoo, she used the tip of the blade to flick away the chunk of gouged skin. "That is repulsive," she said with a snarky titter. She left the wound to bleed freely as she walked around to his other side. "Now, let's see here, probably the flame next." She pinched his skin where the spiral of flame was inked.

Adrian ignited a ball of fire around his clenched fist.

Honey gasped and drew back, shaking out her hand where the flames had singed her fingertips.

Then she laughed. "Oh, what a darling trick," she said, stroking the back of a black hornet with the pad of her thumb. "One that deserves punishment."

The hornet buzzed at Adrian, and it suddenly felt like a searing poker was being jammed into his neck, just below his ear. He screamed, struggling to get away, but the ropes didn't budge.

"Honey!" Nova screeched. "Stop it!"

The hornet flew away, but the venom continued to burn and throb. Adrian squeezed his eyes tight as hot tears started to brim.

The upside was that he hardly noticed the next cut of the knife as Honey Harper carved out the flame tattoo.

As the burning venom spread down his torso and into his arms, Adrian dared to open his eyes. He sought out Nova again, desperate.

She had her back to him, though, doing nothing as Honey scraped the edge of the knife down his forearm.

He thought her shoulders might be shaking, but it could have been his own blurry vision causing the distortion.

"That actually is pretty gross," said Honey, when she'd finished with the flame tattoo. "Maybe we can wait and have Leroy do the rest. What do you think, little Nightmare?"

Nova didn't respond.

Adrian cast his attention up to the high ceiling beams, which converged into a single point over his head. His whole upper body was on fire now, but as the venom spread, the intensity of the pain lessened, if only incrementally. Inhale. Exhale.

"Interesting," Honey murmured. "The swelling is already going down. Usually it lasts a day or more."

The immunity tattoo, Adrian thought. It was protecting him, ridding his system of the venom faster than it otherwise would.

But he kept his mouth shut. No point in reminding her about it. Instead he muttered to himself, "The Renegades will come for me, you know."

Nova spun around so fast he'd hardly realized she was moving before she was crouched in front of him, her eyes bright with fury and wet with unshed tears. "No," she spat. "The Renegades *aren't coming.*"

He held her gaze, grateful to have her attention for once, despite the vitriol in her words.

"Yes," he said, "they are, Nova." His mouth curled in a weary smile. "Maybe they're already here."

Her brow furrowed briefly in confusion, then she let out a rattled scoff. "Me?" she said, standing again. "You think *I'm* going to help you? After all this?"

"Clearly, I don't know you as well as I thought I did," said Adrian, "but I know you're not one of them, not deep down. You're better than this, Nova."

She scowled. "From the day I met you, you've been saying how Nightmare is a villain. It's practically been your life's mission to hunt me down and destroy me. And now, suddenly, I'm better than this?"

"*Yes*," he said emphatically. He'd been having a lot of revelations since he was dragged into this chapel, and a lot of things had begun to make sense. Nova had told him that her uncle rescued her from the murderer who killed her parents. And during the fight at the arena, he was sure he had heard Nightmare called Ace Anarchy "Uncle."

"Ace Anarchy is your family, and you want to be loyal to him. I get that . . . sort of. But this isn't you."

She leaned toward him and hissed, "You have no idea what I am."

His eye caught a glimmer of a chain around her neck, disappearing into her collar. His blood ran cold. "Is that the Vitality Charm?"

Nova straightened, one hand going to her shirt where the medallion must have been hidden underneath.

She didn't have to answer. Her expression was all the response he needed. Anger stampeded through him, and he pressed forward against the ropes. "You had it this whole time, even though you knew it was the only way anyone could get close to Max!"

She looked momentarily taken aback. Then, setting her jaw, she pulled her jacket's zipper to her throat, glaring. "You can get close to Max just fine."

It was Adrian's turn to be surprised.

"The Sentinel wasn't affected when he carried Max halfway across the city to the hospital," she said. "How long after discovering the charm did you decide to give yourself that tattoo?" She jerked her chin toward the immunity tattoo. "How long were you planning on keeping it a secret?"

His lips pressed tight. He didn't offer an explanation, not when she hadn't bothered to give him one. He only said, "We needed it."

"So did we," she spat. A simple statement that did nothing to quell his rising fury. Then Nova waved a hand at Queen Bee. "I'll find some bandages."

Adrian shivered, startled that Nova would leave him here alone with Honey Harper and her knife. "Nova—wait."

She ignored him, but had only gone a few steps when Phobia appeared in the corridor, towering over her.

Adrian drew back against the altar, snarling.

"Ace wishes to speak with us," Phobia said. His hood fluttered, and Adrian had the uneasy sense that Phobia had turned his focus on *him.* "I'll send one of the Rejects to stand watch."

CHAPTER FORTY-ONE

Nova passed by the room that had once been the cathedral's treasury, where ancient tomes and fine statuary depicting angels and saints would have been stored. Now it was where Oscar and Danna were tied up, their hands and knees bound with nylon ropes.

They both glared at Nova as she passed.

She gritted her teeth, wishing she had taken a different path around the nave so as not to have seen them at all.

Honey, walking a few paces ahead of her, didn't seem to notice.

"Honey?" said Nova, jogging forward to be beside her. "Can I ask you a question about Phobia?"

"Sure, but I probably won't know the answer." Honey flashed her a spooky look. "All these years later and he still scares me as much as the day he joined us."

"How *did* he join the Anarchists?"

Honey cocked her head, considering. "He just showed up during a fight, against Thunderbird and Lady Indomitable, if I remember right. We were getting whupped—it was me and Animus—he was killed not long after that, I don't think you ever met him. Anyway, I thought we were both dead, when Phobia showed up, creepy as ever, and suddenly the Renegades were running away, terrified. Phobia said he wanted to meet Ace, so we brought him back with us."

Nova frowned, not finding the clues she wanted in Honey's story. Why had one of Adrian's own creations wanted to join Ace?

"He killed Lady Indomitable, didn't he?" Nova said.

Honey glanced at her, surprised. "How did you . . . ?" She paused. "Did someone tell you that?"

"Adrian told me about a note that was found on her body."

"Ah yes, his *notes*. I'm glad he stopped leaving those. They were so pretentious."

So it was true. Nova had known, and yet, a small part of her had held on to the hope that maybe she wasn't allied with the villain who had killed Adrian's mother.

"Does this have anything to do with whatever the mirror walker found in your boyfriend's mansion?" said Honey, eyeing her suspiciously.

Nova swallowed.

"Now, now," continued Honey, "before you start spouting off more of your lies, I heard the two of you blabbing while we were at the pawnshop. Something about the Everhart boy and Phobia and . . . comics?"

"It's . . . complicated," said Nova, having the sinking feeling that she did *not* want Honey to know the truth of Phobia's origin. "I think they might be connected somehow, but I don't know. Maybe I'm wrong."

Honey stopped walking suddenly. Nova froze at the abruptness.

"Really?" said Honey, an edge to her voice. "You think our ghastly friend is connected to the Everhart boy? Tell me, what else did you learn from all this detective work?"

The hair prickled on the back of Nova's neck. She had the distinct impression that Honey was fishing for something in particular.

Was it possible she already knew about Phobia's origins? That Adrian himself had created the villain?

Or was it something else?

"Not much," she lied. "Only that Phobia joined the Anarchists not all that long before I did. I wanted to check with you, see if that was true."

Honey's gaze was long and searching, before a subtle smile pulled across her glistening lips. "It's true. And just like you, he's been an invaluable member ever since."

She pushed open a large oak door, leading them into the arcade around the cloister. Nova hesitated, sure there was something Honey wasn't telling her. But the click of Honey's heels on the pavers quickened, making it clear the conversation was over.

By the time Honey and Nova reached the chapter house, nearly all their allies were already gathered. Beyond the cathedral, they could hear the first sounds of war pummeling against the barrier Ace had erected. The Renegades had arrived and were attacking the wall with a barrage of explosions and weapons. Each impact rattled the ground beneath their feet. So far the barrier was holding, but Nova knew it wouldn't forever. The Renegades may have been weakened, their numbers reduced, but they still weren't powerless.

She couldn't help revisiting the conversation in the bell tower again and again, and wishing that things had gone differently. They could be halfway around the world by now, already working to start their new life. Instead, they were under siege, Adrian was their prisoner, and Nova felt smothered under everyone's expectations.

Ace expecting her to be the little Nightmare he'd raised her to be.

The Anarchists expecting her to finish the job she'd started and bring down the Renegades once and for all.

And Adrian expecting her to . . . what? He couldn't possibly expect her to help him. He must know better by now. She could still feel his stare digging into her. Judging and disgusted.

But then there were times when he seemed almost hopeful.

Always so unnervingly optimistic.

Being in Adrian's presence had left her feeling about as strong as a slug in a salt bath. Now, with some distance, she tried to focus on the sounds of war outside their protective shell, and the prodigies who were gathered at her side, preparing to win the battle that would give them all a chance at a better life.

She was here, with Ace, and she was ready to fight, as she'd always intended to do. Soon this would be over and she could be at ease again. She could be herself. She could be the Nightmare the world feared.

"I will not wax poetic about our chances for victory," said Ace, once everyone was present. "I know we will succeed. The Renegades will fall." He spent some time questioning everyone on their respective roles. Had Cyanide prepared the necessary chemical reactions? Had Locksmith secured the eastern entrances? And on and on until he met Nova's eyes. At that moment, there was no familial gentleness in his expression, only an intensity that stopped Nova's heart.

"I will commence negotiations once the Council have revealed themselves. Is our leverage ready?"

She gulped. The leverage was Adrian. He was an asset now, a bargaining chip. Just as Ace had always known he would be. For months he had encouraged Nova to get close to Adrian, knowing he could be used against his fathers.

Somehow, she'd never pictured it coming to this, though she probably should have.

The words caught in her throat, and it was Honey who answered for her. "He'll be ready."

Ace held Nova's gaze another moment, before nodding. "Take your positions and await my signal."

They dispersed. Nova dreaded going back to Adrian, to again be accosted by those looks of hope sprinkled with loathing. She was relieved when Narcissa jogged up to her in the cloister, clutching a stack of familiar comics.

Relieved for half a second, before Honey called back to her, "I'll go ahead and check on the prisoner. You take your time, sweetness."

Bile rose up in Nova's mouth, thinking of Honey and that stiletto knife. But it wasn't her concern, she told herself, fighting every instinct to chase after her.

Adrian was no longer her concern.

Burying her apprehension, she turned back to Narcissa. "Glad to see you stayed."

"Yeah, well . . ." Narcissa kicked at the stone floor. "I promised the Rejects I'd help them secure a better future for themselves. We haven't accomplished that yet."

"You're right," said Nova, a little darkly. She wondered if any of them, when they'd been plotting their revolution, had foreseen *this*.

"You know now, don't you? About the Sentinel?"

Nova tensed. "Yes," she said slowly. "You knew already?"

"That's what I wanted to show you the other day."

Narcissa started to flip through one of the comics, but a particularly loud explosion above the barrier made her jump and she dropped the stapled pages. They fell at Nova's feet. When she stooped to pick up the comic, the air caught in her lungs. The pages had opened to the final spread. It showed the main character, the young boy known as Rebel Z, as he transformed into a superhero. The superhero he needed to become in order to seek vengeance on the mad scientist.

In the image, he was donning an armored suit, one that was remarkably like the Sentinel's.

Nova examined the picture, wondering if this would have changed anything if she'd seen it before the attack on the arena. She wondered if it changed anything now.

"The comics are actually pretty good," said Narcissa. "It's a shame he never finished the story."

Nova swallowed, wondering if it was okay for her to hope that maybe someday he'd get a chance to. "Thanks for showing me this," she said. "But you were right before. It doesn't change much at this point."

Nova started to head back to the chapel where Adrian—kind, righteous Adrian—was shackled to a cold altar, but as she rounded the nearest corner, she crashed into Honey Harper. Without pretense, Honey plucked the comic book out of Nova's hand.

"Hey!" said Nova, too late to grab it back as Honey spun out of reach and started making her way down the corridor, flipping through the pages.

"So this is what's caused so much interest between you and the mirror girl?" said Honey, turning the pages this way and that, inspecting the drawings with an air of derision. "What is it, exactly?"

"It's . . . nothing," stammered Nova. "Give it back, Honey."

"I take it our young artist drew it," she continued, ignoring Nova. "Must have been a while ago. He's certainly improved, hasn't he?" She chuckled. "Not that I can do any better."

She suddenly stopped walking. She was gripping the comic in both hands, carelessly creasing the brittle pages in her fists. "Is that who I think it is?"

"Doesn't really matter," said Nova. "We already knew he was the Sentinel, so . . ." She trailed off, noticing the page that Honey had landed on. It didn't show Rebel Z in the Sentinel's armor. Rather, it showed a shrouded figure with bony fingertips and nothing but shadows where a face should be.

"He . . . drew that when he was, like, eleven," said Nova. "He'd probably heard about Phobia, from back during the Age of Anarchy. He could have inspired this . . . this villain . . . thing."

Honey shut the comic, her eyes shimmering with a glee that sent a chill down Nova's spine.

"You don't believe that," said Honey. "I overheard you two talking. There are more drawings, aren't there? Some not quite so recent?" She didn't wait for Nova to answer, which was just as well because Nova wasn't sure what to say. She didn't want to lie to Honey, but she could already see Honey's mind calculating what this meant.

Suddenly, Honey let out a barking laugh and clapped one hand over her mouth. "My, my," she said through her fingers. "That little *artiste* . . . and he has no idea, does he?"

"It doesn't matter. There's no reason to—"

"Oh, I beg to differ!" she said, pivoting on her heels. "I cannot wait to see this."

"Honey, no, wait!"

Nova chased after her and grabbed the comic, hoping that would stop Honey, but she hardly seemed to notice as she made her way back through the cathedral's corridors.

"Honey, please! We need to stay focused. This doesn't mean anything!"

Honey cast a smirk at her. "Careful, Nightmare. I'm beginning to think you might actually feel bad for the hostage."

Nova winced and ceased her pleading, but she stayed on Honey's heels, dread filling her with every step.

◇◇◆◇◇

Adrian had never been afraid of bees before. But then, he'd never had the creatures crawling over him like tiny guards with fat, striped abdomens and needle-like stingers that twitched every time he moved. Though one of the villains had put gauze over the deep gashes in his arms, the blood had soaked through in spots, and the bees seemed particularly attracted to it, forming little clusters on the bandages.

He tried to distract himself by thinking of the creatures not as harbingers of venom and pain, but rather of little miracles of nature. He didn't know how many species Queen Bee had control of, but he'd counted nine different varieties while he'd been sitting here by himself. Some all black and fluffy like a caterpillar. Others that were sleek and metallic blue, with a wingspan as wide as Danna's butterflies. Black and yellow stripes. Black and red stripes. Long, narrow bodies that looked more like a dragonfly, and thick, shiny-shelled bodies that looked more like a beetle, and everything in between.

He was beginning to think his efforts at distraction might have been misplaced when he heard footsteps in the hall. Queen Bee appeared with a toothy grin that immediately set Adrian on edge again, wondering what new torture she was devising.

It was foolish, he knew, but he couldn't help but be relieved when Nova came in right behind her. Not that she'd done anything to stop Queen Bee from cutting out his tattoos.

"I've just learned the most delectable secret about you!" Queen Bee said, clasping her hands in front of her face.

Nova opened her mouth to say something, but stopped herself and shut it again with a grimace.

"I wonder if you can guess what it is." Queen Bee sat down beside Adrian, her arm pressed against his. Hairspray clogged his lungs and he angled his head away, but she didn't seem to notice. "I'll give you a hint. It has to do with our eerie skeletal friend, who likes to go on and on about *fear* and *courage* and *bleh*." She rolled her eyes in mock disgust.

Jaw tightening, Adrian glanced up at Nova in disbelief, before glowering sidelong at Queen Bee. "Phobia killed my mother," he said through his teeth. "It's not a secret anymore, but, wow, I sure am glad it's been so amusing for you."

Rather than seem disappointed, Queen Bee gasped and pressed a hand dramatically to the base of her throat. "That's *right*, he did kill Lady Indomitable. Why"—her eyes glinted cruelly—"that just makes all of this even richer, doesn't it?"

"Honey," said Nova, her voice cutting. "It's not a game."

"Oh, lighten up," said Queen Bee, flicking a few fingers toward her. "You've been frolicking around the city with your Renegade friends for months now. It's time I got to have some fun, too." She winked at Adrian, but then her expression became thoughtful. She placed a hand on his forearm, right over his wound, squeezing just enough to make him flinch. A few of the bees deserted him and started making their way up her limbs instead. "I've just had a thought. Do you believe in archenemies? You know, that a hero and a villain are destined to be locked in an eternal battle forever and ever until they finally destroy each other? Because I always thought the idea was a bit too clean-edged, if you know what I mean—Ace

Anarchy and your dear dad notwithstanding—but I'm beginning to wonder. Because it's just so . . ." She tapped a finger against her shiny, sticky lips. "*Perfect.* Your own mother, the person you must have loved more than any other in this world, cruelly snatched away from you by . . . your very . . . own . . . creation."

Adrian blinked at her and would have gone on blinking at her, except a hornet decided at that moment to try and climb into his ear and he let out a yelp and roughly shook his head.

"Oh, allow me," said Queen Bee, scooping her finger against his earlobe and lifting the creature away.

Adrian shuddered. "What are you talking about? My creation?"

"See for yourself. Nightmare?"

Nova hadn't moved from the entryway and for the first time Adrian noticed she was holding something. A stack of papers. She seemed reluctant to give them up. She seemed reluctant to do anything more than stand there, shoulders tensed and face borderline apologetic, but he didn't think it was the capturing, the tying up, or the torturing that she was sorry for, which made him go cold with suspicion.

"What is she talking about?" he demanded.

Nova still didn't move. Still didn't speak.

"Don't be shy. Our guest asked you a question." Honey got to her feet and grabbed the papers away from Nova, who didn't resist. "Now, let's see, where was it?"

As she started flipping through pages, Adrian realized what they were. His comics.

He sneered. "The Sentinel isn't exactly a secret anymore, either, you know."

"Patience, patience," said Queen Bee. She flipped through the whole comic, the third and final one Adrian had made, the one where

Rebel Z first donned the armored suit and transformed himself into a superhero intent on revenge. Reaching the end, she frowned and started flipping back the other way, turning the pages carelessly in her haste. He heard some of the paper rip. She reached the front again and heaved a sigh. Holding the comic up by just the front cover, she tilted her head to the side and started flipping through the pages *again*, as if this new perspective would help.

Adrian raised an eyebrow at Nova.

Groaning, Nova finally stepped forward into the room and yanked the pages out of Queen Bee's hand. Dropping to her knees in front of Adrian, she set the third issue of the comic aside and found the first issue in the stack, the one where Rebel Z was captured by power-hungry villains, kept locked up, and tortured while all his friends suffered around him.

It was all sounding eerily prophetic.

Adrian tried not to think about that as he watched his old drawings flip past. Though he knew it hardly mattered at the moment, he couldn't help cringing at the awkward facial features and the hands that resembled pudgy starfish.

Nova stopped on a page where one of the kidnapped kids was being tortured and turned the book around, holding it up for him to see.

He took in the drawing, and couldn't help the twinge of surprise that coursed through him. One of the kidnapped children was dead, still strapped to a medical table while the doctor and a nurse watched in the background. A shadowy figure was rising up from the boy's body, like a wisp of formless black smoke, but with a single bony hand pointing at the boy's dead eyes.

It had been a long time since Adrian had seen the comics. He vaguely remembered the skeletal hands, the dark shadowy cloak. He vaguely remembered how this phantom creature was intended to get stronger over the course of the series and become one of Rebel Z's most feared enemies. He vaguely remembered what the creature became—a villain crafted from fear and death, who had no face, no soul, and a mean-looking scythe that Adrian had thought would be fun to use in future epic fight scenes.

It took only a second to guess at what Nova and Queen Bee were suggesting.

But . . . what they were suggesting was ludicrous.

"What's your point?" he said, glaring at her over the top of the page.

Nova lowered the comic. "I think this is Phobia," she said, with such tenderness that he felt his fury flare irrationally.

"That," he said, nodding toward the book, "is the disembodied soul of a troubled kid who's been used as a science experiment by an evil branch of the government."

"Oooh," said Queen Bee, clapping her hands. "I would read that."

Sighing, Nova set the comic back on the floor. "It's not just these comics. I've seen your drawings from when you were little. Really little. The phantom from your dreams? You drew it, a lot. And over time, it was turning into *this*." She pointed at the page again.

Adrian let out a hoarse laugh. "Hold on. You really think I created him? Phobia?"

Nova pressed her lips until they went white. There was so much pity in her eyes that Adrian wanted to scream. Had he really been relieved to see her only a few minutes ago?

"It fits the timeline," she said. "It fits what little we know about Phobia. It explains why no one has any idea who he was or where he came from. He just . . . appeared, out of nowhere, and right around the time that you would have been old enough to start drawing him."

"I would have been four!" he said. "*Maybe* five. I might be good, but I'm not that good."

She shook her head. "It's not about skill though, is it?"

He scowled, biting back his irritation. She was right. His super-power didn't work based on how good of an artist he was. It worked through his intention, though what he believed his drawings could become.

"No," he said, shaking his head. "I would remember creating . . . that."

"Would you?" interjected Queen Bee. She was still smiling, as if she were enjoying a particularly saucy soap opera. "Do you remember every drawing you made when you were four years old, *maybe* five?"

He glared at her, even as his breaths began to quicken.

Of course he didn't remember every drawing. His mom had once joked that Gatlon City would have to open a new paper factory with how many pages and pages of crayon scribbles he was creating.

"There's also that phrase he uses," said Nova. "The one he would leave on his victims?"

Adrian glared at her. "What about it?"

"You told me it's like something your mom used to say, about being brave. I think you fed him that line, or your brain did, when you were little. You created him with that thought in mind."

His heart was pounding hard now, threatening to break through his own rib cage. "No," he said firmly. "It's impossible."

"And . . . Adrian . . ." Nova's face contorted, twisting with pain. "He works through people's biggest fears, and you told me that, back then, your greatest fear was . . . was that someday your mother would leave, and she would never come back."

A shiver raced down his spine. He tore his gaze away from her, staring instead into the shadowed corner where Phobia had loitered not all that long ago.

His mother's murderer.

It wasn't possible. Adrian didn't . . . he couldn't have . . .

"I'm so sorry," Nova whispered.

"What's to be sorry about?" tittered Honey Harper. "We should thank you. Phobia may not be the most charming of roommates, but he has proven to be an effective villain."

"Honey, *please*," said Nova. "Could you just go away?"

Queen Bee flashed Adrian a haughty, victorious smile, and it was that look, filled with such delight, that made it seem almost real.

His lungs spasmed, pushing out what little air he had left.

"Of course, Nightmare," said Honey. "I'll just give you some time alone, let our young hero come to terms with the fact that, when you think about it . . . he pretty much murdered his own mother."

"Honey!"

Queen Bee left the chapel, her own squealing laughter echoing after her.

Nova rubbed her temple. "Adrian, it isn't your fault. You have to know that. You were just a kid. There's no way you could have known what you were—"

"Stop."

The sound was so cold, so harsh, Adrian almost didn't believe it had come from his own mouth.

But it worked. Nova fell silent.

His lungs were no longer cooperating. It felt impossible to make his chest expand enough against the ropes. Ropes that were growing tighter by the second, digging into his flesh. Cold sweat was beading across his bare back. The altar had suddenly become unbearably cold.

Phobia was a villain. An Anarchist responsible for countless deaths, including Adrian's own mother's.

Nova reached for him, but he whipped his head away and she froze.

"It's impossible," he said again, more viciously this time. "My creations don't last this long. They die. They . . . fade away, after a few weeks, *maybe* months. But not years." He shook his head. "There's no way I created Phobia."

"Adrian . . . ," Nova started again, her fingers twitching, as if she wanted to comfort him. But how could she?

They were enemies.

That was much was perfectly clear. "If that's true, then how do you explain the drawings? The timing of it all, the similarities . . ."

"Coincidence," he spat.

Nova rocked back on her heels, and he could tell that she wanted to believe him, but didn't.

He snarled, his voice rising. "I didn't make that monster, Nova! Do you really think I'd be capable of that?"

After a hesitation, she slowly shook her head. "No," she whispered. "But . . . I'm not sure I believe in coincidences anymore, either."

The clatter of Honey's shoes reverberated through the chapel again, and she appeared in the doorway a moment later.

"I know that probably wasn't enough time to come to terms with this dreadful new information," she said, smiling sweetly at Adrian. "The good news is, you'll soon be put out of your misery." She beamed at Nova. "Ace wants us in the bell tower."

CHAPTER FORTY-TWO

Nova seemed sensitive to the ragged wounds on Adrian's fore-arms, but Queen Bee showed no qualms about grabbing his bare arms as they hauled Adrian to his feet.

"What's happening in the bell tower?" he asked.

"Only your *doom*," Honey said with a giggle.

Adrian glowered at her. "Is that a dressy occasion? Because some-one sort of destroyed my shirt."

"Believe me, that's the least of your worries," said Honey, patting him on the shoulder.

Nova took a handgun from her belt, and though she didn't aim it at him, the threat was implied.

Adrian shook his head at her, still reeling from the absurd sugges-tion that he might have created Phobia. "You're not going to shoot me."

Nova gave him a look, and it was so hollow and unfamiliar that Adrian immediately wanted to take the words back.

At least she was looking at him, though, and with something

more than just pity over his supposed creation. He held the gaze until she was forced to turn away.

Despite everything, it remained impossible for him to imagine Nova shooting him. He had been wrong about her, in so many ways. But this, his mind refused to compromise on.

Nova was not going to kill him. This much, he had to believe.

But would she stand by and do nothing once the other Anarchists decided he'd served his usefulness? That, he couldn't be so sure about.

It was very likely that he was going to die in this cathedral. Maybe it would be Ace Anarchy himself who did the honors. Or even Phobia.

Phobia. His mother's murderer. An abomination, maybe, but not one that Adrian had anything to do with. He was sure of that.

Wasn't he?

He couldn't fend off a sting of doubt. Honey and Nova had been persuasive, and the drawings *did* look like the villain . . . but Phobia had been tormenting Renegades for years. Probably Adrian's art had been inspired by the villain, on a subconscious level. It didn't prove anything. Besides, nothing he'd made had ever lived half as long before. Why would Phobia be different?

He shuddered at the very implication—that if Nova was right, he had created his mother's killer.

But it wasn't true. It couldn't be true.

He tightened his jaw and tried to convince himself that this was just a mind game they were playing with him. Something to distract him. To leave him disheartened and hopeless. That's all this was.

Nova and Queen Bee took him down a corridor of watchful statues and past the main altar, then into the north transept. Queen Bee carried the lantern, which offered them enough light to see by, if not enough to fully illuminate the shadowed corners. Nova pulled open a heavy wood door and cocked her head, indicating for Adrian to go first.

He found himself trudging up a marble staircase that wrapped the walls of a large square tower. He could hear the Renegades from here, their attacks drumming against the erected barrier. Though the leaded windows were too narrow to escape through, he kept searching the world beyond them for any sign of what was happening outside. But all he could see were glimpses of the dome and the darkness that filled it. The Renegades hadn't breached it yet.

They passed two stories and then ducked through another narrower door into the top half of the tower. The steps changed from marble to wood. They had reached a place where visitors and worshipers would not have entered, where only bell ringers might once have trod.

The staircase seemed to spiral into eternity, disappearing into shadows overhead. The windows were still Gothic style—leaded glass surrounded by stone moldings—but otherwise, this section of the tower was simple and utilitarian. Undecorated walls and supportive wooden beams crosshatched between the rickety stairs.

Adrian climbed. The wood beneath his bare feet was worn to velvet smoothness and he was grateful that Honey hadn't started her mutilations with his feet, otherwise this trek would have been torturous. They rounded a corner to another flight of steps and he took the chance to glance back at Nova. She bristled and jabbed the barrel of the gun into his back.

At the top of a particularly steep, narrow section of the staircase, they came to a solid wooden platform overhead. Nova reached past Adrian to push up the trapdoor, doing everything in her power to avoid touching him as she did.

The door fell back with a thud and a cloud of dust rained down through the opening. Adrian angled his face away, coughing.

"Heroes first," cooed Honey Harper.

It was awkward to climb the last of the tiny steps without being able to use his hands for balance, but Adrian managed to do it without falling on his face. He found himself in the belfry, where two enormous bells hung in the center of the tower, along with a series of smaller bells suspended in the openings around the exterior walls. The windows here had no glass, allowing the bells' music to ring outward over the surrounding neighborhood.

Back when there had been a surrounding neighborhood.

Up here, the sounds of war were more pronounced, each strike on the enormous shield reverberating through the floorboards at their feet. Explosions. Grinding and chopping. A steady clanging that battered against the dome again and again. Adrian couldn't help but wonder what sort of damage the Renegades could have done if they hadn't suffered so many casualties at the arena. As it was, he was proud to hear them putting up such a ferocious fight.

He was led to a window where one of the smaller bells was hung a few feet overhead, where he could view the dead, faded wastelands. Ace's barrier rose up a couple of hundred feet ahead of them, blocking out the city. Blocking out the sky.

To his surprise, Queen Bee extinguished the lantern. Though it wasn't pitch-black, it was dark enough that, for a moment, Adrian could barely see the Anarchists' outlines. Then Nova lit a few of her micro-flares and tossed them out the window. Some landed on the pitched roof of the cathedral below, a couple on the wide arcade that ran along the northern side of the church. A few more fell into the barren land beyond. Though they succeeded in pushing away some of the darkest shadows, their faint light only served to make the atmo-sphere even more menacing.

Realizing that Nova's attention was on the front of the cathedral, Adrian followed the look and saw figures emerging onto the roofs of the two western towers that framed the grand cathedral entrance. His blood cooled to see Phobia among them.

Ace Anarchy himself appeared, recognizable by the helmet that seemed to have its own faint glow. The villain lifted his arms dramati-cally, and Adrian felt both Nova and Queen Bee tense beside him.

The collection of debris that had been forged together to build the dome began to rattle. Rivulets of dust streamed down.

Straight ahead, directly facing the cathedral's western facade, a slim shard of light appeared unexpectedly from the base of the bar-rier. Not sunlight, but something blinding white and artificial, as if there were a giant spotlight trained on the barrier. Like massive doors opening, the wall peeled back on either side of the breach. Metal and wood and stone grated against one another, folding inward until an arched tunnel had opened between the wasteland and the world beyond. Adrian squinted against the unexpected onslaught of light, a swath cutting its way straight through to the main entryway of the church.

For a moment, all fell still. Adrian wondered what the Renegades would do with this open invitation, one that could only be a trap.

As soon as the pathway had been cleared, the assault on the dome's exterior ceased. A heady silence filled the space. Adrian felt the hair standing up on his arms, apprehension hanging in the air with an electric charge.

They waited. In the stillness, he could hear Nova's breathing. Though she was right beside him, she seemed to be taking care not to touch him and, strangely enough, he translated this as a sign that she still cared for him. He had a heightened awareness of her proximity, and he couldn't help believing that if she felt nothing for him, then she wouldn't be taking such care to avoid an occasional brush of skin.

He stopped himself before his thoughts could travel much further down that path, because it raised a series of uncomfortable questions about his own feelings, questions he wasn't prepared to face. Not when Nova was wearing a black hooded jacket and holding a gun to his side.

Funny, he thought, how he'd been so ready to write off their relationship as nothing more than a game to her back when she'd been arrested, but now he found himself resisting the idea. Maybe, after having gone through those doubts once already, his heart was refusing to go through them again. Maybe denial was easier.

His dangerous thoughts were interrupted by a cruel chuckle from Honey Harper.

"Jackpot," she whispered.

A figure had appeared in the opening. A single silhouette, and one that Adrian recognized immediately. Broad shoulders, accented by armored pads. Muscled arms and legs in skintight Lycra. Hair glinting gold in the light, not a lock out of place.

Captain Chromium entered, his head high as he stepped through the tunnel into the wasteland. He carried a long chromium chain in one hand and the Silver Spear in the other, every bit the superhero who had first risen to power in the Age of Anarchy.

As soon as he crossed the threshold of Ace's barrier, the wall rumbled and closed up tight behind him. An enraged cry could be heard from the Renegades left behind on the other side, and Captain

Chromium paused. When he realized he was alone, he squared his shoulders and faced the cathedral, taking in Ace Anarchy and the villains gathered on the front towers.

He stopped halfway across the wasteland and plunged the end of the pike into the ground. He looked ready to destroy the Anarchists single-handedly, and Adrian almost believed he could do it.

"Hello again, dear friend," said Ace, his voice echoing in the vast chamber. "Are you missing something? Or . . . someone?"

If the taunting had an effect on the Captain, it was impossible to tell. He kept his gaze locked on Ace Anarchy, cool and unflustered. "We've had this fight too many times already, Alec," he said. The silence, combined with the enclosed dome, made for an echo that carried his voice all the way to the top of the bell tower. "Are we really going to have it again?"

"Oh, I hope so," said Ace. "I have plans for a different outcome this time."

"You know you can't defeat me."

Ace laughed. "It is refreshing to see that your arrogance has not changed in all this time. Let's remember, last time we stood here, you only bested me with the help of a *baby*."

Adrian shivered at the mention of Max.

"This is pointless," said Captain Chromium. "You know you can't kill me. What are you hoping to accomplish here?"

"Well, to start," said Ace, "I've long harbored fantasies of chaining you to a tank and watching you sink to the bottom of the ocean, never to be heard from again."

"All so you can have control over a city that doesn't want you?"

"I'll be satisfied with revenge at this point. Revenge for ten years of being powerless, while *you* ran around belittling who we are and what we are capable of. Your trials have turned prodigies into a sideshow, and the way you pander to the media is disgusting. You care more for your own reputation, for the citizens' approval, than for taking care of your own. And maybe that was going well for a while. You were idolized. You were adored. But how has it been working out for you lately?"

"My job is to make this world safer for everyone, civilians and prodigies," said the Captain. "Which would be a lot easier if we weren't always having to defend ourselves from villains like you!"

"Those civilians treated as like abominations!" Ace roared. "Don't you remember what it was like before I decided it was time for things to change? They hunted us! They tortured us! They murdered innocent babies, all in fear of what they might become! And they will turn on us again if we don't keep them in their place."

"What place is that? Should we just enslave them for our own purposes, then?"

"Why not?" said Ace. "You know it's what they would have done to us if they'd been able to manage it."

The Captain shook his head. "With you in power, all anyone knew was fear. I've worked too hard to clean up your messes. I won't let you do this again!"

Ace scoffed. "I'll admit, I did make some mistakes, but I've learned from them. It isn't enough to destroy the existing world order. You must destroy it—and then rebuild the world to fit your vision."

"No, Alec. We have been given a gift. We should use these gifts to better society, not just to stoke our own egos. Not just to put ourselves on pedestals."

Ace chuckled in amusement. "How trite, coming from you. I have never known a time when you didn't put yourself on a pedestal. Besides . . . you're wrong, my old friend. We have no obligation to use our powers to help the people of this world, not after what they did to us. Our only obligation is to ourselves. And once prodigies are no longer governed by fear or arbitrary *codes*, they will recognize their place. We will soon be in a second Age of Anarchy, but this time we will not be villains. We will be gods!"

The Captain shook his head. "You're delusional, Alec. You can't defeat me."

"I don't have to defeat you, my old friend. You are going to defeat yourself. Soon, you will know what it means to feel powerless, just how you left me all those years ago. Cyanide, if you'll do the honors?"

Cyanide reached into an inside pocket of his trench coat. Captain Chromium tensed, eyes narrowing. The villain pulled something small from the pocket and held it up.

Adrian leaned forward. "Is that a flask?"

Queen Bee shushed him.

The flask was lifted from his grip and sent drifting toward the Captain below. Hugh snarled and braced himself, angling the pike toward the flask as it came to hover an arm's length in front of his face.

"My chief chemist has distilled a particularly potent batch of the substance you call Agent N," said Ace. "We wanted to try a little experiment, to see if you are, in fact, invincible to your own poison. All you have to do . . . is drink it."

"Why would I do that?"

"Because if you don't," Ace said slowly, "we're going to kill your son."

This, too, brought no reaction from the Captain, who had probably been expecting it. His voice remained steady, if also cut through with a new edge. "For all I know, he's already dead."

"You think I would waste a perfectly good hostage?" Ace swept an arm toward the bell tower. "Behold. Safe and sound."

Queen Bee reignited the oil lantern, filling the belfry with its subtle, steady light and drawing his dad's attention up to them. Relief brightened the Captain's face.

"I'm fine!" Adrian yelled. "Don't worry about me!"

He was surprised at how confident he sounded.

Beside him, Nova lifted the gun so his dad could see it, holding it against Adrian's temple.

Adrian turned his head to look at her, not shying away even as the cool barrel pressed into his forehead. "You're not fooling me with that."

She ignored him, her focus on the scene below.

Ace chuckled. "As you can see, he's very much *not* fine. Which leaves you with a decision to make. Sacrifice him to protect your own powers, or sacrifice yourself and save the boy you raised from childhood, who has already suffered so much in his young life. It is a difficult choice. Let us see how much you truly care for your *greater good*."

Hugh scrutinized the side of the bell tower and the roof of the cathedral, and Adrian could imagine him trying to plot out another option. A way to be the hero, as he always was.

"Don't waste our time," said Ace. The flask bobbed in the air. "This deal comes with an expiration. Besides . . . it may not even affect you. Your invincibility may yet hold. How will we know if we don't try?"

"Don't!" Adrian yelled. "Don't do—"

Queen Bee grabbed his head and slammed it against the stone window frame. He grunted and fell to one knee, his head ringing like the bell above. The blow throbbed through his skull and into his teeth.

She held him down with his head bent over the windowsill.

Adrian was about to lift his chin again, prepared to show Honey and Nova, Ace and his dad, just how defiant he could be, when he heard a click and felt the gun pressing against his scalp.

He released a dry laugh. "Come on, Nova."

"Stop talking," she growled.

He lifted his head as much as he could. Hugh was watching him, horror pulsing beneath his strong exterior.

Maybe he'd been wrong yet again. Maybe Nova would kill him.

Maybe that, too, would be its own sort of justice. He had trusted her so deeply. Welcomed her into the Renegades without hesitation. Begun to fall in love with her. It was, in part, due to his own blindness that she'd managed to cause so much grief.

Adrian forced himself to be calm. He let his body relax. He lifted his chin, pressing the back of his head hard against the gun. He held his dad's gaze and tried to convey what they both knew to be true.

Hugh Everhart could not sacrifice himself. If Adrian was going to die today, he needed to die knowing that the Renegades would persevere. That they would stop Ace Anarchy. That they would end this war between heroes and villains . . . again. For good, this time.

He wished he could convey these thoughts to his dad. He believed in him and the organization he had created, even if he had fought against so many of their rules. He wasn't afraid to die. He was a superhero. The son of Lady Indomitable . . . and also the Dread Warden and Captain Chromium. Being prepared to sacrifice himself for the greater good was a part of the job description.

And they both knew that Adrian was not the superhero this city needed. Captain Chromium was.

As he stared, he saw something enter his father's eyes. An apology?

Driving the pike back into the ground, he grabbed the flask from the air and unscrewed the lid with his thumb.

"No!" Adrian screamed.

His father threw his head back and drank it.

Heart pounding, Adrian watched, they all watched, as Captain Chromium turned over the flask to show that it was empty before dropping it into the dirt.

They waited.

Adrian wondered what the physical indications would be. Would his muscles begin to shrink? Would the chromium chain and spear melt away, as Ruby's bloodstone had?

Captain Chromium yanked the spear from the ground, gripping it in his fist while the seconds ticked by.

Ten.

Twenty.

Thirty.

The air came rushing back into Adrian's lungs and he found himself laughing as the truth sank in, for all of them.

It hadn't worked.

His invincibility had held.

"How disappointing," said Ace. "But there is more than one way to destroy a hero." He gestured toward the bell tower. "Nightmare, you were once forced to watch as your loved ones were murdered in front of you, due to the negligence of this man who calls himself a hero. Today, you will have your revenge! Today, Captain Chromium will know what pain you felt, as he, too, witnesses the death of the person most precious to him. I sentence Adrian Everhart to death! Nightmare, you may have the honors."

"NO!" Hugh screamed.

Even as Adrian lifted his head, refusing to cower from his fate, Captain Chromium pulled back his arm and heaved the spear with all his extraordinary might at the bell tower.

He sent it straight at Nova.

CHAPTER FORTY-THREE

NOVA STUMBLED BACK from the window, at the same moment Adrian shoved his shoulder against her side, knocking her to the floor. The javelin flew over Adrian's head, missing him by inches, and lodged itself into one of the wooden beams supporting the bells. A cloud of dust exploded across the belfry.

Dizzy with the rush of adrenaline, Nova pushed herself onto her elbows and gaped at Adrian.

He stared back at her, seemingly as surprised as she was.

Honey Harper laughed. "What was *that*? Did you just save her life? Oh, darling, if you weren't so disgustingly noble, I'd be half in love with you myself."

Adrian didn't look away from Nova. "She saved my life once," he said. "A few times, actually."

Nova swallowed. Outside, she heard the Captain, still screaming. The sound was rife with anger and fear and the promise that he would annihilate anyone who laid a finger on his son.

Catching her breath, Nova forced herself to turn away from Adrian and all the emotions scrawled across his face. The intensity, the openness.

She saved my life once . . .

She had not dropped the gun, though her hand was trembling as she climbed back to her feet and returned to the window. The Captain was sprinting toward the entrance of the cathedral. The villains stood motionless on the western towers, watching him come. Nova couldn't tell if they were nervous that this supposedly invincible superhero was ready to demolish the church in search of Adrian, but they did still have strength in numbers, and the advantage of the higher ground, and familiarity with the cathedral, and . . . Ace.

They still had Ace.

But Ace wasn't paying any attention to his archenemy, Nova realized with a start. He was watching *her.* His mouth moved, but in the burgeoning noise, she could no longer hear him. He frowned and beckoned to Megaphone at his side.

A moment later, Megaphone's voice boomed through the enclosed space. "You did want to see an execution, didn't you? Then so be it!"

Ace nodded at Nova.

Shivering, she lifted the gun. Adrian didn't move as she angled it against his temple again.

Her heart ricocheted inside her chest.

Captain Chromium released another war cry. Dragging the chain behind him as he ran, it seemed like he intended to tear the church apart stone by stone. Anything to stop Nova. Anything to keep Adrian safe.

He was halted as a series of wooden timbers dislodged from the arched dome and crashed in front of him.

He roared, and with a single punch, the first beam splintered. The Captain grabbed another and heaved it aside, then planted his palm on the third beam and launched himself over it like a hurdle. But for every obstacle he crossed, another was ready to take its place. Rubber tires. Iron gates. Cinder blocks.

Ace was toying with him. He wasn't worried that his longtime rival was using all his strength to get to the church, to get to Adrian.

Ace cast Nova another questioning look, this one tinged with suspicion.

She adjusted the gun in her hand. Put the barrel against Adrian's skin. He was facing forward, his focus locked on the struggle below. His glasses had slipped slightly down his nose. Nova watched the dip of his lashes as he blinked. The steady rise and fall of his shoulders.

Pull the trigger, Nova.

The gun became heavy. The handle felt slick in her palm.

Adrian's lips parted. His gaze shifted in her direction. He was still shirtless, his wounds still bleeding through the gauze, and she knew he must be in pain. And yet, he was so still. So steady.

Just waiting.

Pull the trigger.

"His father made the choice for you, little Nightmare."

She startled. Ace had taken to the air. He was levitating over the nave's steep roof.

"And now," he continued, "we must keep our word. We do not make idle threats."

She tried to nod, but wasn't sure she succeeded. This time, she didn't look down at Adrian. That would make it easier. To not see him. To not feel his breaths moving through her. To not remember the steady drum of his heartbeat as she'd once rested her head on his chest.

Her lips moved this time, saying the words to herself. *Just pull the trigger.*

That was all she had to do and Ace would be proud and Captain Chromium would be devastated and the Anarchists would win. Her family would finally win.

Her own breaths came in strangled hiccups. She was that frightened little girl all over again, staring at the unconscious body of the man who had murdered her family. She was petrified, unable to squeeze her finger, to take that one small action that would avenge her family's deaths.

Her father. Her mother. Evie. All that she had loved, stolen from her, so brutally, so carelessly.

Her arm started to shake.

This was supposed to be her revenge, and yet . . . it wasn't the revenge she'd longed for. This was pain of an entirely new sort.

She couldn't lose Adrian, too.

A roar came from below, followed by a crash. Ace turned back. The Captain had made it around the front facade and begun scaling the cathedral's northern wall. The crash had been a saintly stone statue being thrown to the ground and shattering.

Ace's hands curled into claws. He lowered himself onto one of the stone buttresses, snarling as the Captain launched himself from pillar to window arch, gargoyle to finial. Every time he landed, he punched a new hole into the stonework, forming handholds for himself as he pulled his body higher.

Ace lifted his hands toward the Captain, but Nova wouldn't know what happened next.

A hand snatched something from her belt. She gasped and swiveled around. Honey had taken her knife.

"For all the diabolical schemes," said Honey. "If you can't do it, then I will!"

Honey grabbed Adrian's forehead and yanked his head back. She reached around, prepared to drag the knife against his throat.

"No!" Nova grabbed Honey's arm and wrestled it away. Swinging them both around, she gritted her teeth and shoved Honey back against the wall. "Please."

It was a pathetic plea—a begging, desperate plea.

Honey's expression was startled, though it quickly darkened. She shoved Nova away. Nova stumbled, but caught herself. She still held the gun, but she wouldn't aim it at Honey. Her ally. Her friend.

"I thought we were past this," Honey growled. "He's a Renegade, Nova. He's one of *them*."

"I know," she said, her voice sounding weak even in her own head. "I know."

It was all she could think to say. Because Honey was right. And there was no way for her to explain that at this moment, she didn't care. She couldn't even ask Honey not to hurt him. She couldn't suggest that they let him go, because where would he go? And what would Ace think?

But still.

Still.

She'd thought she could do it. She'd thought—for Ace. For the Anarchists. For her family. For this world. She could do it, if that's what it took for Ace's vision to come true. For the Renegades to be destroyed once and for all. For all prodigies to have freedom from tyranny. For the balance of power to tip back toward actual balance.

But she'd been wrong.

She couldn't kill him.

She couldn't do it.

And she couldn't stand there and watch him be killed, either. Not this boy, who had given her a quiet, dreamless sleep. Who had given her a star. Who had given her hope.

Not him. Not Adrian.

Honey's face twisted.

Then Nova heard the buzzing.

She had barely cocked her head when the first wasp landed above her elbow and drove its stinger into her skin.

Nova had seen Honey's bees at works, had heard the screams of agony—but nothing had prepared her for this. It was a burning nail being plunged into her flesh.

Nova screamed. The gun clattered to the floor.

A second sting pierced her thigh. A third beneath her shoulder blade. A fourth on her shin. Each one speared into her, more painful than she could have imagined. And they kept coming. Scorching needles being driven into her again and again and again.

"Stop!" she wailed, collapsing against a wall. "Honey—stop!"

Every instinct told her to run, to throw herself from the tower if it would only get her away from here. But one thought kept her there, despite the pain. If she ran, Honey would kill Adrian.

"*Please,*" she cried, swatting away a crimson hornet. "Honey—" She gasped as a stinger burrowed into her chest. "This is wrong, Honey! We don't need to—fight them—anymore!"

"Is that so?" Honey yelled. "So what, you thought you'd keep one as your boyfriend? Or forgive his Councilman father? You've never understood, Nova. You were always too young to understand."

Another sting plunged into the soft flesh behind Nova's ear. She tried to cover her head and neck as hot tears blurred her vision. She could feel them everywhere. Not just the venomous stings, but their legs crawling across her skin, their wings beating against her hair, the deafening buzz all around her.

Her hazy vision landed on the bare skin of Honey's ankle. Her power pulsed through her, more desperate than she had ever felt it before.

She only needed to touch her—

She threw herself forward, arm outstretched.

Honey lifted her foot and slammed her heel down onto the back of Nova's hand. Nova screamed.

"Nice try," said Honey. She lifted her shoe and kicked Nova's hand away. "Ace gave you an order, and if you can't follow through, then I will. Captain Chromium took everything from us. Everything! And now . . ." She rounded on Adrian, still leaning against the wall, his hands bound behind his back. "Now I will take everything from him."

She lunged.

Adrian sidestepped. Honey crashed into the window ledge, knocking over the oil lantern. The flame extinguished as it fell and rolled a few feet across the timber floor, oil spilling behind it. Honey pivoted, swinging the knife gracelessly through the air. Adrian kept backing away, dodging her swings as best as he could, watching his footing on the uneven boards. The blade nicked his shoulder.

Nova tried to focus, but her thoughts were dull with pain, her movements involuntary as she contorted and writhed, trying desperately to escape the swarm.

Her blurry attention landed on the gun.

Her brain was slowed by the agony, the way her entire body felt like it was smoldering from within.

Adrian's back hit a wooden support beneath the bells.

Honey grinned.

Adrian buckled forward suddenly, crying out in pain. A black wasp was crawling over his shoulder. He spun, trying to knock it away—driving himself right toward Honey.

A howl tore from Nova's throat. She raised the gun, sweat dripping into her eye.

Another stinger stabbed Nova's wrist.

Honey lifted the knife, preparing to drive it into Adrian's chest.

Nova locked her jaw around another scream and pulled the trigger.

The kickback sent her flying into the stone wall. The gun blew out of her hand, ricocheting off one of the smaller bells with a resounding clang before it careened out of the tower window.

Nova fell onto her side, just as another sting shot through her knee, and she whimpered, wishing it would stop, pleading for it to stop.

And, suddenly, it did.

Not the pain, but the volley of stings, at least.

Nova sobbed and trembled as the hornets covering her body began to take flight.

They returned to Honey. Returned to their queen, whose body lay crookedly across the old wooden floor. A small pool of blood was forming beneath her cloud of yellow hair. Nova blinked back her tears, watching as the bees moved across Honey's flesh. They seemed to be inspecting her.

Nova started to cough. She used her sleeve to wipe away the snot from her nose. She could not stop shaking. She couldn't think of much beyond the agony working its way through her system. Her body felt like a series of open wounds that someone had dumped acid into.

One bee left Honey, buzzing up toward the central bells for a moment and waiting there, uncertain. Nova moaned and shrank away from it, terrified, but the bee took no notice of her. The others began to leave Honey's body as well. Only a few at first, then more, dozens at a time, dispersing through the open windows of the tower. Abandoning the cathedral. Abandoning their queen.

Only once the last of their buzzing had faded away did Nova know for sure that Honey Harper was dead.

CHAPTER FORTY-FOUR

NOVA RESTED HER cheek against the rough wooden floor and sobbed. She was aware of nothing but burning and stinging and throbbing. She wished she could put herself to sleep. She would rather be unconscious and vulnerable than have to endure this. She would rather be dead.

Something clattered across the floor and bumped her stomach.

Shuddering, Nova peeled open her swollen eyes and saw her knife. Adrian was inching toward her on his knees. When he got near enough, he lay down so their faces were inches from each other. There was so much concern written into his features that she started to cry harder.

"Nova," he said. Gentle. Kind. "I can help you, but you have to untie me. Can you do that?"

She bent her head and coughed into the floorboards. His words felt distant. Impossible. She didn't even think she could sit up, much less handle a knife. Much less do anything useful.

But she had to do something. She couldn't just lie here sobbing.

"I know," he whispered, nudging his forehead against hers. "I know."

She sniffled. Choked some more. Nodded shakily.

Though her skin was aflame and her muscles as sturdy as string, she worked her elbows under her head and forced herself up, then back, resting on one hip. She bit back a cry of pain as each movement sent the venom searing through her veins again.

Adrian sat up so she could see his hands. She stared at the ropes for what must have been ages. Her vision was blurry. Her mind refused to function.

"The knife?" Adrian said.

Nova picked it up and gripped it as tightly as she could with one hand. With the other, she held Adrian's wrist as she began to saw through the ropes. It took her forever, but Adrian was patient. He angled his body as best as he could to make things easier for her, though the bindings must have been digging into his arms.

When the last rope fell away, Nova dropped the knife and collapsed with a groan. Adrian turned and swept her into his arms. She couldn't return the embrace beyond burying her head into the space between his throat and his chest. She was crying again.

Keeping one arm around her, Adrian moved his other hand to her waist, searching for something along her belt.

A gurgling, hysterical laugh spilled out of her as it occurred to her that this, all of this, might be nothing more than Adrian preparing to betray her. He could kill her easy enough, or tie her up with her own rope, or pick her up and toss her from the tower.

It was probably what she deserved.

Instead, she felt the touch of a pen on the skin behind her ear. Adrian shifted slightly and she felt him draw something on the back of her neck. After a moment, she felt something cold and damp and soothing pressed over the puncture wound.

She sighed, practically in ecstasy at such comfort.

"The Vitality Charm is protecting you," said Adrian. "Otherwise you'd probably be dead from having this much venom in your system."

"It feels like I'm dying," she said, the words slurred together into something almost coherent.

"I'm sorry it doesn't do more to help the pain, but trust me, it would be worse without it." Adrian unzipped her jacket and eased it off her shoulders, peeling each sleeve carefully away from her arms. She whimpered each time the material brushed against the swollen welts.

Setting the jacket aside, he shifted her body so she could stay cradled against him while he worked on her arms. Nova watched, speechless, as he used her own pen—the one she had long ago installed a secret blow-dart compartment into—to draw a fat teardrop around each swollen wound, before tenderly rubbing it in with his thumb. The sketch became a cool salve under his touch. Then he drew a series of neat bandages, covering each sting.

"This is an ointment against the venom," Adrian said, finishing up with the first arm and starting a new teardrop on the other. "Honey and antihistamines. And this"—he drew another bandage—"is an icy-cold compress, to bring down the swelling and take away some of the pain."

Her lashes dipped. They still felt damp and heavy from the tears, but she wasn't crying anymore. Though her body ached and burned, the pain on her neck and arms had already dulled significantly.

"Okay," he said, finishing her arms. He cocked his head and she could feel him watching her, but she kept her attention on the compresses that now dotted her limbs. "Where else?"

She grimaced and bent forward, peeling up the bottom of her

shirt so he could see the welts along her back. He worked his way through them, steady and meticulous, and when it was time to do her legs, Adrian looked away while she wriggled out of her pants, hissing and flinching the whole time. He handed her the jacket to cover herself as much as she could while he treated those wounds, though she felt the modesty was for his benefit as much as her own. She didn't much care what he saw, so long as he made this agony go away.

Distantly, she recognized the thunderous cacophony of a raging battle. Though they sounded miles away, she knew it was much closer than that. It didn't sound as if the Renegades had yet breached the makeshift barrier over the cathedral, and she imagined the villains standing at the western towers, waiting to see if Ace's structure would hold. Ready to defend their newly earned territory, with their lives if necessary.

That had been the plan. In the event that the Renegades did make it through Ace's wall, the villains would hold the cathedral at all costs. Ace had been insistent that they not lose their sanctuary. The Renegades were weak, anyway. Nearly half of their numbers were neutralized. Holding the cathedral should be easy.

Nova found herself hoping that the Renegades never made it inside. She couldn't stomach the thought of another battle that nobody would win.

By the time Adrian was finished, the pain had become a distant, dull thrum throughout her body.

Again, Adrian allowed her privacy while she stood and pulled her pants back on, busying himself with finally addressing his own wounds. Nova swiped the backs of her hands across her cheeks.

"Thank you," she murmured, and felt tears welling up again.

Tears of gratitude, but also tears of guilt. A part of her wanted to lie down on this dirty, ancient floor and do nothing but sob until this whole miserable ordeal was over. It was all she could do to stay standing. "You didn't have to . . . after everything . . ." She buried her face in her hands. "I don't know what I'm doing anymore. I don't know what's right or wrong or—"

"Nova, stop. Listen to me." Adrian took her wrists and pulled her hands away from her face. "I can only begin to imagine what your life has been like, but none of that matters right now. What matters is that you are good and strong and brave and willing to fight for the people you care for. Right?"

She gaped at him, not at all sure his description of her was accurate. Who *was* she? Who had she become?

"Oscar and Danna are down there somewhere. And my dad . . ." His voice wavered. It seemed like an eternity had passed since Captain Chromium had started scaling the cathedral walls in an effort to get to Adrian.

He was battling Ace, perhaps at this very moment.

But he was invincible. Ace couldn't hurt him.

Right?

"Help me," said Adrian. "Ace Anarchy wants us all dead. Please, help me stop him."

"He's my uncle," she whispered.

"He's an Anarchist."

"*I'm* an Anarchist."

"No. You're a Renegade."

She grimaced. "Adrian—"

"You *are*, Nova. If you don't believe it, you're just going to have to trust me."

She hesitated. His words reminded her of what Ace had said, what felt like eons ago. *You cannot trust them, Nova. You are not one of them, much as you might wish otherwise.*

But she did trust Adrian. She always had. Even if he was a Renegade. Even if he hadn't told her about the Sentinel. She trusted him.

She just wasn't sure how it was possible that he could still trust her.

"Adrian, I need you to know that I really am sorry. For everything. It wasn't all a lie. My feelings for you—"

Adrian cupped her face in his hands. "I know. And when this is all over, we are going to have a serious talk about keeping secrets from each other."

She laughed, though it was a nervous sound. "How can you still trust me? After everything?"

"We've got nothing else to lie about, right? You're Nightmare. I'm the Sentinel. Ace Anarchy is your uncle. You and I might be archenemies. And yet . . ." He shrugged, a little hapless. "Somehow, I still want to kiss you."

Her skin tingled. "You do?"

"As much as ever."

And then, he did.

The kiss was more tender than the passionate kisses they'd shared before, full of hunger and urgency. This was more patient. More knowing.

Utterly devoid of secrets.

He started to pull away, but Nova stopped him, wrapping an arm around his neck and pulling his lips down to hers again. She melted against him. A kiss full of far more words than they had the time to say.

She couldn't keep the overwhelming emotion from her voice

when they separated, the disbelief and hope that coursed through her. "I was sure you would hate me when you found out the truth."

Adrian grimaced. "I tried to, at first. But it's like you said. Everyone has a nightmare." He pressed his forehead against hers. "Maybe I want you to be mine."

Her heart swelled, but she still couldn't help a teasing smile as she leaned back. "You've been holding on to that one for a while, haven't you?"

"Just a few hours." He beamed. "But I sure am glad I got a chance to use it."

Nova was tempted to kiss him again when footsteps thundered beneath them. The noise pounded up the wooden staircase. The trapdoor crashed open and Leroy emerged, panting. "What in the name of—" He froze. His attention skipped from Adrian to Nova to Honey and the blood-soaked boards. The right side of his face twisted with rage as he hurled himself up onto the floor of the belfry. "Get away from her!" he shouted, reaching for one of the vials attached to a bandolier across his chest.

"Leroy—" Nova started, stepping toward him. "Wait!"

Adrian lifted a placating hand.

Leroy uncorked the vial and hurled it over Nova's shoulder.

Nova spun around in time to see a shimmering wall spread out from Adrian's palm, just like the one that had protected him and his father at the arena. Leroy's vial smashed into the invisible bricks, painting them with a splotch of yellow liquid that hissed and sizzled.

Nova cringed at the rank odor of tormicene acid, one of Leroy's favorite concoctions. It was known for the instant boils that formed on human flesh, that would begin to decay and rot within an hour.

"Leroy, please listen. Please stop—"

"He's manipulating you, Nova," he said. "Brainwashing you to think they're the good guys. Trust me. All he cares about now is saving his own skin." He shoved Nova away—away from him, away from Adrian.

The wall shimmered, the golden mortar dispersing into the air, and Adrian took a hesitant step forward. "I'm not manipulating anyone. I care for Nova, and I think you do, too. If we could just—"

"Talk?" suggested Leroy with a high-pitched laugh. "Like you talked to Honey, who loved Nova like she was her own daughter?"

Nova shook her head. "Honey tried to kill—"

She didn't finish. In a blink, Leroy had thrown a second vial—not at Adrian this time, but at the floor near his feet, where a puddle of oil had spilled from the broken lantern.

The moment the two chemicals mixed, they exploded with the force of a stick of dynamite. The ancient wooden floor crumbled like tissue paper. Adrian shouted and fell through.

Nova screamed and tried to lunge for him, but Leroy stopped her, both arms wrapping around her waist to hold her back. She stared, gasping, as Honey's body slipped into the void, as timbers and stonework caved in around them and clouds of dust filled the air, invading her lungs.

"He's our enemy, Nova. You need to understand. I hope you will someday."

A heavy thump sounded below, a series of crashes—then a figure emerged from the void. Adrian, practically flying. He landed hard on one knee, just outside the chasm. The floorboards creaked and groaned from his weight.

"No, Leroy," said Nova, her voice raw with emotion. "I hope you'll understand someday."

She brushed her fingers against his leathery hand.

"Nov—"

She didn't see whether his face held anger or betrayal. She let him crumple to the floor, his arms slipping from her waist, and then dove for Adrian.

"Wait!" Adrian yelled, too late, the word muffled by the noise of splintering wood and groaning framework. He caught Nova in his arms. This corner of the floor, compromised from the hissing chemicals, began to cave. "Hold on!"

Then they were falling. The blast had pierced the top level of wooden stairs, leaving a mess of sharp edges and teetering beams beneath them. Wood chips and stone dust rained around Nova's head as she wrapped her arms around Adrian's neck, bracing for the fall to end. She spotted Honey's body on the next wooden platform.

She looked up, to where she could hear bells jostling overhead, and saw Leroy's body slipping over the edge.

Unconscious Leroy, falling.

"No!"

Adrian hit the wooden platform with an impact that clattered through her bones. He used the momentum to spring upward again. It felt like flying. Their heads crashed through falling debris. The air whistled past her ears. The narrow windows of the tower blurred in her vision.

With one arm locked around Nova, Adrian used the other to catch Leroy around his middle. Clearing the destroyed floor, they tumbled together to the edge of the belfry, where one small section of floorboards had yet to give in to their weakened joists. Nova landed on her side with a jarring crunch. Leroy's body smacked the stone wall beneath one of the outer bells.

"The floor's not going to hold," Adrian shouted, as the telltale groan of wood and nails echoed beneath them.

Ignoring her throbbing rib cage, Nova hoisted herself to her feet and reached for the open sill. With the mortar and stonework, it was easy for her to find fingerholds, and in seconds she had climbed up onto the crossbar that supported the enormous bronze bell. It swung beneath her weight, the bell ringing like an alarm.

Squinting through smoke and debris, she saw that Adrian had Leroy draped over one shoulder while he used the chromium pike that had been lodged into an overhead beam to haul himself onto the enormous timber frame in the center of the tower.

"Don't hurt him, please," Nova said, gripping the walls to keep her balance.

Leroy started to slip. Adrian barely caught him, grunting from the effort. He managed to secure Leroy on the crossbeam before leveraging himself up the rest of the way. Slumping in exhaustion, he looked at Nova.

Clouds of dust spun in the air around them. Wood continued to groan and creak in the floors below.

"You okay?" Adrian asked.

She laughed and pushed her bangs back from her brow. "No," she said. "Leroy's been like a second father to me." She hesitated, before adding, "Him and Ace both."

Adrian stared at her. "I don't want to sound mean, but I think we need to get you new role models."

She scowled. "Your dads aren't perfect, either."

"I know they aren't, but come on." He gestured at Leroy's slumped body.

Nova adjusted her balance so she didn't feel quite so precarious, her ankles locked around the sides of the bell. "I know it may not seem like it right now, but he's actually a good guy . . ." She trailed off, wondering how she'd never once, in all the time she'd felt herself falling for Adrian, considered what it would be like if he ever met Leroy or the rest of her "family." It had never been worth considering, because she'd known it would never happen.

"Well then," said Adrian with a dry chuckle, "I hope we'll have a chance to get to know each other."

She focused on him again, grateful that he hadn't outright dismissed the idea. "Thank you for not letting him fall."

"We're not safe yet." Adrian peered down into the jagged hole beneath them. "I'll have to transform. I'm stronger with the Sentinel's armor. I'll be able to get him down to safety, but I don't know if I can take you both at once."

"I can get down," Nova said, testing that the pouch with her gloves was secure at her hip. "Just let me catch my breath first."

At least her body was no longer throbbing from the wasp stings, she realized, pressing a hand over her shirt where the Vitality Charm was tucked away.

Things could be worse.

"Nova?" said Adrian. His expression was worried. "What is Ace planning? What is all this for?"

"He wants to destroy the Renegades, especially the Council, so we can take control of the city. He sees the Renegades as tyrants who are oppressing prodigies everywhere and . . . and he keeps saying that we're going to be gods."

Adrian made a sound of derision. "And he calls my dad arrogant."

A sudden crash shook the tower. Nova yelped, sure that the aftermath of the explosion was about to bring the bell tower toppling around them. Then she glanced across the expanse of the cathedral's roof and her heart launched into her throat.

Captain Chromium was on top of the southern turret, gripping the tall pinnacle with one hand while spinning his enormous chain overhead with the other. Ace levitated above the roof's peak, using his powers to peel off stone gargoyles from the architecture and lob them at his enemy. The Captain was attempting to strike Ace with the chain while blocking the constant assault.

Nova shuddered. Not from seeing the two in a battle, but because Ace was cackling as he tore into the clay tiles that lined the roof.

"My masterpiece, so recently rebuilt, and so easily destroyed once again!" said Ace, sounding more gleeful than distraught. "All that matters now is that you Renegades are buried in its rubble. It will be a fitting end, after what you did to me ten years ago!"

"Nova," said Adrian, "we have to stop him. You know that, right?"

Her mouth ran dry.

It was impossible. Them? Stop Ace Anarchy?

And yet, she knew he was right.

No more heroes.

No more villains.

Inhaling a shaky breath, she met his gaze and nodded. "I know."

CHAPTER FORTY-FIVE

A STARTLED CRY drew Adrian's attention across the cathedral
spires. His dad was falling, tumbling down the steep incline
of the cathedral's roof. He caught himself on a flying buttress
and dangled for a moment, before swinging himself back up. With a
grunt, he tore an openmouthed gargoyle from the structure and
heaved it at Ace's head. It was easily deflected. Ace didn't even flinch.
But in the same moment, the Captain lashed out with the chain, striking Ace in the chest. The villain was blown backward, his back
crashing against the inside of his makeshift dome.

"Ace can't control your dad's weapons, can he?" asked Nova.

Adrian shook his head. "He never could. They aren't made of
normal metal."

"Yeah, I know. Your family is kind of scary."

Adrian gawked at her. "*My* family?"

She dared to let a hint of a smile show through. Adrian hesitated,
and then started to laugh. A long, tired, gasping laugh. "I'm going to

turn into the Sentinel now," he said, reaching for his sternum. "You sure you can get down okay?"

Nova smirked. "Don't you know who you're talking to?"

She started to dig through a pouch on her belt, when the noise of splintering wood and screeching metal shook the tower. The two gigantic bells in the center of the belfry were being pulled from their timber framework.

Adrian tugged on the zipper at his sternum, and within seconds, the armor had engulfed him. He scooped up Cyanide's unconscious body, hefting it over his shoulder again, as a series of steel bolts pried free and dropped into the depths of the disemboweled tower.

He leaped from the beam, barely managing to grab hold of the bell adjacent to Nova's. It shifted from his weight, the clapper banging against its sides. He held tight to the crossbar, his other hand securing Cyanide's dead weight, and looked back in time to see the center bells angling upward, pulling unnaturally against their restraints. The wood gave out with a thundering crack, and the bells soared straight for the side wall. Adrian tightened his hold as the bells burst through the stone exterior of the belfry with a ringing cacophony. Stones and mortar exploded outward, raining down on the rooftop, as the bells hurtled through the open air, heading for the Captain.

His dad braced himself on top of the buttress. He ducked, letting the first bell sail over his head and smash into the dome, then reached up with both hands and grabbed the rim of the second bell. The clapper inside gonged against the bronze shell. Using the bell's own momentum, he spun in a circle and threw it at Ace.

Ace dodged. The bell missed him by inches and crashed into the barrier. A jettison of debris trickled down to the wasteland.

Adrian was still holding Cyanide, still watching the bells, when the tower began to groan.

It had taken as much destruction as it could.

He looked at Nova—but she was no longer silhouetted in the next window frame.

"Nova?" he yelled, searching the inside of the tower, but there was no sign of her. "*Nova!*"

The roof above him gave out. The tall spire fell forward, tumbling past the demolished windows, pulling apart joists and beams. The off-kilter weight of it started a chain reaction that pulled at the weakened walls. Stones crumbled into the void. Ornate moldings broke free and disappeared into the chasm below.

Adrian was still searching frantically for Nova when the sill he was perched on tipped, and he was falling.

Please oh please let her not be doing something reckless right now, he thought, watching the fast approach of the cathedral rooftop and trying to determine a safe place to jump to. He adjusted his hold on the unconscious villain, muttering to no one in particular, "Hold on . . ."

They crashed into the roof and it caved from the force. Chunks from the tower hailed around them, beating against Adrian's suit, and he did his best to shield Cyanide from the deluge.

He tried to twist his body to get his legs beneath them so he could use the springs to absorb the shock of the fall, but there wasn't time. They crashed onto a stone floor inside the cathedral, landing with a jolt that ricocheted through his body. The rest of the falling tower tore through the weakened roof, smashing into the church's northern wall. It exploded outward, scattering across the wasteland. The remaining bells landed with such force they cratered the floor and fractured stones.

Adrian lay amid the rubble, every inch of him aching.

"Nova," he groaned. He checked to make sure Cyanide was okay, before stumbling to his feet. He could barely see for the cloud of dust surrounding him. "Nova!"

"I'm . . . fine," came a weak reply. Heart soaring, Adrian stampeded through the debris in the direction of her voice.

He was a few feet away when a bell that had landed upside down rolled off the broken stone wall it had crashed into, striking the floor with a clang.

"*Ow*," Nova groaned.

Adrian froze. He stooped to look closer, and there she was. Her body tucked inside the bronze bell, her arms and legs braced against its curved sides.

"Nova," he whispered, sweeping forward and helping her climb free. He pulled her against his chest, though the embrace wasn't quite the same now that he was wearing his armor.

"Your suit gave me the idea," she said, her voice muffled against his breastplate.

"Genius," he replied. "Are you hurt?" After a moment's consideration, he amended, "Badly hurt?"

Nova groaned, but followed it with, "Not really. Leroy?"

"He's alive. We should find a place to put him before the whole place caves in."

Nova pulled away and shook some of the debris out of her hood, while Adrian scoured the dust from his helmet's visor. They scanned the wreckage. The collapsing bell tower had torn a hole through this part of the cathedral, demolishing nearly the entire northeastern corner.

Adrian's body stayed tense, waiting for the next catastrophe to strike. But there was only the ongoing trickle of dust and clattering debris.

"We can put Leroy inside one of the bells," suggested Nova. "I think he'll fit, and it will be as safe a place as any."

Cyanide did fit inside the bell, though he would probably have a terrible crick in his neck when he came to.

"So," said Adrian, watching as Nova grabbed a few vials off Cyanide's bandolier and shoved them into a pouch on her belt. "How do we stop Ace?"

A frown flitted over her face. It took him a second to remember that she couldn't see his face behind the visor. He pressed a button on the side of his helmet, retracting the face shield. "Sorry."

She shook her head. "I'm not sure Ace can be stopped, not while he has the helmet. Unless we can find a way to neutralize him."

"Is there any more Agent N?"

She considered this. "Do you still have my pen? I have one blow dart with Agent N in the chamber."

"Yes, I have it. If we can get you to the roof, do you think you can get close enough to use it?"

"Maybe," said Nova, "but if he figures out what we're trying to do . . . he'll snap that dart like a twig."

"If anyone can do this, it's you."

She shot him a wry look.

"What about Oscar and Danna?" he asked. "Where are they?"

"They were locked up in the treasury when this all started. Come on." She led him up a short set of steps and down a curved corridor, through a chapel that was only slightly less dreary than the one he'd been kept in earlier.

Then Nova froze, staring into the room attached to the chapel.

It had once had doors of stained glass enclosing it, but the glass had been shattered. The room beyond was barren and tidy compared with the destruction wrought on the rest of the cathedral. And it was empty.

"They were here," said Nova, her boots crunching over broken glass.

Adrian noticed frayed ropes tossed across the ground. "They must have found a way to escape."

Nova seemed unconvinced. "Maybe."

They shared a look, laced with a question.

Find Oscar and Danna . . . or try to stop Ace Anarchy?

Adrian sighed and tucked a hope into the back of his mind that his friends would be all right, wherever they were. "The roof?"

Nova's expression hardened and he recognized the same resolve that had made his heart skip when he saw her at the trials.

She gave him a nod. "Let's end this."

They raced back through the chapel, but as they were passing the choir, a shrill scream made them both skid to a stop. Adrian peeked around the wall toward the high altar.

He gasped, pulling Nova back into the corridor.

"What is it?" said Nova.

"Birds!"

She hesitated only a moment, before shoving Adrian's arm away and looking for herself.

The sanctuary that surrounded the altar was full of enormous black crows. Everywhere, shining black eyes and sharp black beaks and scaly black feet. They perched across the rails that divided the sanctuary from the choir, along the moldings of the grand pillars, and on the tall windowsills stretching to the top of the vaulted ceiling. Their black wings drummed against the air as they flocked in and out of the space, like a blizzard of ink-black wings. A clamor of angry caws echoed through the chamber.

In the center of the tumult, clinging to each other at the base of the altar, were Danna and, of all people, *Narcissa*. Danna was curled into a ball, her head in Narcissa's lap as she tried to protect herself with her arms. Narcissa had one arm around her, though her own face was pale with terror and her other arm kept swiping aimlessly at the air to keep the birds away.

It wasn't working. Their feet dug into her limbs. Their beaks nipped at Danna's legs.

"Oh, come *on*," Narcissa pleaded to no one. "Birds were the one thing I *wasn't* afraid of!"

Adrian was still trying to figure out what he was seeing when a figure emerged from behind a pillar, wielding an antique candelabra like a sword. Oscar roared insensibly at the flock, trying to beat them back as he made his way toward the altar. "Monarch!" he yelled. "You have to get up!"

As soon as Oscar stumbled onto the dais, the crows converged into a whirlwind, trapping all three of them inside a funnel. Their wings and bodies so dense it seemed impenetrable.

And then the birds caught fire.

"It's Phobia," said Nova. "Danna had a fear of birds, and I'm pretty sure Oscar is afraid of fire."

Adrian's skin prickled at the mention of his mother's murderer, the phantom that was so eerily similar to his childhood nightmare.

"I need something to draw on," he said, pulling out Nova's ink pen. "We need water. A hose or some sprinklers?"

Nova's face pinched. "He'll just morph into something else."

"Then what do we do?"

"I don't know. He isn't a normal prodigy. As far as I know, no one's ever managed to actually hurt him, not with weapons or even superpowers." Her gaze grew intense. "But . . . Adrian . . . if you *made* him . . ."

"I didn't make him!" he snapped.

Nova shrank back. "Okay," she said, placating. "But I'm just saying, if you did, then maybe there's some way you could destroy him?"

"Except I didn't—"

Narcissa screamed, a sound of pure agony, as the fire drew closer. Adrian was never sure how much of Phobia's ability was simple illusion, but the girl's pain sounded real enough. He cringed. "I didn't create him, and even if I did, I still wouldn't know how to stop him."

"Well, start thinking of something," said Nova. "One thing I do know, the best way to fight Phobia"—she squared her shoulders—"is by being brave." She descended the stairs into the sanctuary and stood facing the searing-hot flames. They were so bright Adrian had to lower his visor again so he could stand to look at them, but Nova didn't flinch away.

"Nova?" He could feel the heat of the flames even through his armor, and she was standing so much closer than he was. He was amazed she could stand it.

Then, she stepped into the fire.

CHAPTER FORTY-SIX

"NOVA!" ADRIAN YELLED—and his scream split through the sudden, unexpected silence. The inferno had disappeared as quickly as it had come.

Nova, untouched, stood only a few feet from the others, who were clutching one another on the floor. Their faces were ashen, their hair drenched with sweat.

How long had Phobia been tormenting them? How long had they been trying to stand up to their greatest fears, as the Anarchist slowly wore them down to their greatest weaknesses?

BANG.

They all jumped at the gunshot. It was earsplittingly loud, and Adrian spun around, trying to find its source, sure the gun had been fired only inches from his head. But the sanctuary was empty.

BANG.

Nova whimpered, bringing his attention back to her. Her eyes were shut tight and she was trembling from head to foot, both hands gripping her head.

BANG!

A shadow rose up in front of Nova. For a moment, Adrian could see the hazy outline of Phobia forming, the billowing cloak, the sharp scythe, but then he morphed into something else.

A man. A mammoth of a man, towering over Nova's small frame. His chin was rough with stubble. He had pale hair tied at the nape of his neck. There was a splatter of dried blood on his brow.

He was holding a gun, pressing it against Nova's forehead.

A hatred like Adrian had never known surged inside him and the next thing he knew, he had crashed into the man's side. They both fell. The man landed on his back beside the altar, but Adrian's momentum sent him rolling across the floor. He struck a column that shook from the impact of his armor.

On the other side of the sanctuary, Nova released a shuddering breath and fell to her knees.

The man started to cackle. His body dissolved into wisps of shadowy smoke, before re-forming again into a long black cloak. The gun elongated into a staff and a hooked blade.

"Master Everhart," said Phobia, his raspy voice making Adrian twitch with loathing. "I had hoped our paths would cross again before this night was through."

Adrian climbed to his feet, one hand braced on an intricately carved cabinet. He peered into the blackness where a face should have been and realized this was the moment he had spent years imagining. He had found his mother's killer. Justice was within reach.

"You killed my mother," he said through gritted teeth. The image came unbidden to his mind. His mother's broken body, her silent scream. Dread filled him all over again, but he needed to stall. He needed time to think.

Behind Phobia, he saw Nova urging the others to run. Narcissa seemed keen on the idea, but Oscar and Danna were staring at Nova in disbelief. They didn't trust her. Why would they?

But then . . . how on earth had they come to trust the mirror walker?

"So I did," rasped Phobia. "It might have been my favorite death of all. Do you know what her greatest fear was?"

Adrian clenched his fists.

"It's an easy one to guess. It usually is with *mothers*." Disgust and boredom oozed over the word. "She feared losing you. She feared that this dark, cruel world would ruin her darling little boy. Ruin him or kill him, whichever came first." He chuckled. "Would you like to know what was the last thing she ever saw?"

Adrian said nothing.

"*Me* . . . holding the body of her dead son in my arms. I didn't even have to say anything. She took one look and started to scream and then . . . she just gave up. I think she might have actually forgotten that she could fly." He made a quiet tsking sound. "Her scream was a symphony. I can hear it to this day."

With a guttural roar, Adrian grabbed the narrow cabinet beside him and flung the whole thing at Phobia.

The villain dissolved before impact, wisping away in a cloud of smoke. The cabinet crashed onto its side, its door swinging open and an assortment of chalices and urns spilling across the floor.

Phobia appeared again, rising up on top of the altar. "You're very much like her, you know."

Adrian ripped a statue from a nearby alcove and threw that, too. Phobia blocked it with the handle of the scythe, sending the marble figurine skittering into the choir. "You also fear losing the ones you love. It's a common fear. One shared by prodigies and humans alike. But for you there is an added element of . . . responsibility. Your greatest fear is to lose your loved ones, while you are powerless to stop it."

Adrian sprang upward, vaulting himself onto the altar. This time he reached for Phobia's throat, as if to strangle him, but again the villain vanished the moment he touched him.

He reappeared behind Danna and grabbed her forehead with one skeletal hand. He pulled her back against his cloak, angling the scythe so that the tip of the blade pressed into the soft spot at the base of her throat.

"Nothing is quite as debilitating," whispered Phobia, "as seeing a loved one suffer."

Adrian called for the concussive energy beam in his arm, only too late remembering that Queen Bee had cut that tattoo from his skin. "No!"

Snarling, Danna grabbed two of Phobia's skeletal fingers and bent them back as hard as she could. The fingers snapped off in her hand. Phobia hissed, his grip loosening enough for her to slip out from his choke hold. The moment she was clear, a volley of throwing stars sliced through Phobia's cloak. He evaporated into the air again, as did the bones Danna had ripped from his hand. The stars struck the wall on the other side of the sanctuary—one lodging into the mortar between stones, the other two rebounding and skidding across the floor.

"Danna, Oscar, get out of here!" Nova shouted. She raced past the altar and gathered up the discarded throwing stars. "You're not superheroes anymore, and he's just going to keep using you against Adrian if you don't leave!"

Oscar sent her a frazzled look, then turned to Adrian. "I'm sorry, is this a thing we're doing again?"

"What?" said Adrian.

"Trusting her!" Oscar yelled.

Before Adrian could respond, Phobia re-formed, towering behind Oscar. He raised the scythe, and Adrian gasped, already envisioning the swing of the blade coming down on Oscar's throat.

But then a war cry erupted through the chamber, and Danna came charging down the aisle. She launched herself into a series of forward flips that took her beneath Phobia's outstretched arm. It happened so fast it wasn't until Danna had lobbed herself onto a shrine, scattering unlit votive candles, that Adrian realized she had stolen the scythe.

"We may not be prodigies anymore," Danna said, casting a glare toward Nova, "but we're still superheroes."

"How quaint." Phobia jutted a pale finger toward her, and the scythe became a twisting serpent in Danna's grip. She cried out and dropped it. The moment the creature hit the stone floor, it scattered into a million black spiders, scurrying in every direction. Narcissa and Oscar both screamed.

The spiders merged with Phobia's cloak, and he seemed to grow taller, as if he were pulling the very shadows around him.

Adrian's mind searched his options. He could jump high, he could lift heavy things, he could crush his gauntleted fist through concrete walls, he could . . . draw things. What could he draw? It all seemed useless against Phobia.

"All right, *Nightmare*," said Oscar, his voice thick with disdain. "You must know his weakness, right? How do we defeat this guy?"

Phobia continued to grow, darkness surrounding him like mist. His body stretched upward until he seemed to take over the whole sanctuary. He was a giant composed of shadows and smoke, about to engulf them all.

"Well?" Oscar said.

Nova shook her head. "I don't know."

Her panic was evident.

How do you kill a phantom? How do you kill a nightmare?

"Helpful, as always," muttered Oscar.

"I told you to run!" Nova shouted.

Adrian took a step back, craning his head as Phobia's massive form expanded, a living black hole sucking the light from the room. The scythe was in his hand again, a blade hanging ominously overhead.

Blood pounded against Adrian's temples.

How do you kill a phantom?

"You want to know fear?" said Phobia, his voice bellowing from all directions. His form engulfed them, blacking out the rest of the world. "Fear of the dark. Fear of being trapped. Fear of death. I am master of them all." As the sanctuary succumbed to impenetrable darkness, Adrian and the others were forced together, crowding against the altar.

"I'm not afraid of you," said Adrian, daring to step forward into the shadows. His heavy boots clanged on the stone floor.

"Actually, you are," said Phobia, with a low, sinister laugh. "But you are even more afraid to know the truth."

Adrian hesitated.

Phobia's voice dropped to a whisper. "Or do you already know?"

Heat climbed up Adrian's neck. It wasn't true. It couldn't be.

"I suppose I should be grateful," Phobia rasped. "It's a rare gift indeed to meet one's maker."

Adrian shrank back, colliding with the wall.

Another game, he told himself. Phobia was toying with him.

"It's impossible," he said. "You would have died years ago. Faded away to nothing, like all the rest!"

"Is that so?" Phobia's hood had reached the vaulted ceiling, so that the blackness enguled the room. Nothing but shadow in every direction. It felt like death itself closing in on them, sucking the warmth from the air, suffocating them, slowly, agonizingly. . . .

"I suppose I should be dead," said Phobia, "but you were so clever in your fearful youth, to imbue me with an endless source of strength. A bottomless well of power. Your . . . own . . . fears."

Adrian shuddered. "What are you talking about?"

"I used to worry that they would fade as you got older, but I needn't have bothered. Fears might change, but they never go away. You once feared losing your mother above all else, but once that nightmare came to pass . . . there was another lurking to take its place. Fear that you would lose your new family. Fear that the Renegades would collapse. Fear that Ace Anarchy would win. Fear that you would always be in your fathers' shadows. Fear that you would lose more loved ones. Fear that you would be weak and helpless when it mattered the most." He cackled, almost delightedly. "There is no end to your fears, Master Everhart, and there is no end to the life they give me."

Adrian tried to swallow, but it was like swallowing a mouthful of sand. He started to choke.

The refrain persisted in the back of his thoughts—*impossible*—but he knew that was only because Phobia was right. He was terrified of this truth.

Because if he had created this monster, that meant he had created his mother's murderer. But instead of the anger that had propelled him in his search for the killer, all he felt now was a deep, weary distress. He had created this thing. On some level, *he* was responsible for every unspeakable act Phobia had ever committed. His imagination had rendered a soulless creature and set it loose on the world. He had made him to be a villain, a killer, everything Adrian loathed.

Adrian clenched his jaw until he thought his teeth might break.

Phobia was his own worst nightmare come to life, and it was entirely Adrian's fault.

And now, Phobia was going to kill him, his friends, Nova. People he would give anything to protect.

It had a sick sort of completeness to it. Adrian even found himself wondering if maybe he deserved to die, now that he knew one of his drawings had been the cause of so much suffering. The guilt of it settled into his core.

Maybe a death at Phobia's hands would be fitting. He even suspected, though he didn't know for sure, that all his creations might perish, too, when his own life was ended. That would provide its own sort of justice, if Adrian's and Phobia's deaths were intrinsically knotted together. It lacked only that moment of satisfaction that Adrian might have known to see his mother's killer ended once and for all. It lacked only his own yearning for revenge.

Nova believed there was a way for Adrian to destroy Phobia. Perhaps this was it. Perhaps his own death was the only way.

A rumbling laugh shook the wall. "Ah, the sweet bravery of one who is ready to die," crooned Phobia. "But don't overindulge your self-sacrificial fantasies just yet. I'm not going to kill *you*." The enormous scythe swung lazily overhead, a shard of silver light glinting in the blackness. "I'm going to kill *them*, while you watch, and know that you can do nothing to stop me."

"No!" Adrian jerked forward, but collapsed to one knee. The darkness had thickened to something tangible, rendering him trapped. He could barely make out the stricken faces of his friends through the shadows. "No . . . you can't . . ."

Phobia knew his fears too well. He knew how this would torment Adrian. To be powerless, to lose his loved ones and be unable to stop it, just like he'd lost his mother. His rib cage squeezed inward, suffocating him. He couldn't let this happen. He couldn't let Phobia win. There had to be a way to defeat him. He would do anything. *Anything.*

Then, suddenly, he knew.

Or, he hoped.

Because if this didn't work, it would be the biggest mistake of his life.

Coughing against the press of shadows, Adrian reached for the plate of armor and retracted the protective suit. It clanked inward along his limbs, leaving him in the remains of his Renegade uniform, still shirtless, his skin dotted with dried blood and the bandages he'd hastily drawn on himself in the belfry.

"Adrian!" Nova yelled through the chasm. He could barely see her in the gathering dark. "What are you doing?"

"I have an idea," he yelled back, pulling out Nova's pen, the one with the hidden blow-dart chamber. He opened it up and pulled the single dart from the chamber, sloshing with familiar thick green liquid. His mouth ran dry.

"No, it won't work!" yelled Nova. "Don't waste it!"

Ignoring her, Adrian grabbed a massive leather-bound tome from the shrine and spread it out on the floor. Pressing the pen against the pages, he started to draw.

Phobia's voice boomed through the cathedral. "I'm impressed." Adrian's gaze traveled up the length of the shadows, into the emptiness beneath Phobia's hood, which now brushed the ceiling beams so far above them. "Your courage is remarkable, for such insignificant creatures. But you know what they say about courage. One cannot—"

"—be brave who has no fear, yakkity-yak," said Adrian, remembering how Winston Pratt had once mocked Phobia's favorite saying. "But do you know what they say about fear?"

The hood fluttered around Phobia's obscured face.

Adrian pressed his hand into the book and pulled his drawing from the brittle pages. A narrow rod, the length of his forearm, with a flat cross at one end. It glowed like a lit ember in the darkness.

His hand started to shake.

"Adrian," Nova croaked. "Is that a *firebrand*?"

Adrian ignored her, facing off against the shadows. "One cannot be afraid," he said, "when they have nothing left to lose."

His gut lurched, even as he angled the brand toward himself.

"Adrian!" Nova yelled, her voice hitched with panic. "*Adrian!*"

He braced himself and, before he could talk himself out of it, thrust the heated iron against the immunity tattoo on his chest. A cry of pain ripped out of him. Almost immediately, the sickening aroma of burnt flesh filled the sanctuary.

When he pulled the brand away, a deep red X had destroyed the tattoo.

He dropped the firebrand with a shudder. He felt suddenly dizzy with pain, white spots creeping into his vision, but adrenaline and will kept him standing.

Closing his fist around the dart full of Agent N, he searched the depths of Phobia's hood. The phantom who had haunted his childhood dreams. The nightmare who had stolen his mother from him.

The monster he had created.

Phobia hissed, sounding almost worried for a moment, before his low cackle shook the sanctuary again. "Don't be a fool. More than any prodigy I have ever crossed, *you* fear being powerless. You would never—"

Adrian set his jaw and drove the needle into his own thigh.

CHAPTER FORTY-SEVEN

ADRIAN SANK TO one knee, knowing there was nothing else he could do. Either this worked, or he'd just given up everything on a whim. On a chance. He didn't even know if it was a good chance.

That, and his chest was burning and he thought he might pass out from pain and blood loss, and the shadows of Phobia's cloak were still engulfing him, still closing in around him and his friends, still swallowing them whole.

When the effects of Agent N began, he was almost too weak to notice them. The sensation was reminiscent of being in the quarantine with Max, before he'd discovered the Vitality Charm and given himself the tattoo. It was like a spark extinguishing inside him. A chill sweeping through his body. A slow draining-away of strength, concentrated in his hands. The fingers that had sketched so many amazing things in his nearly seventeen years.

The fingers that had sketched Phobia himself.

They tingled and grew cold, until he almost couldn't feel them at all.

He heard a rattling cough. "No," Phobia whispered. "This isn't . . . you can't . . ."

He wailed as he began to fade away. His cloak vanished like fog on a breeze, a cloud of ash billowing across the sanctuary floor. The cloak, the skeletal fingers, the shadowed hood, and, last, the scythe—a curl of candle smoke wisping into the air, before it, too, was gone.

Adrian held his breath. He counted to ten.

Phobia did not come back.

Adrian slumped forward. Warmth was returning to his fingers, but it didn't come with the sensation of power he'd known all his life. He knew beyond doubt that he could draw a hundred flowers or a thousand weapons or a million dinosaurs, and none of them would ever come to life again.

And everything he'd ever made before . . . would it all be gone? All the work he'd done rebuilding the mayor's mansion . . . the jungle in his basement . . .

Even as he thought it, Nova gasped and something clinked, hitting the floor. She bent down and picked up her bracelet. The clasp was broken again.

The star, however, was still there, glowing brightly, indifferent to their victory. He had drawn this, too, and yet . . .

His thoughts caught on themselves.

No. He hadn't drawn it. In the mural, the statue had its back turned, so its hands could not be seen. The star had been Nova's dream, not his.

Nova shoved the bracelet into her pocket and crouched beside Adrian. "I can't believe you did that," she said, inspecting the burn on his chest. "Sweet rot, Adrian. A firebrand?"

"It was the fastest method I could think of," he said. "It's not that bad. I think it singed off the nerve endings. Really. I can hardly feel it."

Nova sat back on her heels, staring at him with something like awe. It wasn't the first time she'd looked at him that way, with something more than admiration, more than respect. With something akin to amazement.

He would do just about anything to keep her looking at him like that.

He was still tense, his whole body strung tight, half expecting Phobia to reappear, howling his dark laugh.

But only the sound of their own uneven breaths persisted and, after a moment, Oscar's voice cutting through the gloom. "That was simultaneously the bravest and stupidest thing I've ever seen."

Adrian tried to smile, though he knew it was weak. "I created Phobia. It had to be me."

Oscar opened his mouth, but Adrian raised a hand. "I'll explain later."

Harrumphing, Oscar said, "There's a growing list of things you'll be explaining later." He grabbed the altar and pulled himself up, weak on his feet. As the rest of them stood, too, Adrian wondered how long Oscar had been without his cane.

A faraway rumble shook the walls of the cathedral. Adrian glanced toward the nave. In the struggle against Phobia he'd nearly forgotten that his dad was still out there, battling the most infamous villain of all time. He knew that Ace Anarchy was powerful, but it was still unbelievable to him that anyone could be a match for the Captain.

Then he remembered that his dad had given up his favorite weapon, the Silver Spear, when he'd thrown it at the bell tower. The pike must have been buried beneath the tower's wreckage.

Was there any hope of finding it? Would it give his father the upper hand again? Surely no one could defeat Captain Chromium, not even Ace Anarchy.

"Adrian," said Nova. "That was the last of the Agent N. The only way we can stop him now is if we can somehow get the helmet, but—"

"I have Agent N," said Narcissa.

Nova froze, then spun to her.

"You do?" said Adrian, at the same time Nova said, "Why are you helping us?"

Narcissa crossed her arms. "Could ask the same of you."

"She helped us escape," said Danna. "Well, I mean, we only made it this far, but she broke the doors and cut our ropes. And she doesn't even have to stay—she could leave through a mirror anytime. As far as I can tell, she's a few steps ahead of you as far as trustworthiness goes."

"We're all trustworthy," Adrian insisted. "We're all on the same side." He gave Narcissa's shoulder a squeeze. "Thank you for helping my friends."

"I didn't do it for *you*," she said. "I just . . ." Her attention traveled from Adrian to Nova, Oscar to Danna. She cleared her throat. "My grandfather was a lot of things to me, but I never thought of him as a villain. I know he did some bad things, but he was just trying to survive, to take care of me and the library. I don't think he would want this for me, and . . . I'm not sure I want to be a part of it." Guilt scrawled over her face. "Any more than I've already been."

"We've all done things we're not proud of today," said Nova.

"Speak for yourself," Danna muttered.

"Danna's right," said Oscar. "I've been pretty awesome today."

"You said you have Agent N?" said Adrian.

Narcissa reached into a pouch at her waist and pulled out a dart full of green liquid. Adrian recognized it as the projectile Frostbite had given him, the one he had brought with the intention of neutralizing Ace Anarchy from the start. "I swiped it when we were carrying you back to that chapel. I figured they'd give it to Cyanide, but"—she frowned at Nova—"after Ace Anarchy's speech about us all becoming gods, I worried this whole plan might be going off the rails. I thought this might come in handy at some point, and . . . I wasn't entirely sure I trusted anyone else with it." After a moment's hesitation, she held it out to Nightmare. "Please don't make me regret this."

"I'll do my best," said Nova, tucking the dart into her belt. "Now, to figure out how I'm going to sneak up on him."

Oscar held up his hand. "Just so we're clear, you are officially on our team again, right?"

"Of course she is," said Adrian, more defensively than he'd intended.

"No," said Danna, pressing her hands into her hips. "There is no *of course she is*. She betrayed us. She let them neutralize us! She doesn't get to just—"

"She killed Queen Bee," said Adrian, "and she saved my life. I know things are messed up right now, but I trust her."

Danna's glare only intensified.

Nova took a step forward. "I know it doesn't mean much, but I am sorry."

Danna huffed, but Oscar made a face like maybe the apology meant *something*.

"Look, we're going to have to work this out later," said Adrian. "The three of you"—he gestured to Oscar, Danna, and Narcissa—"you're with me. My dad threw his spear into the belfry before it collapsed. It's his strongest weapon, and one that Ace can't control. We're going to see if we can find it and get it back to him."

"Spear, belfry, got it," said Oscar, saluting. He cocked his head toward Nova. "What's she doing?"

Adrian turned to Nova.

She took in a steadying breath. "I might be the only one who can get close enough to Ace to neutralize him. I have to try."

Adrian had been so focused on making sure Nova was okay after the bell tower collapsed, he hadn't fully grasped the extent of the destruction. The tower had crashed through the roof of the transept, leaving a gigantic pile of rubble beneath a split roofline. The dust had begun to settle, but Adrian still covered his mouth to keep from inhaling too much as he made his way through the treacherous landscape. He could see the doorway that led down to the catacombs, now largely covered up by debris. A handful of the bells stuck out from the mayhem, silent where they had fallen.

"Whoa," said Oscar, who had taken a floor candelabra from the nave to use as a makeshift cane . . . and possibly a weapon, in case it was needed. "I think I found a body?"

Adrian cringed, not eager to see Queen Bee again. But Oscar had crouched in front of one of the fallen bells, where a foot was dangling from the opening.

"That's Cyanide!" said Narcissa.

Adrian nodded. "He was trying to kill me, so Nova put him to sleep. We thought he'd be safe inside that bell, in case the whole cathedral collapses around him."

They started sifting through the wreckage, searching for the chromium pike. It wasn't long before Adrian began to realize how much he was going to miss the strength that had come with his alter ego's suit. Each stone block, every ancient timber, seemed heavier than the last. He was already exhausted, and it wasn't long before his muscles were groaning at him to stop. He was glad Oscar was there. He, at least, had actually bothered to spend time lifting weights in the training halls. Unlike Adrian, who had just gotten really good at drawing weighted barbells.

"There!" Danna cried, standing on a bank of rubble.

Adrian scurried up beside her and saw what was left of the wooden scaffolding that had supported the tower's central bells. The pike was still stuck in one of the timbers.

In the end, it took all four of them and an embarrassing amount of straining and grunting for them to pry it free. When the spear finally came loose, they fell backward with a cry, landing in a heap among the stones and mortar. A broken gargoyle dug into Adrian's hip. Hissing, he grabbed it and threw it back into the pile.

"Phase one complete," he said. "Now, to get it to the Captain."

He started to scramble back up when a pair of bare feet appeared a couple of steps away. He froze and let his gaze travel up long golden robes until he was staring into the face of a boy who was probably a few years younger than he was. Despite his age, the uniform suggested that he was a Harbinger, one of the most powerful gangs from the Age of Anarchy.

He wasn't alone. Villains surrounded Adrian and his friends, including at least one other Harbinger, many of the Cragmoor inmates he recognized from the arena, and a couple of prodigies he vaguely recalled being rejected at Renegade trials. But there were also men and women he had never seen before in his life. A few dozen, at least. Some carried weapons—guns, blades, a tall staff. But most, he knew, would have no need of weapons.

He wanted to believe they'd appeared from the shadows like Phobia would have, because that's the sort of creepy thing villains did. But no. He and his allies had simply been too preoccupied with getting the pike to hear them approach.

Adrian swallowed, all too aware of his lack of superpowers.

He spread his fingers in what he hoped would be seen as a supplication for peace, but he couldn't bring himself to put down the spear. Instead, he used it as a prop as he rose to his feet.

"So, um, you might want to put on some shoes before coming any closer?" said Oscar, his voice cutting through the tension. "There's, like, a lot of jagged pieces around here."

The two Harbingers studied him, but said nothing.

"Narcissa?" said an older woman who had a shotgun slung over one shoulder. "You're helping them?"

Adrian cast his gaze to the side. The mirror walker pulled herself from the debris and stood facing her previous allies, her expression distressed. She opened her mouth but hesitated.

"She is," Adrian answered, with enough conviction to surprise even himself. "And I would ask each of you to help us, too." He saw a few lifted eyebrows and a few suspicious glares. But no one had attacked them yet, and he couldn't help but see that as a good sign. "We've been enemies a long time. Some of us"—he glanced at the two younger boys—"were probably born enemies. We were raised to hate one another. I've been told my whole life that Renegades are the good guys and any prodigy who defies us is an enemy who needs to be destroyed. Or, at least, locked up, far away from the rest of society. But what if we've been wrong? I don't want to fight you. Just like I don't want to fight Narcissa . . . and I don't want to fight Nightmare." His knuckles whitened around the spear. His muscles tightened, preparing to wield it to defend himself, even as he pleaded with the universe that he wouldn't have to. "We can stop this. No one else has to die today."

A man snorted. "Fine speech, Renegade. But it's easy to make fine speeches when you're outnumbered."

"I hate to break this to you," said Danna, stepping beside Narcissa. "But we aren't the ones who are outnumbered. The Renegades may not have broken past that barrier yet"—she gestured toward the world beyond the cathedral—"but when they do, there will be thousands of superheroes charging in here, ready to demolish everything they see."

"Thousands?" said the Crane. "We were at the arena. We saw what those bees did to your ranks."

"We've received reinforcements," said Danna. "They've come from every syndicate around the world. They weren't going to stand by and let Gatlon City fall. Not to Ace Anarchy."

The villains exchanged looks, but Adrian couldn't read them.

"The Renegades are right," said Narcissa, finding her voice. "When I brought you together, I promised we would find a way to have a better life for ourselves. I still want that. I still believe in that. But Ace Anarchy isn't the one who's going to get us there." She lifted her chin, prepared to accept her fate should her allies turn on her. "Maybe the way we change things is by finally crossing the divide between heroes and villains, rather than blindly lining up for battle, again."

"We know, Narcissa," said the older woman. "Believe it or not, we didn't come down from that tower so we could pick a fight. Not even with the Everhart kid." She smirked at Adrian. "We joined this mad crusade because it's time things changed. We deserve a revolution, and that, we're willing to fight for. But Ace Anarchy . . . all he sees up there is revenge. All he cares about is destroying Captain Chromium. He's not doing this for us or for a better world. This isn't what we signed up for."

"And now you're telling us we're under siege by thousands of Renegades?" said a woman with long wooden fingernails. "Well, what do you think's gonna happen to us when they get here? You can talk all you want about peace and forgiveness. They'll slaughter us on sight."

"And any they don't," said a man with neon-yellow skin, "will be shipped right back to Cragmoor." He shook his head. "I can't go back there. I'd rather die."

"So, pretty Everhart boy with the pretty words," said the older woman, tapping the gun against her shoulder. "You got any other options for us? Because we're not looking to die today any more than you are."

Adrian's mouth had run dry. They were right. He could plead for a truce all he wanted, but as soon as the Renegades arrived, they wouldn't stop to listen to these prodigies or their requests. They didn't care about revolution or freedom or acceptance. This was a war. Their enemies must be vanquished, before they could do any more damage.

Would *he* be able to stop the Renegades? Could he persuade them to put their hatred aside long enough to find resolutions beyond death and imprisonment?

Not today. Not so soon after the battle at the arena. Not with the deaths, the neutralizations, the fight still raging between Ace Anarchy and Captain Chromium. The hatred ran too deep, and change would take time.

But things had to change. And if he wasn't the one to start it, then who would?

"You can escape through the catacombs," he said. "Go out through the tunnels into the subway. You'll be long gone before the

Renegades realize it. And if our paths ever cross again . . . maybe it won't be as enemies."

"We can't go out through the catacombs," said Narcissa. "Ace closed off the tunnel, piling up a bunch of those marble coffins. To get through there, we'd need—"

"Dynamite?" said a tired, scratchy voice.

Adrian wheeled around. Cyanide was sitting cross-legged inside the bronze bell, his fingers drumming against his knees. When they had been in the bell tower, Cyanide had been intent on killing Adrian. Now he was watching him with an appraising look.

"Uh . . . yeah," stammered Narcissa. "Dynamite would probably work."

"Unfortunately, I don't have any," said Cyanide. "But I have a few other concoctions that will do just as well."

"Settled, then," said Adrian. "You all get out of here and when this is over, I'll be the first among the Renegades to advocate for tolerance . . . or prodigy rights . . . or whatever it takes to end this war between us. For good."

Cyanide flashed him a lopsided smirk that showed a few missing teeth. He peeled himself out of the bell and limped toward Adrian, then settled a hand on Adrian's shoulder. "Just remember. If Nightmare gets killed out there today, I will find you, and I will douse your extremities in an acid that will eat away at your flesh until all that's left is those fine pearly teeth of yours."

Adrian pressed his lips together, not so much from fear, but rather to keep from smiling. Funny how a threat could suddenly make him like a guy. "Duly noted."

Cyanide led the group of villains toward the staircase and the catacombs.

Narcissa hesitated, caught between old allies and new. It was with an apologetic look that she faced Adrian and the others, with a particularly regretful glance at Danna, one that made Adrian suspect the trauma of the past hours had done more to draw them together than any amount of talking ever could.

"I have to go with them," said Narcissa. "I know I'm not much of a leader, but . . . I made a lot of promises when I brought them together, and I want to keep those promises. I'm supposed to make sure things change for us, for the better."

"You will," said Danna. "And you won't be doing it alone." She held out a hand. "Friends?"

Narcissa wilted with relief and took the hand. "Friends."

After she had gone, Adrian said, "You two could go with them, you know. Might be safer down there."

"Yeah, nice try," said Oscar. "Ruby's somewhere on the other side of that barrier. When it comes down, I'll be waiting."

Danna grinned determinedly. "Heroes to the end."

CHAPTER FORTY-EIGHT

NOVA SPRINTED UP the steps to the northwest tower. When she reached the roofline, she peered through one of the narrow windows. Ace and the Captain were on a flat rooftop that ran beneath a series of Gothic-style flying buttresses. The Captain's head was lowered as he slammed his way through every obstacle Ace put between them, his fists shattering stones and lobbying thick pillars halfway across the cloister. Despite his strength, Captain Chromium was red-faced, his brow glistening with sweat. Even he was becoming exhausted against Ace's relentless attacks.

Nova scanned the stairs' landing. A stone niche held a statue of a praying woman. She tore it from its base and hurled it at the window. The statue burst through the stained glass, littering the rooftop below in colorful shards. She kicked out the remaining edges and climbed through, dropping onto the rooftop.

The Captain had pulled himself up onto one of the buttresses, trying to find a way to get to the villain.

"Ace!" Nova screamed.

It was a sign of his exhaustion that Captain Chromium startled and nearly fell from his perch. He grabbed a gargoyle's head for purchase.

Nova ignored him. Her attention was on her uncle. She still didn't know what she could say or do, but if she was going to neutralize him, she would have to get closer.

Maybe she could get close enough to put him to sleep, even, which would make everything a lot easier.

But first, she needed him to come back down to the roof.

Ace peered at her, his eyes thinly veiled with suspicion. "Why, if it isn't my dear little Nightmare. How thoughtful of you to join us." He scanned the tower behind her. "The Everhart boy isn't tagging along?"

Nova lifted her chin, drawing on all she'd learned these past months about lying and betrayal. "He's dead," she said, her voice rigid and calm. "I killed him, just like you asked. I'm sorry I hesitated before. It won't happen again."

She could see Ace considering her words. Perhaps wondering if he could trust her.

"You're lying!" Captain Chromium screamed.

Nova looked at him, and though she wished she could convey that yes, she was lying, she couldn't risk it in front of Ace.

Instead, she raised her voice. Made it colder. Harsher. "When he died, all the things he'd sketched before died with him." Reaching into her pocket, she pulled out her bracelet, its clasp broken but the star glowing bright as ever. "He fixed the clasp on my bracelet once." She shrugged. "I guess this time I'll have to take it to a jeweler."

The Captain dropped to the rooftop, raging, and grabbed the chromium chain. Nova barely had time to blink before the end was flying toward her with enough force that it probably could have taken off her head.

A stone spire snapped off from the tower behind Nova and intercepted the chain, shattering into a thousand bits.

Nova stumbled back into the wall, feeling the crunch of glass under her boots.

"You dare attack my own flesh and blood?" Ace roared, dropping between Nova and the Captain. Her pulse skipped at the opportunity—but he was still at least ten steps in front of her, not close enough to touch.

The pouch with the last Agent N dart felt heavy on her hip. She checked that the zipper was open and started to creep forward while Ace's back was turned.

"No more games, Captain," said Ace. He glanced back at Nova. She froze, feeling caught, but Ace was smiling. "Do you know how my brilliant niece was able to retrieve my helmet? She told me about your little box. I suspect you thought it was as invincible as you are . . . but it wasn't, was it? You see, we have a new weapon, the last that my brother ever made, and the most powerful."

Nova cringed, wishing she'd never told Ace about the star and what it could do . . . what she thought it could do.

"Perhaps," Ace said, enunciating carefully, "it is even powerful enough to destroy *you*." Ace extended an open palm. "Give me the star, Nova."

She instinctively clamped her fist around the bracelet.

Ace frowned. "Nova. Give me the star."

The star pulsed against her skin, almost like a heartbeat. Or perhaps it was her own heartbeat thundering through her limbs.

"Let me do it," she blurted. "My dad left the star for me. And . . . and Captain Chromium needs to be punished for what happened to my family."

Ace still appeared doubtful, bordering on angry.

"Niece?" said Captain Chromium, his tone full of disbelief. Only a few moments before he had looked ready to tear Nova in half, but now his head was cocked to one side, a wrinkle stitched between his brows. Staring intently at Nova, as if seeing her for the first time.

Ace tensed, as if he realized he'd said something he shouldn't.

"But that means . . . you're David Artino's daughter."

The name coming from him was a shock, this man who was supposed to protect her family. Who was supposed to be a superhero.

But he hadn't come.

"Yes," she said defensively. "I am."

"And I could not be more proud of her," said Ace, shooting her a doting smile.

She tried to return it, but hers became more of a grimace. All her life, she'd longed for those looks from Ace, the recognition that she had done well. He had taken her in, given her a home and a family when all was lost. And now she was going to betray him.

There was no other way, though. He was hurting too many people. He was no longer seeing a better world for prodigies. All he could see was his own revenge.

Sudden anger eclipsed the Captain's boyish features. He bared his teeth at Ace. "Does she know?"

"Know what?" Ace said. Quietly. Harshly.

The Captain bellowed, "Does she know you killed her family?"

Nova stumbled back a step. "*What?*" She swiveled toward Ace, but he was watching his enemy.

"A desperate, pathetic lie," said Ace. "He would say anything to turn us against each other. Anything to save himself."

Nova riveted her attention on the Captain again. "I witnessed their murders. My family was killed by an intruder, an assassin hired by the Roaches when my father refused to keep crafting weapons for them. Ace saved me."

"No," said the Captain, shaking his head. "*He* sent the assassin. A lowlife gun for hire that wouldn't be traced back to the Anarchists."

Her throat constricted. She glanced at Ace.

"You know it isn't true," he said, but he still wasn't looking at her. "You know that I killed the Roaches in retaliation for the deaths of my brother and his family, whom I loved."

The Captain's expression became almost gentle, Nova thought, which might be worse than his anger. Worse than the shock. He was watching her with pity. Captain Chromium, the one who had not come, even after she had put every ounce of faith into him . . . he *pitied* her.

"Your father regretted making the helmet," he said. "He felt responsible for the things Ace had done. He came to us and begged us to stop his brother. He told us about the helmet—before then, we believed Ace Anarchy's strength was inherent, but when David explained that most of his powers were a result of the helmet itself, it allowed us to formulate a plan to defeat him. But David knew . . ."

He hesitated, his handsome features twisting with grief.

"David knew that Ace would seek revenge for his betrayal. In exchange for the information, we promised . . . to protect his family." His voice broke. "But we failed. I'm sorry, Nova. I'm so, so sorry."

"No!" Nova yelled, surprising even herself with the outburst. Tears flooded her eyes, and she swiped at them with her fist. "You don't get to apologize! Why didn't you save us?" Her voice rose, ten years of rage storming inside her. "Why weren't you there? *Where were you?*"

The man's ruthless stare.

Bang.

Her mother begging for mercy.

Bang.

Evie's cries, silenced forever.

Bang.

"Why?" she murmured as the first tears escaped.

"We were there," he whispered.

"Liar!" she shrieked.

Hugh Everhart's voice remained steady. "We had someone posted at your apartment building day and night. For weeks."

"No. No one came. No one——"

"Lady Indomitable was there the night of the murders."

Her breath snagged. "What?"

"She was killed that night, too," he said. "And though I've never known for sure, I always wondered if Ace had orchestrated that death as well. I believe he sent another villain to distract Georgia while the murders took place."

Nova felt suddenly dizzy.

A Renegade had been there that night? To protect her family, to protect *her* . . .

Not just any Renegade. Lady Indomitable. Adrian's mother.

Phobia killed her . . . that same night . . .

Her lungs throbbed, expelling the air as fast as she could gulp it down.

"I'm sorry, Nova," Hugh said again. "I failed you. I failed your whole family. Not a day has gone by that I haven't regretted it."

Nova turned her head, focusing on Ace. "Is it true?"

He watched her. Unmoving, unmoved. And, when he finally spoke, remorseless.

"Your father betrayed me," he said, speaking in the low, soothing voice Nova knew so well from her childhood. "He sold my greatest secret to my worst enemy. Such treason could not go unpunished."

A cry fell from her lips. "You had him murdered!" she screamed.

"And my mom and"—a sob swelled in her throat—"and . . . and *Evie*. How could you?"

"I know," said Ace, still disgustingly calm. "It's awful. I know. But you understand how our world works. It is necessary to send strong messages, lest others think to one day betray you as well."

Nova pressed her palms into her eyes. "What about the Roaches? You told me you slaughtered them, the whole gang, in retaliation . . ."

"And I did, every last one," said Ace. He shrugged, remorseless. "I couldn't have you guessing the truth. Not after I'd seen what you could do."

"What I could do!" Nova's pulse stammered. "My father never told you I was a prodigy, did he? Because . . . if you'd known . . . you would have tried to turn me into a villain." Her lip quivered as she realized that she'd become exactly what her father had tried to avoid. "I was supposed to die that night, too. You only saved me because . . ."

"Because I saw your potential," Ace insisted. "Because you were my little Nightmare. Listen to me, Nova. I know how much you loved your family, and how the tragedy of losing them has driven you all these years. But for all your father's talents, he was weak. He did not belong in our world. Your family was not like us. And now . . . look around. Look at what we have achieved, together. We have torn the Council apart. The Renegades are in shambles. But we still stand, Ace Anarchy and his Nightmare." He raised his arms toward her. "We are strong, and we have conquered today, because of *you*."

Her blood congealed, with revulsion, with dismay.

But in all the tumult of her raging thoughts, she had a flash of clarity.

This moment was what she had been working toward her whole life.

Vengeance.

"No," she said, her voice shaking. "*I* am strong. You are a murderer and a liar. You were defeated once. You can be defeated again."

In a blink, his warmth vanished, masked over with calculating precision.

"It saddens me to have been so wrong about you. Still, you will always have my gratitude for bringing me to this moment. And . . . for bringing me *this*."

He stretched his fingers toward Nova.

The bracelet flew out of her hand. Nova cried out, but was too late to grab it from the air as it sailed into his waiting palm.

She released a war cry and charged for him, no longer thinking strategy, only that he couldn't have it, she would *not* allow him to abuse her father's last gift—

Ace sliced his hand through the air. The star flashed, briefly illuminating the atmosphere in blinding electric waves.

An invisible force struck Nova and she was thrown backward. Her body tumbled, weightless, for nearly twenty feet before her back struck the stone wall of the nave, forcing the air from her lungs.

Ace laughed. "Finally! All these years, being limited to only the control of the inanimate. My brother truly was a genius."

Nova struggled to breathe, but her lungs wouldn't expand.

Nova!

The scream was muddled in her head, eclipsed by mounting panic and throbbing pain.

"Adrian! You're alive!" yelled Captain Chromium.

She peeled her eyes open, wincing from the effort.

A figure was sprinting toward her. Tall and broad-shouldered. Dark skin and thick glasses and a metal pike gripped in one hand. Sweet rot, but he was the most handsomely heroic vision she'd ever seen, and Nova was filled with abject terror that he was there.

Ace would destroy him.

CHAPTER FORTY-NINE

"DAD, CATCH!" ADRIAN yelled.

Captain Chromium caught the pike one-handed.

"Don't get overconfident," said Ace, humoring himself. "The rules of this game have changed." With the star in one hand, he stretched his other toward the chromium chain that was coiled not far from Adrian's feet. It sprung to life, slithering like a snake toward Ace, one end coiling around his waiting arm. Ace pulled his arm back and lashed out at the Captain.

The Captain blocked with the spear—once, twice—the sound of metal striking metal rang across the wasteland. But Captain Chromium was losing ground, each blow pushing him closer to the edge of the roof. He looked down once to gain his bearings, when the chain reared up and circled around his throat.

Adrian cried out and ran to him. He tried to dig his fingers between the chain and his dad's skin, even as the metal squeezed tighter. His dad fell to one knee, suffocating.

The most ear-piercing, skin-crawling screech echoed from overhead. Adrian flinched and resisted the urge to cover his ears, still pulling at the chain. It started to come loose as Ace shifted his focus to the barrier overhead.

With a reverberating groan, the enormous back end of a rusting semitruck that had been attached to the barrier pried loose and fell. It landed with a resounding crash in the wasteland, mere feet away from the cathedral's side wall, sending up an enormous cloud of dust.

Captain Chromium ripped the chain over his head and tossed it away, panting and massaging his throat.

Adrian squinted toward the gigantic hole left behind by the semitruck, taking in the patch of night sky. There should have been stars, but some artificial light was being shed on the dome, blocking them out.

"Who dares interfere?" Ace growled.

As if summoned, a head appeared over the edge where the trailer had been. With the figure silhouetted by the glaring lights, Adrian couldn't make out any details, but he would know that fluffy hair anywhere.

He didn't know if he was more elated or horrified.

"Sorry!" Max shouted. "Is everyone okay? It didn't hit anyone, did it?"

In response, Ace released an enraged scream. He took to the air. Gripping the chain, he reared his arm back and sent it whipping toward the opening. Max's eyes went wide and he vanished.

The chain struck the barrier, knocking loose an aluminum wheel. Ace froze, hovering over the cathedral as the chain swung beside him. He scanned the barrier, tense and watchful, as he gradually lowered himself back down to the roof.

A tall, narrow spire snapped from the western tower and plummeted toward Ace. He sneered and sent the chain soaring for the spire. The chain lit up, as if made of molten gold. When it struck, it sounded like a bomb going off. Stonework cascaded around them, chunks of shrapnel, some as big as Adrian's head, raining across the roof and down to the wasteland.

Adrian heard a cry of pain. He blinked back the dust as he searched the roofline of the cathedral.

Max flickered back into view. He had followed Ace, trying to get closer, and was now caught in the deluge. He lifted his arms to protect himself from the blast.

Ace roared at the sight of the boy. "I'd hoped we would meet again! You and I have unfinished business."

Max startled as he realized his mistake. He winked into invisibility again, but the chain was already careening through the air.

It crashed through a window, catching the wall above the jagged stained glass as Ace yanked it back. Stones blew outward, leaving a crater where Max had stood.

Adrian searched the cloud of dust, his body trembling with fear and adrenaline.

"I'm fine!" said Max, his disembodied voice a little breathless. "Don't worry about—"

Ace swung the chain again, aiming for the air where Max's voice was coming from. It crashed through one of the flying buttresses, sending more stonework and a hefty gargoyle toppling over the side of the cathedral.

"It shouldn't be possible," said Hugh—drawing Adrian's attention to him—aghast and pale, red impressions on his neck where the chain had dug into his skin. He was watching Ace. "He could never use my weapons before. They always defied his telekinesis."

"It's the star," said Adrian. "It's changed him somehow."

It was difficult to see his dad this way, weaker than Adrian could even have imagined him looking.

"You think you can stop me?" Ace bellowed. "A child?"

"I did once, didn't I?" Max appeared again, crouched on the edge of a tower, holding on to one of the decorative spires for balance. "Besides, you'll have to kill me to stop me. All I have to do is get close to you." He stood, his jaw set. His feet lifted off the roof, and he hovered there a moment, before sinking down to Ace's level. A few feet closer than before.

The sight left Adrian awestruck. Max was wearing a Renegade uniform. It might have been a little long in the arms and legs—Adrian guessed it was Ruby's—and yet, for all the greatest skies, his little brother really did look like a superhero.

Hearing a groan, Adrian glanced at Nova. She had been slumped against the wall on the opposite side of the roof, too far for him to reach her. Relief welled inside him now to see her conscious, using the wall for support as she staggered to her feet.

He wanted to tell Max to be careful, to not get too close to Nova, but he bit back the words. She still had the Vitality Charm beneath her jacket. It would protect her.

Besides, Max had enough to worry about, facing off against Ace.

All he had to do was get close . . .

Even as Ace was taking a step back, keeping the distance between them, he curled one finger toward the nave. An arched window of stained glass shattered. Max ducked, protecting his head as the glass drove toward him, sharp edges slicing through his skin, one shard lodging itself into his thigh. He hollered in pain.

With an enraged scream, Hugh took off running, charging toward Ace with renewed vigor. He brandished the pike, holding it like a javelin, ready to spear the villain through the gut.

Ace spun to face him, the chain swinging overhead.

Captain Chromium leaped, at the same moment Ace lashed at him with the chain. Another flash from Ace's fist, igniting the weapon.

The Captain was in midair when the chain struck him squarely in the chest. The golden aura rippled outward, an explosion of light and sound, burning the air where the invincible chain met the Captain's invincible body.

Then his dad was falling, his body limp as it was thrown backward, tumbling head over feet off the side of the cathedral.

Adrian wasn't sure if the scream was his or Max's, maybe even Nova's. He didn't remember sprinting to the edge of the roof. Desperate hope surged through him as he leaned over the short stone balustrade. He imagined seeing Captain Chromium, as ferocious as ever, already scaling back up the wall.

But that's not what he saw.

Captain Chromium was on his back, eyes closed, the Silver Spear a few feet from his limp hand. A cloud of dust billowed around his body.

Adrian stood motionless, waiting. Waiting for his dad to wake up. Waiting for him to groan and shake it off and get back into the fight.

But Captain Chromium didn't move.

"Incredible," Ace murmured. "I remember this feeling."

Adrian stumbled back from the edge of the roof.

The villain was levitating again, his eyes half closed in euphoria. "The first time I wore this helmet, I was a changed man. Everything that I am, everything I ever hoped to be, was within reach. And now I surpass even those bounds. The world at my fingertips, malleable as clay . . ."

A hiss of pain drew Adrian's attention to Max. He watched as Max pulled the shard of glass from his thigh, then stood on weakened legs, dozens of cuts leaking blood into the gray suit. He kept cough-ing. Beads of sweat dotted his brow. But still, he scrunched his face in concentration, and the wall behind Ace began to tremble. A small vibration at first, until, all at once, the great slab of stone pulled free from its mortar and launched itself at Ace.

He was too distracted by his own glory to notice. The block hit him in the back and Ace fell, sprawling onto his knees as the rest of the wall clattered around him.

For a moment, the villain didn't move, and Adrian could almost hope that this would be enough—he was still just a man, wasn't he?

But then Ace released a guttural scream, and the stones shot back at Max.

"Max!" Adrian cried, unable to do anything as the stones collided into Max's slim form. He fell, curling into a ball as the storm rained down around him. Adrian sprinted across the rooftop, in agony to know there was so little he could do. What he wouldn't have given to have the powers of the Sentinel again . . .

"I will not be defeated!" Ace yelled. "Not by you! Not again!"

Adrian skidded beside Max and started pulling the rubble away. He was relieved when some of the stones moved of their own accord, Max lifting them with his powers.

"I'm . . . okay," Max muttered, clearly not okay.

"Stop wasting your energy on attacking him," said Adrian, scoop-ing one arm around Max's shoulders and helping him sit up. "Focus on getting close. You're the Bandit, remember?"

"Not ready to surrender?" said Ace, chuckling as he watched Adrian and Max stumble to their feet. "You have no idea what I'm capable of! No idea of the power—!" He cut himself off and a wicked gleam entered his eyes. "Perhaps a demonstration is in order."

Adrian and Max took one step forward, and Max's body collapsed against him from the effort. Adrian realized that Max wasn't putting weight on his right foot. Was his leg broken?

Lifting his head again, he locked his attention on to Ace Anarchy, who stood at the far end of the rooftop. The distance could have been miles.

"I've got you," said Adrian. "We can do this."

A shocking burst of light drew Adrian's attention back up to the overhead barrier. His feet stumbled. The barrier was shifting. Starting from the opening that Max had created, the whole thing seemed to be splitting open. Sewer pipes, utility boxes, traffic lights. Jumbled architecture and found machinery, abandoned vehicles and wrecked buildings. All peeling outward toward the city. Being dismantled, bit by bit. The glare from enormous floodlights that had been erected on a series of trucks cascaded over the wasteland, making Adrian squint against their brilliance.

As the hole grew larger, it revealed the city skyline in the distance and a night sky with the faintest haze of electric blue along the eastern horizon.

Media helicopters circled overhead. It was disorienting, after having the battle relegated to Ace's small bubble, to suddenly be thrust back into the real world.

That is, until Ace snarled and waved his arm as if swatting at mosquitoes. Both helicopters careened off course, plummeting from the sky.

Adrian ground his teeth. No time to worry about whether or not the pilots had parachutes. He tightened his arm around Max and started moving again, when he heard a new sound—a war cry, blaring from all directions.

His heart leaped. The Renegades had been waiting outside the barrier, desperate to get in. Now, with the wall torn down, they wasted no time in charging across the wasteland. The sight was mesmerizing—wave upon wave of identical gray uniforms. Thousands of superheroes from every corner of the world. Even many of the Renegades who had been neutralized at the arena were still among them, ready to be heroes with or without superpowers. He spotted Tamaya Rae, wingless and hoisting an electric trident that he recognized from the artifacts department.

She wasn't the only one. The mob was brandishing an assortment of weapons and artifacts. Powerful ones.

They must have raided the vault.

The mob raced forward, more unified than ever. Though it was chaos, Adrian couldn't help but seek out the people he cared for most. He found them easily, as if drawn to them. Simon. Ruby. And in the wasteland, preparing to join them—Oscar and Danna.

He was glad the villains had abandoned Ace and the cathedral. Seeing the Renegades now, Adrian knew this fight would have become a massacre.

Now, the only enemy left was Ace.

"Isn't that charming?" said the villain, watching the Renegades come. The way he said it, unconcerned, even amused, sent a chill into Adrian's bones. "Unfortunately . . . I fear they're too late."

Ace let the chromium chain slip from his hand and cupped the star in both palms. It flashed, and for a moment, Adrian saw streaks of energy in the air, flickering all around them, as far as he could see. Then Ace stretched his hands toward the city.

CHAPTER FIFTY

THOUGH SHE COULD barely stand, Nova forced herself away from the wall. One knee buckled and she half fell onto the hard stone. A chip from a broken spire caught under her kneecap and she flinched. Planting both hands on the ground, she pushed herself back up. Wobbled unsteadily for a moment, then kept going. One foot in front of the other, even as a wave of dizziness washed over her. Step by step, even as her muscles rebelled.

Movement in the distance made her hesitate, the small momentum she'd picked up nearly sending her crashing down again. She barely caught herself.

Her jaw fell as she took in the sight.

Beyond the cathedral, beyond the wasteland and a rush of Renegades, more Renegades than she'd ever seen in her life, the city skyline began to rise upward. Hundreds of buildings shuddering, undulating, lifting into the air. Nova watched a multistory hotel torn from its foundation. She saw the stately courthouse, with its Roman pillars, disconnect from the imposing front steps. She saw the enormous backlit *G* on top of the *Gatlon Gazette* building topple over, while the structure underneath swayed upward. Building after building succumbed to Ace's power, sending bits of concrete raining down on the streets below. Plumbing pipes ruptured, spewing water and sewage into the craters of empty foundations. Wires and rebar dangled from the bases of the levitating structures.

The power grid was disrupted, plunging whole swaths of the city into blackness. It was like watching someone flick off the lights neighborhood by neighborhood.

From the sudden blackness came screams. The screams of people who appeared at their apartment windows and saw the ground suddenly too far away. The screams of those below as they sensed the ominous weight of the buildings above them, with nothing to keep them from falling.

It was the screams that made the Renegades in the wasteland hesitate. They turned to see what was happening. To their city. To the people they'd sworn to protect.

A strange sense of déjà vu flickered through Nova's memory, and she thought of the night she had caught Max practicing his telekinesis in the quarantine. She had seen him lift up the miniature glass buildings of his miniature glass city, letting them hover weightless in the air around him, almost exactly as Ace was doing now.

Nova had been surprised at the time that Max was powerful enough to lift so many glass figurines at once, a feat few telekinetics could have mastered.

But this . . .

She stared at Ace Anarchy, her uncle, and her anger and loathing were momentarily dwarfed by fear. Of who he truly was. Of what he could do.

Thanks to her father and his weapons.

Thanks to *her*.

She stumbled forward a few more steps. She was far closer to Ace than Max was, and she didn't know how close Max would have to be in order to have an effect on her uncle.

Her fingers twitched, tempted to make contact, to put him to sleep.

But what would happen to the city if she did? Without Ace, it would come crashing down. All those buildings, all those lives. There would be no stopping it.

"Great powers," she whispered, realizing the terrible inevitability of it. Ace was going to destroy the city. The few who survived would have no reason to stay, surrounded by rubble and ruins. Gatlon would become nothing more than a forgotten legend. A nighttime story to warn children of the dangers of power—having too much of it, or having not enough.

She remembered Callum's words, as if he were standing right beside her. *He killed and he destroyed and he left the world in shambles.*

Nova tried to gather her emotions into a tight ball and spoke with all the calmness she could muster.

"Ace," she started, taking another step forward. "Think about what you're doing. You love this city. You want to rule this city. If you destroy it, then what's been the point of any of this?"

He chuckled deeply. Though she couldn't see his face, she could picture his expression—a cruel, crooked twist to his lips. "Oh, my wise young niece. You saw what I could do to this cathedral, and that was before I had this gift. Before I understood what was possible." He clicked his tongue. "I can destroy this city. Tear it apart brick by brick. And when I am done . . . I will rebuild Gatlon to fit my vision of perfection." He tilted his head back, as if basking in sunlight that wasn't there. "The world will have learned its lesson. No one will dare stand against Ace Anarchy."

The star in his palm pulsed, and one final tower rose up toward the sky. The tallest building in the city. Renegade Headquarters, its glistening glass facade an icon of hope to the world.

Nova watched its ascent, dwarfing all that surrounded it.

"Hang in there, Max."

Adrian's voice startled her. He and Max had covered half the distance but were still at least fifty paces away. They both looked ready to collapse.

How much farther did they have to go? How long before Ace felt the slow drain of his abilities?

It wasn't going to be enough. They wouldn't make it in time.

In the wasteland below, the Renegades were divided. Some had taken up the charge again, but Nova knew they would never make it in time to stop Ace. Others were rushing back toward the city, desperate to help the people caught up in Ace's approaching catastrophe, but what could they possibly do against such power?

She reached for the pouch on her belt and wrapped her fist around the projectile inside.

She calculated the distance, focus shifting from Ace to Max and back again.

Clenching her fist around the dart, Nova lunged.

The needle was inches from Ace's shoulder when he turned and grabbed her forearm, locking her in a debilitating grip. While his other hand remained outstretched, holding the star toward the city, he forced Nova's fist to eye level, studying the syringe. The bright yellow liquid sloshed inside. He frowned.

"That is not the neutralizing agent," he said.

"No, this is one of Leroy's," said Nova. "*This* one is Agent N."

She drove her other hand forward, jamming the dart into Ace's side.

Ace released her arm and drew back. In the same moment, Nova reached up and snatched the helmet from his head. Ace cried out in surprise but she was already sprinting, both arms crushing the helmet to her chest.

Her feet were lifted into the air as Ace summoned the helmet back to him. Nova held tight, curling her body around it as the helmet flew back to Ace, taking her with it. She somersaulted in the air. Her shoulder crashed into Ace, knocking him against a column.

Nova fell to the ground, but her body had dulled to the constant battering and she stayed folded around the helmet, bracing to be thrown halfway across the roof again.

But another attack did not come.

Daring to lift her head, she saw Ace examining the fingers of his open hand, his face wrinkled, his hair gray and unkempt.

Agent N was working.

She had no time. Springing to her feet, Nova swiped one hand at her uncle's, snatching the bracelet from him.

He hardly seemed to notice.

In the distance, the first buildings began to fall, slipping from the sky.

"Adrian!" she screamed, hurling the helmet as hard as she could across the roof.

Adrian caught it one-handed. "What—"

"For Max! Quick!"

Even as Adrian's face tightened with confusion, he planted the helmet onto Max's head. The kid gasped, both hands reaching up to pull it off.

"*The city!*" Nova screeched.

Max froze. He looked out at the city. At the hundreds of structures that were slipping from Ace's control, being claimed by gravity, starting to plummet back toward the earth. A strip mall struck the ground with concussive force. A bank tower speared through Mission Street, forty floors of glass and steel caving in on themselves.

Max recoiled from the sight at the same time he lifted his arms toward it.

The crumbling buildings slowed their descent, and gradually stilled.

Max groaned. His entire body shuddered.

"Adrian, this too!" Nova threw the star.

Adrian caught it and immediately dropped it with a yelp, shaking his hand as if it had burned him.

He looked at Nova and she looked back, baffled.

Setting his jaw, he went to pick it up again, but Max stretched out his own hand and the star leaped into his grasp. There was a flash, and Nova saw those flickers of energy again, swirling through the wasteland like a brewing storm.

Max's limbs stopped trembling as the star lent him strength.

In every direction, the buildings haltingly, tentatively, began to settle themselves back onto their foundations.

Nova exhaled, feeling the first wave of relief, when her fingertips began to tingle. She gasped and looked down at her open palm.

A sensation of fragility streamed through her limbs, even as a foggy, sleepy weakness seeped into her mind. It felt like powerlessness. It felt exactly like when she had once gotten too close to Max inside the quarantine.

She pressed a hand to the Vitality Charm under her shirt. It should have been protecting her, but . . .

The helmet.

It was amplifying his powers.

Perhaps the charm could no longer protect her.

Max, focused on resetting countless buildings back in place, seemed oblivious that he was even doing it. Nova took a step back, then another, wondering if she had the strength to get away from him before he absorbed everything.

She didn't get far.

Nova yelped as her feet were suddenly lifted from the ground. Ace had one hand on her upper arm, the other scooped beneath one leg as he lifted her over his head. Nova screamed, thrashing in his hold, swinging her arms in an attempt to find skin, any skin.

Adrian screamed her name, but she barely heard it over her own panic. Ace stormed toward the edge of the roof and she realized that he intended to throw her over the side.

She used every technique she knew, kicking and flailing, trying to curl herself into a smaller target or rock her body from side to side. But her thoughts were too frantic, too scattered, and Ace's grip was iron, his own scream an animal's wail as he reached the ledge and prepared to heave her to the ground eighty feet below.

Something glinted in the blinding floodlights, driving straight toward them.

Nova felt the impact slam into Ace's body. She heard his strangled cry.

His grip loosened, and Nova arched her back, rolling out of his hold and landing on all fours at his side.

Her jaw fell open.

Ace Anarchy stood at the ledge of his cathedral. A god among men. A revolutionary. A visionary. A villain.

With a chromium spear impaled through his heart.

Nova scurried backward, colliding with another body, and a pair of arms wrapped around her from behind. She screeched and spun out of reach, already calling on the well of power in her gut.

Adrian grabbed for her again, his face wild with worry.

Adrenaline draining from the tips of her fingers, Nova swiveled. Ace seemed frozen in time. His head was cocked back. His eyes on the brightening sky. The great floodlights around the wasteland lit up the metal driven through his chest.

Ace Anarchy tipped forward and fell.

CHAPTER FIFTY-ONE

"EVERYONE OKAY UP there?" called a ragged voice.

Nova peered over the ledge, avoiding the sight of Ace's broken figure below. A surge of relief rushed through her to see Hugh Everhart on his feet, if only barely.

With an exhausted grin, he wiped an arm across his brow. "I once swore to protect you. I'm sorry it came so late."

She laughed, half delirious with gratitude that it wasn't *her* broken body at the base of the cathedral.

"Dad!" cried Adrian, throwing himself against the balustrade a few feet away. "You're alive!"

Hugh chuckled. "Yes. But not invincible anymore, I don't think." He tried to disguise the pain that flashed over his features as he shifted his attention to the other side of the roof. "How's Max doing?"

Nova studied Max, taking in his shuddering limbs and the helmet that was far too big for him. Little ten-year-old Max, who was clever and brave and now might very well have stolen the superpowers of

Ace Anarchy and Captain Chromium, arguably the two strongest prodigies in the world.

And Nightmare's, too, she knew with absolute certainty. There was no need to test the theory. When she called for her power, that subtle strength that had always pulsed beneath the surface of her skin, it was no longer there.

She would never put anyone to sleep again.

But what surprised her more than anything was that she suddenly recognized Max in a way she had never recognized him before. Watching him was like watching an illusion.

He stood as still as the gargoyles that surrounded them, his face shrouded by the helmet, his arms stretched out like offering a gift to the world. The star hovered a few inches above his cupped palms.

He looked like the statue. The one she had once conjured in a dream. The one who had held a star in its hands.

The star brightened, and for a moment, she saw the flash of energy lines again, the coppery-gold strings her father could manipulate, the remains of a supernova that had brought superpowers to humanity. The lines were still there, but more sparse now than she'd ever seen before and—unnervingly—they were all flowing in one direction.

They were all flowing into Max.

She blinked, and the vision was gone. She was left gaping at the boy, afraid of what it could mean.

"Adrian," she whispered. He was focused on his brother, his face pinched with concern. Nova stepped closer and tucked a hand into his, but he hissed in pain and pulled away. Nova started. Adrian flashed her a sheepish look and flipped his hand over, showing her the blisters on his palm where the star had burned him. "It's not so bad."

She linked their elbows instead. "Don't panic," she said, "but I think Max might be absorbing all the superpowers that are left . . . maybe, in the whole world."

Adrian frowned. "What?"

"The helmet is amplifying his power," she explained. "He took my power already, and your dad's."

His eyes widened.

"I think he's taking them all."

In the distance, the final building fit into place. Shattered concrete and snapped rebar melded back together. The skeletons of broken scaffolding and discarded fire escapes climbed back up their facades. Erupted asphalt streets sunk into smooth, level grades. Collapsed walls righted themselves. Bricks and mortar fused like puzzle pieces. Sludge-filled water drained into the sewers. The whole world knit itself back together, as if the wounds caused by Ace Anarchy had been nothing but a long nightmare they could finally awake from.

Electricity had not been restored, leaving a city that would once have been aglow with a million golden windows instead awash in the light of a million stars and an indigo sky. The horizon was glowing with the promise of dawn. It was absolutely breathtaking.

"He did it," Nova whispered.

Adrian didn't respond.

She cast a look up into his face and saw that he wasn't witnessing the same amazing sight she was. His attention was trained on his little brother, his lips parted with growing horror. "What's happening to him?"

She followed his gaze.

Shining rivulets appeared beneath the skin of Max's hands, like veins of melted gold disappearing into the cuffs of the Renegade uniform. More were on his throat, where the helmet didn't cover. They glowed with an iridescence that was both beautiful and terrifying, its warmth pulsing in time with the star.

The star, too, had begun to change. It was larger now, roughly the size of a walnut, and its color had changed to a writhing orange-red mass. Like a sphere of molten lava.

"Max?" Adrian called uncertainly. He pulled his arm from Nova's and approached his brother. Nova followed, and as she got closer, she could see Max's eyes open through the cut in the helmet.

She gasped, at the same moment Adrian froze.

The irises of Max's wide brown eyes were gone, replaced with liquid gold. A few droplets had leaked down the corners of his eyes like tears.

A shiver cascaded through her body.

"MAX!" Adrian cried, running the rest of the way to him and grabbing his elbow. He gave him a shake, but the boy didn't respond. Adrian looked at Nova, panicked. "What happens to someone who absorbs too much power?"

She shook her head. How should she know? Had anything like this happened before? Closer to Max now, she sensed an electric current in the air, a charge that made the hair stand up on her arms.

Adrian grabbed the helmet, pulling it from Max's shoulders and tossing it across the roof.

"Max . . ." He squeezed the boy's shoulder, pleading. "Max, talk to me. Tell me how to help you."

For a long moment in which Nova suspected even her own heart had stopped beating, Max remained unresponsive.

Hovering a few inches beyond his fingers, the star continued to grow, now almost as big as a hand grenade.

"I . . ."

Nova and Adrian both jumped, pressing closer to Max. His voice had been so small, as if being dredged up from somewhere deep inside.

"I'm here, Max. Talk to me," said Adrian.

"I . . . don't want . . . it . . ."

A golden tear dripped from the bottom of his chin and Nova instinctively reached out. It landed in her palm, warm, but not burning. It reminded her of the golden threads of energy she had watched her father pull from invisibility and craft into toys and armor and jewelry and . . . weapons.

She pictured him sitting alone at their small table, coppery strands illuminated between his fingers. He'd been working on something special that night. He'd told her as much. She thought that she solved the mystery, but no—her father wasn't creating the star as a weapon to destroy Captain Chromium. He'd wanted to stop Ace.

What are you making, Papà?

Something I hope will put to right some of the great injuries I've caused this world.

The great injuries he'd caused this world.

He had so much guilt for making the helmet. He wanted to counteract the enormous power he'd given his brother. So he made a new gift for the world, crafting it from light and energy and stardust.

The droplet seeped into her palm and Nova felt a twinge of familiar power tingle in her fingertips. She squeezed her fist shut and gulped.

"I'm going to knock it out of his hand," said Adrian, picking up the remnants of a broken stone pinnacle.

"Wait," said Nova, looking from Max to the dark city, the ocean, the vast world beyond.

She had once dreamed of a statue surrounded by ruins, but that dream had never been about destruction. It was about the hope that persisted when all else seemed lost. It was about the hope that the world might yet be saved.

It was about putting to right the great injuries Ace and the helmet had caused, and seeing her father's final wish fulfilled.

Nova looked at Max again. She took in his eyes, glazed with liquid gold, and the star, which had darkened to a rich, crimson red.

He would absorb it all, every drop of power in this world. She didn't know if this is what her father had intended, but she knew it was for the best. Soon, there would be no more prodigies. No more heroes, no more villains. It was the world Nova had longed for, convinced it was the only way for humanity to ever achieve some semblance of kinship and equality.

But no human could possibly hold so much power and survive. If Max did this, it would kill him.

Nova shuddered.

The Anarchists believed in sacrifices.

The Renegades believed in a greater good.

Nova wasn't sure what she believed in anymore, but she knew she believed in Max. And Adrian. And herself.

She couldn't let this happen.

The surface of the star cracked loudly, making her jump. Black fissures marred the bloodred surface.

"It's okay, Max," she said, slipping one arm around his shoulders, amazed at how small and fragile he felt. She stretched her other hand along his arm until she felt the heat of the star beneath her palm. "You don't need to carry this. You can let it go."

She glanced over at Adrian, who was still clutching the spire, and beckoned him closer with a nod of her head. Though he was dubious, he set down the stone and mimicked her actions on Max's other side, wrapping one arm around Max's shoulders, settling his palm over Nova's.

There was another fracture from somewhere within the star, and a wave of energy pulsed outward. She felt it in the joints of her knuckles and the spaces between her ribs. Power incarnate. Infinite strength. Boundless wisdom. Clarity cascaded through her mind, and she felt like she could understand every mystery in the universe if she only paused to consider it. But at the same time, she didn't want to pause for anything. She wanted to run and fly and *soar*.

Tears blurred her vision as the sensation of strength expanded through her limbs and it occurred to her that this must be only a fraction of what Max was feeling. Endless potential. Fathomless power.

In the space between their hands, the star had darkened. It was nearly black now, but with a web of hairline fractures burning white.

This power, this feeling—it didn't belong to her, and Max couldn't contain it much longer.

"Now, Max," she said. "Just let go. We'll do it together."

He whimpered. The veins of gold pulsed under his skin.

The star began to cave in on itself, and then—

A flash. An explosion of energy—not just gold, but shades of aqua and amethyst, deep magenta and metallic orange, surging outward in every direction. The shock wave rolled across the wasteland, washed over the city, filled the rivers and the bay and tinted the water coppery gold as far as Nova could see.

It was destruction and creation at once.

It was a supernova.

And then . . . it was over. In the wake of the cataclysm, the star shrank back into the confines of Nova's broken bracelet, looking like a chunk of polished lava rock.

Nova exhaled. She felt like she was releasing a breath she'd been holding on to for ten years. She covered the dead star with her hand and watched as the last remnants of its light faded away into the ocean beyond the city's ports. There were a few more sporadic flashes of color, of brightness beneath the water's surface, and then all fell still.

For a moment, it was peaceful on the cathedral's roof. The whole world felt quiet. Waiting to see what would happen next.

Max groaned and slumped forward. Adrian barely managed to catch him before his head struck the stone banister.

"Max!" they shouted simultaneously, crouching at his sides. Adrian pulled him into his chest, pushing back his mop of sweat-drenched hair.

"Is he breathing?" asked Nova, checking for a pulse. The golden veins were gone, and his skin was now pale as parchment.

But yes, he was breathing. Yes, his heart was beating.

"Max!" Adrian yelled. "Come on, kid, stay with me."

Max's eyes started to open, fluttering warily, and Nova could feel her relief mirrored in Adrian. Not just to see his eyes open, but to see them returned to normal, if a bit bleary and unfocused.

"Were we heroic?" he croaked.

Adrian laughed and crushed the kid against his chest. "I think you just redefined *heroic,*" he said through an onslaught of tears.

"Max! Adrian!"

Nova propped herself against the wall, feeling like it would be weeks before she could stand without her muscles wobbling, and turned to see Hugh Everhart and Simon Westwood racing across the roofline, though Simon hesitated when he was halfway to them, his expression torn.

"What was that?" said Hugh, falling to his knees and wrapping both of his sons in his broad arms. "We were coming up the stairs when we felt it and now—" He pulled back, bewildered. "What did you do?"

It took a moment for Nova to understand. She'd been so overwhelmed by the surge of inexplicable power that was inside of her, even for such a short time, she had failed to notice the change that still lingered inside of her. Swallowing, she flexed and straightened her fingers. They tingled encouragingly.

A laugh tumbled from her mouth. Her power. It was back.

She could tell that Adrian was having the same realization. They were prodigies again. Elation rushed through her, and the first thought that crossed her mind was that Adrian would be able to fix her bracelet.

But that was a request for another time. Beaming at him, she slipped the bracelet into her pocket.

The star had returned their gifts.

And yet. Adrian still had his arm around his little brother, and nothing was happening. Nova felt no weakness in his presence.

Could it be that Max was no longer the Bandit?

Simon continued to approach them, cautious, and seemed bolstered by every step in which Max's power had no effect on him. Then he was laughing, too—they all were, as their family crowded in together, embracing amid the broken stonework and shattered shards of glass.

Feeling like she was intruding on an important moment, Nova heaved herself onto her feet and stumbled across the roof. She stooped to pick up Ace's helmet. She peered into the opening where her uncle's eyes had once looked on her, doting and proud.

But his pride, she could see now, was never for who she was. It was only for what she could do. What she might be able to do for him. She doubted if he had ever truly loved her.

"It was indestructible when I took it the first time."

Nova spun around. Captain Chromium had extracted himself from his family and was standing warily a few feet away. Was he worried that Nova still despised him? Now that he knew the truth about who she was, she supposed it was impossible for him not to think of how she had tried to kill him in front of thousands of adoring citizens.

"I doubt we'll have any luck destroying it now," he added.

Nova angled the helmet one way and the other. She could feel the weight of the dead star in her pocket, and wondered whether it could have been used to destroy the helmet. But it was too late now. Whatever power that star had held, it was gone, spread out across the world.

"We can put it down in the catacombs," she suggested. "We'll bury it down there, and hope no one will find it."

"In a chromium coffin?" Hugh suggested, and though his eyes twinkled as if it were a joke, Nova actually liked the idea.

"With Ace," she said.

The humor faded from Hugh's face.

"Any public grave will be defiled," she said. "I can't forgive him for what he did to my family—" Her voice caught. Inhaling shakily, she forced herself to continue, "But he *did* give me something to believe in, and to fight for. His vision for the world wasn't all bad."

Hugh nodded in understanding. "A chromium coffin, for Ace Anarchy and his helmet." He started to turn away.

"Captain?" said Nova.

He paused.

"What would you think if . . . if a villain happened to fall in love with your son?"

He stared at her, a twitch at the corner of his mouth, though he fought to remain serious. "To be honest, I'm not sure there are such things as villains anymore." He shrugged. "Maybe there never really were."

He walked away, returning to his family. Adrian was watching them, an arm around Max, a question in his eye.

Nova smiled, hoping that Hugh was right. Maybe there were no villains.

But watching Adrian and Max, she knew there were heroes.

She was beginning to wonder if she might be one of them.

EPILOGUE

WE WERE ALL *heroes in the end.*

At least, that's what people liked to tell themselves.

Which, in her humble opinion, was a heaping load of garbage.

She missed the days when the Renegade Parade actually meant something. Back when people would watch the floats passing by and be awed by what they represented. Gifts and abilities that were truly extraordinary. Power too great to be quantified. Back when the word *superhero* was more than a marketing device.

That was before "the Supernova," as they had taken to calling it.

One minute, the world had been in an uproar over the return of the greatest supervillain of all time. Mass panic, mass terror, the media drawling on and on about the end of the world.

And then—destruction collided with creation. Devastation met rebirth.

Suddenly, everyone and their mom had superpowers.

It was the end of heroism as she'd known it, which was pretty sad, given that she hadn't been too impressed with heroism to begin with.

This year, the Renegade Parade had a different feel to it. Rather than putting the Council and their cohorts up on a pedestal, it was about the celebration of *all* prodigies, of all gifts, extraordinary and otherwise. It was full of peppy good vibes and people saying things like, "Now anyone can be a superhero!" and whatever other mumbo-jumbo they were buying into these days.

The spectacle was still impressive, to be sure. The floats were alive with flames and ice, lightning and fireworks, towers of suspended water and gravity-defying props and the prodigies at its center—the gears that made it all work.

But they'd gotten rid of the villain floats, which were now seen as disrespectful and uncouth. She wasn't sure who, exactly, they were supposed to be respecting now. The Anarchists? The villain gangs? Ace Anarchy himself?

Please.

Instead, the villain floats had been replaced with memorials for the warriors who had been lost. Blacklight. Queen Bee. Even that jerk, the Puppeteer, which was the height of irony, given that he'd attacked this same parade just one year before.

There was even a float with a statue dedicated to Callum Treadwell.

Her heart did jolt at the sight of it, but she'd never tell anyone that. Sweet marvels, Callum may have been a ridiculous nerd, but he deserved better than being lumped in with these goons.

She watched from the jostling crowd, arms crossed, scowling at each float that passed. What were they supposed to be celebrating now? The idea that they'd all gone from helpless civilians to courageous superheroes? Laughable. So what was it? The second fall of Ace Anarchy? The great equalization?

A return to mediocrity?

No one else seemed to have figured it out yet, but she knew they would soon enough. The facts were inescapable.

If *everyone* is special . . . then no one is.

A float rounded the corner, bringing with it a chorus of eager shrieks.

The Council, naturally, every bit the political figureheads they'd ever been. Without Blacklight, the float was lacking a certain flair— no more strobe lights and fireworks and sparklers. Otherwise, not much had changed.

Despite having their own superpowers, people still tried to emulate the Council. Scanning the crowd, she picked out at least a dozen Captain Chromium costumes, along with branded light-up wands and plastic masks. She also saw a large banner hung from a nearby storefront.

BOLD. VALIANT. JUST. DO YOU HAVE WHAT IT TAKES TO BE A HERO?

YES, YOU DO!

But it was a lie. For starters, not all powers were created equal, and she knew the hierarchy would start sorting itself out soon enough, once all this chumminess over "equality" wore off. And not everyone was cut out to be heroic, even if they could boil water with their breath or hypnotize puppies with their magic kazoo or whatever. They weren't all empowered, no matter how much they wanted it to be true.

Empowered. Gross. She wanted to vomit every time she heard that word.

The crowd broke into another round of cheers. A parade float came into view displaying a miniature model of Gatlon City, crafted entirely of glass, just like the one she remembered at headquarters. It was pretty, sparkling in the bright afternoon light. It took her a minute to notice the boy in the center of the city. He seemed a lot older than the last time she'd seen him.

Max Everhart.

The haunting recluse she'd so often seen watching the Renegades from behind his quarantine walls. He was a legend now. If *anyone* was a hero, it was him, after he single-handedly rebuilt Gatlon City when Ace Anarchy had tried to tear it apart.

The funny thing was, Max Everhart was quite possibly the only human being on the planet who didn't actually have any superpowers. Not anymore.

He could have had them all, but instead, he chose to give them up. To give them away.

She sort of admired him for it. She sometimes wondered whether he had regrets. She sometimes dreamed of having chance encounters with Max Everhart where she could ask him what it had been like to have that much power, even if just for a moment.

Actually, she thought a lot about Max Everhart these days. At some point in the past year it had occurred to her that he was actually kind of cute, and she wondered if he had always been cute and she'd just never noticed it before because, well, no one really noticed Max Everhart before.

But people noticed him now, and she couldn't help the fact that she had, too.

She'd never tell anyone *that,* either.

Next came a float that was painted all in black, with light shining through a million pinprick holes, reminiscent of the night sky. A giant five-pointed star stood in the center of the float. On one arm of the star stood Monarch, alongside a shorter girl with red hair that hung to her hips in a long, narrow braid both of them waving exuberantly to the crowd. On the opposite side of the star were Smokescreen and Red Assassin. Grinning his dopey-eyed grin, Smokescreen pointed a finger at the sky and sent off a stream of fluffy white clouds that folded in on themselves to form the shape of a heart. A second later, a second burst of smoke sent an arrow piercing the heart, and Red Assassin gave him googly eyes like he'd just ended world hunger or something.

On the topmost point of the star stood another happy couple.

She scowled. Her lip curled in disgust of its own accord, even as the crowd roared gleefully in her ears.

They were the proof, people kept saying. Adrian Everhart and Nova Artino were evidence that there could be common ground. That the divide between heroes and villains wasn't as wide as they'd always thought.

That love conquered all.

She didn't know about any of that, but it was clear enough that the two were disgustingly infatuated with each other.

Her attention landed on the bronze-filigree bracelet Nova was wearing. It was still pretty, and a twinge of desire still coursed through her every time she saw it, but not nearly as much now that the stone had been swapped out. She never could pinpoint what had been so alluring about it before, other than she had a sixth sense for the value of things, and that stone had been worth more than any trinket she'd ever lifted before. Than all the trinkets put together.

It was gone now, though, replaced with a hunk of onyx or black sapphire or something. She couldn't tell from so far away.

There were a lot of rumors circulating about what had happened at the cathedral that day. Rumors about a star, an explosion, a new weapon made by David Artino himself. Rumors about Ace Anarchy and Phobia and Captain Chromium and Max Everhart.

Rumors about Nightmare.

On the float, Nova leaned over to speak to Adrian, and something passed between them. A softening of the eyes. A widening of smiles.

Then they were kissing, and she had to turn away before she gagged.

She'd seen enough. Any hopes that the Renegade Parade might still be worthwhile were smashed. She shouldered her way through the crowd, dodging people who were drunk on excitement and cheap beer, kids propped up on their parents' shoulders for a better view.

She wasn't sure which of the rumors were true, but the only ones she cared to pay much attention to were the rumors about Ace Anarchy's helmet. They were saying it still had not been destroyed. They were saying it was indestructible, and that the power contained within it would never fade. She had even heard whispers that the helmet had been hidden beneath those cathedral ruins. Buried deep in the catacombs.

It made her pulse race to think about it.

She'd had more than one fantasy lately about being the one to excavate such a treasure.

If the rumors were even true.

A sparkle caught her eye and she paused, noting a fancy brooch pinned to a woman's gray blazer. It was the iconic Renegade R, set in red rhinestones. Probably not real gems, but pretty enough to give her pause.

She angled her way forward, focusing on the jewelry. She pictured the sharp little pin pushed through the fabric of the woman's lapel. She imagined the clasp peeling back. The pin popping free. The brooch slipping out of the fabric.

She bumped into the woman at the same moment the brooch tumbled down, landing in her open palm. She wrapped her fingers around it too fast and felt the stab of the pin against her finger. She flinched, but the woman was watching her suspiciously, so she changed the grimace into a brilliant smile and dashed off an effusive apology before ducking back into the mass of bodies.

She felt someone's gaze on her then. Daring to glance up, she spotted a man tucked into the crowd, a worn trench coat draped over his bulky figure. He was staring at her like he recognized her, though she knew she'd never seen him before. One doesn't forget a face like that—a patchwork of blotchy skin, with one cheek that drooped lower than the other, dragging down the left side of his mouth, missing eyebrows and raised scars crisscrossing his brow. She wondered what sort of sad superpower would manifest like *that*.

He smiled at her. A knowing, lopsided grin.

Feeling self-conscious and worried that maybe he'd witnessed the theft and was about to raise an alarm—which was extra risky now that *everyone* saw themselves as part vigilante—she pivoted and hurried off in the other direction.

She waited until she was half a block away before she opened her hand and inspected the brooch. Definitely cheap costume jewelry, but it would fetch a few bucks at the pawnshop, at least.

She held the pin up against her own shirt, right over her heart, and used her mind to slip the sharp point through the fabric and twist the clasp back into place.

Popping her finger into her mouth to suck off the drop of blood, she dug her other hand into her pocket to pull out the rest of the day's treasures. A wallet, two watches, and a gold wedding band. She felt a little guilty over that last one, but without knowing what was to become of the Renegades, she figured she had to go into survival mode.

If she was good at anything, it was surviving.

She tucked away her findings, but kept out the last item she'd dug from her pocket, the good luck charm that was always with her, hidden away for safekeeping—a small silver bullet. The one that should have killed her. When she was just a baby, she'd been shot by a burglar breaking into her family's apartment. That night, her parents had been murdered. That night, her older sister had disappeared, either run away or kidnapped, and never heard from again.

That night, her own dormant powers had been awoken.

Of course, she didn't remember any of this for herself, only what the staff at the children's home had told her. They said she'd been found by the landlord, drenched in her own blood and screaming her head off, the bullet clutched in her pudgy fist. They told her that was less than an hour after Captain Chromium himself had stopped by to investigate the crime and declared her and her parents dead.

And the Renegades wondered why everyone thought they were inept.

For years, she had dreamed of her sister coming to claim her. Of . . . anyone, really, coming to claim her. But eventually she had realized that no one was coming. No one cared about one more orphaned, unwanted prodigy.

She could only rely on herself.

Which was fine. She didn't need anyone else. She was a survivor. The bullet was proof enough of that.

Squeezing her fist, she shoved the bullet back into her pocket and started making her way to the pawnshop to sell her goods before she got caught with them.

She knew she wasn't a Renegade anymore. A lot of people were saying they didn't even need Renegades now, just as they no longer needed to fear villains. There were no longer prodigies vying for power or non-prodigies being caught in the middle. They could reclaim control of their own city, their own society, their own lives.

But it was only a matter of time. The greed would come back. The power struggles. The conflicts. This phase would pass, and the problems would still be there. Only now, each side would have a bigger army, with stronger weapons.

When it happened, they would see that not everyone was willing to protect the innocent, defend the weak, fight for justice. They would realize that some prodigies are stronger for a reason. Braver for a reason. Some people were always meant to be heroes.

Just like some people were always meant to be villains.

ACKNOWLEDGMENTS

ANOTHER BOOK SERIES completed (celebrate!), and I don't know that it would have happened without the incredible support of so many people. Mostly I want to say thank you to my agent, Jill, who helped me see the true heart of Nova and Adrian's story, and my editor, Liz, who helped guide me down its path, even when it became far longer and more winding than I think either of us expected. I might have given up on these books without the wisdom from both of you, and I am so grateful for your constant encouragement.

I also want to say thank you to everyone at Jill Grinberg Literary Management—Denise, Katelyn, Sam, Sophia, and Cheryl (I miss you!), as well as Matthew Snyder at CAA—you guys are unequivocally the best.

To my entire team at Macmillan Children's—Jean, Jon, Mary, Jo, Morgan, Rich, Mariel, Allison, Caithin, Jordin, Katie H., Katie Q., and so many others—who are true heroes in the world of children's literature. Thank you for helping me craft my stories into the best books they can be.

I am eternally grateful for my longtime beta reader, Tamara Moss, who not only helps me see the weaknesses in my writing, but also gives me the confidence and motivation to make them better.

Many, many thanks to my extraordinary copy editor, Anne Heausler, for bringing such thoughtful comments and suggestions to the text. It is always such a comfort to have your eye on it!

I offer immense gratitude to Laurel Harnish, whose entry in my "Create Your Own Superhero" contest resulted in the creation of Callum Treadwell. Callum has become, in my mind, one of the greatest heroes in this saga, and it was a privilege to write him.

Thank you to my wonderful group of local writers: Gennifer Albin, Kendare Blake, Jennifer Chushcoff, Kimberly Derting, Corry Lee, Lish McBride, Lily Meade, Sajni Patel (we miss you!), Rori Shay, Breeana Shields, and Emily Varnell—for the many afternoons of productivity and camaraderie, the thoughtful advice, and the friendship.

Last but never least, I am grateful for my family and friends, who have been such incredible advocates and cheerleaders for me since the beginning: Mom and Dad, Grandma, Jeff and Wendy, Bob and Clarita, Connie, Chelsea, Pat and Carolyn, Leilani, Calli, Sarah, Steph, Matt and Melissa, Ash and Christina, Eddy and Melissa, and I'm sure I'm forgetting someone (gah, I hate that feeling!). And of course, thank you to my lovely daughters, Delaney and Sloane, for the unspeakable warmth and joy you bring into my life, and to Jesse, my husband, my best friend, my favorite travel buddy, and all around my favorite human being on this planet. In the words of Sandol Stoddard Warburg: *I would go on choosing you and you would go on choosing me over and over again.*